For Michael

Audio log

7 Feb 2016 18:32

This will be my last audio log. I've been thinking about how to explain, though perhaps it doesn't matter now anyway – you didn't come, and it is too late to make a difference. So I think I might end with the story of the indigo hamlets. You remember – those luminous tropical fish I used to talk about? For ten years I've kept them in my aquarium in the outhouse. When I stand between those four walls of Caribbean Sea I can imagine myself in a coral reef with no glass keeping me separate. I suppose they'll be dead by the time you hear this, but that's probably for the best. Fish should not be kept in a tank any more than animals housed in a cage or humans confined to a role. We all of us need our freedom, sooner or later. Don't you think?

I went out to the rocks this morning, before sunrise. It is not as dark as you might imagine, when your eyes are accustomed and the moon is past waxing gibbous. But I do realise that a fall could kill me and I am not ready to die, not just yet, so I wore my head torch and carried a hand-held beam strapped tight to my wrist. The path out to the black coast is muddied and frozen this time of year. Covered in thin sheets of ice that crack under my feet and puddles that trap my ankles, sinking me shin-deep into half-hearted bog.

I call it the black coast for the rocks, fractured and pitted as they are. Deep like charcoal but sharp as etched glass. Sheets of them stretch out when the sea is away, lives upon lives of sediment. This morning, though, the sea was close in, and the waves were thrashing against the dark sandstone. I wondered if they were trying to claw their way right up into my lighthouse.

I feel alive, standing at the coast, my feet planted – like this – on the rock and my body braced against the wind. It believes I am not a challenge, that wind. It sees only an old woman but it has not blown me over yet. It stings my eyes with grit-salt until they're raw in the corners and weeping but it does not blow me over. It is hard to imagine anywhere else when you're facing those waves, standing on those rocks. But even there – even now – there are times when I am in two places at once. When I am living in two times. I am an old woman standing alone with her scowl and I am a young woman sitting among the dark wood and towering bookshelves of that basement room in King's. The feel of all that cold stone underfoot, the echo of it, the smell of the professor's tobacco mixing with a hint of stale chlorine that could have come from the lab or from the clean floor in the corridor. That room is as still and timeless, in its way, as the ever-changing black rocks of the peninsula.

'You can have the post,' he says to me. His beard doesn't move as he talks and it obscures his lips – I only see the flash of teeth. 'Fixed term,' he says. 'Three years. You will be expected to publish.'

'Of course,' I say, not wanting my excitement to show.

'I see you have a reference from our Dark Lady.'

He chuckles. His eyes are amused. He seems to find himself amusing.

'Though Rosy's not working on cell fertilisation, is she?'

I give a clipped smile as my excitement changes into something vaguely sickening. These are the names they call her, behind her back. The Dark Lady. 'Rosy'. I've heard them before – everyone has – and we all understand the implied insults, too. What an affront, to be a woman. To be that type of woman. I chose to use her reference for a good reason.

He leans across the desk with a reassuring expression, like you would give to a child.

'Well, let's see what you're made of, eh?'

I think he might be about to pat my hand, so before he can I snatch it away and push my chair further back from the desk. It scrapes, nail-like, along the floor. I can hear the screech even now.

I meet his gaze.

'Thank you,' I say, standing up, keeping my back rigid and my expression professional. I want to get away from this man, who makes me feel small even as he gives me what I came here for. But if I am to work here, I know that I must be able to work with him.

He stands too. Towers over me. Holds out his hand, expecting me to shake it. I haven't accepted his job offer, though he assumes that I have.

I am hesitating.

The world spins. The bookshelves grow until they meet in an oppressive arc over my head. I'm trapped in a labyrinth of dark wood and pristine white, of labs and stone and chemicals, and I know, with my arm half raised to take his hand, that my decision in that instant will be the decision that makes the difference. But the flagstones are turning to sharp black rocks that glisten in the sun and my fingernails are aching in the cold. Way out to sea, far beyond the rocks and the whites of the waves, I can see dense storm clouds gathering. I am an old woman again and I start to make my way home, thinking about the indigo hamlets.

I wish I'd told you more about them when you were young. You would have listened then – remember how you used to listen to me, as though my ideas could change the world?

Truth is, it's been a long time now since I spoke to anyone. I am alone here, quite completely. I've made sure of that. The storm has been threatening all day and the lamp glasses are rattling in their frames – perhaps there is an earthquake shaking the foundations of my lighthouse. But I'm going to imagine instead a sea so warm it caresses my toes, a landscape of gently ribboned anemones and shoals of lilac-moon jellyfish, a glowing world of multicoloured coral where I wouldn't have had to fight in the first place. That is where the indigo hamlets live. And now I'm going to finish where I started, with their story. Close your eyes, just for a moment. Forget how angry you are.

They leave their home ranges before sunset to search for a mate in the warm saltwater reefs of the western Caribbean. When they find a partner – and they find true partners – they wrap their transparent tails around each other and use their blue-white fins to swirl themselves through the sea. They turn together so close that their love dance spins the water into a vortex. It's beautiful to watch: an extraordinary combining of colour and soft threads of DNA in the sheltered valleys between tall mountains of snowflake coral. They share, the indigo hamlets. They take turns. That is what makes them so special. They release alternating sets of gametes, male one moment and female the next, and it seems to me that they whisper the truth of how it can be. I want to join them but I can't because suddenly I am back, transported against my will, standing in that room surrounded by the smell of stale chlorine. I have a choice and I must make it. I can walk away to live my life elsewhere. Or I can stay, and become a scientist. This is where the path splits. The world changes.

But now I hear the wind shaking the window glass and feel the air thickening around me. It is no use. The dense purple clouds have reached the black rocks and I made my choice a long time ago and I understand that the storm has finally—

Chapter 1

EVA OFTEN FELT THAT THE entrance should be dilapidated in some way – paint chipped off, perhaps, windows in need of a clean. Nothing too dramatic, just a hint of changing circumstances. They had a local community group, though, like most neighbourhoods, and it was very well funded – her windows were cleaned regularly, fresh paint applied each year at the start of spring. Apparently it was more important to make sure the building looked good than to fund the work being carried on inside. It wasn't even the government she was most angry with.

The winter sun made the window glass shine, glint gold as she glanced up. One of the shelter vans drove past behind her; there must have been a report of someone sleeping rough last night. No sign of them now though – the street appeared flawless. She unlocked the front door, which was painted a deep olive green, and collected her post at the reception. There were flowers on the desk, luminous oranges and purples with each petal larger than the head of a rose. The heating was on full blast. Eva reluctantly smiled at another smiling woman and headed for the stairs. Sometimes she felt like something had gone very wrong with the world.

Her mum had told the tale of how she started the group so many times it had become a sort of genesis story, to their family at least, to their supporters. Women, it always began. We are women. Eva held on to the banister as she climbed, almost pulling herself up the stairs. She felt tired. Was tired. And frustrated, and more beyond that. The staircase was so familiar she could have walked it with her eyes closed, though what she did instead was stare at the small square patches of light that came in from the windows at either end of the stairwell. The beams of sun were strong, low-angled, bright enough to catch the tips of her eyelashes when she blinked. As she reached her floor she noticed, with relief, that the air was colder there – the landing window was open, letting in a breath of December. She felt it cooling her neck, straightened her back then checked with an open palm that her hair was suitably spiky today.

Once inside the office, Eva dropped her bag on the floor by the desk and took a seat. It was a large, light-filled room that ran the length of one side of the building. Large, and empty. Recently she'd repositioned the desk and chair so she could look out – different to how her mother had it arranged, with multicoloured furniture and throws and cushions, scarlet and purple and turquoise, every seat facing inwards, a welcoming circle. No, Eva wanted to look out, to be able to stare out at the world and watch what was happening face-on.

The windows overlooked a small park, though park was probably too grand a name for it – every spare space in London had been turned green over the last few years. So much planting had been done, so many new patches of grass sown, and all those bulbs resting quietly under the ground, waiting for spring. She thought the office had once had a view over a car park, but she couldn't quite remember. Perhaps it had just been a bit of street where cars had parked. Now it was an elongated triangle of grass with chestnut and cherry trees along the sides and neat wooden benches in between. People went there for picnics, in the summer, parents and children. Today there was just a couple walking their dog. She looked to see if they were carrying anything, but saw to her relief that they weren't.

She began with the slim white envelope, slid her finger along the seam and pulled out the contents. Next she did the same with the handwritten one, and then the brown envelope with the pristine address label on front – she didn't bother to read the words, just placed the bill and another two letters of disagreement on her desk and clicked on the screen. Her long coat was starting to feel heavy on her shoulders and she could feel a trickle of sweat running down her spine, but she wouldn't take it off. It had belonged to her mother, and perhaps her mother's mother before that. The screen lit up, but didn't show the login box. It was an old computer. Probably needed an upgrade it would never get. She pummelled the enter key, even though it was useless. Then stopped.

Leaning back in the chair, which adjusted for her comfort, she allowed her eyes to linger on the factory-set pale blue screen of her computer. There had been a photo there once. She closed her eyes, just for a second. There was no point in feeling sorry for herself, but she wanted to take a moment to listen. She listened to the soft pad of footsteps walking across the shared office space upstairs, to the drone of traffic outside, the murmur of indistinct voices from the start-up across the hall, the whisper of warm water flowing through cold pipes. And her own breath, the only sound coming from her office as she drew air into her lungs and held it there, imagining the oxygen passing into her capillaries, travelling, eventually, to the left side of her heart.

Enough.

She pulled open the empty bag that she'd carried from home and stood up, shrugging the coat from her shoulders. Walking around the edges of the room she ripped the last of the brightly coloured posters off the cream walls. It didn't take long.

Eva could remember coming into the headquarters with her mother when she was a child, how full of people it had always seemed. There were several desks in the room back then, though people rarely sat at them, preferring the comfy chairs and low sofas arranged all around for volunteers and visitors. They came to help with campaigns, sometimes, to raise awareness. They came because they needed to talk or because they were unsure, because the facts seemed to say one thing while their instincts were saying another. They came with ideas and with doubts and her mother offered a place where they could be shared, and where they would be welcomed. Where had they all gone, those people?

We are women, her mother would always begin.

And then, four years ago today, her mother had died.

An old-fashioned stapler. A note pad, phone recharger, pens, some letters of support from years ago, all went into the bag along with today's post and her favourite chipped coffee mug with the half-handle that no one else could hold. She checked her email, though she didn't know why she was bothering. Clicked through to watch the latest vlog from FullLife: another beaming couple, another newborn. The comments had been disabled. Below that, an interview with the FullLife director calmly reassuring everyone that nothing had been stolen during the break-in last week. Eva stared at her face. At her smiling, lying face. They had probably been going for the newly released covers. The ones that everyone wanted, and some could not afford.

She imagined the laptop making a sigh as it shut down, though it was perfectly silent. She slipped it into her bag. There was hardly any furniture left. The single empty desk and chair she would leave for whomever it was that came next. They would know nothing about her. Or her mother.

She stood up and pulled the bag onto her back.

How easy it was, to bring something to an end.

As she walked to the station, no idea what she was going to do next, Eva found herself standing underneath the railway bridge, looking up.

One hundred thousand lemmings can't be wrong.

That's what it had said – Eva remembered it from when she was a child, though she hadn't heard the phrase for years. How had they done it, she'd wanted to know, how had they hung one-armed off a bridge and maintained stability enough to write? Such determination to break the law must come from somewhere. And now, standing under the same bridge, painted a soothing pale green – it was the most relaxing colour to view, and so it had become a very popular colour to use – her eyes searched under the layers of paint, under the years, the decades, for that same scrawl.

It was gone, of course.

A couple walked past, the man's hand cupped affectionately – though not protectively – around the curve of their unborn child. Five months, Eva thought, perhaps six. Enough that the pouch looked full but still comfortable. Very comfortable, she knew. They had chosen a winter cover of fluffy red fleece. Christmassy. Festive. The last few years had been all about the accessories.

They saw her staring.

'Are you OK?'

They asked kindly. So kindly her reply came out more wistful than angry, though she wasn't wistful, and she was angry.

'No one makes graffiti any more,' she said.

The man looked up at the bridge then over to the woman beside him, questioning, and she explained.

'She's talking about vandalism.'

He looked a little shocked, though he hid it well. Eva could imagine his thoughts: Perhaps she was a historian. Perhaps she was writing a book – doing research.

She adjusted the bag on her back. It was larger than she'd needed, and awkward on her shoulders. Beams of light shot through the gaps in the bridge's security barriers.

'Why would anyone want to vandalise anything?' he asked.

Eva didn't reply. She didn't think she had the fight left in her.

The man stood still, an uncomfortable smile on his lips. She knew that he didn't need to adjust the straps of what he was carrying.

She had tried one on once, years ago, when she was young and would happily have argued with any stranger in the street. She'd wanted to understand – what it felt like to wear one, but more than that as well. The appeal of it. It was before all the different textures were available, though there was a range of colours. Bright yellow, she'd requested, fluorescent, like one of those tropical fish.

'This is the equivalent of six months,' they'd told her, as they let her strap it on over her T-shirt. In the early days the FullLife doctors had helped people position it, over the shoulders, snug on the belly, but they realised it was making people nervous – much better to do it yourself, they decided, then you can see how easy it is. How versatile. How safe.

Back then they'd used them in schools as well, as props – teenagers given the chance to see what it's really like, carrying an unborn child. It didn't put them off, although whether that was really the intention she'd never been sure. These days, celebrities made a show of designer pouches, of being friends with their children as well as parents – holding hands down the street in their matching outfits, courting the paparazzi. The pouch had become trendy, especially among the young – why wait, when you could study part time and still have your career, now parenthood was equal; and it came in such pretty colours. There had been FullLife sponsorship for all baby pouchers at first, to make financially feasible what today was offered as a free-of-charge benefit to every health-care plan. And if you didn't have a health-care plan, there were always used pouches available. FullLife were very generous with them.

The texture was almost butter-soft, but padded too, and it slipped into place so easily it terrified her. She'd made a mistake with the colour. Tropical-fish yellow was what she actually might have wanted, had she been a different sort of woman who was not horrified by the baby pouch. Instead she should have gone for a deep black-red, like the colour of the inside, to remind herself of what it really was – to make sure she didn't slip, quietly, into feeling at ease with it. Even though there was no baby inside the trial pouch she was wearing, she knew she could not let herself relax.

But she had persevered. She'd worn the pouch for the full day, felt the weight and warmth of it, the way it moved against her skin. She'd recognised the feeling of selflessness that would come from carrying something precious. As night fell she'd hung it up on the pouch stand, just like they told you to, turned on the incubator and attached the nutrient bag to the feed on the pouch's surface. It provided more than food to her imaginary baby; it was what the pouch needed to sustain its cells, its entire biological environment. She closed her eyes thinking of every way that it was wrong. But in the morning it was still there, waiting for her. Warm and inviting. Despite everything, she knew the comfort of waking after a peaceful night's sleep to reach out a hand and stroke.

The couple wanted to leave, she realised, but didn't want to be impolite, having started the conversation.

'I should get going,' she said, and held out her hand.

He reached forward to shake it, but before she could step away her hand was pulled closer and placed on the soft, synthetic fleece of the pouch. She could feel it, gently pulsing between her fingers. Had to force her eyes away from the subtle stretching and contracting of the fabric back to the man's face. He seemed to be watching her earnestly.

'She was kicking,' he said. 'I think she wanted to say hello to you.'

He smiled, openly this time.

'Goodbye,' Eva managed, pulling her wrist from his grip and backing away.

*

At home, after a busy Tube ride and an empty train journey out of the city, Eva sat at her piano and rested her fingers over the keys. For the first time in a long time, it was the middle of the afternoon in the middle of the week and there was nothing that she had to do. She didn't even have a plan. The book was open at the Adagio of Mozart's D major sonata, but she didn't start to play. The instrument had intricate carvings in the wood, swirls and leaves outlined on either side of the front panel.

There had once been silk behind the carvings, so she'd been told – delicate handmade silk from China, from the nineteenth century. The attachments for the candleholders were still visible, though the candleholders themselves had been lost years before she inherited it. Her mum claimed that her great-grandfather had been given the piano as a gift from the tsar, but it was hard to know when to believe what Avigail Goldsmith said. She'd enjoyed her mysteries. It was old, though. You could tell, from looking at it, from the feel of the wood, the way the pedals didn't work, the sticking of the notes because the felt had long since rotted away. There was no value to it at all now. The world was full of old, broken pianos. Nevertheless, as she started to play, she smiled at the distinctive, incorrect sound that it made.

Walking into the kitchen that evening, the last rays of sun reaching the windowsill, she switched on the radio more out of habit than for any particular programme. The voices in the background kept her company while she cooked, though today they felt intrusive in her kitchen. She chopped an onion coarsely, turned on the hob to heat some oil.

She was trying to work out what it was that she felt. She was not sentimental, and there had been no satisfaction in her job for years. You couldn't keep doing something if there was no demand for it to be done – and you can't help people that don't want to be helped, either. Her grant had been cancelled eighteen months ago, and she'd hardly been surprised when the last of her private funding was withdrawn. This month, for the first time in her life, she couldn't even afford the rent on her office. She had asked for more time. They had asked her to leave. It was over.

Guilt, was that it, for letting her mother down? For failing to preserve what she had been asked to protect?

We are women, her mother would say. Life grows inside us, and we protect it. Now, more than ever, we must protect it.

Perhaps she had failed twice over, then. Though she didn't stop what she was doing – red pepper and sugar snap peas were quickly chopped and thrown into the pan, with noodles and dark soy sauce. Her mother didn't know what it was like to receive the letters she'd been getting, for years now. Polite, kind, well-meaning letters telling her that she was wrong. That the pouch was beautiful. That it had changed the world for the better. That everyone was equal now we had moved beyond natural birth. That they could help her. That they *wanted* to help her. The pouchers had no doubts any more; they were happy. The women – and the men. They were happy.

Yes, closing down was the right decision. She couldn't have taken the futility any longer. She needed to have purpose, needed to feel like she was getting somewhere. An image flickered in her mind, not of where she was going but of where she'd come from. Perhaps she should visit the home where she'd lived for the first three years of her life – so far from where she was now, but only a bus ride away. She shook her head. Going backwards wasn't the answer. It was something new that she needed. Something totally different. She would take a week. Rest, and think, and make a plan. She piled her stir-fry into a bowl and threw in some extra chilli.

Sitting at the table with the fading light outside, the sound of leaves rustling in her front garden and the gentle voices coming from the radio, Eva tried to enjoy the crunch of a sugar snap pea. She allowed herself to close her eyes again. She allowed herself to imagine how things might have been. And she listened.

She listened to a voice on the radio, so soporific she leaned forwards over her bowl, resting her head in her hands.

Then, she heard the words.

Natural birth.

'Natural birth,' they were saying – she was saying, it was a woman in an advert on the radio, a young woman, presumably an actor – 'that's why we chose natural birth instead of using the pouch, with the new FullLife *NaturalBirth* plan.'

'And we couldn't be happier,' the man joined in, backed by the sound of young children running into the room.

What were they doing?

Natural birth. It was what she'd been fighting to preserve her entire professional life. It was everything her mum had believed in. It was what no one wanted any more, what FullLife had destroyed. So why were they promoting it now – in a new health-care plan, no less? Were they scared of losing their customers? Or trying to gain more? With FullLife, it was usually about money.

She realised her hands were clenched around the edge of the table, so she sat back and consciously released the pressure in her fingers. The advert had finished, and a DJ was talking about Christmas and pop charts in a voice that seemed to belong to a different time. As if nothing had happened.

Should she be pleased? Perhaps she should, but she couldn't be. If women were being encouraged to return to natural birth, then there must be a reason. Hardly anyone had listened to her arguments in favour of it, not for years, and none of her campaigns had made it onto the radio. But this wasn't about her. Neither Eva nor her mum was responsible for this. FullLife had spent decades – billions – promoting the pouch as the better way, and now they seemed to be doing a U-turn all on their own. For reasons of their own. Someone, surely, should be asking why.

Still, it was none of her business. Not any more.

She stood up, walked across the room and filled the kettle. It was something to do, a distraction from the unease she'd been feeling all day, that had just intensified. There was the piano room. She could use that as an office. There was the last of her mother's money. Outside the sun fell below the fields on the horizon and the kitchen was suddenly dark, the moon no more than a sliver. She touched the backs of her fingers against the kettle. The heat emanating from it was still a few degrees short of burning her knuckles.

Chapter 2

EVEN AT SEVENTY-SIX, HOLLY BHATTACHARYYA was amused by the thought of being a matriarch. To be seen that way by her family was one thing, but quite why the rest of the world had to join in she had no idea. Silly world, she thought with a smile as she deliberately made her way down the staircase much more slowly than she needed to, her walking stick planted firmly on each step in front of her. Holly liked to make an entrance. And there was some fun to be had today.

She'd tried to take down the framed print of that first article many times now. The most recent time she'd gone so far as to take it out of the expensive frame and hide it under the squirrel-patterned cushion on her favourite armchair so she could sit on it while her family tried to search without her noticing. She didn't let on that she could see them doing it. Instead she pretended to doze, even let her mouth droop open and faked a snore, while they were leafing through the magazines under the coffee table. She could hear her daughter's whisper – 'She's sleeping now, Rosie, go and search her room' – and Rosie's loyal reply that she would do no such thing. If she'd had a favourite out of all her grandchildren, which of course she didn't, then Rosie, with her deep hazel eyes and easy smile, would have been it.

But as Holly pushed open the door, readying herself for another interview, and walked serenely into the front room where Rosie and the journalist were waiting, there it was – cleaned and gleaming – hanging right bang centre over the mantelpiece. *Holly Bhattacharyya and her husband Will*, it read in the caption beneath her determined twenty-three-year-old face, *this morning became the first couple to give birth using the new and still controversial baby pouch.* She looked for her squirrel-patterned cushion and noticed that it had been relegated to the long sofa, where it was now being squashed behind the journalist's substantial back.

'Oh, crap,' she said, letting the metal walking stick clatter to the ground and standing in the middle of the room with her hands on her hips.

Rosie took her arm and guided her to the comfy chair. She was late already. On purpose, of course.

'Nana?'

Rosie was wearing the pouch, and had even dressed to match. Holly felt a swell of pride. Her granddaughter was so good with these journalists – she was a natural.

She turned her eyes towards the middle-aged man interviewing them, and the sleek charcoal-grey phone he'd placed on the coffee table. It was already recording. Hopefully Rosie had done most of the interview already.

'So, er, you were saying William . . .' the journalist began in a softer voice than she'd expected him to use. More accented, too. Still, his words were wolfish.

'I'm not talking about Will,' Holly said abruptly.

'We were all very close to Grandpa,' said Rosie, glancing reassuringly at Holly, and shaking her head just slightly. 'That's why we've chosen his name.'

Holly's face softened as she realised what they'd been talking about, and moved her hand to touch the soft, warm pouch that was cradling new life – her great-grandson. Will. Like the man she had loved. Rosie had attached the portable nutrient bag for the interview, and a muffled gurgle came from the pouch. Now she thought about it, Holly rather fancied a biscuit.

'Well,' she said, looking back up at the journalist, 'that should give you a nice sense of closure for the article. Full circle, wouldn't you say? Mr . . .'

'Filipek.'

He gave a smile that seemed to Holly to be hiding something as his pen scratched away in his notebook. The pages were angled away from her, so that she couldn't read what he wrote. Hardly in the spirit of the times. She reached up to her head and touched her fringe, making sure there was still a bounce in her hair. She'd had it cut very short, all over, a few years ago – there does come a point when it simply seems like a waste of time to be styling your hair every morning – but she'd kept her thick, bouncy fringe, which covered her forehead in one gentle inward-facing grey curl to sit just above her eyebrows. She liked to pat it.

It still seemed miraculous to her, even after all these years, that humanity had found a way to share the creation of life. When she was young it had seemed impossible, as if the inequality so blatantly visible all around was an innate part of what we are, as a species.

She could remember one day in particular. It was a late afternoon in September, right at the end of the school holidays. She'd been sitting out with her parents, their deckchairs arranged on the slabs of cracked concrete that served as a patio behind their home in the council estate. A trickle of autumn sun from overhead and similar houses in every direction. It was a small space – there was just enough room for them to sit between her mum's potted fuchsias and planters of herbs – but then it was the small things that Holly was angry about, that day. Simple things that should have been so easy to change. Like the way her mum made every single meal and her dad sat upright – pressed shirt and tie, as always, clean-shaven like a matter of pride – and never offered to help. How ridiculous.

There he sat, assuming his meals would be cooked for him. And there was her mum, quietly fulfilling his assumptions.

It had never been any different in their entire marriage. Her mum up at 5 a.m. to make the bread, her dad teaching at the grammar school he'd joined as a trainee when he'd first arrived in London. He was the deputy now, having worked his way up doggedly over the decades, still hoping for the headmastership that would never be given to him. He was not English, not even after thirty years of citizenship, and it made no difference how carefully he pressed his tie or how straight he kept his back. She could see that, even if he couldn't. But retirement was still ten years away, as they sat on their inappropriately bright striped deckchairs on the concrete. They were intelligent people, she knew. So what was it that made them both fall into these roles? What was it that made them both cringe and dismiss her views when she used the word feminism?

'Don't you want to do something else?' she asked her mother quietly, when her dad seemed to have closed his eyes.

Her mum smiled and shook her head.

'You could do anything,' Holly said, trying to imagine it. 'You could . . .'

'Oh, Harshini,' her dad said, opening his eyes.

'*Holly,*' said Holly.

Her dad sighed. 'These roles, as you call them, are useful. We're doing what we want to do. Someone has to earn money, and someone has to stay home with the children – that's how it works in a family.'

If he'd stopped there, she might not have lost her temper. But he went on. Told her the story of how she and her brother had been such *different* children. How she had been too scared to go on the climbing frame at the park – your brother would just run off, he said, he was fearless! But you preferred to stay close to your mother, play with your dolls.

'And that's OK,' he said, as though trying to get her to accept who she was and just be happy. As if this story was proof – imagine it! – that little boys and little girls were intrinsically different. No acknowledgement of learned behaviour, of the impact of society, of school friends, of the clothes they were dressed in, of the way her brother had been thrown into the air and told he could do anything, while she was told to be careful, always, be careful. No, as far as her parents were concerned, boys and girls were simply different. That was what they actually believed.

She'd argued. She'd shouted. She'd felt something slipping away – she was sixteen years old and that was the moment when she realised that despite her love for them she fundamentally disagreed with her parents.

'Keep your voice down, dear,' her mum had said, and Holly's reply had felt like it defined her:

'I do *not* keep my voice down.'

Her dad had stood, turned his back, and walked away.

It had been coming for a while. That afternoon on the concrete was the last of a long series of arguments, and non-arguments: of those barely noticeable details – injustices was too grand a word – that add up over years to form who a person is and how they see the world. But she remembered the day not for the words she'd used but for the recognition that it would be the last time she tried. She gave up hoping to get through to them. It wasn't the beginning of their argument. It was the end. That day she dismissed their views, as they had dismissed hers.

She'd always believed she could make things different in her own life, though. She'd kept searching for a way – and this was where it had led. The problem wasn't simply a society sculpted around the needs of men, forcing women into the roles of wife and mother. It was deeper than that. No matter how well they argued, or how hard they worked, women would always be the primary caregivers while they were the ones *having* the children. They would always have to take more time off work while it was their bodies that needed to recuperate; that were expected to breastfeed. She couldn't deny it: men and women were different in one way. Not in their minds, or their taste in toys, and certainly not in their abilities – but in their physiology. If equality was to be achieved, the physiology, the *biology*, had to evolve.

And what a difference it had made! Society at last expecting – no, assuming – that fathers played an equal role to mothers. Businesses offered full parental support, flexible hours, actual understanding. Having a baby wasn't something you had to work around any more; it wasn't a difficulty that forced compromise. The rest of life was organised to fit naturally around raising a child.

Not that this journalist was going to get to hear anything about her long-gone anger. None of them had. From that first article onwards, she had been calm and assured. That was who she was able to become, thanks to the FullLife baby pouch. And thanks to another woman, an extraordinary woman who, unlike Holly, had never appeared in a newspaper.

'Do you have children?' she asked, and the journalist looked up at her in surprise. Perhaps she wasn't supposed to be asking questions. His eyes were grey, like his suit, and his case, and his phone, but his hair was a thick, rich brown that curled around his face, giving a hint of someone young, playful. She liked him a little more for it.

'No, I . . .'

She nodded – she had known what his answer would be before asking him the question. Still, she wanted to delve a little deeper. He seemed different to the other journalists that she'd known over the years. There was something else going on in his head, she was sure of it. She smiled, mischievously, and felt Rosie's eyes watching her. How often the young imagine they need to protect the old. She reached out again to stroke the warm bump of her great-grandson.

He would be able to feel her affection from inside the pouch; it worked both ways, that closeness.

'Have you ever tried one on?' she asked, her eyes flicking back to the journalist.

He didn't reply, but looked horrified. The warmth Holly had felt for him a second ago evaporated, and she withdrew her hand and repositioned the cushion behind her. She remembered the judgement, especially with her first child, the looks certain people had given her. As if she were doing something unnatural. She had even been attacked on the street, once, when her first daughter was still in the pouch, before they'd even chosen the name Daphne. A woman ran right up to her, screaming in her face: 'It's not God's way!' She was one of the hardliners, the kind of woman who hated other women so much she was against the epidural. It was frightening. Those people had been proved wrong long ago now, of course, but you still met them occasionally – people who thought that women were supposed to feel pain, that the pouch made things too easy. Though whether it was the baby pouch or babies in general that this man disliked she wasn't sure.

'I published a series of books on the psychology of childbirth, you know? I wrote the first one after I got my PhD. The last after I retired.'

'I know.'

'Hmph.'

So what if he knew about her books. Holly was fairly sure he hadn't read them. He was just here to write a silly website article. Ha!

She leaned back in her chair and decided that she wasn't going to make any more conversation. And if he insisted on taking photographs, she was going to have her eyes shut in every single one of them.

*

Piotr Filipek was uncomfortable. He hadn't asked for this assignment, and had put off the interview twice already, but Rosie

Bhattacharyya's baby was due to be born tomorrow and, well, you had to have the before as well as the after. Celebrity culture was what it was. There was nothing special about this family, just the fluke of timing and a media desperate to put mediocre people in the spotlight.

So what that Holly Bhattacharyya was the first woman to give birth using the pouch. So what that Rosie was her granddaughter. If it hadn't been them, it would have been others. This idolising of a perfectly ordinary – and unusually wealthy – family was nothing but a lack of imagination on the part of the human race. No, he didn't much care about Holly Bhattacharyya, who he was fairly convinced was smirking at him, or her innocent, open-faced granddaughter. What he cared about was more out of reach now than ever. Six years. He hadn't seen her for six years. That was longer than the time they'd been together.

'Would you like to tell me about your wedding?' he said to Rosie, since it seemed totally impersonal and, as such, would probably get a long and detailed response.

He let his mind wander as she described walking down the aisle hand in hand with Kaz – stupid name – and something to do with the music, which sounded like a kind of reggae fusion so far as he could tell. His research had told him that Rosie was only twenty, but he had forgotten how young twenty could be. She was *giggly*. The colours of the wedding flowers were inspired by Mexico, apparently, where they'd been on their gap year before getting married. The press hadn't been invited to the big day, thank God, or he would have had to endure the wedding itself as well. He couldn't understand why anyone would want to go through with it. After hundreds of years of obligatory marriage society finally gives people the choice not to bind themselves to one another for life and what do they do? He glanced up, and there they were – Holly Bhattacharyya's piercing eyes fixed on him.

Rosie had finished about the wedding now, and was standing up, stroking the pouch. 'Next year we're both going to uni, of course,' she said. 'Part time, here in London. We just love it here.' She paused. 'It's great, isn't it, the way universities offer childcare and stuff? It's like, there's no need to choose between . . .'

Piotr closed his eyes, just for a second. Pressed the heel of his hand into his forehead as she chattered away.

' . . . and we'll be able to really relate, you know, be friends with Will, as well as parents. Do you want to meet Kaz now?' And without waiting for a reply she was skipping her way out of the room to fetch her husband. Well, not skipping, obviously.

'I wonder . . .' he began, then stopped and waited until she had shut the door. Now he was alone in the room with Holly. He had thought for one awful second earlier that he was going to be asked to *wear* the pouch – he'd heard more and more about friends sharing with each other, extended family units being formed, though to offer a pouch to a stranger would have been surprising. Still, that was what he'd thought, and he sighed in relief now that the pouch, and the mother, were out of the room.

'I read . . .' he started again, cleared his throat.

It was colder than he'd expected in this house – freezing outside of course, bloody Baltic, with that stinging clear sky, but he'd thought the central heating would be maxed up in here. No such luck. And the entire family seemed oblivious. The last few years he'd found his fingers were getting numb in the cold, completely numb. He clasped his hands together to try and bring back some circulation.

'There's been some speculation, possibly nothing—'

'Come on, out with it,' Holly snapped.

He studied his hands for a moment, flexed his fingers. He might be about to get thrown out.

'Do you – did you stay in touch with Freida at all?'

'No.'

No was good. Much better than the off-limits-to-the-press response he usually got when interviewing anyone who had known her personally. He tried to sit up but only sank further into the pile of cushions in a way that he imagined looked fairly ridiculous. So instead he leaned forwards, attempting to give the impression they were co-conspirators, that he was a man she could confide in.

'You fell out?'

'Now why would you think that . . . ?'

Holly paused, as if about to say more, and suddenly he wondered if she had forgotten his name. She was an old woman, after all. Just a forgetful old woman. Ridiculous for him to have felt so awkward earlier. Had he actually been intimidated by her? He smiled what he hoped was a warm, open kind of smile.

'She'll be one hundred this year, I believe,' he continued. 'If she's alive.'

Holly raised her eyebrows at him – he wondered if it was subconscious – but she didn't reply and her silence eventually pushed him to give a little more away.

'So, *you* don't know where she is, then?' He found he was unable to stop the smile that was creeping around his mouth. He'd been looking into Freida's whereabouts for quite a while.

Holly's feet suddenly seemed to be planted firmly on the floor, which was strange because, up until now, they had been dangling a few inches above the ground.

'Do you?' she asked mildly, as if making idle conversation, but beneath it he saw the curiosity in her expression, guarded and alert.

'No one knows, exactly . . .' he replied enigmatically, but she didn't seem to register his response.

'I'm very proud of this picture,' Holly said, suddenly standing up and walking over to the mantelpiece. 'Do you see? The one up here on the wall?'

An old newspaper article had been cut out and framed – expensively, as far as he could tell – with the photo centre stage. He recognised Holly's eyes, her stare. There was something confrontational in it.

'I don't mean me, of course, don't bother looking at me,' she said, and she actually grabbed his chin – the way his granny had done when he was a little boy, when she'd decide he had some dirt on his face and then spit on a tissue to wipe it off – and moved his head a few degrees to the left, adjusting his line of sight. 'Now you see this arm here, around my shoulders? Someone just out of the frame?'

'Oh, yes. I see.'

He took a step away from her, rubbing his chin where her hand had touched him. The jolt of memory had left him unbalanced.

'Well, that,' she said, turning to face him with something like defiance, 'is Freida. And that is all you will be getting out of me.'

*

When Rosie walked back into the room, Kaz carrying the pouch behind her, her nana was pretending to be asleep in her comfy chair again. Rosie wasn't going to let on she knew it was an act – she never did. And she had an idea. Pausing by the door, she beckoned the journalist playfully, who raised his eyebrows and didn't get up.

'We could do the photos outside, what d'you think?'

She beamed and nodded at him. It would be great to do the photo shoot outdoors, in the open, in the middle of winter. Much better than in the front room. Days like this were her favourite – ice cold and bright. She took hold of Kaz's hand and swung his arm back and forth before pulling his fingers towards her lips and giving them a quick kiss. He was wearing his dreads down today. She loved that. And there was some almost-blue sky visible, a light turquoise winking at them between the sheets of white.

'It's the perfect day for it,' she said with a grin.

The journalist nodded and stood up, slowly, as if his joints ached, gathering his notebook and phone into his bag and pulling out a small camera instead. She thought about asking him if he was OK, but she didn't. He gave the impression of someone who didn't want to be approached. Strange, for a journalist – usually they were practised at drawing you in. She rather liked the difference.

'This way, Mr Filipek,' she said, turning back to the door and putting her hands on Kaz's shoulders as he stepped through to the hall. She reached up on tiptoes to kiss the back of his neck.

They went out beyond the lawn of the back garden, past the apple-tree orchard to the shiny holly bushes by the fence. The berries were bright red now, and would look pretty beside the dark red-brown of her hair and the soft mauve of their pouch. Plus there was the satisfying poetry of the name; her nana would be in the photo even as she faked sleep to avoid it. Kaz was carrying Will, with her holding his hand – she directed both her husband and the journalist into the positions she wanted them – and for the shoot after the birth she would hold baby Will in her arms, while Kaz held his hand. She'd got the idea for the symmetry of it as soon as she agreed to the interview. Next year she'd be studying for a BA in textile design – the combination of the way things looked and the way they felt, that was what she loved. Their pouch was an inspiration for a lot of her designs actually; she was so glad they hadn't waited. If becoming a parent changed your life then she wanted to be one right now, so it could shape her entire life. The journalist took a step back and aimed the camera. Rosie tucked her hair behind her ear.

'So, are you nervous?' he asked, filling the silence as he stepped around them in a semicircle, snapping away. Rosie squeezed Kaz's hand and they looked at one another.

'You mean about the photo shoot?' she asked. 'I've been doing these with Nana for years. Someone always wants an article . . .'

'No, I mean are you nervous about the birth tomorrow,' he said.

'Why would we be nervous?' Kaz grinned, before pulling Rosie towards him for a kiss, the pouch pressed momentarily between them. 'We can't wait.'

When Rosie stepped back, she thought she saw the journalist rolling his eyes, but couldn't be sure. She looked at him through the lens, her smile subsiding. She wasn't so young she couldn't give a serious answer to a question – and now she thought about it, it was the most interesting question he'd asked. Her mind ran through the several types of answer she could give.

'Nana must have been nervous, I think,' she said. 'Being the first, y'know? It must have seemed like this massive risk. But now – well, there's no need for anyone to be nervous, is there?'

He had dropped his arms, was now holding the camera in front of his chest.

'I do think about those other women though,' Rosie continued. 'All those women from before the pouch. The pain of it was one thing, I know, but what must have been terrifying was the thought of something bad happening, some harm coming to the baby.'

Her nana had told her stories, and there was something about them that seemed so personal she wasn't going to repeat them here. Stories of women who had to be cut open, women whose bodies were so damaged they were left incontinent for life. Then there were the women whose babies had died, who had to go through with the pain of childbirth even though their children were already gone, suffocated in the womb. Suddenly, she wanted to cry for all of them.

The journalist was looking down at his camera, seemed to be scanning through some images. Then he buried it away in the bag slung over his shoulder.

'Right then,' he said.

'Are we finished?' she asked, surprised.

'That's it for today,' he said. 'See you Saturday. Good luck.'

Then he turned and just walked off. Rosie looked at Kaz, still standing as if posed for another photograph.

'Well, he was rude,' Kaz said, wrinkling up his nose.

Rosie laughed and shook her head.

As they watched, the journalist reached the locked gate at the end of the path, rattled it a couple of times, then leaned down to inspect the padlock.

'Should I go and tell him . . .' Kaz began – there was an open gate on the other side of the house – but before he could finish his sentence the journalist had dropped his bag over to the street and begun climbing. Rosie tilted her head as he reached the top and swung his leg up, revealing a striped green-and-yellow sock. Then he sort of tumbled his way over the gate, stood up, slung his bag over his shoulder and strode off. They looked at each other, stunned into silence for a second before the giggles came.

'I guess he *really* wanted to get away from us,' Kaz laughed.

'Was it something I said?'

He shook his head. 'You were perfect and charming and lovely,' he said, pulling her in for a hug around the pouch.

'And you are sweet, and a little soppy.'

'Yes I am,' he grinned. 'And he was weird.'

They both stood still for a minute, gazing in the direction that the journalist had disappeared in, though there was no sign of him now. The gate, so far as Rosie could see, was unharmed.

'Come on, let's go find Nana,' she said. 'I expect she's trying to hide all of Mum's favourite newspaper cuttings again.'

She pressed Kaz's hand, still held in her own, gently onto the curve of the pouch he was wearing, then slid her palm further round so they could feel the warmth of it together. The texture had changed as it expanded over the months, as baby Will grew and the pouch filled with amniotic fluid. In its squidgy early days she'd gently pressed her face onto the soft cover and felt the pouch shape itself around her features, but now it was firmer, fuller, velveteen. The pressure of her touch passed through the cover and bio-membrane, just like through clothes and skin. In response she felt baby Will give a soft, impatient kick.

'This time tomorrow,' she smiled.

'This time tomorrow.'

Kaz put his arm around her and they strolled back to the house through the surprising warmth of the winter's sun.

Audio log

24 Nov 2015 19:04

It is a soft, watery kind of sleet that is falling today – still not the
snow that was promised in the clouds, though the wind is getting
up to no good and my rowan tree is aching because of it. My night
was interrupted by gusts in the chimney, a wheezing through the
walls that turned into nightmares, though in the stunning low
light of the morning I could see that my nightmares were foolish.
My lighthouse was standing on this spot long before I was born,
the wind can't harm it. Besides, as I watched clouds racing the
wave tips over the black rocks, I was grateful for the wind, despite
my stinging ears and raw eyes.

    I walk every morning out to the rocks. In the summer, the miles
of purple heather smell like honey and butterflies dip through the
bushes. Now, though, the gorse is dominant. Its silver-green blades
edging onto my path, sharp and unforgiving, held firm with
inexplicable shapes of wood. I once burned it back, and the
branches were fragile as hollow bone, shades of silver and white
and such curves and angles to them – I felt I had destroyed
something beautiful, and was seeing beauty in the scars. I haven't
burned it back since, though the wood shapes decorate my home.
Their twists and turns make, one day, the shadow of a wolf, the
next, a beckoning hand. Or a smile. I'll show you when you arrive.

    Perhaps we can collect driftwood together.

    Would you like that?

I have decided to record this new set of logs as I wait for you. It will help me mark the time, as much as anything. I'm getting forgetful and sometimes I do not know the days. Sometimes I miss the passing of weeks. I've wiped all the old logs, to clean things up a bit – there was nothing much there except my ramblings, my doubts. I expect I'll delete all of these as well, when I see your car pulling in through the gate.

I sent the letter with the Asda man, who promised to post it for me in the village. The postman doesn't come any more, though I don't know if that's because he's stopped making the journey or if there simply haven't been any letters to make it for. It doesn't really matter, though I suppose if you reply by post I might not receive the letter. But of course I wasn't asking you to write to me, I was asking you to visit.

Perhaps I should have made it sound more beautiful. It is beautiful here, as well as brutal. You'll see. It is the kind of landscape that inspires. We'll walk out towards Rockfield, perhaps, scramble over the rocks and search for fossilised remains of giant coral and ammonites . . .

My own coral reefs are surviving, but they need so much care they will never be truly independent. I keep the conditions as close to perfect as I can for my indigo hamlets, and for the exquisite corals themselves. The tanks are maintained at 1.023–1.025 specific gravity, which you'll need to know if you ever want to keep a reef tank yourself. Calcium at 425 ppm and magnesium at 1300. I can teach you, if you like. The corals need the constant challenge of turbulent water, did you know that? Wonderful, from something so delicate. Their requirements are contrary to their appearance.

It feels so very important that I talk to you now. There was so much I couldn't say in the letter, since I don't know really where it will go or what will happen to it. The Asda man is a decent person, I think, but after he posts it . . .

Well, I hope you will come. I've been thinking about you all day today, and for many of the days before that.

Hold on a minute. I'll be right back.

. . . I just went to put more logs on the fire there – it's been on since the morning so the embers are glowing, but the cold really is bitter now. I can feel it in the tops of my feet, spreading through my ankles and shins, curling up to settle around my knees. If you come soon you will be arriving in midwinter, so perhaps we'll not go to the beach. I'm sorry about that. I'm sorry about a lot of things.

I hope the journey isn't too treacherous.

I hope you can forgive me.

Well.

I think I should eat something.

Chapter 3

EVA WOKE WITH THE SUN in her eyes and the curtains wide. The chill was noticeable through the blankets and sheets she'd pulled up to her mouth in the night.

She slept in a single bed. She'd had a double for a while, thinking the space would be a luxury, but it wasn't. Even though she'd been sleeping on her own for years – the last six years of her forties – she always kept to one side, noticing the cold of the unused portion of bed when she dipped a toe across. The habit was frustrating. She didn't feel like she was occupying half a house, living half a life, so why this ritual with her side of the bed? Then a few months ago she'd arranged for a single to be delivered, and the old double removed. With the extra space, she'd brought plants into the room: an avocado plant that sprouted long thin leaves, chilli plants of varying oranges, red, purples – like the colours of her hair – and a peace lily. They were standing on small, circular tables of different heights and woods that she got second-hand, from charity shops or street markets. She liked the splashes of green, the terracotta and black pots. She liked the idea of some new life occupying the room.

She sat up, swivelled around to face the door. Soft slippers, placed the night before, were waiting for her feet. Time to get to work.

Four years ago Eva had inherited her house from her mother. She'd never really intended to live there long term, but in the years since her mum's death she hadn't quite been able to move out. The house connected her to a past that was out of reach – perhaps it always had been. She'd moved in a couple of years before her mum died, at a time when she'd had nowhere else to go and she'd been grateful, for the company as much as the roof over her head. But the house was more than that, and had been passed down in their family for generations – she didn't even know who had first lived there, whether it was the grandparents she'd never known, or generations before that.

She'd driven her mum mad, when she was little, wanting to know who everyone was, where they were. Of course she wanted to know. She wanted them to be her family. But her mum never gave a straight answer to anything. 'Tell me about Grandma Goldsmith,' she'd plead. 'Tell me about Grandpa and Great-Grandpa, tell me about Great-Great-Great . . .' Her mum would lift her up and spin her around, but she didn't tell her what she wanted to know. 'Can we *visit* Grandma and Grandpa Goldsmith?' she'd ask every holiday, eyes wide until, once, her mum looked at her and said, 'My dad died when I was young.'

Eva hadn't known what to say. She'd shuffled closer to her mother, put her head on her shoulder. 'But what about Grandma?'

'Enough!' her mum had said, pushing her away and standing up, leaving Eva gaping in shock. Her mum was everything to her. She didn't want to make her angry, she hadn't meant to. She'd have stopped her lip wobbling if she knew how. Her mum had come and knelt down in front of her. 'It's OK,' she'd whispered. 'I'm sorry. I didn't mean to shout.' But after that, Eva stopped asking. Even as a teenager, it was the one subject she knew not to approach. And now? Whatever the history of their beautiful house, it had been home to Avigail and Eva Goldsmith, and that was all she needed to know.

Downstairs a large living-dining room ran the length of the house, with bay windows looking over the herbs in the front garden and glass doors opening onto a patio in the back. Paved with red and grey stones, weeds long since settled in between them, it led to the wonderfully overgrown wilderness that stretched all the way down to the stream. She didn't use it as a living-dining room though; instead she had her piano in there, and some of her mum's old paintings on the walls. There were layers upon layers of wallpaper. She'd peeled back a corner once to find an emerald-green stripe, and something with roses in red and gold beneath that. The top layer was pale blue with curved grey branches and light pink cherry blossom. With the dark wood floor and large, empty space, she liked it. Besides, it had been her mum's favourite room. Aside from the piano and the old sofa in the corner, the only piece of furniture was the roll-top desk, and Eva found herself looking at it now, her fingers running over the curved slats before turning the key in the small lock.

She wanted to find out what was behind the new advertising campaign. There had to be some motivation there – financial? political? Once she knew *why* they were doing it, perhaps she'd be able to work out how she felt about it. But she didn't want to start by looking through her own correspondence. It was all too . . . polite. FullLife had always responded to her emails, given answers to her queries about specific aspects of the technology, the statistics. She'd been given no reason to suspect they were doing anything wrong, or that they were lying to anyone.

But she did suspect they were lying. All their perfect data, all the smiling faces in their adverts – where were the parents who felt a lack of connection to their child in the pouch? Where were the side effects? There had to be something. She needed to look further back, to find someone who had hidden the truth and been bad enough at it that the truth had been visible. One of the scientists, maybe. Not PR, not publicity – they were too good at staying on message. She wanted someone who couldn't follow the rules quite so well. She felt something leaning on her, a pressure on her chest as she pulled out folder after folder of her mum's notes, piling them around her in disordered stacks. She would go through everything, and somewhere in among it all she would find a name. A starting point.

She sipped her coffee, then stood up and headed to the kitchen for the radio. Unplugging it, she carried it to the piano room – her new office, she corrected – and plugged it in next to the desk. Sooner or later there would be another advert. There had to be. Because one thing she knew for sure when she woke up this morning was that if FullLife had announced a new 'NaturalBirth' plan, then something was going on.

*

Rosie rolled over and curled her body around Kaz, the way she did every morning in the half-sleep she passed through before waking. The warmth of his body and the rhythm of his breathing helped her open her eyes. She kissed the curve of his neck and rested her head against his. She loved mornings. Mornings were the best.

'Kaz,' she whispered.

'Mmmmm.'

'It's today.'

'I know, baby.'

She inched her head closer to his arm, which he lifted so she could lie on his chest. Her fingers touched his belly, stroked the smooth dark skin she was so fond of.

Downstairs most of the family were up already. She could smell coffee, hear the swish and churn of the bread maker. Nana still insisted that fresh bacon roti was the way to start a birthday. And was she singing? Rosie hummed along quietly to the tune. Her nana was the best, and she was going to be just like her.

Rosie loved living in this house, with all her family. But once Will got older, perhaps had a baby sister or brother, they'd start looking for their own place. Once they were qualified, after uni, and when they both had jobs. Perhaps another house along this street. West London was so beautiful, and the Thames nearby. Maybe they could teach Will to row – there was a club that she'd seen out on the river. They'd have to learn themselves, though, since she'd never actually been in a boat. And she didn't know how to swim. She'd learn, they both would. That's what was so great – they'd learn everything with Will and Will's baby sister or brother. There was so much she wanted them all to learn together, and today was the start of it. Today she was going to learn to be a parent.

She felt Kaz's body move beside her.

'Are you imagining holding Will again?' she said.

'How did you know?'

'Your shoulder wobbles when you smile.'

Rosie leaned up on an elbow, looked down at him with her hair falling around his face.

'You are sooo sexy,' he said with a grin, wrapping his arms around her waist and slipping his hands under her vest top.

She was glad they'd chosen natural conception for Will, and fairly sure it'd be the same for all their other children. It was special for them, for their generation – in the early days, almost all the pouches began with IVF. But now that the transfer process had been perfected, loads of people opted for natural conception. The hard bit was waiting two weeks for FullLife to monitor the completed transfer. They used the time for screening too, so they could confirm the baby was healthy and everything.

'Are you ready?' Rosie said, kissing the tip of his nose.

'I'm ready,' Kaz smiled. 'I've been ready since the day I met you.'

'You mean when I accidentally hit that rounder's ball into your face in PE?'

'OK, the day after that.'

'You mean when you came to school with a bruised eye?' she said, eyebrows raised.

'And you looked like you were about to cry.'

'I was *not* about to cry.'

'You reached up to touch it, but didn't,' he said. 'I think it was because you were scared of hurting me again. So your hand just kind of hovered there, by my face, like time had stopped.'

Rosie paused for a minute, listened to his breathing, felt the warmth coming from his body. 'That's when you knew?'

'That's when I knew.'

'Shall we have a baby today, Kaz?'

He pulled her closer, kissed the side of her ear, pressed his face against her head.

'Yes please,' he whispered, his voice muffled by her hair.

'Right then!'

She leapt up and pulled the covers off him, jumping out of the bed and laughing as he clutched on to the sheet.

'Better get up,' she grinned.

He threw a pillow at her, but she caught it and held her finger to her lips, turning to the pouch stand. The legs of the base were the only part of the stand outside the incubator; inside it their pouch was gently supported by the soft shoulders and central padded shelf. They'd chosen a pale blue for the stand itself – it toned so nicely with the mauve of their pouch – and the transparent incubator was almost like a bubble in the way it refracted the light. She could see little rainbows on its surface as she moved her head from side to side. Then she slid the front panels open and felt the warmth on her skin, just enough to mimic the closeness of a human body, as she reached in to gently stroke the curve of their child. The shape of the pouch really was beautiful, like a painting or something, the way it rested there just like when she or Kaz were wearing it. She could imagine nutrients flowing from the nutrient bag, down the matching mauve tube cover, through the feed and into the pouch itself, giving baby Will everything he needed. The pouch was more than a painting – it was like a beautiful living sculpture that you could touch, that you could hug. And outside the incubator it actually shared heat with the person carrying it. She loved that idea, the transfer of warmth between them.

'Good morning, baby Will,' she said, kissing the pouch, feeling it softly flex beneath the pressure of her lips. She'd put it on soon, so he'd feel the heat of her body, hear the beat of her pulse on the morning of his birth. 'We love you,' she whispered, as close as she could get. 'We'll see you soon.'

*

There were no more natural-birth adverts on the radio. Eva listened all morning, and while there were radio plays and music and adverts for furniture sales and Christmas trees, there was nothing about FullLife. Nothing, for hours. From the serenity of the broadcasting, you'd think there was nothing new going on in the world.

From searching online she found some chat rooms full of the crazy accusations she'd always tried to distance herself from – FullLife were experimenting on babies in the pouches; babies were disappearing; babies were being replaced with something non-human. It all sounded a bit like alien abductions. Of course none of it was true. She had checked, she'd even met up with a few of the most vocal users, but all they had were urban legends and sci-fi plots. FullLife never even got involved. They didn't need to – no one believed any of it anyway, and there were plenty of people willing to leap to FullLife's defence in the discussion groups. You could find anything online, if you looked for long enough, but rarely anything of use.

She did find some information in her mum's notes, though she wasn't sure how much help that would be either. There were folders full of letters of support, which must have been important to her mum, but Eva couldn't bring herself to read them. There were newspaper cuttings from when she actually managed to get some good press, back when papers were still being bought and sold. Articles raising questions that no one seemed to want to raise, about the clinical trial periods, care homes, pouch abuse, potential long-term effects on human fertility. They were from decades ago. And there was an address book. That's what Eva had been hoping to find. Her mum had known a lot of people, and some of them, surely, would talk to her.

As she flicked through the pages and read the names, she could imagine herself back there, watching as a child in awe of her mum who had no end of phone calls and letters – she'd had so many friends. The house was full of them, as well as the office. Her mum had loved it when people came to stay. They didn't have to agree with her – in fact she'd relished the chance to stay up late and drink and argue, Eva listening, usually, from her bedroom upstairs, wishing she were old enough to join in.

One night she'd crept down in her pyjamas and sat in the corner without her mum noticing. They were smoking something sweet and leafy, she thought, too young to place the scent, and they were talking about Freida. One of her mum's friends was claiming to have met her – she could tell the story was important, even though she was only nine – everyone had heard of Freida, and no one knew where she was. Except that man with the long moustache and the beads around his wrist and the kind eyes, who winked at her. He was describing an old woman, it seemed to Eva, an old woman who was lonely and lost. Not the arrogant, single-minded scientist her mother had told her about. Her mum stood up, arms wild like she was about to say something *really* important, but then she saw Eva and started trying to hide the joint behind her back.

The memory made Eva smile. She was like a teenager, her mum.

Rebellious. 'Now my daughter's caught me at it,' she'd said. 'My moral high ground slipping ever further away . . .' And Eva had been allowed to stay, to listen to their talk of island communities, living off-grid, carrying life inside you. Seemed a bit icky to think of it like that, though Eva knew better than to say so. Besides, she was happy to stay quiet and watch. Her mum was radiant, at the centre of a group of hippies and artists who thought they were on the right side of a peaceful but essential fight.

And here were their names, catalogued in the address book along with journalists and parents of her school friends. But they were not the people Eva needed to speak with now. She found the FullLife staff her mother had known listed, beautifully and arbitrarily, under F. For FullLife? Fools? Fuckers? Knowing her mum, it could have been all three. Each had a name and a label: receptionist at London office, fired technician, research lab student (see Q), cleaner at birth centre, marketing intern. She must have started the list fifteen, twenty years ago – actually Eva had no idea when. Her mum had been monitoring the work of FullLife ever since Eva was old enough to ask what she was doing. The list could be forty years old, but it was possible that the research lab student might be a scientist now. Might still be working there. Or might remember something that had been brushed under the carpet, a shortcut taken . . . She flicked to Q and there was just one entry: Quentin. There was a personal mobile number.

Eva sat back on her heels and took a deep breath.

*

Piotr was taking the day off. He'd been interviewing the Bhattacharyya women yesterday, and would have to do more of the same tomorrow, but today they were having their perfect baby (perhaps he should pity the spoiled little thing) and Piotr – well, he was walking aimlessly around London in a foul mood. Sometimes he missed the manual labour of his teenaged summers and today, in particular, he would have liked to vent his mood on something productive, something literal. His fingers were aching in the cold.

His flat was at the wrong end of Angel, small and increasingly dusty and he suspected there was a leak from upstairs rotting the inside of his bathroom wall. He could smell the damp, but not see it. A bad sign, surely. Even Sweet Potato roamed around with her nose in the air, letting him know that she wouldn't put up with this substandard life for much longer. He was surprised – though grateful – that she hadn't run off years ago. And then this morning he'd left the flat to find that his bike, which he kept chained up in the communal stairwell along with several others, had been stolen. Not just the bikes – they'd stolen the whole banister. Sawn right through it with a hacksaw, at both ends, and then lifted the whole lot. Must have been two of them at least. Shit's sake, was it a gang? His wasn't even a very good bike. Not that he would be able to afford a new one. He needed to get this article about the baby finished and filed as soon as possible – he needed the bloody money.

Perhaps it was the unashamed wealth of the Bhattacharyya family that had annoyed him. Perhaps it was the self-satisfied money of the whole of west London. No, it wasn't that. He wasn't like that. At least he never used to be. He was just unnerved by Holly, by the way she'd looked at him as if she knew everything about him and was profoundly unimpressed. And he would have bet everything he'd ever owned on the fact that Holly Bhattacharyya's wide-eyed granddaughter had never had her bike nicked.

He criss-crossed through the greens and parks of Islington, mostly empty in this weather – there was frost on the grass, crunching beneath his feet. Avoiding Holloway Road, he found himself walking around the outskirts of Paradise Park. He pushed the gate and walked over to one of the benches.

The wood was damp, cold, unpleasant to the touch, but he

wanted to sit down – he was unfit, he thought to himself, and not for the first time. He'd been in good shape once, when he was younger, and it wasn't just from working with his dad on the building site. He'd been a runner, back when he had the enthusiasm to get somewhere quickly and the right kind of competition beside him. That was how he thought about Eva these days, not about her face or warmth or even her smell – though her smell was something he missed deeply, achingly, when he woke – but as a sort of presence who had been there when he was better at life. Who'd made him better at life. No, he wasn't that pathetic – he'd been good on his own, too. She'd liked something about him.

He patted down his pockets, looking for anything to sit on to avoid the damp from the bench seeping into his trousers, but his pockets were empty apart from his keys, phone, and equally empty wallet. There wasn't even a tissue to wipe it down. He shrugged off his jacket despite the cold and laid it over the slats, then sat down heavily.

He tried to get back the irritation that had spurred him on to walk in the first place – the stolen bike, was it? Or the girl, Rosie, with her oblivious confidence? But it was no use. His annoyance had dissipated already, and been replaced with a loneliness that seemed to linger, on some days, in his lungs. And then it popped into his head, that ridiculous thing with the gate yesterday. He didn't know why he hadn't just walked around to the front, but he couldn't do it – couldn't backtrack, couldn't turn after having made the initial mistake. Then he'd fallen. They were watching him; he'd heard their laughter. But he'd got up from the ground quickly. At least he had that.

He'd been a good reporter once. Been able to hear the words that people left unspoken in their sentences. Eva said he made it too personal sometimes, but he thought that journalism had to be personal – if you don't care about what you write, with personal intent, then what is the point? Though he was struggling to find any interest in Rosie and Kaz. They had no need for his article; perhaps that was the problem. In fact, the world had no need of him to write it at all. It wasn't personal. It wasn't important. It was filing yet another page on a computer screen. And paying the bills. Bloody insurance. Bloody FullLife. It had never been more imperative to have a job, and his was sinking.

Holly had been testing him, he realised suddenly. She was never going to ask him to wear the pouch – they would never let a journalist wear their pouch, not a family like that. She'd wanted to see his reaction. He didn't know why.

He stood up. His jacket clung to his trousers, damp from the wet wood he'd been sitting on, but he didn't notice. He took a step away from the bench, looking carefully around the park. Trying to remember how to look at things properly. The trees, the fence, the farmyard animals they kept in the corner. The huge, bright billboards along the tops of the buildings across the road, advertising films and department stores and shampoo. It wasn't the advert for FullLife and their health-care plans that caught his eye, though. Not exactly. It was what had been done to it.

First the bikes and now this.

What was going on? Something had changed these past few months and, whatever it was, it was getting worse. There was more petty crime. There were more conspiracy theorists online. Last month he'd pitched an article about the used pouches, the new social divide, and now this ... This was blatant vandalism. He hadn't seen anything like it in years.

As he stared up at the poster he wasn't sure if what he was feeling was unease or an illicit thrill. The words written in friendly green letters advertising the FullBirth 'baby pouch' plan had been spray-painted over. Someone had climbed up there to graffiti over the advertising, to block out the word 'Full'. And in its place they had scrawled something else, something that he thought was a signature, like a tag. But then it jumped out at him. It wasn't a tag, it was a word. There, in an ugly black scrawl, someone had defaced the ten-foot-tall FullLife advert.

Not with art. Not with colour or imagery but a word.

Still.

The word was 'Still'.

And the poster said: Still Birth.

Chapter 4

IT WAS THE DAY OF his first grandchild's birth, and Karl was balancing on the top rung of a ladder putting the final touches on the elaborate sea mural he'd painted for baby Will's new bedroom. Of course, he understood that Will, Kaz, and Rosie, would be living at Holly's place once he was born, same as they were now. And that was totally fine. He just wanted them to know they'd always be welcome here. Here, there would be purple mer-people and bright yellow butterfly fish on the walls. Here there were glowing stars on the ceiling. OK, so secretly he wanted this to be Will's favourite bedroom. That wasn't so bad, was it?

Karl had always imagined he'd have a large family. Four, five kids at least. He'd been the youngest of seven, the quiet one, always smiling and watching the rest, and always getting tickled too. As his siblings left home one by one he'd missed the laughter, the company, the sense of being surrounded by people – so he wanted to fill his own house with the same boisterous noise. Then he'd met Cris, who made a fair bit of noise on his own. And as things had turned out, Kaz was their only child. He and Cris spoiled him rotten. They couldn't help themselves.

And now Kaz, their baby Kaz, was having a child. The first of many, he secretly hoped, though far be it from him to interfere. He'd already got all the old toys out of the attic – they'd never been thrown away, of course – and he'd even started playing with some of the

Lego. Just to remind himself, so he could help build the houses, the farmyard, the space station ... Yes, he'd spent a while playing with the Lego. And he'd introduced himself to Will, his grandson-to-be, through the pouch. It was therapeutic, to whisper to someone through the pouch like that, palm-to-palm. Easier in a way than talking to someone face-to-face. Though Cris liked to call out to him from across the room: Good morning, baby Will, Grandpa's arrived!

Karl himself had been a natural birth, as had all his brothers and sisters – his parents were traditional, at a time when it was still the old versus the new. He'd been born a month premature; his parents liked to tell the story. It had a happy ending. There were pictures of his tiny black body looking all wrinkled in one of those transparent cots they used for babies in the neonatal ward – just like in the leaf-lets about the risks of natural birth you got at school. He didn't think it had affected him, but then how could you ever really know? Perhaps, given that extra month in the womb he'd have grown up to be a six-four prop for Harlequins like Cris, rather than a choreographer. Put like that, he was rather glad to have been born premature.

By the time he was an adult, though, everyone knew the baby pouch was the safest, the best way – it wasn't just accepted, it was preferred. So he and Cris hadn't had to fight for their right to have a baby with the pouch. FullLife had frozen eggs available for anyone who needed them. And they knew there'd be no trouble get-ting milk, since genetically engineered milk was available to all parents, specifically tailored, the healthiest option. They hadn't had to suffer looks of surprise or, worse, activists telling them they had no right to jointly father a child. Incredible, how far human-ity had come in a few generations.

He climbed down from the ladder, one careful foot at a time, and stood back to survey his work. It was pretty good, if he did say so himself. Beautifully colourful. He would have loved a room like this, when he was young. Kaz was going to love it too. They'd kept it secret, so it could be a birth day surprise. He could imagine Kaz's face, as Cris held his hands over his eyes and they led him in – he could hardly wait. He sat on the floor and looked up to the solar system on the ceiling.

There had been some difficulty, for Karl and Cris. Twenty years ago now, but still fresh, still sore. There had been a baby girl, before she was even a baby, their daughter who never grew to be more than an embryo. She'd died just six days after implantation in the pouch. Before they'd even been able to carry her. It didn't happen often, but when it did it always happened within the first fortnight. It was the most difficult part of the whole process, that initial attachment. He still missed her as if he'd known her all his life – he could picture her perfectly, even though he'd never seen her at all. He wondered why it was, that love should work like that. The next time they tried, Cris acted as the biological father instead, and Kaz was born. Strange words those, 'biological father'. Parenthood wasn't about being a blood relation, he knew – and he knew it deeply, in the same place he knew love and fear and hope. It was about intimacy.

The pouch itself allowed him to have an intimacy with his son that he wouldn't have otherwise had. To feel what it was like to carry an unborn child, his tiny fists pressing against his belly – there was nothing like it. He'd written to Holly about it once. They'd lived not far from each other, and she was famous, so he knew which house was hers even though they hadn't met at that stage. The first woman ever to use the pouch – even now he occasionally felt a little in awe of her. He'd been far too embarrassed to talk to her in person, but he wanted to tell her how wonderful it was, for a man. For two men. How life-changing. It was a gift, he'd written, and he didn't know if he deserved it.

It had probably been a rather gushing letter, quite out of

character. He'd written it just a few days after Kaz was born, overwhelmed with love and wonder and sleep deprivation. Holly had never mentioned it. Not when they met for the first time at that playgroup, not at all the school plays and Christmas concerts over the years. He'd taken that as kindness – as her understanding that he didn't want to make a big deal of things. That he was a little embarrassed.

There was just that one moment, at the wedding. Kaz was in his suit, looking even younger, somehow, than he would have done if he'd worn his school uniform, and Rosie was looking pretty in that simple, elegant dress that had once belonged to Holly herself. They'd finished the main course and were waiting for dessert. Rosie's sweet laugh echoed around the room. Kaz had pulled himself together after crying his way through Cris's extended speeches. Karl hadn't given a speech though, he hadn't said much at all – sometimes he didn't know what to say to anyone – but he had smiled around the table and felt proud of his son. And throughout it all, Holly had been seated next to him at the high table, watching the ceremony with a knowing look on her face. Then, quite unexpectedly, she'd turned her eyes to his, and whispered to him. 'You did well,' she'd said, making sure that no one else could hear. And then she'd winked.

*

Eva keyed in the phone number for the third time, and looked at the string of digits on the screen without pressing call. It was strange, how anxious she felt – she was not normally precious about making phone calls. It probably wouldn't be his number at all, not after all these years. But if it was, she had no idea what to say.

Usually, she would have been direct – told them exactly who she was, listed her questions, requested information. And usually, in response, they were polite and accommodating, and sent her everything that she asked for, together with a promotional pen or fridge magnet. But today . . . She wondered if she should pretend to be a reporter or something, a researcher. Was there a way to make him think she was on his side? Quentin. Perhaps he would let his guard down if she lied, and then she'd be more likely to see a crack, a hint at something buried away from the public eye.

She pressed the call button. She'd work out the best approach once she heard his voice, play it by ear. Perhaps she should hang up.

'Yes?'

The man's voice was breathy and impatient. She hesitated.

'Hello?' he said again, a slight irritation creeping into his tone.

'Hi,' she said. 'Hi, my name's Eva—'

'Who?'

'Eva. I'm looking for Quentin?'

'Yes, this is James.'

'I . . .' It took her a moment to realise that her mother had written only a surname. They can't have known each other well. This was a mistake. 'I'm sorry. I thought you knew my mother. Avigail Goldsmith.'

He didn't reply, and she thought for a moment that he was going to be the one to hang up the phone.

'Why are you calling?'

'I found your number, in my mum's address book and I—'

'Just tell me,' he said, 'please. Just . . .'

The pause seemed endless to Eva, as her mind slowly caught up with the conversation.

'. . . is she ill?' he asked. 'Has something happened?'

Eva felt a lurch in her stomach, wrapped her free arm around her waist to try and stop the reaction. She'd forgotten what it was like, having to tell people.

'Yes,' Eva said.

She heard his breath as he exhaled close to the phone. Was he genuinely upset?

'I'm sorry, she passed away,' she corrected.

Eva hadn't meant to make it sound so recent, or so blunt, but her mum's death was still raw. Besides, she'd never known how to soften the bad news for others. Sometimes, before falling asleep, she'd forget everything that had happened these past six years, and she'd be back to what things were like before. Her mum's face as they argued in the office, eyes blazing, her laugh a crescendo, drinking wine over dinner, Eva confiding in her about how much she missed the garden now she was living with Piotr. Then she'd jolt awake, remember what had happened but think, just for a second, that it had all been a nightmare. That it was OK. That she'd find her mum downstairs making tea. And then she'd feel in her stomach that it wasn't OK at all. None of it was OK.

'Are you in London?' he said.

'What?'

'I'm, unfortunately, I'm very busy, we have . . . so much work but, if it's in London, I'd like to come to the funeral.'

'Oh. God, I'm sorry. It's too late, she . . . I didn't realise . . .'

There was silence on the line while Eva searched, unsuccessfully, for something to say. She couldn't find any words.

'Perhaps lunch then?' he said hurriedly.

'What?'

'I can take a break at one. It's the only time I have . . . Things are busy. Can you meet me for lunch?'

She calculated the time it would take to get to the station, the trains every half-hour at this time of day, but she could get there. Of course she could get there. She didn't know why she was hesitating like this.

'I'd appreciate it,' he said.

He sighed, and she could hear another voice, muffled, in the room he was sitting in – someone on another desk, perhaps, working at another lab bench. She realised she had no idea what he was doing. Was he still at FullLife?

'If today's no good . . .'

'No. Yes,' she said, finally gathering her thoughts and grabbing a pen. 'Today's fine. Yes, of course. Lunch. Where?'

On the train, Eva had a row of seats to herself. Over beyond the doors she could see another passenger, a young man in a suit with bright yellow earphones. She could hear the thumping bass of his music above the smooth glide of the train on the tracks. Her eyes stared out of the window but didn't focus on the fields they were passing – beyond them, in the distance and half hidden by trees, she could see the large complex of care homes on the outskirts of the city.

There was a paper at the end of each aisle, as there always was, even though everyone got their news online. But reading material, recycled of course, was supplied on public transport, to make the carriages feel homely, welcoming. Newspaper was the wrong word for it though, she thought as she picked one up. This was a brochure. A series of glossy adverts. Nothing more. She wished they'd leave the trains out of their bloody PR campaigns. Trains were one of the few places she still loved.

She'd once travelled by train across Siberia, with Piotr. The last time she'd left the country, in fact. How long ago was that? She counted back the years, trying not to use landmarks of funerals and hospital appointments to keep track of the dates. Ten years. Could it really be ten years? Even then the visas had been hard to get. Piotr's credentials got them into Russia – officially he was writing an article about the new canals, unofficially a report on the black market for used pouches. Eva was allowed to go along for the ride. Everyone assumed she was his wife. Still, she wasn't going to miss the opportunity, even if she was infuriated by the way it came about – FullLife were funding the website that had commissioned his report. But the world needed to know how much damage the pouches were doing, and she could write her own articles when she got home regardless of what Piotr decided to publish.

She could remember their compartment as if it had been a few weeks ago. The cooked-vegetable smell that wafted in early evening from the dining carriage, the flimsy curtains that she pulled across every night – except for one particularly clear night, halfway through their trip, when they'd kept the curtains open to watch the stars through their small square window. There were bunk beds that they were supposed to sleep in, each one barely big enough for a person – he'd confined himself to the lower bunk when they'd argued at the start of the trip. But eventually they'd climbed into the top bunk together, enjoying the closeness, laughing at the fun of it, clinging on to each other so as not to fall out during the night.

'It must be possible to sleep like this. Humans used to live in trees,' Piotr had said, his voice softly close, his breath sleepy-stale and familiar.

'No, that was caves,' she'd replied. 'You're so confused, sweetheart. Must be the sleep deprivation.'

'I mean *before* the caves, sweet potato.'

The train's wheels had clanked over some uneven track, both of them opening their eyes wide in alarm. 'Sounds a bit wild out there,' he'd whispered. But the train had carried on.

'So, you mean back when we were monkeys?'

'Apes.'

'Then tell me, how did we balance on the branches?'

'By wrapping ourselves all around them, like so.'

'I see,' she'd laughed quietly, into his chest.

'That's why we have such long arms and legs.'

He'd curled his legs around hers and pulled himself in closer.

'So, I'm like the branch here?'

'Skin smooth as eucalyptus.'

'And that would make you a koala bear?'

'Still an ape.'

'Well, you're hairy enough for it, I suppose.'

'And there I was being so charming.'

Eva closed her eyes and allowed herself to fall back into the memory, just for a moment. She wished the trains into London juddered on the tracks the way the old Trans-Siberian trains did. She wanted to be jolted, to feel the movement of travel while she was travelling. All this gliding was too easy, made you forget the miles that were passing below your feet. It was like the colour green, everything painted green to be relaxing. Where did it come from, this obsession with everything being perfect? She wanted the rough edges back.

The endless birch trees, she remembered, bark shimmering in and out of the winter sunlight as they sped past. She hadn't realised that was what it would be like. When she'd thought of Siberia, she hadn't pictured birch trees – she'd imagined it as desolate and wind-swept. But then they'd passed Irkutsk and followed the shoreline of Lake Baikal, and there were no more trees. It *was* flat and desolate, the expanse of water reflecting the globe of the sun.

He had whispered to her one morning, as they woke in their tiny carriage, entangled, the sun bursting its way through that flimsy white curtain and the snow on the Gobi Desert reflecting more light than she'd ever seen. It wasn't featureless though, wild as it was, it was curved and cupped, that snow. She could imagine movement in it, as if it were flowing, slipping through the air like satin. Yes, she remembered what he'd whispered, as they looked out at the Gobi Desert – she remembered it word for word. It was the moment that had changed everything. His breath tickling her ear, his arm heavy over her chest, the lurching of the cabin.

The train had pulled into London Bridge, and Eva looked up to realise she was the only one left in the carriage. She grabbed her bag and the paper lying beside her, ran to the train door, pressing the button repeatedly to make sure it didn't close on her. It was a panic out of proportion. They weren't supposed to close on a person, these train doors – they had special detectors to make sure they were perfectly safe – but somehow she was never quite convinced about that. Things had a habit of closing on her when they shouldn't have, and she knew that it could hurt.

*

As the rest of the family chatted downstairs and planned the celebrations, Holly stood in front of the long mirror in her bedroom. Every now and then she could hear the pop of a party balloon that had been filled with too much air, followed by a pretend-scream and a giggle. She had bought balloons in every colour and shape she could find, the bright reds and yellows of children's birthdays mixed in with elegant silvers, smiling cartoon faces and friendly monkeys. It had become a family tradition, the balloons, started on the day Daphne was born, her first child. It hadn't been a room full of balloons then, though, it had just been the one.

She had worn the pouch herself as she and Will walked, hand in hand, into the FullLife birthing centre. She'd thought it was an important statement – she needed to show the world that this was *her* choice. She had not given anything up. She was carrying her own child, in the way that she chose. Will had suggested, although it was already what she was thinking, that they take turns carrying their children into the birthing centre to be born. It gave a lovely equality to the matching photos. Holly carried Daphne, and two years later Will carried their second daughter, Leigh. Then Holly carried Aarav but by then the press had cooled off and they'd swapped over in the lift because Holly was better at keeping Daphne and Leigh from fighting.

'It's because I'm the calm one,' she said to Will as she readjusted the pouch straps around his back. 'It's not that I'm strict.'

'Of course not,' he replied, smiling calmly.

'And it's not that you spoil them.'

'No.'

'Though all that maple syrup at breakfast might not have been a good idea.'

But that was all later. For the first time, the birth of their first daughter, there was no joking in the lift. It was as if the world was holding its breath and, even for Holly, the nerves, the spotlight, made her anxious, aware of the importance of what she was doing.

Her mum still didn't understand – neither of her parents ever had. But she didn't expect them to, really. The parents who had explained to seventeen-year-old Holly that they couldn't afford to send both their children to university, but that university wasn't really important for women anyway. Her mother hadn't gone, and things had worked out well for her. Spoken by her father, of course, although her mum certainly didn't contradict him. She felt the injustice so sharply she didn't know how to fight it, so instead she shouted the truth at them.

'That's stupid,' she said. 'I'm cleverer than him.'

Her dad had glared at her and left the room, and her mum had asked her to help chop the vegetables.

No, they'd never understood, but her mum did try, after her dad died, Holly had to admit – and she'd come round to visit Daphne often. She'd accepted Will, in the end. She'd even grown to like him. But her mum hadn't been there to see her enter the building and change the world. That was what Holly and Will had done together.

The press had gathered outside the glass doors, not allowed in except for that one journalist who had been granted exclusive access to take the first photo after the birth was complete. As their camera flashes glinted in her eyes she held her head high but drew her arms around the pouch, as if protecting her baby from the media's glare. She had worn a dress, a bright dress with a bold pattern of flowers, and looking back she thought perhaps that had been a statement too – that she would not hide. They were shouting her name, hers more than Will's, and they walked together up the steps to the entrance as if they were on a red carpet. Then they'd walked through the glass doors and into the most peaceful building she'd ever been in.

It was new. Everything was new, everything felt warm and soft, the reception desk beautifully curved – even the doors had no sharp edges. And these huge, colourful flowers everywhere, it really was lovely. That was the moment when it hit her, just how much was resting on the birth of this one innocent, unaware baby. Will held her hand – his other arm occupied with their bag of supplies – and together they'd followed Freida into their birthing room.

And the funny thing was, she couldn't remember what happened next. She'd seen other births so many times since she knew what must have happened, but all she could remember now was the look of absolute awe, of love, on Will's face as he stared at his newborn daughter. He was almost afraid to touch her. 'She's so perfect,' he kept saying. And she was.

Freida had left to give them a moment, in that thoughtful, sensitive way that she had. Sometimes it seemed to Holly that Freida was everything her own parents were not. And when she came back she brought a balloon with her. A single, deep-indigo-coloured, perfectly round balloon. Holly had looked for a balloon that colour for every birth she'd been to since, but she could never find one.

She had kept the dress, though. She'd altered it a few times over the years, had to re-hem it, and more recently she'd added pockets because she liked to have pockets these days. Perhaps that was some part of the ageing process she didn't understand. But the colours were still there, on the pretty flowers covering the dress that she was holding in her hands. Will had called it her Holly dress.

'There's no holly on it, you know,' she'd said once, many years after the name had stuck, after their children had grown up and they'd been told that his cancer was terminal.

'But it's got Holly written all over it,' he said.

'Unapologetic?'

'Yes. And bold,' he smiled. 'And bright. And so very pretty.'

Now, Holly sat on the edge of her bed and pulled the dress over her head, feeding one arm at a time through the full-length sleeves of soft fabric. She stood up, smoothed over some creases, then turned back and forth to see every angle in the mirror. Yes, it still fitted her. She knew it would. It had to. This was the dress she was going to wear for the birth. For the new baby Will, named for the man she loved, whom she was missing, today, particularly deeply.

Audio log

8 Dec 2015 17:04

It has been two weeks now since I sent the letter and no one has arrived at my door. Still, it would have been out of the blue, I know, and I'm sure there are things happening that you need to be there for. It's OK, is what I'm saying. I'll wait.

I set up the scope again looking out to sea, for the dolphins, and the porpoises, but what I saw this afternoon was a boat of some kind. It was large . . . grey . . . bulky. Reminded me of my husband. It was many miles out to sea and it didn't approach the coastline, but I felt its presence out there like a weight.

After it had moved beyond my field of vision I didn't see anything for an age and then, during the hour or so before sunset, I saw an Arctic skua flying low against the waterline, then pivot high above only to plummet in a dive to the surface. I don't know what it was catching, but I pity its prey – I have never seen a bird twist and dive with such merciless precision. I couldn't look away until the dusk made viewing impossible, and the darkness came as a relief.

Tonight, between six and eight, I'll be getting my delivery. I have a standing order, which means that every fortnight my food arrives. It's especially important in the winter when my own vegetables and fruit trees are not productive. I would so hate to have to leave! And I don't need to, since my order has been delivered reliably every fortnight for two and a half years now. I don't mind telling you that I have come to appreciate it.

It is always the same man they send, the Asda man, and he is usually cheerful and whistling as he walks up the path. At first, I left a note instructing him to leave my delivery outside the front door, saying that I wasn't in. I didn't want to be disturbed, I came here to be alone and I don't care about the rain – what does it matter if things get wet? But these days I usually go to the door myself and open it once everything has been stacked up on the ground, ready for me to bring it inside. I like to make sure, to check everything personally.

The first time I opened the door he said:

'Well, hello!'

I didn't say anything back, but he didn't seem deterred by that. Nowadays he stands with me, him on the outside of the porch and me on the inside, and runs through everything on the list, making sure I have everything and telling me sometimes about substitutions. The substitutions are when they don't have the exact item on my standing order, so they give me the next best thing. He apologises for that, but I don't mind. Sometimes they give me sprouts instead of broccoli. It doesn't matter. Perhaps I'll ask him about the letter, although we've built up such a good understanding I don't want it to seem as though I doubt his trustworthiness. Because I don't doubt his trustworthiness. I'm sure he has posted it for me in the village and that is all he could do.

I wonder how you are. It is not often I wish I had a phone – so rarely I can't remember the last time I thought about it – but if I had one now I would probably be dialling your number. You wouldn't be glad to hear from me. Intrigued though, I expect. If nothing else your curiosity will bring you to my door sooner or later.

At least, that's what I'm hoping for now. I can't do it any other way. I am stubborn, I dare say, but I can't put myself on your doorstep to be turned away once more. Do you remember, what you said to me that last time? Do you remember how completely you slammed the door?

If I had to hear those words again, I honestly think they might kill me.

Chapter 5

ROSIE HAD TOLD THE JOURNALIST that she wasn't nervous, but now it came to the day, there was something - not nerves, exactly, but a sort of tingly excitement. Adrenaline, she supposed, and thought again how the pouch had made everything better. She wouldn't want baby Will to be pumped full of her own silly adrenaline on the first day of his life.

It was a funny phrase that, though, wasn't it? He had so clearly been alive in there for months now. He responded to her movements, kicked about if he was excited, was soothed by her singing and by the music they played him through the audio adapter. She wished she knew what it was like, listening to music through that adapter - like surround sound but so much better, like the world itself was humming and resonating in tune.

They'd played Will all sorts, some of their favourite bands, some of Nana's jazz - they'd even made a recording of Kaz's band playing their own songs. 'Sort of ska,' Kaz had called it, slightly embarrassed but pleased that Rosie had suggested the recording. They'd played at all the school concerts, Rosie and her friends always going along to watch. She'd liked seeing him onstage, though she could tell he was uncomfortable with all the attention - he was the bass player, while the others took turns as frontman. Kaz didn't want to be noticed, he just wanted to keep his head down and play music.

Her mum had already made the coffee when they got downstairs, and Rosie had taken a cup but Kaz had made some ginger tea instead – perhaps he was nervous too, looking over at her and giving his geeky grin. It was strange to think of baby Will being out in the world, where anything might happen.

The world on the whole, Rosie thought, was a good place. But there were accidents, things beyond anyone's control, tragedies. She shook her head – she didn't want to be thinking like this for Will's birth day. And she'd promised herself she wouldn't be too protective a mother.

When she was little she loved going on climbing frames, especially the big ones with metal bars at different heights that they have in playgrounds all around the city. The council made them as safe as could be, with padded mats embedded in the ground and a safety officer on site, but she'd also read somewhere that the bars needed to be all different distances apart, to really help with coordination. It wasn't good for things to be too predictable – better for children to learn to anticipate and adapt. Her mum used to let her play for as long as she liked, as wildly as she liked, while she sat on the bench reading or chatting with Grandpa or Auntie Leigh. She could hang upside down from her bended knees, turn somersaults on the highest bars of the climbing frame, around and around so that the world would spin – blue sky, green grass, blue sky, green grass.

She had been totally fearless, she realised now, as the memory made her heart beat a little faster. She wouldn't be able to perform those acrobatics any more, she didn't even like going on roller coasters. She and Kaz had admitted that to each other last year – after a dizzying ride at Thorpe Park, the kind designed to make you scream. He took her on the horses for their next ride, and they'd sat together with Rosie on the front saddle and Kaz behind, his arms wrapped around her waist as the organ music played and the carousel gently turned.

'This is better,' she'd said, leaning back into his chest. The music had reminded her of a jewellery box she'd had when she was a child, soft and soothing and far away. 'This is exactly the sort of life I want to have.' All around them people had been laughing and playing, children waving candyfloss and those fluffy clouds were in the sky, the kind you get sometimes on a summer's day.

'Time to stop daydreaming, you two.'

It was Rosie's mum, smiling and jangling her car keys. She'd taken the day off to drive them to the birthing centre, to be there for the birth. Kaz's dad and pops were meeting them at FullLife – they'd been texting for updates all morning. Kaz had called them Dad and Pops since he was a little boy so Rosie had adopted the names; she rather liked having two dads, after spending most of her life without even one. Her nana was coming too of course. Nana had been at every birth in the family. She'd put on her favourite dress, the one that she was wearing in the photo. Rosie knew she often crept upstairs to make tiny alterations when she was missing Grandpa. And today she'd chosen her pale yellow-and-navy wide-brimmed hat to go with it.

'Nana, you look like you're going to a wedding,' she laughed.

'Wait.' Her nana held up her hand. 'I still need the finishing touch.' And she stood in front of the long mirror in the hall to pin a brooch to her smart jacket. It was the wise snowy owl, Rosie noticed, the one she'd given Nana for her seventy-fifth birthday.

'Perfect,' her nana smiled. 'Now, what are you all waiting for?'

The whole family piled into the car: Kaz in the front seat wearing the pouch, Rosie in the back, leaning forward to check they were both OK, comfortable, strapped in safe. Nana was sitting beside her with the full skirt of her flowery dress splayed across the back seat. The bag was in the boot, with the bottles and Babygros in different colours – we don't know which one will suit him yet, Rosie had argued, and Kaz had conceded her point. She couldn't wait to feed him for the first time, to give him their genetic blend of milk they'd had specially prepared, to choose the little hat for his head. As they pulled away her nana smiled at her, conspiratorially, and kissed her on the cheek.

*

Piotr scrunched his eyes shut and leaned back on his sofa, only to open them wide again and stare at the ceiling. Which needed painting. Which had a spider's web not exactly in the corner – in the corner would have been more OK – but it was forming around the old light fitting and had developed into a long, thick, hanging thread. It reminded him of the fake cobwebs you get at Halloween. But it wasn't fake, and it was in his goddamn living room. He reached for Sweet Potato and lifted her onto his lap. Her body was warm on his legs, her fur soft and fluffy. She was a large cat, and patient – she allowed him ten seconds before leaving his lap and curling herself onto her cushion.

He'd be laughed at if he took his suspicions into the office, that much he was sure of. A coincidence, they'd say. A bit of graffiti on a poster – it would be cleaned up by tomorrow, they'd say, and of course they would be right. But then there was that advert in the paper on the Tube. He hardly ever read the paper, no one did, it was just something to glance through, to look at some pictures or catch the name of a new restaurant . . . He'd almost flicked right past. It looked so like the adverts they placed for the pouch, for the whole FullLife range of plans, that the words sunk in subliminally. But then he'd realised. They were advertising a new plan: a natural-birth plan. They'd never done that before.

He shook his head, tried to get her out of his mind.

There was something going on. Call it instinct. Call it a hunch. But there was something. And he had to think of someone he could talk to – someone else. He needed to bounce his ideas off other people. That was how he worked. At least it was how he had worked, back when he had done anything worthwhile. It must be some kind of punishment, that he ended up on every assignment alone. Or maybe it was just that no one could predict what his articles would end up saying. He didn't write to a brief, no matter how many times they gave him one.

He needed a name. Forced his mind back through the colleagues he'd had over the years, trying to think of one who might be willing to go out on a limb, do a bit of investigative journalism off the payroll. Or, failing that, someone who still considered him a friend. It was like staring at an anagram and seeing the same word, over and over again. Unable to push past it. His mind was stuck on one answer, which wasn't the one he sought. His thumb hovered over his screen, typed then deleted the first letter of her name. Shit's sake. He should have deleted her number. She was bound to have deleted his. This kind of indecision was not how Eva operated. She was better than this.

She'd been furious, when she stormed into his office that first time. She'd been furious and he'd been complacent, sitting in his fancy corner office with the big windows that now belonged to someone else. Her scorn had hit deeper than he'd ever admitted, though there were times, later, when he'd used the word ashamed and she had looked at him in surprise.

'I never had the power to make you feel ashamed,' she'd said once. But that was exactly the power that she'd had. Still would have, probably. No, he couldn't call her. There had to be someone else.

Twelve years ago the site had wanted to cover all points of view, and so he'd set out to interview the almost-famous Avigail Goldsmith. It was no kind of coup at all – she'd been approaching them with offers of articles for months, and had already been featured a few times on the website. Her quotes willingly supplied and quoted. It had seemed too easy, that was the problem – that was what told him he needed to find something more. It wasn't that he had strong opinions either way. If pressed, he would have suggested choice was the way forward. Give people options, give them choice, and make sure the choice is available to everyone. The middle ground didn't generate much traffic though, and he was in the business of attracting readers.

Avigail had invited him to her house. Not the office – to her house. She was rich, old-money rich, that much he'd known before he arrived.

'Ah, Piotr,' she said, her pronunciation perfect. 'Just like that funny character in *War and Peace*?'

He stood his ground and stared at her.

'We have a rare edition in our library – we have all *kinds* of things in our library. You can use it if you want.'

Her eyes sparkled at him as she spoke, like a laugh she was trying not to let out, and Piotr wondered if he'd just been insulted. It didn't make him feel inclined to go easy on her in the article.

'You don't seriously expect me to be impressed with your inheritance,' he'd said, moving his questions about her personal life and family history to the top of his list. Her smile was already fading. 'Especially not when you're so set against progress. Tell me, what exactly is it you're clinging on to?'

But something about the interview reminded him of how he now felt about Holly and Rosie. Though Holly had been poor once, hadn't she? It was a part of their story – though a part not usually talked about. He wondered if the baby was born yet. Thought again of the puff piece he was going to have to write if he wanted to get paid at all this week. And then he thought about the defaced poster.

It was no use.

He dialled Eva's number, waited with apprehension as it rang. It would be good to hear her voice. Even if she did shout. Perhaps she had every right to shout.

The tone rose. The phone rang again.

His apprehension turned to something else as he imagined what she'd say when she answered. Was there a chance, even now, that she might be happy to hear from him?

He would say her name, then wait to hear what she said. Perhaps, if she thought he was on to something, he would get to see her again. And there they were, five years of life shared that he tried not to remember. Five years of conversation that ran on into the night. She forced him to see new points of view. Forced him to defend his own, questioned everything he said. It had been infuriating. But that's a lie. It had been like waking up to a world brighter than it had been before, living life with Eva. Yes, he wanted to see her again. He couldn't help it.

The phone switched to voicemail.

He didn't leave her a message.

*

The cafe James Quentin had suggested was not opposite the Full-Life birthing centre, it was better than that – down the side street around the corner, out of the way, hidden, but close. So very close. The coincidence was too much – he had to work there. It wasn't that surprising. They treated their staff well, offered good career paths, believed in keeping their students on to become researchers. Eva paused on the corner to look up at the building in all its fracture-proof glory. It made her shudder.

Still, the birthing centre was a building you couldn't ignore. It dominated. She turned the corner and hurried away from its shadow, into the shadow of other, lower, more mundane buildings that housed grocers and a flower shop and the cafe where she was headed. She was early. Once inside, she chose a table near the front windows and ordered a coffee. He was going to stay 'Quentin' in her mind. 'James' was saddened by her mother's death, a man she felt sympathy for already, but 'Quentin' was someone she needed to get information from.

A couple were sitting in the back, fussing over their pouch. Eva didn't mean to stare, but it was one of the oldest pouches she'd seen for a while – and instead of the colourful soft fabric covers most people had nowadays it was coated in its original, synthetic pale green. She still found it creepy that the pouch's bio-membrane could heal itself after birth; that it could naturally re-form. The couple can't have had any kind of health-care plan if they were carrying one of FullLife's used pouches. It must look, she thought before she could stop herself, just like the pouch she was in, before she was in the outside world, before she was Eva Goldsmith. But the comparison ended there. They might not have been able to afford a new pouch, but they clearly wanted their child. They were telling it a fairy tale, whispering directly through the surface of the pouch itself since there was no audio adapter. A story about castles and magic and bravery. She wondered where they lived. Perhaps they'd be raising their child in one of the out-of-city shelter homes.

Eva held the end of the scarf she was wearing, which had been her mother's. She'd watched her make it when she was little, amazed at what she could create – soft silk and rich colours, home-made swirls of indigo dye and delicate gold leaves. 'Will you teach me?' she'd asked, and her mum had nodded, made room for her to stand up at the table on her plastic steps and help. 'Did your mummy teach you?' She hadn't expected an answer so her mum's reply had stayed with her. 'My mum didn't teach me much of anything.' It had made young Eva feel sad, but also grateful. Even now she often wore her mother's old clothes, used her expressions.

The bell above the door announced a new customer, and there he was. James. Quentin. She stood up, found herself walking towards him, clasping his hand in hers.

'It is good to meet you,' she said.

'I am so sorry . . .' He placed a cautious hand, briefly, on her shoulder. 'I'm so sorry for your loss.'

*

James had waited for the lab to empty before slipping out himself. Not that there was any reason to think they wouldn't want him meeting anyone for lunch, or that they might be watching. Though when he thought about it, there was so much expensive equipment in there they probably should be watching. Especially after the break-in. And his data was so important – his research, his samples. If someone made a mess of the lab it could put him back months. So hopefully they were watching, and obviously no one would care where he ate his lunch. It wasn't the company he was worried about. He just wasn't sure where this meeting was going to lead.

Curiously enough, it was his wedding anniversary today. They never made a big deal of it, but there was a restaurant booked for later. Just the two of them, for a change. They'd never wanted to be the kind of parents who went away without their children – they still holidayed together, all six of them, even though the twins were seventeen now and Jules and Sarah already at university. But the house would be quiet after the twins left. He and Julianne would have plenty of time to spend, just the two of them. He'd been lucky with the way things had worked out. He was in no doubt that he loved his wife.

He'd chosen the back door as he left, not for subterfuge but because there was some kind of ruckus out front. A crowd seemed to be forming. Perhaps a celebrity was coming in. He never did read the newsletter that they emailed round every week. Still, on the research floor there was no need to interact with the parents – the photographers gathering outside had no interest in him, or he in them. Must be terrible, being famous. His life was stressful enough, but to add to that a lack of privacy? Poor souls.

It was a phrase he found himself using too often these days. Poor souls. It wasn't meant to put anyone at a distance. Quite the opposite. We are all souls, aren't we, he thought, we are all something more than the physical cells and proteins that compose us.

He'd stopped outside, pausing to inhale deeply, several times. He hadn't realised that he was holding his breath as he skirted the lobby. It looked like they'd repainted the side wall of the building yet again.

But after all this time, and at *this* time, this precise moment, how strange, how haunting to learn that Avigail was gone. He could still picture her as she was almost forty years ago, still hear her voice – confident, determined, unshockable. If he were going to be able to talk to anyone, it would have been her. It had been so many years, though, so many good years that had passed. And on his anniversary . . .

As he pushed open the door to the cafe a bell jangled, too loud and bright. And then he saw her. The image of Avigail, as she was, walking towards him, taking his hand, but speaking in a softer voice, and her hair shorter, spikier, and there was more pain in her eyes. Suddenly he wanted to help her. It didn't occur to him to be careful.

*

Eva steered him over to the table, sat down herself and smiled.

'Thank you,' she said. 'I wish I'd called sooner. I didn't realise you'd known my mother well.'

'Yes, well. Not really . . . A long time ago.'

He seemed anxious, or perhaps unsure of what to say. He had a nervous habit of pushing his glasses higher up on his nose, from where they slipped a few millimetres lower every few seconds, and although he was balding the hair that he did have needed a trim. He looked less like a FullLife employee than an academic, in his knitted brown jumper with a white zigzag pattern across the chest.

'What happened?' he asked.

Eva couldn't lie, not about this. But she paused, and a waitress arrived to take his order. He asked for coffee, then added on a super-food salad.

'My wife's idea,' he smiled. 'I've been . . . run down. Too busy to eat properly.'

Eva frowned. 'What is it you do?'

'Oh, I thought you knew. I thought . . .' His glasses were pushed up again. 'Sorry, I'm the director of scientific research, round the corner.'

'That sounds important.'

He sighed but said no more.

If he hadn't known her mother, if she hadn't got his name from her address book, Eva would have assumed this man had no idea who she was or what she'd been doing for the last twenty-five years. Perhaps they were so confident now, up in their glass tower, it never occurred to them that people might be working against them. But that made it sound too dramatic. Of course, she never had been any kind of threat.

'I hope . . .'

She looked up at him, surprised for some reason that he was speaking again.

'I hope it was peaceful, as far as these things can be.'

Suddenly, for no reason she could put her finger on, she wondered if this was all an act. If they had heard the phone call, given him instructions on what to say, how to play the meeting so as to get rid of her, get her mind firmly away from FullLife and onto more painful subjects. Were they expecting something?

'Not particularly,' she said, aware of how her tone had changed.

He ran his hand through his thinning hair.

'How exactly did you know my mother?'

She stared at him across the table, challenging now, but he didn't rise to it, seemed to diminish even further into himself. When the coffee arrived he looked so grateful she wouldn't have been surprised if he'd stood to shake the waitress's hand, though he didn't. He just said a quiet 'thank you' and began to stir in several heaped teaspoons of sugar. Eva had already finished her cup, but she didn't order another one. The waitress left. Quentin continued to stir.

He had said he was busy, but she couldn't imagine him moving quickly or rushing through anything. In fact, what was it he'd said? We have so much work, was that it? Like what? Maybe she should have asked for ID. But obviously she couldn't ask for ID now, that would be . . . It wasn't the right time. Though it was worrying to think that she had no proof he was a scientist at all. Or that he was actually James Quentin.

He said something she couldn't make out – her thoughts had gathered momentum in her head, and their volume seemed to drown out his words. Perhaps, if he went to the toilet, she could get a look at his wallet. Or was there some other way? She preferred a direct approach, but it seemed inevitable now that he was lying.

He started to speak again, and she listened more closely this time. 'I, er . . .'

His spoon was still held in his hand, resting on the rim of his coffee cup. He looked tired, beaten down.

'I loved her,' he said, meeting Eva's eye. 'I loved your mother. But it was a long time ago, and she never loved me. I'm fairly sure about that.'

The cafe seemed to go quiet. He held his coffee cup gingerly to his mouth, took one sip, and then another. Placed it back down.

'I really was – am – so sorry to hear. If I had known . . . Well, what can you do though?' His eyes searched hers, as if she had any of the answers. 'Probably there was nothing I could have done.'

'She was ill for a long time. Years.'

He swallowed. 'I could have seen her, then.'

She held his gaze, trying to force herself to see some deception in what suddenly looked like the most defenceless and innocent face.

'Although,' he smiled sadly, 'I'm not sure if I would have come to see her. These things are easier to say with hindsight.'

'Yes,' Eva said. 'It was a while ago. I am sorry. I should have called at the time.'

He nodded a bit, as if he wasn't even surprised, as if he'd known that there might have been some other prompt for her to call him.

'I looked it up, after you called,' he said, eyes staring down into the dregs of his coffee. 'So, I know when . . .'

'And you know what my mother did, for a living?'

'Of course.'

'The group, the protests.'

'She was very proud of it.'

'You didn't mind?'

He laughed. 'At times I think she felt rather disappointed in me.'

Eva could relate, though of course she wasn't going to say that here. She did want to say something though, something kind, after how she'd spoken to him before.

'I'm not disappointed in you,' she said. 'Yet,' with a smile.

He shook his head a little.

'You haven't asked anything of me.'

'But I'm going to.'

She thought he was about to speak, but he frowned instead and reached into his pocket, pulled out a phone. Selected the message that must have just arrived. Eva leaned over the table slightly, and then sat back ashamed. She couldn't see it anyway.

'Look, I think I have to go,' he said. 'They erm, sorry, they need me in the lab and I think I should—'

'But you've only just arrived.'

He suddenly looked so nervous it made her doubt his sincerity again. What a strange, jittery man.

'I have work . . . Things are very busy at the moment . . . Particularly busy and . . .'

There it was again. Although this time her thoughts ran in a different direction. They had perfected the pouch technology years ago – so what were all these scientists researching? The technology worked, it was fully legislated, had passed every trial and test for three generations, it was a completed success. It dawned on her, unpleasantly, that while she'd been trying to persuade people the pouch was a mistake, FullLife could have been developing any number of other technologies. What did they spend all their money on? Why exactly were they calling him back to the lab, on his lunch break?

He stood up to leave. 'Really, there is so much I have to do.'

'Like what?' It came out too sharp.

He stepped away but paused, turned back to her, pushed his glasses up.

'Sorry, I'm . . . Can we talk another time?'

'Of course.'

'Your mother, she was . . .'

'Stay,' Eva said, aware that her voice was softer now. 'Just for lunch, James.'

'I can't. It is important research, I promise you. If you knew . . .'

'Try me.'

'Saturday would, erm . . . Are you free Saturday?'

The weekend. He'd be off work. Eva felt a spark of hope. 'Tomorrow?'

'Oh, yes, that's tomorrow, isn't it?' he said. 'Perhaps we could meet here tomorrow then, early . . .'

'Here?'

Surely he'd want to get away from the birthing centre – they obviously didn't want him talking to her.

'Yes,' he shrugged, looking around the cafe as if he thought he'd missed something distasteful. 'It's OK here, isn't it?'

It was nice, in fact – she looked around as he did, noticing the artwork on the walls, the simple but elegant wood furniture, the lighting that managed to be simultaneously bright, warm, and subtle. On their table, in place of a menu holder, was a snow-globe with a tiny, handmade robin in the centre.

'Here is good,' she smiled. 'I'll see you tomorrow then. At ten.'

He took a deep breath, nodded, turned and walked towards the door.

The waitress appeared with his superfood salad.

'It's OK,' Eva said, 'I'll have it.'

She ate as if she'd been starving, and when she'd finished she picked up the snow-globe and turned it, once, upside down. The snow was made of tiny white flowers that fluttered for a moment before settling on the robin's brown back. There were trees in the distance – within the world of the globe – tall coniferous trees dusted with white-flower snow. She covered the curve of the globe with her palm.

'Do you sell these?' she asked, as she got up to leave.

The waitress nodded, added the price on to her meal. It was inexpensive.

Standing at last outside, leaning against the corner of the building and looking over to the reflective curves of the birthing centre, she took the globe out of her bag and tilted it back and forth, making the snow flowers flutter in the sheltered air.

Perhaps she should have been willing to change.

But no, she shouldn't have had to. No one should have to change. That was the whole point.

Some shouting erupted from the entrance to the birthing centre. She looked up, for a second imagining that the voice was familiar. It wasn't though. It was just a group of photographers and journalists, larking around. God's sake, she thought. Piotr's not here and I don't want him here. She scowled at the building, with its tall glass panels designed to reflect the city, the light and the frost, tapered at the top to give the sense of height that pulled you up into the sky. Turning her back, she strode angrily past twinkling trees to the edge of the Thames, still holding the globe, and raised her arm high above her head. She didn't even know why she'd bought the stupid thing, or why she kept falling back into memories she didn't want to keep. It would be good to see it disappear into the water.

But she couldn't do it. She dropped her arm without throwing the snow-globe and faced the birthing centre again. Her back against the wall. Then, slowly, she slid down until she was sitting on the pavement, the globe resting on her knees, and she thought about how much she wanted to cry or, perhaps, to scream.

Chapter 6

THEY WERE STANDING AS A family on the balcony that overlooked the lobby of the FullLife birthing centre. It was huge, the lobby, several floors tall, with golden sunlight streaming in through the windows and digital panels stretching all the way up the central pillars. They were filled with colourful photos of babies. Thousands of newborn babies, smiling and laughing their way into the world.

'Is it that one?' Kaz said, pointing up to the highest photo. 'Is that the first baby?'

Rosie's mum had a smile playing about her lips. She was the first baby, of course, and Rosie knew it was a photo of her. There, right at the top, above the colours and smiles and sunlight: a baby oblivious to what she meant and to all the babies that would follow as she was caught by the snap of a camera, mid-gurgle.

'You were very cute, weren't you, Mum?' Rosie smiled at her mum's raised eyebrows.

'Good thing too,' Daphne said. 'I think half the world was expecting a monster.'

'Don't exaggerate,' said Nana, though she seemed pleased with the conversation. Proud. 'I told them all at the time, we knew you were healthy from day one with all the check-ups . . . But they just wouldn't believe it until they saw you with their own eyes. Bloody journalists.'

'Don't swear, Nana. Not in front of the baby.'

Rosie was joking, but only just. She actually wished her nana would stop swearing so much. She didn't want Will's first word to be 'crap'.

'See that little tuft of brown hair?' Nana was saying. 'Just in the middle of your head there? I always wished I'd put a ribbon on that, for the photo.'

'Thank heavens you didn't,' Daphne laughed.

'It would have been adorable.'

'It would have looked absurd.'

Her nana looked at her mum then, and for a second Rosie thought she might have tears in her eyes. She didn't think she'd ever seen her nana cry.

'You were a beautiful baby,' she said.

Kaz's phone beeped, and she knew it would be from his dad Karl, saying they were nearly there. He'd been messaging daily, coming round to talk to Will, making plans about where Will would go to playgroup, what the best mix of milk was, who would be grandpa and who would be grandad. Now she thought about it, Nana was the last grandparent that she and Kaz had between them – that was another thing baby Will would bring with him, a whole new generation of grandparents. That would make Nana a great-grandma. Though everyone would always call her Nana.

'Come on,' Rosie's mum said, turning from the photo and pressing the call button for the lift. 'Rosie, Kaz. Let's go and meet the newest baby in our family.'

Rosie grinned and blew a kiss to the pouch Kaz was carrying. And once they were in the lift, being effortlessly transported to the twenty-fourth floor, she couldn't help reaching out towards it. During the first few weeks they had both stroked the pouch relentlessly – it was so soft and warm and comforting, and knowing that their baby was in there, she just couldn't stop. Kaz was the same. She'd find him in the middle of the night, sitting on the floor by the pouch stand's legs with the incubator doors open, sometimes whispering to baby Will through the audio adapter, sometimes singing into it like a microphone. Kneeling up so he could lightly rest his head against the curve of the pouch hanging on the stand, just like he did sometimes when she was wearing it.

They'd got used to it of course, everyone did – the novelty of something so tactile was replaced by the life inside, by choosing names and clothes and imagining what he would be like, how quickly he would learn to walk, who he would be when he grew up. They'd imagined entire lives for him, her and Kaz, lying in bed and talking for hours about their baby.

'I think he's going to play the cello,' Kaz had said one night.

'Why the cello?'

'I don't know . . . I've always liked it, I guess.'

'Me too,' she said. Rosie couldn't play any musical instruments – she'd always kind of wished she'd been patient enough to learn when she was younger, but she was in too much of a rush to do other things, to play games and do colouring-in and create cards for everyone she met with bits of fabric stuck on, sequins and tiny beads that they still, occasionally, found underneath their furniture. 'You'll teach him to read music?'

'Totally,' he said. 'When he's really young – the book says they're like sponges at that age, the amount of information they can soak up.'

'The book said "sponges"?'

'No, I say sponges. The book said something about educational psychology and the importance of pre-language development or something.'

'Sponges is better.'

'I thought so.'

'And maybe other languages,' she said. 'It must be brilliant, to speak lots of languages.'

'I can only speak English.'

'Me too. Well, a bit of French, but I'm rubbish at that.'

'We'll get a tutor.'

'Or just ask Mum,' she smiled. 'She speaks Spanish and Hindi.' Rosie had always thought it was cool, that her mum was a translator. It seemed powerful.

'Oh yeah,' Kaz laughed, 'of course.'

'He's going to be a busy baby,' she said. 'Lucky we have a big family to help.'

And they were lucky, she knew. Incredibly so.

She stroked the pouch again, not sure why she was stroking so intently now, but Kaz was watching her and somehow she couldn't stop. She felt the fabric sleek and soft between her fingers, the warmth emanating from it just the perfect temperature to touch. She stroked from the top of the pouch all around in a single, gentle sweep of her hand, and thought – insanely, given that they were in a lift that was about to reach their floor any second – about kneeling down to speak to him, whisper to him for the last time before he was born.

'Rosie?'

It was Kaz. He must have been wondering what she was doing.

'We're here,' he said as the lift doors slid open. 'Dad! Pops!'

'Wait a sec,' she whispered, her hand falling from the pouch. 'Hold on, Kaz?'

But he was already rushing to hug his pops, his dad's arm around his shoulders, smiles passing between them. And Rosie suddenly knew what it was she'd been hoping to feel, why she couldn't stop stroking the pouch, now that he'd stepped away and the pouch was beyond her reach. She'd wanted to feel Will move. Their baby Will, who was going to be a cellist and speak twenty languages and have her red-brown hair and Kaz's dimples – she'd wanted to feel him kicking with his little feet just before he was born, perhaps reaching out his hand, as she was so convinced that he did sometimes, to touch hers. She'd wanted, one last time, to feel him move.

How silly, she thought, as she stepped out of the lift to join her family and they walked together to their birthing room. There were balloons on the door handle, brightly coloured flowers in one of those tall vases beside the entrance. In a few minutes he'd be born, her baby Will, and she could spend the rest of her life watching him move.

*

James Quentin stepped out of the lift on the research floor, keyed his pin number on the entry pad and walked into the anteroom. His coat was still hanging there – he'd forgotten to take it with him. And forgotten to notice the cold. But he removed his jumper now, unlaced each shoe and placed them in his locker before pulling on his cleanroom boots and stepping over the bench into the gowning area.

He'd been part of the team that had redesigned these cleanrooms, fifteen years ago now. They'd had to expand, but that wasn't all – there were increasingly strict requirements and safety protocols for every aspect of their business. It was a good thing. Avigail had been absolutely right about that. He'd demanded more trials with each new development. The safety protocols could never be too intensive, the checks never too robust. They had a series of airlocks, each with pressurisation differentials, separating the outside world – the rest of the birthing centre – from each class of the cleanroom. It was soothing. The airlocks helped to separate the compartments of his life, though it struck him that it would, perhaps, take rather a long time to get out. His lab was in the centre, the highest classification. He worked in the cleanest environment they had ever achieved.

In the lab the atmosphere was tingling, static. Similar to how it had felt down in the lobby, but less excited, more anxious.

'What is going on today?' he asked, finally irritated by what everyone but him seemed to know.

'Holly Bhattacharyya's having her great-grandson,' replied his colleague, Bethan, who always read the weekly newsletter. James fully expected her to be promoted above him at the next cycle. And he didn't care.

'You mean her granddaughter . . .'

'Is in, right now, yes.'

Suddenly the press downstairs, the anxiety here, made sense. He took a moment, during which he sat on his lab stool and pointlessly searched for the newsletter in his messages archive. He must have deleted it. He swore, quietly and uncharacteristically, under his breath.

But perhaps it would be OK. The chances were still excellent, and the check-ups would have shown perfect health. Several months ago they'd moved all delivery dates forward by a day, just in case; that might have helped. But there was that suspicion he had – that they all had, though no one wanted to voice it yet – the connection with the generations and God he hoped he was wrong. He'd seen it though. It was there, in the emergency presentations to the research group, to the board, hidden in the comparisons between new and used pouches, IVF and natural conception, everything they could think of as they searched for the common factor. It was a blip, they said. It was something they could resolve. They had time. At first they'd thought it was just in the used pouches – that might have been containable. They'd even been looking at environmental causes, pouch mistreatment, but found nothing. Still, they had time. Just so long as it didn't happen again. Please don't let it happen again.

He sat back on his stool, rocked on two legs and tried to focus on balancing, but the lurch in his stomach told him he couldn't return to his research. The pouch felt like his personal success in some ways, one he was deeply proud of, one he loved, and now he felt like he was personally on trial. Looking around, he saw that everyone else in the lab was waiting too. They were all invested. He readjusted his hood, loosened the strap under his chin. They were hot, the cleanroom suits, the material designed to stop any molecules passing through. He could already feel the sweat on his back, on his forehead.

The ring of the intercom made him jump in the kind of unexpected-but-expected way that caused his pulse to pound rather than his body startle.

'This is Quentin,' he answered, his voice reluctant, his heart sinking.

'Yes. It's bad news.'

He closed his eyes. Not again, he thought. Not again.

'We're ready,' he said.

Now there could be no more denying it. The intercom had gone silent in his hands, but he didn't hang it up. He turned to the lab and nodded.

'The pouch is going to be sent up,' he said.

He couldn't be sick, though he wanted to be. They mustn't allow any contamination to affect their data.

That's right, he thought to himself. Think about samples. Think about data. Do your job. Block out everything else.

*

Holly stepped away from the birthing table as the doctors began rushing in. Her whole body was shaking. There was something like sea mist filling the room, engulfing her feet, rising and blurring her vision, seeping into her lungs. She closed her eyes against it, but that was no use. There was only one thing she could see when her eyes were closed, and she didn't want to see it. She wished she had never had to see it.

For a split second, he had looked so perfect. His chubby knees were bent, his feet slightly wrinkled the way babies' feet often are. He had deep brown hair lying slick over the top of his head. But his eyes were closed, she noticed, waiting then for the nurse to pat his cheek to get him to wake up, to take a deep breath, to have his first cry. The nurse didn't move. No one was moving.

His colour. Holly saw suddenly that his colour was wrong, he was too . . . he looked wrong, the pallor of his skin, the slightly greasy sheen that she could see, as she stared, unable to move, to speak, as the nurse pressed the alarm and people started screaming and there was the most terrible wail from Rosie. She would never stop hearing it, that cry her granddaughter let out. That awful sound would be with her for the rest of her life.

The pouch was lying to the side, discarded like a used skin. The fluid that had been Will's world was still running through the channels on the birthing table to collect below. And blood was dripping down, from the pouch, from the birth, dark viscous swirls of it that she couldn't take her eyes from.

Holly stumbled away from the table as more people rushed in, as they pulled out from somewhere the tiny pads of a child-sized defibrillator and began to send electric shocks through his limp body. They were so tiny, those pads – she couldn't believe how small they were. Like a baby's toy. No bigger than his tiny, curled-up hands.

She felt her legs giving way beneath her, flopped forward against the windowpane, tried to catch herself on the sill but failed, falling instead to her knees, jolting into the skirting board. And then she just stayed there on the floor. She had no sound to make. She could not cry out the way Rosie had, or the way Kaz was now screaming. She didn't understand how this could have happened.

The machine flatlined. Someone was saying stop. Someone else shouting at them to keep going. She could see Rosie leaning her whole body into her mother's arms, a continuous noise coming from her throat. How dare you, Kaz was screaming at the doctors, how dare you stop, keep going, keep going, how dare you, keep going, his words on a continuous loop. They tried again. Stand back, they commanded the room. It went quieter. They tried again.

But Holly knew it wasn't going to help. She had seen from the angle of his head, the unnatural colour of the skin on his face, around his mouth. He was dead already.

Rosie was looking at her, still held in her mother's arms.

'Nana?' she was saying. 'What's happening? I don't understand. Nana?'

Holly pressed her hand against the wall, tried to claw into it with her fingernails, until she reached the windowsill and could grab hold. Then she lifted her knee, which was suddenly throbbing, and placed her foot flat on the ground. She was going to stand up again. That's what she was going to do first. She was not going to lie crumpled on the floor. She was going to help Rosie, and that meant she needed to stand up.

*

Rosie didn't mean to make things worse but as she saw her nana standing up she knew that she had to do something, she had to do something and she had to save him, somehow, this couldn't be happening. Nothing was making any sense, she had this ringing in her ears that wouldn't stop and there were arms on her that suddenly she wanted to get away from and she was only aware of stumbling towards the birthing table. She didn't mean to push that doctor, she really didn't, but he was in her way and Kaz too, he was shouting, begging the doctors to help, but she pushed past him and she had to get to Will, she had to be the one to hold him, she could save him, no one else could, but she could, she had to – and they had to stop crowding him like that. 'Move!' she screamed at them all. 'Move!' They were all staring down at his little naked body, and so she pushed them away, every last one of them. Every last set of hands, every arm held out to block her, or comfort her, had to be pushed away until she could get to her baby.

He was still lying there, attached.

She had never imagined that the pouch, their pouch, Will's home for nine months, that they had stroked and spoken to and loved – she had never imagined that it could repulse her. The deep sucking red of the insides of it, visible now through that awful cut down the front, wet and dripping. The different skins, the layers that had grown with him, expanded with him. The bio-socket for the audio adapter, useless now. Obscene. And the umbilical cord.

'Get him out!' she screamed – and a doctor stepped forward and she spun round, furious. 'Not you! Get away from him!'

He held his arms up, the doctor, as if he was afraid of her, letting her do what she wanted as he edged away from the bed. And so she reached in and clasped the cord that was sticky and limp in her hands, clasped it and pulled, and pulled, as it leaked on her fingers and fluid ran down to her wrist, but it wouldn't come out of the pouch lining. She screamed as she pulled, but it made no difference. She couldn't free him.

But there was her nana. She had something, was holding something, and she stepped forwards and spoke in a quiet voice and told her that she could help. Without waiting for a response, her nana reached out and cut the cord. And baby Will was free at last.

Rosie held him. Her eyes kept the doctors away, the nurses, even her family, she kept them all away. Her nana stepped back, giving her space. And she held him so tight. She held him and rocked him, she kissed his forehead, stroking his dark, damp hair, and she said, 'Hello, baby Will,' and she rocked him and kissed him with Kaz standing beside her and she whispered, 'Wake up now, baby Will. We're here.' But her words wouldn't come out right. 'We're here,' she tried to say but her whole body was shaking and he did not wake up, he could not wake up. Kaz was reaching out to her and together they held their baby and the room fell silent until quietly Kaz started to sing the tune he'd sung to Will in the pouch, and Rosie started to cry, and then, to break.

*

James waited by the pass-through airlock for the failed pouch to be delivered. It had to be sent through in stages. Each level of the cleanroom had a pass-through, so the scientist from the receiving class of lab collected the pouch then carried it across the lab to where the next level of pass-through was located. Like a relay. A very slow, cautious relay. The pouch had been put in a sterilised box and sealed, of course. It wasn't visible to any of them. Not until it reached James Quentin's lab, and they opened it up.

The first time, they'd decided something physical had gone wrong. Some problem with the umbilical cord, perhaps, something to do with it getting tangled. It was easier that way – they'd thought it was a one-off. It wasn't.

Bethan must have noticed his hesitation. He wasn't sure if she was using the opportunity to take control or simply trying to help, but she carried the opened box from the bench in front of him to the central area, where she began dividing it up. *She* didn't seem to have any hesitation. Her use of the scalpel blade was adept and assured.

Of course, it wasn't an actual living creature, the pouch. It shouldn't feel like having to cut open a person. But James had joined FullLife to help create the new generation of pouches, to make them better for the babies, more inspiring, more enjoyable for the parents. The audio adapter – that had been his idea. People loved it. It had won him promotion to director of research. And yet here he was. Dissecting, not creating.

He was staring at Bethan, though he hadn't realised until she stared back.

'What?' she said impatiently.

He shook his head. 'It's just . . .'

'There's work to do. Come on.'

'Do you not feel anything?' he said, regretting it as the impatience in her eyes turned to shock. She was still in control though – she had accurately sectioned the pouch into the pale green outer skin, the secondary and tertiary bio-membranes that shimmered in the fluorescent light, and the darker pink lining of the inner womb.

'I have a six-month-old, do you know that?' she said.

He hadn't known that, and so he shook his head.

'I could never have carried a child in the past,' she said. 'I wasn't born with the necessary anatomy. But that was what I wanted: to carry a child. If it weren't for the pouch, my baby might not even exist. So yes, I feel many things. Like gratitude.' She placed the scalpel down, waiting as the last of the fluid drained from the membranes and was collected into the vials distributed around the table. 'A lifetime's career as a scientist and dissecting a pouch freaks you out? Grow up, James.'

'It's not that,' he said. 'I'm not . . .'

His voice sounded unsure, unstable.

'Look, I understand,' she said. 'It's awful that a baby has died.' Her voice was quieter now, though everyone was listening – there was no other sound in the lab. 'It's awful that several babies have died. Heartbreaking. But what the pouch means for so many of us . . . for hundreds of thousands of people . . . It has changed everything. It has made my life possible. So don't start getting squeamish—'

'OK,' he said. 'OK. I'm sorry.'

'Forget it,' she smiled, a little too brusquely. 'Just help me, would you?'

He nodded, tried not to sigh again, adjusted his latex gloves, and set to work.

He chose to begin with the attachments, the various ways that the pouch could be connected to the outside world – they were his inventions, after all. The nutrient feed was still intact, so he cut around it with a scalpel then carefully removed it from the pouch's surface, blood from the incision seeping onto his gloves. He isolated each of the tubes that transported nutrients from the feed around the womb, severed them from the feed itself, and sliced them open along their length. The inner and outer substrates of the tubes were composed of different cells, so they needed to be separated. Then he peeled away the thin membrane from inside the audio bio-socket. It functioned a bit like an eardrum, sharing voices and music with the baby inside. It should have been beautiful. He put the thought out of his mind. Bit by bit, the pouch ceased to be a pouch and became a lab full of carefully ordered and labelled samples from all of the components.

Each cell type had to be isolated, as far as possible, while they were still alive. Living cells tell you more about their function – or their malfunction – than dead ones. Then proteins would be separated and studied, DNA and RNA collected and mapped, and they would set to work trying to build a coherent picture of what was different now compared to what was successful in the past. They were still trying to isolate the cause, still at the stage of having to run every possible test, search every element of the pouch's synthetic biology. They needed to find the common factor. Without that, they were lost in the dark.

But he had his suspicions. He didn't want to speak them out loud, but he thought about them, when he stopped working long enough to think, when he lay awake at night. Julianne would stroke the back of his head, to soothe him. It used to help him switch off, that gentle affection from someone he loved – like a lullaby. But it didn't work any more. His thoughts would not be soothed. They were too frightening for that. The problem had to be genetic.

These fatalities must have been caused by something that had been inherited. Not a physical malfunction within the pouch, but a change in human biology, in DNA, brought on by gestation in the pouch, then passed down to the children of parents who had been pouch-born. Nothing else could account for the third generation being suddenly affected. And it was only the third generation; it was only now that this was happening, even though the technology hadn't changed. That meant they weren't going to find the answer by looking in the pouches alone, however much they wanted to. If it was genetic, the problem was in the parents, too. All of them.

He didn't notice how late it was getting, even though he hadn't eaten all day. He didn't even stop for a glass of water. But after hours of work, he realised he'd forgotten something. Walking over to the far end of the lab, he touched Bethan on the shoulder.

'Your baby,' he said. 'I never . . . I should've asked. Your baby's OK, right? Healthy?'

'Wonderful so,' she said.

'I'm glad.' James nodded. 'And, I should have said before, you know . . . Congratulations.'

'Thank you, James.'

'You're welcome,' he said, but his words didn't really come out right; his voice didn't seem to be working the way it should. He wanted to lie down, or beg for help, or find the answer before any more babies died. He wanted to talk to Avigail. But he couldn't help noticing that Bethan's smile when she thought about her child made her look young and wise at the same time, and quite strikingly happy.

Audio log

25 Dec 2015 03:49

You're not coming, are you? I thought I would be despondent if you didn't come, but something must have changed for me because I'm not. Resigned, perhaps. Disappointed. But it is a small disappointment compared to so many others that it feels petty to dwell on it now.

There is good news, though – it seems my indigo hamlets have started mating. It is quite extraordinary, to be able to watch it. What a thing nature is. I noticed at about midnight – I was up, I couldn't sleep, not after what had happened with the Asda man – and I was thinking about going to the rocks with my head torch but I decided to look in on the tanks instead, and thank heavens that I did! Honestly, I have seen photographs and documentaries but nothing prepares you for it, really, when you see it with your own eyes, close up, for the first time. It is exquisite.

Hypoplectrus indigo is their correct name, and I like it more than their common one. It makes them sound electric, doesn't it? Electric, eccentric, hypnotic – they are all of those things, in a way. Their dorsal fin and frayed triangular tail are almost transparent, wispy and fragile, can you imagine? While the broad indigo bars running up and down their bodies are separated by thin white stripes, almost luminous in their lack of colour . . . The indigo is so deep, under my aquarium lights, that the white seems to glow, to carry the current that makes the hairs stand up on my arms as I watch them.

It is the synchronous nature of their hermaphroditism that is so unusual, you understand. Many species change from male to female at certain times in their life cycle, or develop in response to their surroundings, but to have both female and male sexual organs, to be able to simultaneously reproduce as both mother and father . . . to share so completely. Nature really is capable of so much more than us – I believe that now more than ever. When two indigos meet they form a mating clasp, a sort of spinning embrace that churns up the water so rapidly it forms a vortex. Three seconds it lasts, the vortex, that is all – but what a three seconds! They each take on a role, male and female, and release gametes into the vortex where they are fertilised. And then they swap. They join together in their mating clasp again and create a new vortex, except this time the former male acts as the female and the former female acts as the male. Do you see? They are both mother and father, and in being mother or father neither loses the ability to become instead father, or mother.

But I still can't sleep.

When he arrived at the door he rang the bell as usual, but when I opened the door he was standing there, with nothing unpacked, even though I'd given him plenty of time to get back to the van and unload. I couldn't understand it, until I realised he was holding the first crate. A big, olive green, holed thing it was, with a sharp rim around the top. 'This weather!' he said. 'Will I bring it inside for you?'

What was I supposed to say to that? I stood there sort of dumb for a minute, just staring at him. And then I took a step backwards and by doing so, quite accidentally, I left him space to come into the porch.

He left the first crate in front of the inside door – by this time I had been so far pushed back into my own house that I had one foot on the hall rug, while the other was still on the porch tiles. A last stand, if you will. And then he kept returning into the porch with more and more crates. It was a big delivery – it's important to stock up on water bottles since the frost can be a problem here, with the pipes in winter. Then, with the crates stacked up all around me, in my house, I stood there and watched him and even at one point sort of nodded at him for his effort. I regretted it as soon as I had done it.

When he was finished, he stood and looked at me. I looked at him. He looked at me. He has dark blue eyes, deep and wide, the kind that make you not sure where to look because they seem so intense, and they don't suit him – he doesn't strike me in any other way as being an intense man. It must have taken me some time to realise that he needed his crates back. That I was supposed to be unpacking. I bent down to take out one of the water bottles, but he reached down and picked it up first, rapidly emptying the crate and leaving the bottles stacked up along the wall, opposite my outdoor shoes. And then he grinned at me and said:

'You can keep the rest of the crates 'til next time. Aye?'

What a strange effect it had on me. So strange I can hardly describe it here. As he went whistling down the path back to the van, without waiting for an answer, without turning back, I felt like I was watching someone depart. Had he turned, I actually think I might have waved to him.

I was so shaken up afterwards that I couldn't sleep at all last night, or tonight. Which, as I say, turned out to be a good thing, because that's why I ended up outside with the indigo hamlets. They do still soothe me, you know, despite everything. I think I had a good idea, back then. I knew what I was going to do even before I returned from maternity leave. That's when the idea came to me, you know, struggling to breastfeed at four in the morning. I was raw and bleeding, clasping my hand over my mouth so the sound of my crying wouldn't wake my husband. He would get so angry when woken. But the doctors told me I had to keep trying – we were made to feel hauntingly inadequate if we didn't breastfeed, back then. One of so many hauntings that I would have to deal with. So I kept trying, and when I couldn't try any more because the pain was so extreme, I knew what I had to do.

What I'm saying is, it was never intended to be a political statement. It was the physical reality of the situation I was thinking about, at first. The rest came later. Progress doesn't come about through protest groups and the slow, grinding change of democratic legislation. It comes from invention. Technology. Medicine. Invention is how you change things. I knew that then, and I still know it now. I'm not ashamed of being a scientist. I am very proud of it.

And yet, here I am.

Astonishing, how few people have tried to track me down. I'm not really all that well hidden, you know. Have none of you been wondering why I disappeared?

Perhaps no one even noticed. I suspect I've not been missed as much as I like to imagine. I am sorry I shut Holly out the way that I did – I miss her. But she has her family, and they were always more important to her than I was.

I remember that they asked me, when I got back to work after giving birth, if I missed being at home. If I missed it *terribly*, they said. It was shocking, I suppose, for a woman to choose to work rather than stay at home with her new baby. Thank God they never thought to ask me about breastfeeding – they'd have been horrified that I stopped so soon. Formula was my lifeline, as well as my new strand of research.

How does it feel, they kept insisting, to be a mother?

I looked at them with feigned confusion on my face. What do you mean? I said. I'm a scientist.

I wish I'd said it differently now though, looking back with hindsight, at 4 a.m. of another night's dawn, talking to a computer in an isolated lighthouse on the edge of the North Sea.

I'm *the* scientist, is what I should have said.

I'm the one we need.

Chapter 7

AVIGAIL ACCEPTED THE CUP OF tea that was being offered. It came with a plate of custard creams and chocolate bourbons. They were making an effort.

'So few people consider adoption these days,' the manager was saying.

Avigail hadn't told her that she was not considering adoption herself either. She was here for research. It was a new way in, a problem people hadn't started talking about yet. And to FullLife it was nothing but a way to placate their opposition. The new biotech and the old religions working together, now there was a contradiction.

As far as she'd been able to discover, FullLife were donating used pouches and managing the birthing process on the condition that various churches and some of the more progressive pro-life groups covered the cost of care for the children. That wasn't where it had started though. To begin with, FullLife had needed to run clinical trials to test their early-stage transfer process and women considering abortion had been offered a new choice.

'We don't like to call ourselves orphanages,' the manager continued. 'That implies a tragedy, where there has been none.'

'I see.'

'We are saving lives, as you know. And we are called care homes, because we offer home and care.'

Avigail was planning to get some photos, find the saddest,

scrawniest child and make sure the scandal of the care homes was plastered on the front page of every newspaper. Surely people would start questioning the pouch if they knew FullLife had been producing these children then leaving them out here to live where no one would have to look at them. Surely people would see this was wrong.

'Would you like to have a look round the dormitories, and see the canteen?'

'Absolutely.' Avigail stood, leaving the biscuits untouched.

'Let's start with the nursery.'

She was surprised, but shouldn't have been – of course they would be delivered here as soon as the birthing process was finished. Still, she gasped when she saw the room. Flooded with light, painted pale green, and the music . . .

'The synthetic milk is an absolute godsend,' the manager was saying. 'FullLife provide the various mixes – each variety has everything the babies need – and you'd be surprised how quickly they develop a taste for their favourite type. Marvellous, when you think about it.' She chuckled, picking up one of the babies, who was awake and wriggling, then offering him to Avigail, who shook her head and stepped away. She didn't want to hold these pouch babies – she wanted to stop this from happening. But she hadn't found her angle yet.

'What about the older children?' she said. 'How do you feed them?'

'Oh, don't worry, they're all very healthy and well nourished. It's not the food that's a difficulty, it's the space.' She pointed towards the window and Avigail followed her there to look out. 'Our new building site.'

Beyond the edges of the grassy field behind the care home she was standing in, more areas had been sectioned off with wire fencing, and a series of cabins were already positioned for construction workers and on-site management. They were building more.

'My God, how many children are there?' Avigail said.

She stepped back and felt her leg brush against something. Or someone. A child had wandered in from the dormitory opposite. The manager started to usher her out of the room, muttering something about the naptime supervisor, but Avigail stopped her.

'What's your name?' she said, kneeling down to be at the same height as the toddler standing in front of her. She had wide green eyes and olive skin and skinny arms, and she reached out a finger to touch Avigail's brightly coloured dress. 'My name's Avigail,' she said. 'Do you want to tell me your name?'

The little girl shook her head and backed away.

'It's OK,' Avigail found herself saying. 'It's OK, you can tell me your name.'

The manager touched Avigail on the shoulder to get her attention, and she stood up.

'We let them choose their own names,' she said.

'What do you mean?'

'Well, the babies are anonymous when they arrive here, you see, and it gives the children a sense of identity to choose their own names when they're ready.'

'Identity?'

'Or control, if you prefer . . . She can come with us, for a few minutes.'

Avigail looked at the little girl, who was watching with her back pressed against the wall. She felt a surge of anger at the pouch, at that awful synthetic milk, at every way in which women had stopped being mothers.

'Where are the pouches kept? Before the birthing process, I mean.'

'There's another building for that,' the manager said. 'Couple of miles from here. But they get the very same nutrients as everyone else. FullLife deliver fresh bags twice a week, and take away the old ones for recycling. This way.' She was walking through the corridor now, pointing in to the dormitories, each with around ten beds, some occupied by napping children, and each with plenty of toys, plenty of heat. Avigail followed close by her side, passing room after room after room. 'FullLife give them all the same check-ups, too. Completely for free, of course. It's quite wonderful.'

The little girl was walking along behind them, holding on to Avigail's dress – now and then Avigail felt a tug on the hem as the girl's small legs struggled to keep up.

'Imagine, in the past, how parents could be a terrible influence during pregnancy,' the manager was saying. 'Especially the ones who were considering abortion. Think of all the things unborn babies could be exposed to – alcohol, toxins, cold, hunger . . . Now, not only can we offer life, but every baby in the pouch has every-thing it needs.'

'She's not shy,' Avigail interrupted, and the manager stopped mid-stride. 'She's following me around. So why won't she tell me her name?'

'Oh, she hasn't chosen one yet,' the manager shrugged. 'She doesn't like to speak at all. We don't know why.'

Avigail felt her throat clench, but she wouldn't cry. Not here. She would not show this little girl any useless pity; she'd show her some-thing better.

She knelt down and beckoned her closer, pushed her hair back from her face and smiled until she got a smile in return. 'Of course you don't like to speak,' she said, with a wink. 'I bet you'd prefer to shout.'

*

Eva watched the first few reports on her computer at home that afternoon. How Rosie Bhattacharyya had arrived at the birthing centre shortly after noon – she must have just missed her, thank

God – how they'd chosen the main public centre rather than the more exclusive private options because of the history of their family.

She was irritated and impatient. There was something new happening at FullLife, and she wanted to find out what it was. Quentin had seemed nervous, sure, but not dishonest – if anything he'd seemed shaken up and ready to talk. It made sense that her mother had known him. He must have been a good connection at FullLife, especially if he had feelings for her. Presumably they weren't reciprocated – she'd never heard her mother mention him. She'd never asked her to contact him, or tell him about her illness.

A bulletin announced there was going to be an exclusive. Tomorrow morning, the first interview with the new parents. Piotr Filipek gives one of his famous 'interviews at home'. Trust Piotr to be on the front line. She hadn't been that far off, then, thinking he might have been outside FullLife that morning – it was just that he didn't even need to be in the press huddle. Maybe he hadn't changed at all in the past six years. She shook her head, but she was paying attention now, whether she wanted to or not.

Then came the next news cycle. She was expecting an announcement about the birth but instead they just talked about the arrival in more detail: Holly wearing a floral dress – for the love of God, who cared – the pouch being carried into the building by the father, Kaz. At this point she was annoyed enough to stand up and switch off the computer, only then leaning against the table and counting to ten.

How ridiculous, this business with the dress. She remembered it from before – it was a part of the history now. Holly and her bright floral dress. As if that said anything. As if it meant anything.

Her phone started ringing. She stared at the screen, but didn't answer.

The point was, women should never have had to change

anything about themselves. A dress wasn't going to make it OK that they did. The technology had been invented too soon. It had happened too fast. Like an industrial revolution bringing progress on one hand and destruction on the other.

So there was inequality at work – improve the legislation, and enforce it. That was a much simpler solution than an external womb for heaven's sake. Why not try that first? It was as if the science had raced past the common sense, past the socio-economics of the problem. If women were being subject to prejudice, denied promotion for having had a child – or for the potential of having a child in the future – then the prejudice should be removed. Obviously.

How was that not obvious to everyone else?

Of course men and women were different. What was *wrong* with men and women being different? You didn't need to make them the same, you just needed to treat both with the same respect. When a child was born, men and women should be given equal parental leave, take the same responsibility for raising the child, and so be treated with the same respect. That was how she would have done it, if she'd been able to. Although there were people – her mother included – who thought even that was too far. Why should men get parental leave? she'd say. Let them work, and let us women give birth. We should be paid to raise our children for as long as we want to – and then employers should give us back our jobs at the salary we'd have had if we'd never left.

She could see her mother's point, but Eva knew some battles were impossible to win. Their society was still based on capitalism, whatever else had changed.

She looked down at the number on her phone. Shook her head. It was the second time he'd called today.

After all these years, she still knew his number. You can delete someone from an address book but you can't delete them from your memory.

It was an interesting coincidence that he should be phoning now – on the day that she met James Quentin, on the day she realised there might actually be a story, some kind of story, that she wanted to be reported. It was too soon, though. She needed to talk to James again. Quentin. If she knew anything about Piotr, it was that he would have his facts – and they were rarely the facts she wanted. So she needed to have hers ready. She was pacing around the room, circling the piano as she began to organise her thoughts, to make a plan of action. But first, she was going to go for a run. It was starting to get dark, and it was cold out, and she didn't care. She was going for a run, then she was going to do some research. And tomorrow she was going to find out what the hell was going on, and tell the world.

*

Piotr woke up with a start. He was on the sofa. His head was on Sweet Potato's cushion. The cat herself was nowhere to be seen.

When had he fallen asleep on the sofa?

Sitting up, looking towards the window, it was clearly the middle of the night. London never got properly dark, but there was a lull, a couple of hours when you could almost believe that the city was sleeping. Piotr didn't like being woken during the lull. He stretched, trying to feel each muscle all the way down to his toes, then stood and started walking to the bedroom.

On the table, his phone was lit up.

He had a message.

Sitting back down he opened it. Blinked. Read it again.

We have work to do. Tomorrow evening. My place.

He looked, confused, at the phone, at his hands. Then down at his feet. He was wearing his Friday socks: red and blue stripes, with a black heel. He was fairly sure he wouldn't have been wearing his Friday socks if he had actually been dreaming. In his dreams, he was usually more suave than that.

I have no idea what's going on, he thought.

I have absolutely no idea what is going on.

And then: shit.

Tomorrow.

His Friday socks were thrown in the wash, along with most of his clothes, which were all dirty. The spider's web now reached pretty much to the floor. It was almost destroyed with the whack of a book before he changed his mind, put on some bright yellow Marigolds that he found under the sink, climbed onto the sofa, gently removed it from the ceiling, and then trailed it out of the window to flutter, slowly, to the ground. If there were spiders in there somewhere, at least they would have a fighting chance.

Now, he was going to go out for a run. In the middle of the night. And then he was going to have a shower. And then – then – he was going to try to figure out what the hell was going on. Because there were three women he was going to see tomorrow: Rosie in the morning, with her new baby and her innocent smile, Holly Bhattacharyya with her proud stare, and now Eva – Eva in the evening, with her opinions and her ideas and her spiky hair and her voice. God, he missed her voice. And he knew without a doubt that he wanted to hear whatever it was that she had to say.

*

James woke before his alarm, the kind of waking that won't allow you to go back to sleep again, and lay still for a while, the unease making him search for nightmares that he couldn't remember. He thought he'd dreamed that something awful had happened, though as he ran through every member of his family, he knew they were safe and sleeping soundly. The guilt, he thought, as his eyes adjusted to the dark, was probably due to missing dinner last night – well, not so much missing the dinner but having to lie as to the reason. Was that it? He sat up silently so as not to wake Julianne. His feet found their slippers, tucked halfway under the bed. He was glad. The floor was cold.

He could see their point, the directors, which was why he was going along with it. There would be panic that could damage lives – if people stopped trusting the pouch then it would change everything. All he needed was a little more time. To think that, just yesterday, he'd almost spoken to Avigail's daughter about what he was working on. As if he could have a normal conversation about his work and she would just understand that it had to be kept secret. That she might thank him. Had he really imagined she might appreciate what he was doing?

Ridiculous, really, when Avigail would have been horrified and certainly wouldn't have kept it secret. He would have told her, inevitably, and she would have told everyone – he'd never been able to stop himself. He'd been young and naive, but even so, it was absurd the way his words just tumbled out as soon as he saw her. He'd never understood why, had only realised that he had to stop seeing her, had to distance himself from the only woman who got so completely under his skin. Julianne, though – he looked at her, still fast asleep, the duvet bunched around her face but pushed off her legs – Julianne would probably keep the secret if he asked her to. What he was worried about was that if he told one person, he would tell more. He had to keep his silence. And he found it easier, nowadays, to hide the truth when he needed to. Where had he learned to do that? It was one of those slow changes in his character that he'd have resisted had he been aware of it, but having only just noticed how easily he lied to her it was already ingrained. He would have found it more difficult to tell her the truth.

But why? She would have understood. She loved the pouch, and he was trying to save it. That's what he was trying to do. Save it.

If only it hadn't been Holly Bhattacharyya's great-grandchild.

He shook his head, disgusted at himself, and brushed his teeth vigorously. Toothpaste mingled with blood in the basin, and he swished it away with the cold tap, splashing the water onto his face as well. And then he looked up.

There was no mirror above their basin, just a wall of pale blue tiles. They'd done the work themselves, he and Julianne, one weekend a few years ago – toasting their success on the Sunday night with a bottle of wine – and he'd gone into work late the next morning, hung-over and happy. It had been a long time since he'd done that.

He went back to the bed, and knelt down by Julianne's side. She stirred, stretched a bare leg beyond the mattress.

'I'm sorry,' he whispered, keeping his voice quiet, barely louder than a breath.

She said some words that weren't words, just the made-up noises of sleep, as if she was talking to him in her dream. He picked up his bag and keys, closed the door quietly behind him and headed for the Tube.

*

Eva arrived in front of the cafe to meet Quentin. The image of herself yesterday, sliding in a heap to the pavement, was like a half-memory that she was pleased not to remember too well. On the way there, she'd passed a gleaming department store that had police tape zigzagged across its side door. There'd been another break-in. And there were teenagers on the Tube, whispering angrily about something. She'd been in a daze for too long, but she was wide awake now. And she wanted answers.

That morning she'd listened to the radio with half her concentration – background noise while she made coffee, swirled honey in yogurt. Then she'd listened with full concentration to news about a celebrity marriage and the sports results and realised, when they came to their chirpy conclusion, that something was missing.

So she'd searched online for news of the Bhattacharyya baby, expecting the sites to be full of details, name, weight, hair colour. Nothing. A few sites carried a cursory message, hidden far from the home page, about the family requesting privacy. Now, all of a sudden, that family wanted privacy? No. There was only one reason to avoid saying anything – only one reason she could think of for FullLife to pass up the opportunity of this much publicity. Something had happened. For the first time, she saw a shadow falling over their flawless success. And stepping outside, she saw the same shadow falling over their flawless society.

She marched into the cafe, first again, and selected a different seat today – a table at the back, where they could remain unseen, where their voices would be masked from the rest of the room by the grind and whir of the coffee machine. Her eyes scanned the room then she reached into her bag and pulled out the paper from the train. She was planning to look for any more news of the 'NaturalBirth' plan. Whatever that really was.

The editors had managed to fill ten pages without saying anything at all: a new housing development had opened its beige show home, cinemas were screening Hollywood blockbusters and old winter classics, shops were advertising expensive perfume and bright toys. The paper felt flimsy beneath her fingers, slippery from its gloss coating. But there it was, a small advert – eighth of a page, they really were trying to stay below the radar – carrying the FullLife logo and a list of their health-care plans. And buried in the middle was the new NaturalBirth plan. Unlike the FullBirth plan, which was still top of the list. To the side, a man and woman carrying matching pouches with all the latest accessories, dressed in complementary designer labels: *Pop duo prepare for twins.*

The picture was far more obvious, more eye-catching, than the list of health-care plans. The pouch was still top priority, that much was clear. She flicked through the rest, scanning over colour photos and well-spaced text, but there was nothing in there about Rosie Bhattacharyya. Maybe Piotr had wangled the exclusive in print as well as online. It wasn't that she wanted him to fall apart without her, she just hadn't expected . . .

The bell over the door jangled, brightly. She looked up, but it wasn't him.

He was late, which was making her suspicious, and she was in no mood to be patient. In her mind he was definitely Quentin again, not James. She stood up and asked for her coffee to go.

It had turned into one of those bright, crisp winter days that suited London so well, the spires catching the light on their tips like beads of water on needles. The bare trees had ice on their branches. She liked trees better without their leaves, preferred frost and brittle bark to the restful greens of summer. With the same determination she'd had when leaving the cafe, she pushed the large, revolving glass door of the birthing centre and marched, eyes diverted from the tower of baby photos, straight up to reception.

'I'm here to see Dr Quentin,' she announced loudly.

The young man on reception had been looking at his phone, smiling – perhaps messaging someone – but if she'd waited she would have risked appearing nervous. He started clicking through the bookings to check her appointment but, of course, could find no section for Dr Quentin. The reception desk only directed people to the medical doctors who performed monthly check-ups and delivered newborns.

'I know my way,' she began saying.

He was flustered. 'Just give me a minute . . .'

She regretted not making straight for the lift now, seeing if she could outrun him, though she had no idea how to get to the restricted research labs. She'd always avoided this building. Stupid – she should have been studying it, learning her way round for when she needed access. That's what her mum would have done.

'I'll just . . . let me just . . .' he was saying.

He reached for the phone. Well, she thought, perhaps Quentin would actually give her access – he was the one who had suggested meeting, after all. Behind the reception desk, a wall-mounted screen displayed the latest FullLife advert.

She waited. Her eyes fell to the pouch the receptionist was wearing – still small, in the first trimester. Brand new though, with all the expensive extras, audio adapter, portable nutrient feed, the smart-cover that expanded with the pouch itself. FullLife made sure their staff had the best of the best, no used pouches for them. She peered at his mobile and saw he'd been looking at an ultrasound. He'd been smiling at his baby.

'There's no answer,' he said, looking up. 'Would you mind waiting . . .'

He gestured over to the comfy seats that lined the edges of the lobby.

She nodded, selecting a seat as near to the lifts as possible. They all faced the display, the thousands of photographs of newborn babies delivered here. Exactly what she'd wanted to avoid. But she couldn't help it, she started seeing their faces, their curled hands, those little hats in colours selected to match the pouch they'd been carried in. She stood and stepped closer, drawn in against her will. Some of their faces were scrunched up against the world, others' eyes wide and alert, eager to see. Some had their mouths open in a wail but many looked content, peaceful, sleepy. There were babies with dark brown eyes and blue eyes and hazel-green, blonde hair and tight black curls, lying on saris and knitted blankets and grandparents' knees. Suddenly it hit her again, as a punch to her chest.

She heard the smooth swish of a lift opening and turned, blinked. He looked pale. Head down, he rushed towards the emergency exit that she was fairly sure no one was supposed to use.

Eva swallowed, tried to push her feelings away and took a deep breath. Now was not the time to fall apart. The receptionist was talking on the phone, stroking his pouch with every few words. She turned and without rushing, without making a sound, walked towards the emergency exit Quentin had disappeared through. He'd left the door slightly ajar. She pushed it. He was about three steps to her left – she could only see his back. He was leaning into the corner, his head hanging low, his hands pressed against the wall above his head. By his feet was a puddle of vomit, the liquid sparkling where it caught the sun.

'Please no . . .' he was saying, over and over again.

Chapter 8

'THEY'VE DELIVERED THE BABY,' JAMES said.

'So it's OK then?' asked Eva. 'Just delayed?'

'No, no . . . you don't understand.' He brushed the back of his hand against his lips, then turned away from her and leaned his head against the wall. 'They've brought it back here, I mean. It's been brought back here. The . . . the body.'

'What?'

'They're expecting me to do the autopsy.'

'You can't mean . . .'

James groaned again and his shoulders heaved. Eva turned away, repulsed by the sound. She stepped back. He was taking large breaths. Gulps of air that he must have been hoping would calm his stomach. Reaching a hand forward, she touched his shoulder in what she hoped would be a comforting, non-threatening gesture.

The alley they were standing in was dark, shaded by the tall external back walls of the birthing centre on either side – a thin expanse of land that was too narrow to be used for anything. It was like a vertical gutter running between the lift shafts that propelled people between the pristine floors of a building that was beautiful from every other angle than this. Even here it was clean, no litter, no rain damage allowed to linger on the brickwork. Looking up there was nothing to see but sky. The clear, booming blue of it suddenly seemed like a sick joke.

'Let's go,' she said.

He turned, straightened up again, but didn't speak. His eyes were bloodshot.

'We'll get you a drink,' she said. 'Some food. And then you can tell me what's going on.'

He nodded.

He looked helpless. Lost. In a movement that surprised her more than it seemed to surprise him, she took his arm in hers and led him away from the birthing centre. Turning into the maze of backstreets she followed the route that seemed quietest until they stumbled across a grocer's that was serving coffee. Two plastic metal-effect tables were outside, and empty. They sat down. It was not the kind of place that offered table service, but before Eva could ask what he wanted he started talking, as if the words couldn't be stopped.

'I don't understand how they could have known,' he was saying. 'I'm not always here on a Saturday, but I suppose . . . usually, they must have thought, but even I didn't know I'd be here. I should have been out, meeting you, I was about to leave when it arrived, but there were a few of us in the lab today so I suppose someone . . . Why didn't they tell me they were going to deliver it? If I'd known, if I'd been more prepared—'

'Slow down,' she said. 'Start from the beginning. Something went wrong yesterday?'

'A baby died.'

'Rosie Bhattacharyya's child?'

He nodded again, his eyes meeting hers in a way that seemed imploring, although what it was he wanted her to do she had no idea.

'And that's never happened before,' she said.

His head was in his arms, his expression hidden from her as he stared down at the table. She felt sorry for him. They believed so completely in what they were doing, some of these scientists - so many people at FullLife. She'd come across it often, the certainty that they were doing good. To have believed all your life you were doing something right, only to have it go wrong in such a tragic way. It must make you question who you are. She placed her hand on his shoulder again, this time with genuine emotion. There was something surprisingly vulnerable about him. She wondered what her mum had really thought of him. She didn't want to imagine Avigail as someone who used people, although of course she must have done – all her contacts at FullLife were being used, to some extent, as she searched for something to help her fight against them, to slow their unstoppable conversion of the whole population.

'It can't have been your fault,' she said.

He didn't move from his position.

'I mean, I'm sure no one knew there was any danger of this happening . . .'

He looked up then.

He looked up, and she understood, and she pulled her hand away from his shoulder.

*

As Piotr pushed open the gate to the Bhattacharyya family home he noticed, for the first time, the golden-barley colour that it had been painted. Had he been asked before he would have said it was white. A white picket fence. But that's not what it was at all. The fence was low, wooden, yes, but rustic, painted the kind of gold that nature can produce; fresh bailed hay, low sun under gathering clouds. Beyond it the garden hadn't caught up with the December frost. There were leaves on the trees, a large ornamental grass with bright yellow flowers. And the berries – deep purple, wild orange and crisp white – what an astonishing assortment of berries. Perhaps he should have brought something, flowers, some kind of offering, but he was empty-handed. Still, they had their new baby, they probably didn't need anything else cluttering up their home.

He stood in front of the door before ringing the bell, expecting it to be the last minute of peace he'd have until he left again. The silence he heard after ringing the bell reminded him of an empty ice rink. He knew not to press it a second time.

It was Holly who opened the door – opened it just wide enough to look out, but not wide enough for him to step inside. At first her eyes were an accusation, but as she stared at him her expression seemed to soften.

'Nobody told you,' she said.

'Told me what?'

'Not to come.'

Piotr stared at her. She was changed, something was different.

'What's happened?'

'Piotr, isn't it?' she said. 'You have to leave us alone.'

The door was shut again, and Holly was gone, and Piotr was standing on the doorstep bewildered.

He stepped backwards and stumbled down the step. To his right, he could see the gravelled path that led around to the back garden.

Kaz was standing over by the woodpile, holding an axe. It was above his head, hanging there against the backdrop of icy blue sky. And then, as the head of the axe arced down towards the piece of pine trunk at his feet, he let out a low, wordless shout that seemed to come from somewhere deep inside him. The axe struck the wood. It fractured down the middle, and he kicked it over to a haphazard pile of broken logs before dragging the next section of trunk in front of him and raising the axe again.

Piotr crept forwards, half hidden by a laurel bush. What had happened to this family? But somewhere in his stomach he already knew the answer. Piotr hadn't chopped wood when his baby died. He had memorised statistics and stormed from expert to expert, demanding answers. He had lain awake with arguments in his mind, and his shouts had not been guttural and abstract, they had been pointed and utterly misplaced. He wished he'd broken tree stumps instead of the relationship he should have been holding together.

Kaz had realised he was there.

They locked eyes for a moment, Kaz still holding the axe high, Piotr almost hanging his head – a sorry interloper in this garden that he had no right to be standing in.

'It was my fault,' said Kaz.

'What?'

'Have they told you? The doctors?'

Piotr stepped towards him – it was too late to leave now.

'Kaz,' he said as he approached slowly, as the axe was lowered and Kaz's body seemed to sink to the ground even though he stood still on his feet. 'What's happened?'

Kaz looked at his hands, at Piotr's hands, at his bag.

'Off the rec—' Piotr shook his head against the phrase. 'I'm not here as a journalist,' he said. 'I was leaving . . . I'm not . . .'

'He died.'

Piotr swallowed.

'I suppose you know already. I suppose everyone knows.'

'No one knows,' Piotr replied, still shocked, still feeling his own grief. But then he realised that one person did. Eva must know. At least, Eva knew something. How did Eva know? *What* did she know? He had a dry, coarse taste in his mouth. 'I mean, I don't think the public knows anything. I only came here because I thought every-thing was OK . . . that you'd be, that you and Rosie . . .'

Kaz was shaking his head. 'Stop,' he said. 'Stop talking.'

'OK.'

He dropped the axe onto the ground and walked to the only bench in the garden – a carved wooden swing-seat beneath the oak. Piotr sat down next to him. Kaz was slim and neat. Piotr filled two-thirds of the seat by himself and the whole swing creaked when he sat on it, but Kaz didn't seem to notice. And then Piotr waited. Because one thing he had learned was that sometimes you need to leave the space for someone else.

'I was angry,' he said.

Piotr waited, quietly. His feet were firmly planted on the ground – he didn't want the seat to start swinging.

'With the doctors,' Kaz said, looking up. 'I thought they'd done something wrong.'

Perhaps they had, thought Piotr, but he didn't say that. He didn't say anything.

There was a strong wind high above them, clouds moving rapidly through the sky, across the sun, sinking the garden into brief shade before releasing the light again.

'But then, they sent someone round here this morning. Early. And she said that they wanted to take Will. I mean, take him back to the . . . their building.'

He looked so young, Kaz, that Piotr found himself wondering where his parents were. Surely he shouldn't have been left here to deal with this on his own. Where was his wife? Where was Holly? Well, Holly was inside, with Rosie. But he had parents, they would have been there yesterday. Kaz had talked about them at the interview, said how much his dads were looking forward to having a grandson.

'Should I have said no?'

The words startled Piotr, though there was no other sound around them. He looked up, saw Kaz's wide-open eyes, searching his as if he had the answer to anything.

'Rosie said she wanted to know why,' he said. 'So we agreed. But we couldn't send Will alone, with that woman and no one he knew or anything. So I went with him.'

'Back to the birthing centre?'

Kaz cringed. 'That's where they started asking me all of their questions.'

'They did what?'

'They needed to know everything we'd done,' he said. 'That's how . . .'

They'd questioned him? Like he was a suspect?

'I mean, that was when I realised . . .'

'They had no right,' Piotr was saying. 'They had no—'

'It must have been my fault.'

'No.' They were covering something up. Piotr knew it as surely as he knew his own name. He had to talk to Eva, this was huge, this was . . .

Kaz was looking down at his feet now, his head bowed.

Piotr swallowed, placed his hand on Kaz's shoulder but Kaz shrugged it away.

'I must have done something wrong,' he said.

'No. Listen to me.' Piotr was standing despite himself, the swing rocking back and forth from the change in weight. 'Look at me. Kaz?' Piotr knelt down on the grass – if Kaz wouldn't raise his eyes to him then he would have to lower his body to reach them – and clasped the seat to stop it from swinging. 'You did nothing wrong, you hear me?' Kaz turned away, leaned against the arm of the bench. 'You did nothing wrong.' With a silent exhale of breath Kaz started to shake, and Piotr stayed exactly where he was.

*

FullLife arranged for one of the lab assistants to show a tour group around the facility every week. It was no secret – you signed up at the reception desk, were put on the three-month waiting list, and eventually received a letter inviting you at a specified time. Anyone was allowed – they were proud of their public engagement. Avigail joined the fringes of the group outside the glass doors, catching a glimpse of her reflection amid the sea of soothing greens and blues. She was wearing one of her handmade dresses, created from folds of tie-dyed fabric in purples and reds, and a long, looped necklace of shells that Eva had collected on the beach that summer. Avigail had learned long ago she was not someone who could hide in a crowd – her bright red hair saw to that. She also knew the tie-dye made her non-threatening, and the shells made her look naive.

They'd sent a boy to conduct the tour, he couldn't have been more than twenty, and he reddened slightly every time he spoke, the blush spreading up from his chest and flushing his neck rather than his cheeks. He pointed out the lift that was used by the general public, and then guided them towards the one for staff only. Having pressed the call button once, the wait seemed to make him anxious and he pressed the button again, a rapid tap-tap-tap, before adjusting his shirt. When the lift arrived he stood back and gestured for the group to enter first, and so Avigail did the same. They were the last two in, standing side by side almost pressed back into the crowd as they waited for the doors to shut. The insides of the doors were reflective, like the outside of the building, and as they closed Avigail saw the sudden movement of his eyes that told her he'd been looking at her, and did not want to be caught.

She leaned her head closer to him, her eyes fixed on her own reflection in the lift doors.

'I'm Avigail,' she whispered, keeping her voice below the murmur of anticipation coming from the rest of the tour group.

His eyes flicked back to her.

'I'm, er . . .' He swallowed. 'I'm, I'm James.'

She smiled at his reflection, still without turning her head, and waited in silence for the lift to reach its destination. When it did, the doors slid open to reveal a sort of museum. James stepped out, blushing again, and directed people to the first exhibit.

They were looking at the early stages of the development of the baby pouch. It was unrecognisable from where it had ended up. There were none of the friendly additions, soft fabrics, familiar shapes and textures that made the pouch the success it had become. These were the inner workings. Avigail had seen photographs – she'd read all the published papers from before FullLife were involved – but she'd never seen one of the early pods close up, in person.

It reminded her of a rubber dinghy. Except for the colour. It was white and transparent, with an array of tubes attached via valves and pumps. Before the bio-membranes were developed, the outer casing had been plastic. The lid was open in the display, and you could see where the various inserts connected to create the umbilical. If it had been presented to the public in this form, it would have terrified people. No one could feel affection for something like that – it was too alien. It conjured up too many fears of being trapped inside it, of being hooked up to something mechanical. Inhuman. But stepping around the room she could see how each stage had moved closer towards the natural reality of pregnancy, as the plastic casing was replaced by a biological chamber, the rigid technology swapped for smart materials that could grow, flex, respond. The foetus doesn't lie on its back in a real womb, like a baby in a basket, so why should it lie on its back in the artificial variety? People want to carry their child, not visit it in a lab. It must be portable. It must be huggable. After all, the outside of the pod had no effect on the inner workings, so why design it to be inflexible when it could feel comfortable and soft?

There was a commentary being piped out from invisible speakers next to each exhibit. Rigged up to a motion detector, the words began as someone approached, filling the air with a lilting female voice. Avigail didn't pay much attention to what it was saying – that would be the usual FullLife promotional spin. Instead she stayed close to James, ensuring she was in his field of vision, pretending not to notice how his eyes followed her around the room. She pulled her hair up off her shoulders – it had been hanging loose and wavy down to her waist – and twisted it into a knot. He would be able to see her back now, the curls where her hair fell free to form ringlets around her neck. She waited a moment, then turned to look over her shoulder and held on to his gaze. His blush spread again, making its way beyond his neck this time. She walked towards him.

*

James had gone cold. He could feel the frost biting at his fingers, feel the shudder of it down his spine and see his life more clearly than he had ever wanted to.

'You knew, didn't you?' Eva said. Her voice sounded low and level and her eyes were an accusation. 'You knew something was wrong. You knew there was a danger . . .'

'It's more complicated—' he tried.

'Was it deliberate?'

'No!'

'Paving the way for something else, some new—'

'I swear to you, no.'

James reached for her hand, and she pulled away from him with force, bashing her elbow against the arm of her chair. He held his hands out, palms facing her, trying to calm her down. The backstreet they were in was quiet, though he could hear traffic from the main road, and it was shady – the sun wasn't reaching its way between the buildings here. He leaned on the table, which rocked towards him, unstable on its three flimsy legs.

'Well, you're here,' she said. 'Which presumably means you want to talk to me. Otherwise you'd have stayed hidden in your lab?'

'I couldn't stay there,' he said. 'They need to get someone else. I can't do this . . .'

She was shaking her head in disgust. He cringed, pushed his glasses up on his nose, ran his hand through his hair. He could feel the futility of each action as he performed it. A pathetic routine.

'I – we – knew that there might be a problem. A few isolated cases, that's all. We didn't understand . . .'

'So you kept it quiet?'

'I've been trying to find a solution. I love the pouch, you know? I wanted to fix it . . . That's all I've been doing, for years now.'

'Years?'

He cringed again.

'When it first . . . when we had the first . . . fatality . . .' He glanced up at her; she was staring back, unflinching. 'Well, we had no idea what was happening. We started studying the pouch that had gone wrong. There had been no sign, you see. There was no problem in the monthly check-ups – we're very thorough, I promise you – but there was no indication that anything was . . .'

'You've known for years?'

'We thought we could fix it,' he said. 'We thought it was an isolated incident. It could have been anything . . .'

'And then?'

'It happened again, about a year later.'

'Jesus.'

'There haven't been many. I promise, if I'd thought . . . if it was a significant risk . . .'

'It seems like a pretty *significant* risk now,' she said. Her anger made her words clipped and pointed.

'It's getting worse,' he said. 'The number of cases is increasing. There have been three this year. I don't know why. We can't find anything to link them.'

'What do you mean?'

'There must be a common factor . . . We thought at first it was something physically to do with the pouches. A malfunction, in just a few.'

'But it's not.'

'I don't think so. It's not about the age of the pouch, the style . . . I mean, the first three deaths were all from used pouches. Parents who couldn't afford . . . So we thought maybe . . .'

'It's not that either?'

James shook his head. 'And it's not the parents ... I mean, it doesn't seem to be environmental ...'

'You thought they were doing it themselves?'

He closed his eyes for a second. 'We've looked into pouch abuse. But it's not that, I'm certain ... And besides, there are too many cases now.'

'And the Bhattacharyya family are high profile. With a top-of-the-range pouch, I would imagine.'

He wanted to say he was sorry. He wanted this to be over. And he wanted to understand why it was happening. What had he done wrong? What had *they* done wrong? He'd always believed they were doing the right thing.

'Why didn't you tell anyone?'

'Like who?'

'Anyone! Another scientist ...'

'The lab knows,' he said. 'The directors too.'

'A reporter then.'

'I don't like reporters,' he said. 'They make me nervous.'

She laughed, angrily.

'No one ... No one asked me, anyway,' he said. 'No reporters came to me. No one questioned me. No one's ever even heard of me. I was trying to fix it, that's all. I thought I could fix it before ...'

'You're going to talk to the press now,' she said, standing up. 'You're going to tell them everything. I want proof, too.'

'What?'

'Lab reports. Photographs.'

He gaped at her, horrified.

'Get everything you can. You're going to meet me again tomorrow, with a reporter.'

He shook his head, but she grabbed his chin and glared into his eyes and then he was back there, back as a young man who blushed at the thought of speaking to a crowd, who wanted nothing more than not to be noticed, and who had been noticed.

The anticipation of seeing Avigail again was making him extra careful at work. He knew how easy it would be to allow his mind to wander, and in a lab that could be dangerous. So he'd focused his attention on the minute details around him: the exact rpm of the centrifuge, the cautious motion of his thumb as he dispensed the contents of a pipette. He'd managed to push his nerves so far down they didn't show on his face, they just rested somewhere around his lungs to tingle with every breath he took. He'd suggested drinks, but she said no – a picnic.

She was sitting on a red-and-white-checked blanket, laid out over the long grass under the shade of the weeping willow. Her hair looked darker, out of the sun, and her long flowing maroon dress was splayed around her on the blanket where she sat, watching his approach. He fiddled with his clothes, readjusted his collar and started apologising for the frayed edges of his corduroy trousers.

'Sit down,' she said, and his apologies evaporated on his lips. She passed him some white wine and smiled. 'Did you bring them?'

'Oh, yes, I erm . . .' He reached for his bag, but she caught his hand.

'It's OK,' she said. 'You can show me later.'

He nodded.

'There were no problems?'

'You don't understand,' he said. 'It's not secret.'

She sipped her wine, her eyes not leaving his face.

'I mean, it's not public, but it's not secret. We have nothing to hide,' he smiled. 'We're doing the right thing, for everybody.'

'My daughter is staying with some friends,' she said.

'Eva?'

He had never met her daughter.

'Do you want children, James?' she asked, the intimacy of the question all the more intoxicating for how softly she spoke it. He felt the red rising up his neck and tried not to imagine the act of making children with her.

'Yes, I . . . yes,' he managed.

'And you would trust them to a FullLife machine rather than your wife?'

'I don't have a wife,' he said.

'Pretty soon no one will,' she said. 'No wives, no mothers . . .' She put her hand on his thigh. 'No women.'

'It's not . . . no, it's not like that.' He swallowed. 'It's not . . . sinister.'

He could feel the warmth of her hand through the thick fabric of his trousers, and wished he had worn something more lightweight. He wanted to close his eyes, imagine her hand moving further.

'It's not natural,' she said.

'But we're not cloning anyone,' he said. 'We're not conditioning anyone. The conception can be completely natural. And all of it, the whole thing, parenthood, it *is* natural, don't you see?'

The sun had moved lower, was breaking through the branches now and her red hair was ablaze in the light.

'I'm going to stop you,' she said. 'You'll see.'

And although it was absurd – and when you sat in on meetings with the research staff and heard the directors give their speeches there was no way you could doubt that what they were doing was good – when she leaned forwards to him, over that checked picnic cloth with a fork in her hand and a challenge in her eyes, he wanted to say: 'Yes, do it. Give it everything you've got.' And then he wanted to kiss her. He could imagine it, even now, leaning over to press his lips against hers.

But Avigail was out of reach. He knew it as the months passed, as he struggled to keep her out of his mind, his skin tingling with the urge to feel her touch. And he knew she did not long to touch him.

That he wore glasses that fell down his nose all the time and – no matter how often he cleaned them – were covered in smudges and dust, that he stammered when he spoke and she had to bite her lip to have the patience to let him finish, that people laughed behind his back about his knitted jumpers. He knew he would never be loved by Avigail Goldsmith. But she was always there, in his periph-ery, and he spent his life waiting for her to appear, a burst of colour and energy that left him breathless with how badly he wanted her. So perhaps what he should have said to her as they sat on the checked picnic cloth was that he loved her. But what he said was nothing, and what he did was ask Julianne to marry him.

He looked up at Eva, who was in the right – he knew it as surely as he knew, looking at that poor, unnatural baby, that he was some-how in the wrong – who had every reason to go public, who had dyed her cropped hair to the exact same blaze of red that Avigail's had been, and it hit him forcefully that he had spent his entire life loving one woman, whom he hardly knew, and would never be able to speak to again.

Audio log

5 Jan 2016 23:15

Back then you see, when I returned to work, I was still one of the only women in the faculty. Down in the basement, where the physics labs were housed, I was studying early-stage cell development with microfluidic delivery. But King's was an old university, theology its biggest department, and upstairs the seminary dominated.

I felt like I was being followed by those men in their cassocks and collars who paced silently across the stone courtyard. And *watched*. Haunted by the sound of the hymns that resonated through the labs below. When you feel you're being judged, you imagine that same judgement is coming from everywhere. Though there was another type of haunting there, too – Rosalind died the same week my daughter was born. I was grieving for my friend, while my colleagues were still taking credit for her work. To remember how they used to make fun of her behind her back! It made me more angry than ever. I knew that if I gave them the slightest cause, they would push me out. They didn't want me there. They were waiting for me to get something wrong, and so I couldn't. My work had to be perfect.

Still, in some ways King's was progressive, for its time – in Princeton women weren't even allowed to step foot in the physics department. Being patronised was the price we paid for walking through the door. Not that we were allowed in the staff common room. That was the backdrop, you see. That was the world I'd worked so hard to gain access too. It made me different, I think. Different from whom I would otherwise have been. All the time I had to feign a sort of steely confidence, of arrogance, if I were to get any of them to listen to me. And I had to make them listen. I felt like I was on a mission, I was so certain that I knew what had to be done.

Unusually for King's at that point I was more interested in whole cells than in DNA – living cell research was how I wanted to study human reproduction, and I needed the engineering capability as well as the biology to sustain them. I worked with microscopes rather than X-rays, manufactured carefully designed substrates to keep my cells alive rather than wire hooks to hang and stretch molecules from. It wasn't until after I'd built my first living cell chamber that I heard Haldane speak at the Royal Society.

He sounded smooth and assured as he talked about genetics and biostatistics, wearing a deep navy blazer with distinctive white stripes and that full moustache – it was almost a surprise he wasn't holding a pipe. He was something of a celebrity already, being such close friends with Aldous Huxley, but it took me a moment to realise what he meant when he started going on about ectogenesis. I hadn't read *Brave New World* – for the best, I'd say. So as he talked about external wombs and selective breeding and child production rates I thought to myself, no, no, that's all wrong – that's such a man's way of seeing a woman's world. It's never going to be about mass production in all the symmetrical sterility of a laboratory. Human beings, if nothing else, need to feel like individuals. Don't you see? Any change must allow for individuals to remain an intrinsic part of their own reproduction, or it will fail. I wanted to create a liberating form of pregnancy. A genuine equality. A more reliable bond between parent and child. In that moment, I realised that my work was intensely personal. That was why I was the one who would succeed.

I was single-minded in my aims, back then – you've seen it for yourself. I'm not like that any more. Not sure if it's old age or new wisdom, to be honest. But things do seem to have spiralled out of control since I last spoke to you.

It was one of those crisp-as-frost days. The sun was giving out the unnatural sort of light that appears up here – an exaggerated form of colour that takes over the world. The rocks past the gorse were glowing in it, sparkling like quartz rather than coarse battered sandstone. I had gone walking along the coast, thinking myself quite alone until I saw that big green van parked outside my lighthouse, clearly visible against the flat outcrop that is the extended finger of my peninsula.

I thought, there is no need to rush, he's early and will leave my delivery outside the front door. But I turned and began walking back to the lighthouse anyway. The downpour from the day before was still visible in the muddy puddles along the track, in the smell of marsh that seemed more intense than usual. It felt wrong, in that light . . . in the dry clarity of the day. And as I watched, the van did not leave.

I continued towards home, using my stick to test the depth of puddles and propel my steps faster. The gorse was a rich dark green, almost black in places. Black and thick and vibrant in its success. There are not many plants that survive so completely here. The willowherb, with its red tendrils and cotton-wool seed head, when the weather is better, but not now, not in December. This time of year the gorse dominates completely. And still the van was there.

I arrived at the lighthouse to find him, the Asda man, sitting in his driver's seat eating a sandwich. Astonished does not begin to cover it. What was he doing there, parked outside my lighthouse, when he knows I don't like to be surprised, when anywhere else in the world would have been less of an imposition?

His window was closed and his door shut, so when he started trying to speak to me I had no idea what he was saying. I could see his lips moving and I started backing away, but he wound the window down and called out:

'Hello, Freida. How are you?'

I was speechless.

'I'm a bit early,' he said.

Which was true.

'Give me five,' he said, 'and I'll bring your delivery in.'

So, there we were. I nodded, turned, and made my way indoors. I can only suppose, looking back, that it was my shock at him sitting there eating his sandwich that made me forget to lock the door, but that's what I did. I walked inside, leaving the front door open.

So perhaps you can guess what happened a few minutes later. I was making myself a cup of tea, standing facing the kettle, which was just starting to whistle when I heard this noise behind me. In my kitchen. Right inside my kitchen. So I turned round, and there he was. It was the first time anyone but me had stood in my kitchen for over a decade. I kept thinking – how can you be here when I didn't invite you here? But it didn't seem to have occurred to him that he was doing anything wrong.

He placed the crate on my table, the one that I'd made out of the old Scots pine that fell in the storms, and started unloading the contents. I can't tell you what it all was, there were tins and fruit and milk, long-life milk and some other things. 'Plenty more to come,' he said. 'But don't worry, I'll carry them in for you, aye?' I felt unable to stop the scene unfolding before me. He disappeared out the door, but was back a moment later, the next three crates piled high in his arms. When he'd finished he looked around and said: 'You don't mind, do you?' Then he pulled out a chair and sat in it. Smiling. The empty crates were stacked up against the kitchen door like unstable scaffolding.

'It's my wife's fiftieth today,' he said. 'You're my last delivery, I'll be heading into town now to collect her cake . . .' He laughed, a big natural laugh as he dug around for something in his pocket and eventually pulled out his wallet. 'This is us. Handsome couple, eh? Taken a few years ago, mind.'

I looked at the photo, then at him. What did he want from me?

'And this is our husky,' he continued with the family slideshow.

Was I supposed to admire his dog now?

'She's pregnant again.'

'Your wife?'

He laughed his belly laugh at that.

'No, Snowdrop. The dog.'

'The dog?'

'Aye. We're thinking of keeping one of the puppies this time, too. I don't suppose you'd be interested in taking one . . . No?'

What a horrifying thought.

'Not to worry. We'll find plenty good homes for them I'm sure. But to answer your question—'

Good grief, had I asked him a question?

'—We don't have any kids. Bea and I, we're happy with life as it is, see? Plenty of time for gardening. Always time for each other.'

I swallowed.

'Speaking of which, I could help you set up a polytunnel if you like? Out the back there. It's a great way to extend your growing season.'

The door was open, wide open. All he had to do was walk through it.

'Well . . .' he said, standing again now.

I thought he was about to go at last, but instead, casually, like he wasn't even thinking about it, he picked up my one pint of fresh milk, and walked to the fridge. I couldn't have it – a complete stranger opening *my* fridge, looking through *my* cupboards. I moved as quickly as I could from round the counter and grabbed the milk from his hand, holding the fridge shut by leaning against it with my other shoulder.

'There are boundaries,' I said.

But he was still holding on to my milk, a look of total confusion on his face. And so I pulled. I pulled and it hit the floor with a pop and liquid splattered the cupboards and the fridge and leaked out into a seeping puddle on the floor.

'Oh no,' he said, watching the puddle grow. 'I'm sorry, I didn't mean . . .' Reaching for the kitchen towel. 'Let me help. We'll replace the milk, of course, get you fresh. I feel awful bad about this . . .' kneeling on the floor, mopping up the milk. 'Still, there's no point crying over—'

I had to get him out of my house.

'Just go,' I said, my voice rising.

He stood up.

'Get out,' I said. 'I don't want you here.'

He looked at me without moving.

'Why do you live here, all alone like this?' he said. 'I was just trying to help.'

'Get out.' I was shouting now. 'Get out! Get out!'

He left then, and I watched from the window as he walked down the path back to his van. Whistling, again, I could swear to it. Bet you anything he was whistling, as if he didn't have a care in the world.

I cleared up. The kitchen is back to normal and I have plenty of long-life milk so it won't be a problem. Everything is OK.

It has upset me though, and I worry what will happen a fortnight from now when my next delivery is due. At first I hoped they wouldn't send him here again, but then I thought of how they could send anyone in his place, and I couldn't stand that. All of a sudden, I was worried that he would refuse to come back. That they'd send someone else instead, someone with no idea how I like it to be done, some strange person bringing me what I need to survive. How awful. And so now, despite myself, I worry that he will not come back. It's painful to admit, but it seems I cannot live entirely without other people, after all.

Chapter 9

EVA WAS READY. SHE'D SET up her office in the piano room and cleared the kitchen table. Her laptop was on, everything in the correct folders. Emails going back years. The press file with clippings, websites, announcements. She'd drawn up a timeline of what Full-Life had done, from the day they'd been granted the right to human trials, through their introduction of Holly and the protests that followed. Up to the one that had turned violent. She wasn't born at the time but it made her feel sick, when she thought of how they'd slashed open those pouches. Twelve babies dead. Then the backlash, the rallying of support around Holly and her new daughter. The introduction of used pouches for people without a FullLife plan leading to the slow, often unreported, reassignment of contracts from the NHS to FullLife. Not just maternity wards – entire hospitals, every aspect of health care. At first it was presented as a 'partnership'. Then a merger.

She paced from the office to the kitchen and back to her desk again. One hour. She'd told him to come, and he was coming. In one hour. She looked around the office and laughed. Perhaps she wasn't prepared at all, but at least she had done her filing.

It didn't feel good to know that she was right about FullLife, or about the dangers of the pouch. It was too late anyway, for her and Piotr, no point in thinking about what difference this proof might have made. They were over a long time ago, and she had no interest in saying I told you so. In fact, she was going to find it difficult to tell him everything she knew – worried she'd be opening wounds that hadn't healed. At least, they hadn't healed for her.

She forced herself to sit down in one of the chairs she'd positioned by the window. Outside, a robin was pecking at the grass growing between the stones of her patio. It seemed to feel her gaze and sped away almost as soon as she'd noticed it. She was glad. But the memory had already surfaced.

Eva had been sitting on their sofa, reading, when she'd heard the unmistakable thud of something soft, something alive, hitting the window that looked out over their shared garden in north London. She'd known what had happened even as she glanced up wondering what had made the noise, as she walked towards the window to look down at the tiny body of a long-tailed tit lying on the grass far below.

It was the first shimmer of dusk that summoned birds from their nests to the feeder she'd hung outside the window – she loved to see them, taking turns to cling on and scatter the seeds over the ground where others were waiting. They're sociable birds, long-tailed tits, with round bodies and pretty black-and-white tails. The kind of bird she could imagine holding in her palm. She felt responsible, realising it was her own offerings of food that had brought it to the glass.

It wasn't dead. She could see its neck turning this way and that. It looked questioning. Confused. She willed it to gather its wits and fly off, but its wings seemed immobilised and when it tried to get up it stumbled awkwardly on twig-like legs and fell again.

Should she go down? Could she help, or would she just frighten it?

She stood there debating what to do before Piotr came in and realised something had happened.

'What is it?' he asked from the doorway, approaching her gently as though she were the one who'd been injured. They were particularly close, around that time.

'A bird flew into the window,' she said. 'I heard it.'

He joined her where she stood, looked down where she was looking.

'It's still alive,' he said. 'It's stunned.'

'I think it's injured.'

'How do you know?'

'It's just what I think,' she said. 'It can't fly.'

'That's the shock,' he said. 'When they're stunned they need time to regroup. I've seen it before.'

He spoke with such confidence it was easy to believe him.

She wanted to believe him.

'You think it'll be OK?'

'Let's give it a while,' he said. 'We don't want to upset it.'

She hesitated. Surely birds didn't need privacy – they weren't human.

'Should we take it some food?'

'There are seeds on the ground.'

It was true. There was plenty of food nearby that it could reach.

'We'll check on it later,' he said. 'Come on.' Leading her back to the sofa, sitting down with his arm raised invitingly.

She leaned her head against his shoulder, picking up her book again. She was upset, but it seemed silly to show it. So she read for a while, and they cooked dinner, and later she forgot about the bird and slept well through the night. She remembered it in the morning, though, after Piotr had brought her a cup of tea in bed. Slipping on her dressing gown, she went to the window to check and there was no sign of the bird. No body. No feathers either. Just a smudge on the window of where it had hit. She cuddled back under the duvet and sipped her tea. He looked at her, questioning.

'It was OK,' she said. 'That little bird. Just stunned, like you said.'

'That's good.'

'It's flown away.'

They must be more resilient than they look, she'd thought then. It must happen all the time, birds flying straight into windows.

*

The director was waiting for him outside the lab. He wasn't even particularly surprised. She held out her hand, and he shook it.

'Dr Quentin,' she said. 'James. Let's talk.'

She led him to the lift and up to her office, where the chairman and the chief scientific officer were already seated. But James was hardly present at all; he was decades away, telling Avigail he was going to leave his job. Telling Avigail he loved her.

'You do understand,' the director said, 'that we need some confidentiality here. For the sake of the customers, the parents . . .'

He nodded.

'And the research, in the wrong hands, could be dangerous.'

The director was not a woman he knew well, but he knew her enough to believe that she was a decent sort of person. Her speeches, at public events or staff parties, were self-deprecating, warm, and brief. He appreciated all three. She often toured the labs and wanted to talk to the staff, not just the heads of groups, but the students and technicians. She listened to them with genuine interest. She was not a scientist, but she believed in science – he was sure of that.

The CSO was talking about his research now.

'Your colleagues tell us . . .' he was saying.

So Bethan had been talking about him behind his back. He wasn't surprised. She was ambitious. She was better than him too – she could have his job and be welcome to it. He didn't care.

' . . . that you've been getting upset,' he continued. 'Leaving the lab hurriedly. Getting . . . squeamish?'

'You sent me a dead baby,' he said softly, though it was intended to provoke.

'Of course that was upsetting,' said the director. 'And insensitive.

It was my fault – I knew there was a rush.' She smiled in a way that made him wonder if she'd been eager to pass it on, if she hadn't wanted it on her hands any more than he had.

'But even before that,' she carried on, 'I understand there were some problems.'

He was starting to wish they'd just get on with it. He didn't want to be here any more. Why had it taken him all these years to realise that he didn't want to be here?

'Can we move this along?' he said.

She raised her eyebrows, and he did the same – taken aback at his own rudeness. He hadn't meant to say that out loud.

'I'll go quietly . . .' he said.

The three of them exchanged glances, but it was the chairman who spoke, for the first time.

'We don't want you to go anywhere,' she said, with a smile.

'We want to offer you some counselling,' said the director. 'To help you through . . . We know your field is a stressful one.'

'Are you all mad?'

He started laughing, but stopped as soon as he heard how hollow it sounded.

'We need to tell everyone the risks,' he said. 'We can't keep on—'

'The mass concern wouldn't help anyone,' the director said. 'We need calm, and time to resolve the problem.'

'And money,' he said. 'You need people to keep paying, don't you?'

'Well, yes. You know what it costs, your equipment—'

'I'm going to the press.'

'We'd prefer it if you didn't, James,' she said. 'Think of the pain you could cause the parents. And the worry for everyone . . .'

He shook his head.

'What about your research? You don't want to throw that away, after all your years of work—'

'Don't,' he said, standing up.

'We need you, James.'

'I resign.'

'But there's no reason for—'

'Please, James, we can—'

But James Quentin was at the door, where he turned the handle, stepped outside, pulled the door closed behind him, and took the thirty flights of stairs down to the exit. It wasn't until he was outside the building that he realised he'd forgotten to get any evidence for Eva. But what other evidence could he get, anyway? He had all his reports stored at home. It would be perfectly clear that he'd known, that they had all known the significance of what was happening. That it was serious enough for an entire research group to be devoted to finding a solution. That no one had been warned. Besides, there was something else that he had to do, and it seemed at once so futile and so desperately urgent that he broke into a run and didn't stop until he found himself standing on a platform waiting for a train to arrive.

*

Piotr thought about their journey through Siberia often. They'd been together for over a year by then but she was still keeping him at arm's length. He'd stopped researching Avigail's family – that's why he took the assignment in Russia, to get a new angle. He'd heard that used pouches were being passed on illegally in poorer communities. Not properly maintained. Births performed prematurely, while other babies were left in the pouch too long, unable to grow in the confined space. In some cases they didn't even have the correct nutrient bags, or they couldn't afford them. That was why Eva had wanted to come.

She'd been outraged when she saw them, the starving babies, pouch-born but barely able to cry. 'Do you see what it's doing?' she'd said, her voice shaking, though whether it was through anger or supressed tears he couldn't tell. 'Do you see what the pouch enables? Why we have to stop it?'

'But the parents are starving too,' he'd said calmly, steering her away from the slum. He had a report to write. 'They can't afford food either. The children would be dying either way. They're doing what they think is best.'

She paused, reaching for her bag, but he hurried her on.

'Don't give them money or we'll be surrounded. Follow me.'

He understood now how she could have thought he didn't care. That his reaction must have looked cold, heartless. Maybe it was. But he was there with a job to do, he'd told himself then, while Eva was essentially a tourist. She had more time for sympathy. Besides, they had ten days planned together on the Trans-Siberian railway – that should give him chance enough to explain.

On the first day in their carriage, he laughed when the tap that was their only means of washing let out a trickle of water before stuttering to life and splashing his T-shirt. She watched him, stony-faced. She hadn't spoken to him since they'd boarded the train. The next night, when the trickle failed to intensify, he cursed. He needed fresh breath and a decent night's sleep. Arguments about how he'd done nothing wrong ran through his mind as he angled his tooth-brush under the insubstantial flow – he'd wanted to feel closer to her, not push her further away. On the third morning he knew he absolutely needed to wash and made Eva wait outside so he could stand, naked, swearing, scooping palmfuls of cold water from the tiny basin to splash down his body in an attempt to mimic a shower. When she came back in – once he was fully dressed – they seemed like strangers, edging round each other in the confined space and avoiding eye contact. An apology lingered on his lips. That evening, he quietly wished her goodnight and lay awake on the lower bunk for hours, a knot of pain in his stomach as he realised their relation-ship might not survive the trip.

Standing outside her front door now he didn't knock immediately. He knew the house well from weekends spent visiting her mum, but he'd not stepped inside since Eva left their flat and moved back here. He hadn't been welcome after that, and though he'd phoned when Avigail was taken into hospital he knew his help wasn't wanted and his presence wouldn't have been a comfort to either of them.

It was strange to see how completely it looked the same. The large, once-grand window frames, lined and cracked with age, still bore the creases of generations. The round window that looked out of the attic still had its stained-glass bird angled up, a swallow reaching for the sky. The door was the deep red that Avigail had loved. The trees in the front garden must have grown, but they'd been so tall, so unequivocal before, that they seemed to have stayed exactly as they were – the size that serious trees should be. It was like stepping into the past. For a house that had been standing for two centuries, though, the six years of his absence probably seemed like nothing. A blink.

He could remember how he'd felt standing on this step for the first time – no Eva beside him then, no Eva in his life. Just the idea for an article that would expose Avigail Goldsmith. The woman so keen on exposing FullLife herself exposed as a fraud. Except that he hadn't found her to be a fraud, exactly, just someone convinced she was right despite all evidence to the contrary.

Avigail had been so certain there was evil intent behind the baby pouch she'd sounded almost insane when he interviewed her for that article. Raving against a technology that everyone accepted as a benefit to society, unable to accept she'd been wrong. He'd encouraged her to talk about her theories, describe the conspiracies she believed in, requested her 'evidence' – which was mostly leaked memos and research papers about the role of epigenetics and the extent to which the environment of the foetus could alter genetic code expression. It was old research. It was not a smoking gun.

But then there was the noticeable lack of a father for her daughter. He hadn't known Eva was adopted, had assumed a woman like Avigail would only have considered natural birth for her child. And there were the clothes – the hippy dresses and the beads. And this old house that looked as if it hadn't been redecorated for fifty years, the crumbling grandeur, the luxury of old money. The personal story was more entertaining than the research. He'd paint her as the last of an old generation that had no place in the new world. And that moment of spite had brought Eva to his office and changed his life.

He didn't even know if Eva was still running her mother's protest group. He hadn't heard anything about it, but then he'd forced himself not to look her up.

In the end his article about the 'Jewish heiress and anti-pouch activist' Avigail Goldsmith hadn't even been widely read. He'd just put it out there – the nastiness he was capable of – and the only people who noticed were himself and Eva, standing furious in his office as his heartbeat drowned out his thoughts.

'*Her privilege is undeniable,*' Eva read, shouting his own words back at him, '*and it shows her New Age philosophy to be the shallow disguise it really is. Of course she is opposed to change. Those who benefit from the status quo usually are.* Money had nothing to do with it! She believes in something. Not that you'd be able to understand that.'

She glared at him, and he just stared back. For once lost for words.

'*At least I can answer the question of how her anti-pouch protests are funded now: out of her own deep pockets. Even the fundamentalist pro-life groups have started to see her as a liability.* That's a lie! She never took their funding, never. She believes in choice. You're a cheap hack out to discredit my mother for no reason. No reason at all. And you don't even talk about the pouch!'

Actually it was intended to be the first of many articles – there was research he hadn't made public, missing details about her background that he'd not spoken about since. It was meant to start a debate; he would have gone on to talk about the care homes, the inequalities. At least that's what he told himself. At the time he'd taken the article offline and phoned Eva the next day to tell her. Then he'd invited her out to dinner to say sorry in person. She wanted none of it. He hadn't learned till later that Avigail was on to her second transplant by then. That she was being treated in one of the few remaining independent hospitals. That most of her money was gone. He had no idea how deeply he could be changed, and would be.

He used to think that people didn't really change their nature. But that was a lazy excuse, Eva always said. And she was right.

It was Eva who'd changed their dynamic on the Trans-Siberian railway, too. Though Piotr liked to think he'd have got there eventually, if she hadn't done so first. Her actions were so simple. They felt so generous. She stood in front of the basin in their shared cabin, and she didn't ask him to leave.

As she pulled off her clothes they both knew it was a different sort of thing to the mutual undressing that preceded sex. But equally it was different to the brisk, functional undressing of the past few nights with no intention of sex. It was deliberately done. She took her time with each layer, folded it, as you had to, given the lack of space, and eventually stood, naked, unashamed, conscious but not self-conscious, and turned on the tap. Then, without including him but without excluding him either, she began to wash.

Piotr could barely breathe as he watched her; it was such a personal moment he was being invited to share. She'd been angry with him for days but now, was this forgiveness? They were so close to one another, literally, that with her standing at the basin there was no room for him to climb down from the bunk. He could see every goose bump, notice details of her body that he hadn't before. She washed under her arms as best she could, sloshing the soap away before giving up and wiping the soapsuds off with the towel. Her armpits were slightly hairy with four days' growth by then, the same as was on his chin. She washed over and under her breasts, behind her ears, using palmfuls of water she splashed between her legs, soaped, and rinsed. She wiped the fine trails of water from the inside of her thighs. She flexed her bare toes on the thin blue mat under the basin. Combed through her hair with her fingers and, once she was dressed, curled her legs up onto the lower bunk bed to give him space to get down.

She lay back while he undressed in turn and as he stood naked in front of her, close enough to touch – though she didn't reach out a hand – he felt the kind of love that is not dependent on lust to last, and recognised it for what it was. Passing through the Gobi Desert they woke with the sunrise, and he intertwined his legs with hers and asked if she'd consider having a child with him, one day, because there was nothing more beautiful or intimate that he could imagine.

Eva opened the door.

She had a slight frown creasing her forehead, like she was concentrating intensely on something – he knew that look. She had ideas already. She had a plan. But he couldn't help himself when he saw her standing there, he almost fell into her arms and held her in a hug that he knew he needed more than she did. He could smell her skin, feel the fine, soft hairs on her cheek where he allowed his face to brush against hers. The sound of her breath felt like home. Then she pulled away, stepped back, and he swallowed and nodded before she had to tell him that they were not close and they were not together, and that she would not be taking him back.

Chapter 10

HOLLY MADE A POT OF tea and sandwiches: cheese and Marmite, butter and jam. They were Rosie's favourites. She cut the crusts off, arranged them on a plate and put everything on a tray. The tray she carried upstairs. Her slippers almost slipped on the carpeted steps but she regained her balance without spilling a drop, and arrived outside Rosie's bedroom door. She put down the food. She knocked.

'Rosie?' she said, her voice almost a whisper. 'It's Nana. It's your nana. Can I come in?'

There was no lock on the bedroom, but Holly understood that the closed door had to be respected. She wouldn't step inside until invited. But she would no longer wait to be called, and she wasn't above listening in either. She moved the tray out of the way so she could position her ear a little closer to the door.

'Rosie?' she whispered again, louder this time, and prepared herself for the sound of her granddaughter's sobs.

But she couldn't hear a voice inside, or any crying. All she could hear was a very faint tapping like . . . she didn't know what it was like. She couldn't place the sound. It was rhythmical, or perhaps like scraping. She leaned closer to the door.

'What are you doing, Mum?'

Daphne was standing behind her on the stairs. Holly straightened her back, groaning, and turned to face her daughter. Daphne had been the only one of them who didn't break down in the hospital, who had not screamed at the doctors or demanded answers, but silently held Rosie as she wept. When they'd come round earlier, talking about an autopsy, Daphne had dealt with them – she'd invited them in, thanked them for returning her car, made coffee, sat with them at the kitchen table while Rosie and Kaz forced themselves to make a decision upstairs.

Holly hadn't been a part of that conversation, she didn't know who said what, but she knew that eventually they'd both spoken with the FullLife director. Rosie had refused to leave her room since and Kaz had come down, red-eyed and vacant, to tell them they'd decided to proceed with the autopsy. When he returned from Full-Life he hadn't gone up to Rosie's room. He'd gone outside and started on her silver birch.

She prided herself on being the one to open her arms to all her family, to help her children and grandchildren through everything they had to go through. If Rosie fell over as a girl, it was her nana's comforting hug she ran to. If she was in trouble at school, her nana would hear about it first. After Kaz proposed, Rosie had offered to cook dinner for the whole family, to bring everyone together for the announcement, but before dinner she'd crept up to her nana's bedroom and told her what she was going to tell the others – that she was in love, and she was getting married, and Kaz was the sweetest, kindest man she'd ever met. And funny, she'd said, and musical – have you heard him play, Nana? Holly had smiled; she'd heard him at school concerts over the years. She knew, and liked, the man that her granddaughter loved.

'I just wanted to tell you first, Nana,' she'd said.

It had meant more to Holly than she realised at the time, being told first – she hadn't appreciated it fully because she'd expected it. It's easy to be there for someone when they want you to be there for them. Easy to be your favourite's favourite.

But now, she didn't know what to do when her outstretched arms were ignored.

'I thought she might like some tea,' Holly said, looking to Daphne for confirmation.

Daphne shrugged, dry-eyed. 'She's not come out for hours. Enough is enough.'

'What?'

'I'll just go in.'

'Wait, Daphne.' Holly blocked the door. It would be too much of an intrusion. Rosie knew they were here if she wanted them – she'd find her way back to her nana's arms when she was ready. 'She's doing something, listen.'

Daphne put her ear to the door, then stepped back, shaking her head.

'She's wearing her headphones,' she said, and with that she pushed the door open and strode in.

Holly stood back, lingering in the doorway. She wondered if there'd be an argument now – mother and daughter were so different. Daphne sat down on the bed, next to Rosie. Her back was straight where Rosie's was hunched, her expression calm where Rosie's was lost. She pressed stop on the screen that was held in Rosie's hands, and Rosie didn't resist – she just pulled the headphones from her ears.

'Oh, Mum,' she said. Her lower lip wobbled the way it had done when she was a child and Holly felt the same sensation that she'd felt in that hospital room. She leaned on the door frame as Rosie crumpled into her mother's arms.

She was trying to say something through the sobs, but Holly couldn't hear the words. Daphne gave her a slight nod, as if to say, I've got this. You can go. But Holly had no intention of going.

'I think . . .' Rosie stammered. She was trying to stop crying. Holly knew that moment, when you've had enough but your body hasn't caught up yet and you can't stop the sobs. She wanted to join the hug on the bed.

'I think it was . . . I think it was my fault,' Rosie managed, very quietly, the words separated with deep breaths.

Holly held on to the door.

'It was no one's fault,' Daphne said as she rocked Rosie back and forth in her arms. 'Shhh, sweetheart. It was no one's fault, I promise you that. Especially not yours.'

Holly took a step back.

A chill was passing through her body, she could feel it snaking down her spine. That woman who had arrived this morning, who had wanted to talk to Rosie and Kaz in private, she'd said *in private*, what was it about their conversation that had to be hidden from Holly herself?

She was still standing on the threshold of the bedroom, but she walked inside now, invited or not.

'What did they say to you?' she said.

She hadn't meant her voice to sound harsh, but she could tell from the way Daphne's eyes reprimanded her that it had. Her family were used to her being the cuddly one – the one who never told anyone off, who pretended to fall asleep in her comfy chair to avoid the smallest family argument. Well, she was not pretending to fall asleep now.

'You need to tell me what they said to you,' she repeated.

Rosie was shaking her head, burying her face in her mother's arms, and the crying had started up again.

'Get a hold of yourself,' Holly said. 'This is important.'

'Mum,' said Daphne, 'this isn't helpful. Go downstairs, OK? Just give us some time.'

We need more time.

The conversations collided. It was as if days separated by years had reached through to touch one another, leaving Holly reeling. She was back there, and it seemed more present than ever before, more vital.

'We need more time,' Freida said.

'What are you talking about?' Holly held Aarav in her arms – he was still a baby, six months perhaps – while Daphne and Leigh ran between the chairs and the legs of the dining table, giggling. Holly saw Freida's eyes watching them and wondered, just for a second, if Freida was jealous.

'It's moving too fast.'

'Don't be ridiculous, it's everything you wanted,' Holly said. 'It's perfect.' Although sometimes it felt like she'd had an awful lot of kids. She was knackered, Will was knackered, the children were inexhaustible.

But Freida looked old. She was only in her fifties, but she looked in her sixties at least, tired, worn out.

'Look, maybe you *should* retire,' Holly said. She didn't intend to be cruel, she was just shattered, and busy, and didn't have time for a crisis of confidence. Freida was supposed to be strong.

'You don't understand,' said Freida.

'What's going on with you?' Holly snapped. 'Is this about your job? Is this about pride?'

Freida looked hurt, and Holly softened.

'I know you don't get on with Sylvia but . . . Look, everything is beautiful,' she said, trying to be kind now. 'The pouch is perfect. Thanks to you. What FullLife are doing is *good*, and they're good at what they do. Believe me – I should know.'

'I'm going away,' Freida said. Holly didn't realise she meant for ever, of course she didn't think that, but . . . Freida's moods were dragging on her, dragging her down when she didn't have space for philosophy – this was her life.

'A holiday,' she nodded. 'Good idea.'

She didn't ask where she was going. Didn't ask when she would return. They'd been through so much together, taking that first leap of faith that changed the world – that was how it had seemed – and now Holly had built an entire life and she didn't want to hear Freida questioning it, or questioning her motives. There was no point.

Holly stood ready to say a brisk goodbye and get back to her children – Daphne had pinned Leigh to the floor and was intent on tickling her feet until she screamed, one sock already peeled off – but Freida held her shoulders and looked into her eyes as if searching for something there that she couldn't say out loud. Holly looked back, confident and happy, and just smiled. Aarav was starting to squirm, but Freida reached around awkwardly to give her a hug that seemed now to have lasted longer that it felt at the time.

'There we go,' Holly mumbled, putting Aarav into his baby boun- cer then kneeling on the floor to untangle her other children. 'You should visit your daughter,' she called over her shoulder, as Freida lingered in the hall. She hadn't meant anything by it, except that everyone needed their family, didn't they?

'Perhaps it was my fault,' Freida said softly, turning back just for a second before she left.

Holly didn't reply, because it wasn't spoken as a question. Besides, she had no idea what Freida was talking about.

*

'The babies are dying,' Eva said.

If Piotr found her too blunt, he hid it well.

'I only know of one.'

'There have been others.'

He blew out his breath like a sigh and leaned forwards. They were sitting either side of the kitchen table, which was large enough to keep some distance between them. Eva had been caught off balance by the hug. She'd thought he'd come bursting into her home with ideas; she'd assumed he would try to take control. But he didn't. If anything, he seemed less confident. A diminished version of him- self. Fatter, though.

'They don't know why it's happening,' she said.

'I think they're trying to blame the parents.'

'You spoke to Rosie Bhattacharyya?'

He shook his head. 'Kaz.'

She didn't ask how he was doing. How Kaz was doing. Or how Piotr felt. There was no need – she could see it clearly. And she knew how Rosie would be feeling too. Though, she couldn't help thinking, that didn't work both ways. Rosie didn't know the full extent of how she had felt, wouldn't be having to cope with the excruciating blood, the deep ache of it. Her body wouldn't still be trying, uselessly, to mother. Would the emotional trauma be the same? She wouldn't wish that on anyone. But she realised, as she sat not quite looking Piotr in the eye, that her plan was flimsy, to say the least. Write an article. That's all she had. Go public. Suddenly it seemed callous. Superficial.

There had only been three hospitals left in London that catered for natural births by the time Eva was pregnant. All were private of course – the government hadn't funded any kind of health care for years – and more expensive than FullLife. But Eva could afford it. They'd chosen the hospital together, she and Piotr, after visiting maternity wards and midwives. 'Although there've been no recent medical advances,' their doctor explained with a smile, visibly pregnant herself, 'we women have been doing this for a long time. We have everything we need.' Piotr had been full of questions, of course: what happens if, and how do we know, and what other options. Eva was so happy she just put her arm around his waist as he quizzed the doctors and inspected the facilities. His questions showed how much he loved his baby. He was protective, nervous. Though Eva wasn't nervous. She wasn't looking forward to the pain, but she'd never really believed the pain could be all that bad anyway. It was natural, as her mum said, it was what our bodies were designed to do. And to Eva it had felt right, being pregnant. She'd felt healthy, grounded – the world made more sense than it had done before. Where was the sense in the world now?

Piotr's chair screeched back against the tiles and he stood up, exhaling loudly. He stared at the kitchen wall, his eyes resting on the unadorned paintwork before turning to her. He looked tired. Tired, and older.

'I want to prove it's not the parents' fault,' he said. 'That there was nothing they could have done differently.'

It looked like his hands were shaking, but that must have been an illusion of the light. It was shimmering through the late mist outside, the low-lying cloud that seemed to be clinging to her home.

'I have a contact,' she said. 'One of the scientists. High up. He has proof it's happened before.'

'And that the pouch is at fault?'

She hesitated. 'They don't know why it's happening. They don't know—'

He raised his eyebrows. 'You believe *that*?'

Suddenly the old Piotr was back, was looking for an angle to the story, for someone to blame. But, she realised, she did believe FullLife – or at least, she believed James Quentin.

'Maybe,' she said. 'I'm meeting him tomorrow, and you're coming with me. He'll go on the record.'

'Does he have proof? Or is it just his word against theirs?'

'I'm . . . I don't think it's quite like that. But he's bringing evidence that they knew there was a risk. That they've known for years.'

They needed to search carefully, methodically, through her mum's old notes. Avigail had known James when he was a student, he could have given her all sorts of information without thinking. She'd not wanted to do it before, not fully. She'd been putting it off, even though it was her most obvious source of information. It had felt too intimate, going through her mum's desk. She didn't know what else could be hidden. Would Piotr help, she wondered, without needing to criticise?

'So there was a cover-up,' he said.

'They've been keeping things quiet, away from the public.'

'And now a very public baby . . .'

'They must be heartbroken,' Eva said. She didn't mean for it to come out sounding as cold as it did.

Piotr looked at her, his gaze penetrating.

'That's why we can't bring them into this.'

'What?'

'I think we should keep Kaz and Rosie out of this. Let them grieve.'

'But that's . . .'

She looked at him in astonishment.

'What?' he said.

'That's the story.'

He shrugged. 'Then we'll tell a different story.'

They stared at each other for a moment, both only just realising that their voices had been raised. Then Piotr sat down again. Looked at his hands.

'They're just kids,' he said, shaking his head. 'It's . . .'

'It's OK,' she said. If Piotr had developed a professional conscience Eva didn't want to be the one to break it. Besides, he was right. 'We'll focus on the cover-up. Hiding the risks from the public, misleading parents. Making them feel responsible. We won't mention any names.'

Piotr nodded.

'And we need to work out exactly how long this has been going on.'

He didn't say anything for a while, and Eva wondered if she should put the kettle on for some tea, just to break the silence. Perhaps he'd changed more than she realised. She shook her head, not wanting to see him, however fleetingly, as a broken man. She had never wanted that.

'What is it that you're trying to achieve?' he asked eventually. 'Is this about bringing down FullLife? About stopping the pouch from being used altogether?'

Eva didn't answer straight away. She hadn't yet asked herself the question, and she didn't know how to respond.

'I just think people should know the truth, that's all,' she said, looking into his eyes without turning away for the first time that evening. He looked back. For a moment, they allowed themselves to hold each other's gaze. 'There are risks,' she said. 'I want people to know that, either way, there are risks. There is no easy choice. There never was.'

*

By the time James arrived home, he felt like there was something inevitable in the way his life was about to fall apart. It didn't feel like his choice, although he knew he would be the one saying things, and doing things, that would cause the destruction.

But he loved his wife. He kept telling himself that he loved his wife. They had shared . . . well, not dreams. They had shared a home. They had built a home together. They'd raised their children together, shared the joy and the sleeplessness, the birthdays, the chickenpox. She had helped him wash when he broke his shoulder, and she'd done so without ever making him feel like he needed help at all. And when her mum died, he'd been able to sit beside her and ask: how can I help? And she had replied that he couldn't, not really, but at the same time that he had helped already.

They had never even asked him to lie.

For years, he had been lying to his wife about the work he was doing, hiding his fears from her, his suspicions – telling no one what was really going on. He had decided to keep the way he spent the majority of his time, the questions he thought about every day of his life, a secret. Why?

He'd thought it was because FullLife were making him lie. But they weren't.

Yes, everyone knew it would be frowned upon to talk to a journalist about company policy. Everyone knew that their research was confidential – they'd all signed the forms when they took their first job there. That would have been the same in any research post. Even at a university your research belonged *to the university*, not to you – you were not free to give it to anyone you chose. But it had been him, James Quentin, who he'd always thought was a decent kind of man, who had decided to lie to his wife. To pretend he was still working on audio and visual connections to enhance brain development, when for three years the only research he had done into brain development was to ask if the lack of it had caused a stillbirth.

Perhaps it was the reality of letting everyone down that he couldn't stand. All those people who loved the pouch, who trusted it so completely – himself included, Julianne, his children . . . He had let everyone down.

He rang the doorbell.

It was an odd thing to do, given that he had his keys in his pocket, but he already felt unwelcome. This was no longer his home. He didn't deserve it.

Julianne answered the door.

She was wearing smart black trousers and a navy shirt with red birds on – in the shape of swallows, he thought, but red. Red swallows, flying. And a red silk scarf tied loosely around her neck. He looked up at her face.

'Did you forget your keys?' she said.

He shook his head, and followed her indoors.

They sat side by side on the pale green sofa, facing the bay window. The light was lower now – it made the tracks on the windows glitter like snail's trails. Sometimes he wished that the sun would just go away. It felt like every corner of London had the power to blind. He remembered history lessons about the smog, the yellow-grey cloud of pollution that had once darkened the streets. Hard to imagine.

He took Julianne's hand in his, and she let him, though he felt her resistance. Perhaps it was obvious what was coming. Or obvious that something was coming.

'I need to talk to you,' he said.

She pulled her hand back, and waited.

'There are two things, actually.'

He wanted to do this logically. To explain. He might not get another chance.

'There's been something happening at work,' he said.

She frowned, but didn't interrupt. Had he wanted her to interrupt?

'I'm sorry I didn't tell you before. But there's a problem with the pouches. A baby has ... actually, over the past three years five babies have died during their birth. We don't know why. I think the numbers will increase. And now I've been fired.'

'You've been fired?'

'No, that was another lie. I don't know why I said that. I resigned.'

'Why?'

'Because I couldn't do an autopsy on a newborn baby.'

'Oh, James ...' She reached forward to take his hand now. 'Of course you couldn't, that sounds—'

'You don't understand,' he said. 'It's been happening for years. I've been lying about my job for years.'

'Are you sure?'

He stared at her.

'I mean, we'd have heard about it, surely?'

And so he sat back and started at the beginning, told her everything about his job, from the first time a birth had gone wrong, the way the pouch was delivered to him, the way he accepted it and didn't tell her when he got home, and the way he'd told no one and had kept on doing his research, studying the faulty pouches, ever since.

'That's awful,' she said. 'Those poor parents. No wonder they don't want to talk about it.'

She looked a little upset, but didn't seem as horrified as he'd expected. Perhaps it was too abstract – the idea of a dead child is different to the reality of seeing a child, dead. Human empathy doesn't extend that far. It needs personal experience. But even so, he began to feel a little worried she simply didn't believe him.

'Do you believe me?' he said.

'Of course,' she replied.

He didn't know what to say next.

'I've got proof of everything,' he tried. 'So we can make it all public. I've got records of when the babies died, which pouches failed, internal reports showing that everyone knew what had happened. Standard memos sent every year reminding us that our research was confidential. It's all on my computer, saved on the hard drive somewhere. I'll sort through it all. I'll show you everything.'

She shook her head.

'What?'

'It's just that, well – they are trying to fix it, you said. And that's good. They'll work out what's happening, and if the pouches are faulty they'll fix them. There are thousands of healthy births every year, though. Hundreds of thousands . . .'

'But people are being lied to,' he said.

She smiled at him then, as if she found him naive.

'People are always being lied to, one way or another. I'm sure it's not a conspiracy.'

'You're missing the point.' He was irritated now. He stood up, strode away from the sofa, then turned and sat down again. 'Sorry,' he said. 'It's just—' But how could he tell her about his fear, about what all this really meant? Because James Quentin was born via the pouch. And James Quentin's daughters were born via the pouch. And he knew, deep down, that if third-generation babies were at risk, then his children would suffer too. It could be the body of his grandchild that would, one day soon, be delivered through a series of cleanroom hatches to the scientists working in the research lab on the fifteenth floor of the FullLife birthing centre.

'What's wrong, James?' she said quietly.

She sounded like she was still trying to coax the truth out of him – as if everything he'd said about work, about the pouches, had been some kind of midlife crisis and she'd help him through it. He was finally telling the truth and she didn't believe him.

'I'm having an affair,' he said.

'No you're not.'

'Fine, I'm not.'

He sighed, ran his hands through his hair.

'What is going on with you?'

'But I was,' he said. 'I did, I mean.' He took a deep breath. This was happening now. After the initial burst it was harder to continue than he'd expected. 'I had an affair.'

He hadn't wanted it to come out like a punchline in an argument. But it was wrong, being lied to. And he had been lying to everyone. He had to put all that right.

Her posture hadn't changed, but her expression had. Somewhere behind her eyes she knew the conversation had changed from something that could be fixed to something that might be broken.

'So that's what all this is about,' she said.

He shook his head. 'No, not all of it. Everything I said about work, that was true. I'm sorry I lied.'

'When?'

He looked at her, momentarily confused. His glasses were dirty. There were smudges in his field of view.

'When did you have the affair?' she said, as if clarifying her question to a child.

'Thirty-six years ago.'

'We weren't married thirty-six years ago.'

'No, it was before we got engaged.'

'I don't understand,' she said.

'When I asked you to marry me,' he said, 'I was in love with someone else. I was running from someone else. She was . . . I . . . No, sorry, it's not about her, but I was . . .'

'And this continued for how long?'

'Oh no, it stopped. I mean, I didn't see her after we were married.'

'So you were sleeping with someone else, while we were engaged?'

'No, it was never like that.'

'What?'

'There was no sex.'

She closed her eyes, and the way she was breathing made her sound like she was trying to be patient. It reminded him of when the twins were babies and they had screamed, *screamed* night after night, and when she went to help them, picked them out of their cots and rocked them one by one, they would go quiet, but when he did it – which was half of the time, they took turns – they wouldn't stop. He tried everything. He begged them. He rocked them and sang to them, offered toys and milk bottles but it hadn't helped. And eventually, as any hope for sleep was abandoned, Julianne would come in to the babies' room and take the children from him, and she would breathe slowly and deliberately until they stopped crying.

It was the same kind of breathing she was doing now.

'Why are you telling me?' she said.

'Because it's the truth.'

'Why now?'

'Because I can't stand lying any longer.'

'But there's no point,' she said angrily. There wasn't the pain in her eyes that he'd feared there would be – instead, she seemed furious. 'What is the point in telling me this now? Do you want me to forgive you, is that it?'

'No.'

'Do you want to hurt me?'

'Of course not.'

'Then there was no point.'

'But I still love her,' he said.

'Then walk out the door and be with her.'

'She's dead.'

'Then you're a fool.'

'And I still love you, Julianne.'

He looked up at her, suddenly feeling it again, believing in their marriage, and simultaneously feeling that cold, bitter chill that told him it was over.

*

The results of their search were piling up on the floor around the walls. They had emptied Avigail's desk, and now they were emptying Avigail's house, from attic to cupboard and drawers in their search for anything they could use. While Eva's research was ordered and filed and told them nothing new, Avigail's was chaotic, everywhere, in every part of her life; the randomness itself seemed to hold a potential clue. They couldn't stop until they had searched every possible hiding place, and neither of them needed to say so to the other. Eva worked silently, and Piotr respected that need for silence.

Bags were filled for charity, other boxes for the dump – Eva was brutal, even with this – while papers, notebooks, and letters were piled in the living room. She pushed her sleeves up to the elbows, and he knew he was lucky to be allowed to stay and observe, let alone help. He wasn't needed, but it's hard, going through the remnants of a life. He hoped, perhaps selfishly, that having him there was a kind of support.

It felt strange to Piotr that Avigail wasn't still around. He and Eva had broken up two years before she'd died, and so not seeing her – not thinking about her, if he was honest – was something he'd become used to. She had been absent from his life before she became absent from the world. And she'd never liked him anyway.

He'd liked her, though. That was his first thought when he heard about her death. There was an email from Eva, and a brief report online. He'd tried phoning. She hadn't answered. Why would she? But he wished he had told Avigail, just once, how much he liked her.

After his ill-judged exposé, Avigail's reaction was unexpected, especially given that he was meeting her again as the new boyfriend of her daughter. She'd looked at him, standing there on the doorstep – he'd gone to some trouble, in his new suit, his brushed hair, his beard trimmed and almost neat – and as he'd waited, his hand outstretched in the formal offer of a shake, she'd laughed. Not a curt laugh, quite the opposite. A big, full-bodied, fully enjoyed laugh. Then she'd grabbed his hand and used it to lead him into the front room, instead of accepting the handshake.

'I don't mind telling you, Piotr,' she'd said, the laugh still playing about her lips. 'I have not the faintest idea what my daughter is thinking.'

'Nor do I, to be honest.'

'Precisely!' she'd replied, taking wine from the rack, turning over her shoulder to glance at him with the bottle of red held high.

And now she was gone. It was like her death had just happened for him. How awful, the way we can push things out of our minds. So easy not to face something unless it is standing in front of you. And while he was sitting on the floor, thinking about death, Eva was searching through cupboards, and he saw flashes of colour, caught glimpses of fabrics that were so reminiscent of Avigail it felt like she was there. I always liked you, he wanted to say. I liked you. Does that help, at all?

Eva handed him an old calendar, some notes for essays that had never been written. He read them then carefully added them to the right pile. He didn't interrupt her with suggestions about what to do next. She showed him Avigail's descriptions of the care homes she'd visited – details of their funding, too, from private investors whose money had long since dried up to the more liberal pro-life groups while their movement was splitting down the spine. After the pouch was invented no one had known which way they would go. After all, if what you really cared about was the life of every foetus, then the pouch gave you a way to save every one of them. But some believed that women were supposed to give birth, that women only existed to give birth ... Thankfully society had turned away from that. The result was the rapid acceptance of the pouch, in the UK at least. And as for the care homes ... He knew they were struggling.

He read it all in silence, then looked up at her.

'This one,' she said, glancing away from him as she took the papers back and added them to her file. 'That was where I lived. But it's not going to help us today.'

He just nodded and left her the space to talk if and when she wanted to. Twice today, he had managed silent support. And it must have helped – why else would Kaz have talked to him, or Eva let him stay?

'More letters,' she said. 'Just read some of these.'

And there were loads of them, the letters, some genuine, some offering help, some that sounded like they'd been written by deranged fans. Then there was one, handwritten on yellowing paper, and Piotr wasn't sure but he thought it was different to the rest; it hadn't even been signed. 'Have you seen this one?'

She looked over her shoulder and waved her arm impatiently.

'Mum had friends all over the place,' she said. 'She was always going off somewhere. Just put it on the pile with the others.' Then she stopped, stood still, and Piotr knew she'd found something else. Slowly, she sat down next to him.

'Mum's old photographs,' she said.

They were in a white envelope. Eva showed it to him without opening it. He knew, from the look on her face, that this was the moment when he could help. They sat side by side, their backs leaning against the wall, their shoulders not touching. Then Eva opened the envelope and pulled out the printed photos that Avigail had decided to save.

The one on top was a photograph of their house, taken from the back garden looking in, on a summer's day when the yellow rhododendrons were in bloom. The French windows leading into the living room were thrown open and the angle of the shot led you inside, through the long room of wood floors and flowing light. Eva glanced at him, lifted the photo from the top of the stack to place it at the back.

There were group shots next – old and unfamiliar to Piotr, but Eva seemed to recognise them. She smiled, softly, reached out a finger to touch her mum's face, the decades-old images of her mum's friends who had made her childhood so colourful.

'That's Ina,' she said, showing him one. 'She was my mum's best friend.'

Piotr smiled at the photo of them, arms round each other, Avigail and Ina, both with long flowing hair, Avigail's red and Ina's grey.

There were photos of Eva when she was a teenager, dressed in tie-dye like her mum, with dangly earrings and frizzy hair. In one she was wearing faded denim shorts and thick black tights, a flowery purple shirt tied in a knot at the waist, DM boots laced halfway with orange laces and graffitied with swirls of bright paint and glitter glue. And then the images became more recent.

He'd known it was coming, of course.

First there was a photo Eva had taken one Christmas, Piotr and Avigail sitting either side of the dining table with paper hats on – Piotr's balanced precariously on top of his head. It was too small to fit on properly; his head was too big. On the table were the remnants of pulled crackers, Christmas pudding half eaten and swimming in brandy. Eva touched the image, passed it to him. He took it, held it, and waited.

A photo they'd taken in Norfolk, both of their faces too close to the lens, behind them a view of the beach, white satin, windswept and overexposed. It looked like there were smudges, like something had been spilled on the picture. She passed it to him by the edges and he took it too eagerly – his thumb went into the frame, leaving a clumsy thumbprint on the paper. He kept hold of it though, placing it neatly on top of the Christmas dinner before looking up for the next photo.

And then his heart stopped. He'd been expecting more of them, or more of Eva and her mum, but it wasn't that. It was a printout of their first ultrasound. He heard Eva swallow. She hadn't been expecting it either.

'I didn't know she'd kept this,' she said, her voice quiet but even. Perhaps, after what they'd been through, a small picture didn't have much power to hurt.

She passed it to him, and he took it. His hands were shaking but he made himself look. Hardly recognisable at all, at that stage. But he recognised his daughter the way you do a tune you haven't heard since childhood.

Eva was standing up. He couldn't. He just looked up at her from the floor, his eyes pleading.

'You can keep those,' she said, with a shrug. 'I don't need them any more.'

The pain of it knocked the breath out of his lungs.

Audio log

9 Jan 2016 02:15

I realised something today.

At my interview, back at King's, the professor thought I was being quiet because I was nervous. He must have thought I idolised him. Actually I thought he was flirting with me and so I wanted to keep my distance. But we were both wrong, I think. Both wrong about each other's motivations. He imagined he was being encouraging. I was uncomfortable about being spoken to in a way that had simply never occurred to him was wrong.

As we got to know each other it turned out we were rather alike – that is, he was strident, ambitious, brilliant, and I was difficult, calculating and opinionated. When I was directing my own research group, long after my husband had died, he asked me why I always spoke as though I expected a fistfight. I told him I had no idea – so far as I could tell, I was in the middle of a war. He did not ask me to elaborate.

There is no greater patriarchy than London. Who said that? Well, whoever she was, when she spoke those words she was right. It wasn't easy. I don't want anyone to think that my life, or my research, was easy.

I did inherit money, though, from my husband. I'm not sure how I'd have continued my work, during his illness or after his death, if it hadn't been for the money. Even facing prejudice I knew it was privilege that allowed me to be there. And I tried to reach other women, to make my choices available to them. I think we have an obligation to ensure the next generation does not need our levels of privilege to succeed.

But now I am thinking about you. My daughter.

I try not to, most of the time. I talk to you, but I try not to think. To dwell.

What use is it, really? What good does it do?

But it's impossible to train yourself not to think of someone, even when it's someone who's been gone for so long. Especially when it's someone who could choose to come back. I don't believe I did anything so very bad, to deserve this silent treatment. That's what you used to call it as a child. When you were angry with me. When you thought I had been away at my work for too long, or when you felt neglected. It must have been a lonely upbringing, with your father gone and your mother . . . Well. I believed in what I was doing, but you decided to take it all so personally.

Was it that *awful*? you said to me once. Was I really such an *awful* experience?

Of course, it wasn't really about you. Certainly not by that point – the body has a way of forgetting pain and I loved you, deeply. You know that, don't you?

I shouldn't say it wasn't about you, though – you wouldn't like that. I think it might make you angry with me all over again. Perhaps all children want their parents' lives to be all about them. Perhaps they're right – maybe parents' lives should be all about their children. It's possible that I got more things wrong than I know. But it makes no difference, to be wrong or right. The fact is you haven't spoken to me in a long time.

You'll be quite old by now, I suppose. I forget my own age altogether most days, but it's particularly hard to imagine you in your sixties. It's easier for me to picture you at sixteen. Easier and harder, at the same time. Whatever happened, you know, no mother wants to be estranged from their child.

But it's surprising, how I've started to hope that perhaps you will still arrive. I don't know if it's because of my troubles with the Asda man – after all, if you don't come, it is possible there will never be another visitor to my lighthouse. Perhaps I'll die here alone and no one will even notice. But I don't believe that will be the case. I think you're going to come. I'm even starting to have some kind of faith in it. Perhaps you will arrive today, or tomorrow. Perhaps you're on your way already. Perhaps you've been here before, many years ago. Could I have imagined that? Was the wind through the rocks beating like fists on the lighthouse door? I hope I will recognise you. It has been so long. If I don't recognise you I'm afraid I might not even want to let you in. Please don't take that the wrong way.

I want you to know that you are, and always will be, welcome in my lighthouse. I am a difficult old woman – though I am a different kind of difficult now. Less confident in my creation and more confident in my doubts. And still no one can tell me what to do. You wouldn't want them to, would you? There will be no old folks' home for me. Perhaps, when I am ready, I'll walk straight into the sea. Though I worry sometimes that I would float. I wish I had more weight to me, to my bones and muscles. Terrible, the way we become smaller like this.

There is a buzzard sitting outside on the fence post. I have seen her a few times now – I think it is the female, though to be honest I couldn't tell you how to distinguish between them. I can watch her, watching me, from the window opposite my chair, when I turn my back to the fire, which I like to do sometimes – it warms the back of my neck, then, and the back of my neck feels the frost like a paper cut.

Once, when I was out walking the black rocks, I saw a pair of them, sitting in a crevice on the cliffs. They didn't look anything special like that – just birds of prey, a medium-brown colour, large enough to stand out but not the size of an eagle, nothing like that. An average bird of prey, I would have said, from seeing them huddled against the greyish rock face. But then the wind resonated and they both took flight and, while hardly moving at all, seemed to glide towards me. They were so low, as they approached, I could see the extraordinary white crescent markings on their chests . . . the patterns like delicate carvings on the underside of their wings . . . the extent of their elegant wingspan itself. I craned my neck, following their flight, staring straight overhead as they passed. And then they were gone, distant, brown average-sized birds of prey again. As though the display of their captivating beauty was for me alone.

I don't know if I am trying to assert a cause and effect here where none exists, but I'm fairly certain that it was after that day that she began to perch, usually first thing in the morning or at the tail end of dusk, on my fence post. Perhaps – just perhaps – we reached some kind of understanding that day. I think she has come to keep me company. She watches me as I wait for you, and as she watches me I start to hope that my waiting is not futile.

If I see her stretch out her wings again I may start to hope that there is no such thing as futility.

Chapter 11

JULIANNE QUENTIN HAD NEVER LOVED her husband. She was a pragmatic woman, and she judged relationships in the same way she judged everything else in her life: with good sense, a strong belief in right and wrong, and an acute understanding of the practical realities of the world.

She believed in partnership, though. She believed in respect. She believed in treating people with decency and equality and receiving the same in return. James had seemed like such an honest man, when she first met him. So nervous, with that stammer and his habit of pushing his glasses higher up on his nose all the time, so nervous that she couldn't imagine him having the ability to lie at all. And he had been clever. He'd got the internship at FullLife and the competition was fierce. His intelligence was an interesting counterpoint to her own common sense; he'd never made her feel anxious. She couldn't have spent her life with one of those men who need to control others, and she'd known a few of them, when she was younger. The ones who insist carrying the children is their *job*, because they're the *man*. The ones who put their hand on the small of your back to guide you across the road, as though without their guidance you might inexplicably leap in front of a car. Sometimes she wondered if there *was* some kind of basic male instinct at play – though she had to admit things were better, now. The pouch had evened the playing field.

But James had never been like that. He'd never – not once – expected her to look to him for the answers to her own questions. And in return, she had never tried to tell him the answers to his. They had given each other independence. So really, what in heaven's name did he think he was doing?

He'd shut the door quietly when he left, first thing this morning. Creeping out before dawn without waking her. She had no idea where he'd gone. And it was none of her business anyway – he was a grown man and would make his own decisions. Just like she'd make hers. But still, this was totally out of character. Had he lost faith in his work so completely he was on some kind of crusade? He'd signed a contract, though, and he had a duty to keep the details secure for the parents, the children . . . They were a medical facility, of course their data was confidential.

Suddenly everything that her husband had said and done the previous night seemed absurd. He was not someone who leaked information to the press and went around acting like a misguided hero. He didn't have affairs or harbour unfulfilled love for some woman he knew when he was a student. Their life was not that kind of story, and she wanted no part of it.

She went upstairs and packed his clothes into suitcases.

She checked her schedule, saw that she had a midday meeting to discuss the latest flight routes, and was booked into the control room on the 2–7 shift. Fine. She'd travel in early, have time for a coffee and sandwich in her favourite cafe. Her life was going to be just fine.

But she didn't know *how* to wipe a hard drive.

That was OK. How difficult could it possibly be?

She went upstairs, clicked on the computer to wake it up, and searched: how to wipe a hard drive.

The computer told her how to wipe a hard drive.

Calmly, she wiped the hard drive.

She didn't think it was anger that made her do it. It was simply the right thing to do. The information was confidential – personal, private and rightly so – and clearly James was having a breakdown that he would later regret. She'd just saved him from doing some irrevocable damage.

Then she went to the kitchen to make herself a cup of coffee. Toast, butter, jam. And she did not think, not for a second, about the irrevocable damage that James had done to her, to their family, or how it had – in one brutal swipe – changed everything.

*

When Eva woke up there was the strangest sound in her home – unsettling, haunting, but absolutely right at the same time. It took her a moment, in her half-sleep, to place it. It was not a CD, it was not the radio. Someone was playing her piano.

It was a tune she didn't know. It was melodic. They had a touch on the keys that was firmer than hers, a heavy tread on the pedal, but there was depth too. It had been so long that for a moment she could hardly believe it. Piotr was playing her piano.

As she reached for the glass of water beside her bed, caught a glimpse of the sky, like layers of oil paint, she realised that he was doing more than playing. He was composing. He could never remember how to play the notes of others without sheet music, but he could do something better, something she'd never been able to even though she played better than him. She couldn't deny it; he was creating something beautiful. There was emotion in the way his notes fled from one another, a deep sort of ache in the sustained bass. She closed her eyes, imagined that she could touch her hands, briefly, on his shoulders while he played. But no.

They had a meeting to get to. Besides, she'd let him stay the night – on the sofa downstairs – and that was quite enough. She got up, pulled on her jeans, chose a purple shirt, a jumper, and stood at the top of the stairs.

Step by step she tiptoed down towards the sound, the speed of the high notes now making her afraid as they raced across the keys, the contrast with the full pedal making their immediacy blur. She didn't know how he was going to react when he saw her. From the door she could see his head was bowed. His back hunched down, his face too close to the keys.

She swallowed.

He stopped playing, abruptly, and stood up.

'Do you want to get going?' he said, as the piano lid slipped silently from his fingers over the keys.

She could see that the sleeping bag was folded neatly on the sofa. The cushions carefully arranged back into position.

He didn't look her in the eye. His hands rested on the lid as he took a step to the side, away from where she was standing.

'We don't want to keep your Dr Quentin waiting.'

For a second she didn't trust herself to speak.

Instead she nodded.

And just like that they were two strangers again, with nothing but an old moth-eaten piano standing between them.

*

Holly left her house furtively. At least, she imagined she was being furtive, but perhaps it was just that no one in her family was paying much attention to her at the moment. And that was as it should be. Rosie needed to be with her mum, and Kaz needed to find a way to speak to Rosie, and Daphne needed to support her daughter. Holly needed to stop feeling useless and get some answers. Starting with Freida. She didn't want to speak to FullLife – and she was fairly sure they wouldn't tell her anything even if she tried – but Freida was a different matter. Freida had disappeared and asked her not to follow and Holly had gone along with it. But not any more. Freida was alive out there, she was certain, and now she was going to start talking. Holly was going to see to that.

She was wearing an inconspicuous long navy raincoat, comfortable trousers, her wide-brimmed hat, and her house trainers. She tended not to go out in sports shoes, but they did allow you to tread so quietly and walk so freely, and stealth and freedom were what mattered to her on this journey. At the corner of the road she waited patiently for the bus that would take her into central London – she simply hated the Tube, the pushing and the shoving, the blind claustrophobia of it all. Much better to be able to see where you're going. She calmly showed the bus driver her over-sixties pass, climbing the step with the aid of her walking stick, which she didn't actually need but liked because it helped her to go faster. She enjoyed stamping it firmly on the ground, to really make sure that the floor was solid. There was strength enough in her arms to give it a good testing. And today it was helping a bit with her sore knee. She ignored the pensioner seats and made her way to an empty pair halfway along the lower level. The morning light was streaming through the windows. She wondered if she should put on her sunglasses, but she had a feeling that might make her conspicuous rather than furtive. A step too far, perhaps.

Freida had written to her a few times over the years. Never with a return address. Never with an invite to visit. When the first letter arrived, six months after Freida had gone away, Holly ripped open the envelope with relief that at last her friend was going to explain. But she didn't. She just waffled on about needing to be alone and what a pleasure it was to be away from London – from Holly's home! *I hope you are well*, she wrote, *and I'm sure you're all better off without me.* The neediness itself was enough to annoy Holly. The self-pity! But most of all she had hurt Holly's feelings. So Holly had shut them away and lived her life, and loved her family, and never gone looking.

But now, she was headed to the offices of the news website that had sent Piotr Filipek to her door. She'd walk in and claim Piotr had invited her. She was an old lady – they had to believe what she said. At the very least, they'd have to produce him, even if just to prove she had no appointment at all. Then she'd insist that he help her find Freida. She'd seen that look on his face during the interview. He knew *something*, that was for sure, and if her suspicions were correct he had a pretty good idea where she was hiding. Once they found her, she'd demand that Freida tell her everything she knew – starting with why she left, and ending with exactly what was wrong with the pouches.

But what happened when she arrived at his office was unexpected. They simply had no clue where he was. They were happy enough to talk to her – in fact, once the receptionist realised who she was all the staff clustered around her, wanting photos, quotes, asking her about Rosie . . . And then they were asking about the baby, why no one was being allowed to see baby Will. She had to put her foot down.

'I will speak to no one but Piotr Filipek,' she said loudly, rolling the 'r' and projecting her voice the way old ladies can do. When she was younger she'd always imagined getting one of those buggies as an old person, so she could race through the streets shouting gossip and cackling. She'd never got the buggy but she could shout with the best of them – and she found it was most effective in front of people who thought you maternal and sweet. Having got their attention, she made her demand.

'Tell me where I can find him,' she said. 'Now, please.'

And the receptionist started typing on his computer, the other journalists tapping into their phones to get contact details. They even wrote it down for her. She quickly had a mobile phone number, an email address, and a home address for Piotr Filipek.

'Are you sure you should be giving this information out?' she said, folding up the paper and burying it safe in her trouser pocket. The receptionist looked so upset then that she patted him on the head a couple of times, just for reassurance, and held on to his chin as she said a sincere Thank You. They all kept out of her way as she swept through the lobby. Ha!

Next she made her way straight to his flat. She pressed all the buzzers until someone let her in (it was that kind of neighbourhood, full of students) and in she went, climbing the stairs to locate his front door and hammer on it with her walking stick.

There was no answer.

She hammered louder.

Nothing.

She listened close to the door, peered through the letter box. From somewhere out of sight there came a miaow. Other than the cat, it seemed there was nobody home.

Very well, she thought, and sat on the stairs to wait. It looked like the banister had just been replaced – it was shiny and clean, unlike the rest of the drab stairwell. Twice people walked past, heading down from the flats above, stopping to ask if she was OK, if she needed help, if she was lost . . .

'I'm perfectly well, thank you. I have an appointment,' she replied each time.

An hour passed.

Her bottom started to ache from sitting on the cold stair. Her knee felt tender where it was bruised. Her stomach was growling for some breakfast, but she didn't care. Sooner or later, he'd have to show up.

*

Eva and James had planned a new venue for their early-morning meeting, an impersonal coffee chain near Waterloo. But as she sat opposite Piotr in the cafe, resisting the urge to comment on the latte that was larger than his entire face, she began to worry. James was late. Ten minutes so far, but she'd expected him to be there first, after the horror in his eyes the day before. He needed to tell her everything, she'd seen it, the release that comes from finally accepting that a secret cannot be held any longer.

Maybe he'd gone back to work first thing for the evidence and got held up. Or maybe he was in the lab, trying to find a solution. Could they have got to him? She checked her watch again.

'Don't worry,' Piotr said. 'I'm sure he's on his way.'

'You've never even met him.'

He nodded, looked away, scooped some of the foam out of his cup. Suddenly, irrationally, she wanted to grab him by the shoulders and shake him. Her own black Americano was still too hot to drink, so she decided to wait till it was cool enough, drink it, then suggest they leave.

'Do you have his number?' Piotr asked.

'In my mum's address book.'

'Do you have it with you?'

'Yes.'

'So you could phone him?'

Eva's phone was on the table between them, she'd been picking it up and putting it down again since they'd arrived. She *could* phone him. But somehow she knew that wasn't going to make any difference. If he wasn't here, he wasn't going to be answering his phone. And if he'd decided not to talk to her, there was no way they would get admittance to FullLife either. Not now.

'Do you want me to leave?' Piotr said suddenly, and she realised she hadn't answered his suggestion, and had been ignoring him since they left the house. She didn't want him to leave, though. It was ... reassuring, having him here. She just didn't particularly want him to talk while she was thinking.

'No,' she said. 'No, it's not that.'

He sat back and regarded her, as if trying to anticipate her next move, and she saw a flicker of the old journalist back in his eyes. It made her smile.

'I'm trying to have an idea,' she said. 'And you're distracting me.'

Now it was his turn to smile, and he didn't try to hide it – he beamed at her from across the table.

'Shall we go to FullLife?'

'They won't let us in. Especially now.'

'Then if you won't phone him . . .'

Eva picked up her coffee, expecting it to scald her tongue again, but it didn't. The coffee was rich and she held it in her mouth for a moment – as though savouring it would bring James Quentin to the cafe, along with the certainty of what to do.

'You try.'

She'd been carrying her mum's address book with her for two days. Since finding it she hadn't wanted to let it out of her sight. It felt like a connection, the one thing still joining them together despite the soil between them – the handwriting, the notes she'd made beside certain entries. Sometimes she reached into her bag just to check it was still there, ran her finger over the comforting creases in the spine. Without showing any of this sentiment, she passed it to Piotr.

'He's under Q,' she said. 'For Quentin.'

He flicked through, overshot then pushed the pages back until the address book was lying open at Q in his palm.

She looked again at the door, willed it to open while she sipped her coffee.

'Erm . . . Eva?'

'What?'

'Have you seen this?'

And she knew what it was before her eyes moved to the page – she'd known all along, but had forgotten, or chosen not to remember, because for some reason she hadn't wanted to go there. To his home. But that was where they would have to go. If he didn't turn up.

She looked down at her empty cup.

'Want some of mine?' Piotr said, offering a half-full cup of caf-feinated milk with a smile. 'Don't think I can handle it after all . . .'

She put her hands on his over the handles of the giant cup, and steered it down to the table.

'Are we going to try his home?' she said.

'I think we're going to try his home.'

'Then let's go.'

*

Karl had not slept in forty-eight hours. He had lain in bed. He had tried the sofa, the spare room that had once been Kaz's bedroom. He'd leaned back in his armchair in the lounge and closed his eyes and prayed that he could sleep, just for the fleeting peace it would bring. He'd stumbled his way into the painted room, unable to call it the baby's room even in his mind, surrounded himself with the sea crea-tures and distant stars, curled up on the floor beneath them. None of it made any difference. The scene in the birthing centre played over and over in his mind, as he imagined things he could have done to help despite knowing there was nothing anyone could have done by the time they were assembled in that room, waiting, expectantly.

It was no one's fault. There was no one to blame. He had tried – blaming the doctors who came running, the nurse who was there, the ineffective resuscitation pads, and once, in a particularly dark moment, he had wondered if Rosie and Kaz had done something wrong. He was ashamed of that, but the thought had dug its way into his mind and he had to struggle to keep it flattened down. He told himself he must never think it – and, when that did not work, he swore to never speak it out loud.

He wondered if it was something that had been passed on. From Cris. He retreated deeper into his thoughts and shook his head as Cris offered lunch, a walk, a talk. None of it was any use. Karl would not sleep.

He had tried so hard, throughout his adult life, to be a good parent. He could remember when Kaz was born, how he'd sat up late at night with him, when he was restless, and formed lists in his mind of what he'd do for his child. Some nights he imagined teaching him to swim. Sometimes it was picking him up from school in the car to save him cycling home through heavy rain. His father had done that for him once, and he still remembered the gratitude of seeing that car, its windows misted and its lights on, outside the school gate. He'd spent ages running through all the possible types of advice he could give – advice about school, relationships, work, how to fix a leaking tap, repot a house plant, how to dance, how to be gentle, how to be strong. But it wasn't the advice he could give that really mattered. What he wanted to do was listen. He would listen to his son, he promised himself. He'd be a father who knew how to listen without offering advice. But the thing was, now he needed someone to do that for him. He achingly wanted his own father to sit down opposite him, to remind him of the beautiful feeling that came from knowing there was someone who would appear just when he needed them, in the car, its windows misted and its lights on, offering him a drive home.

He looked up at Cris and felt his eyes starting to water before he blinked that away – he shouldn't be the one crying about this.

'I know,' Cris said.

But Karl hadn't spoken. When was the last time he had spoken?

It was the day of the birth. The day his grandson died. The day they had stumbled as a family, numb with disbelief, out into a world of sharp biting sunlight and traffic and the chattering of journalists waiting on the other side of the building. The nurse had guided them out of a side entrance, where no one would see them, and they would be driven back to their homes so they could have some time, some rest, some space to recover. Had she actually used that word, recover? He couldn't remember. What he remembered saying was:

'Come home, Kaz.'

And it had been the wrong thing. So utterly the wrong thing. Kaz was clutching on to Rosie, their heads pressed close together as though they wanted only each other in the world and everything else to disintegrate. And they had been ushered towards two cars – of course, he'd thought, we have to take two, there are too many of us – and he'd watched as Kaz and Rosie climbed into the back of the first car along with Rosie's mum and Holly, who was impenetrable now, her eyes locking on to no one. And they'd driven off. The driver of their car was motioning to them, but Karl just stood there watching his son drive away with his other family.

Of course, Holly had invited them back to the house as well – of course, they were all one family. Except you never really were all the same family, were you? Because there'd only been one time when he'd felt that completeness, and that was many years ago, when he'd been surrounded by brothers and sisters, and he'd known with a deep certainty that his mum would always comfort him when he was sad, and that his dad would always know the right thing to do. He'd looked at Cris, seen his red eyes but felt too exhausted to pull him close. He had run out of whatever it was that propelled him. In the car, sitting together on the back seat as the driver made his way through the busy roads towards west London, he'd looked at Cris and said: 'I don't know what to do.'

*

Eva and Piotr were standing on a quiet residential street of semi-detached Georgian houses, with neat, walled front gardens and well-shaped shrubs. It was not quite suburbia – the gardens were too small for that, the houses cuddled too close – but it was a different world to the gritty north London of their old flat, or the gently preserved spaciousness that surrounded Eva's home.

'I guess FullLife pay well,' said Piotr, and Eva nodded but pulled her coat closer, keeping her arms crossed around her body. He'd always felt peeved that he didn't get paid more – not quite a chip on the shoulder, but enough that he felt the need to let out a whistle when he saw something he couldn't afford. It irritated her.

'Do you think that's why he worked there?' he said.

'No.'

'So he believed in what he was doing?'

Eva thought about that for a moment. 'Yes, I think he did. Or he must have done, to begin with. Number 38.'

Eva marched up the path and rang the bell. Together, they waited.

She checked her watch – it was gone ten. If he was here he surely had no intention of speaking to her. There was a letter box, silver against the deep blue wood of the door. She pressed the bell again. It made a ding-dong sound like Big Ben.

Certain no one would be there, she leaned down and pushed on the letter box, which opened easily against her fingers, and peered inside.

Two eyes peered back.

Eva gasped and stumbled off the red-tiled step she was standing on, falling backwards into Piotr.

'There's someone in there,' she said, as the door opened a fraction.

'Can I help you?'

It was a woman, mid-sixties, about her mum's age. Just before she'd died. She was dressed in smart black trousers and a white shirt with a silk scarf tied around her neck.

'I have to get to work soon, so if you're selling—'

'It's Sunday morning,' said Eva uselessly.

'No, no.' Piotr stepped towards the front door, holding out his hand and introducing himself. 'We're looking for James Quentin. Ms . . . ?'

'He's not here.' There was hostility in her tone, and she left his hand hanging.

'Do you know when he'll be back?' Eva took over from Piotr.

The woman's eyes narrowed.

'Who are you?' she said to Eva.

'I'm a . . . I'm . . .' She knew instinctively that to say she was a friend of James would be a problem. Something had happened, though she didn't know exactly what.

'We're journalists,' said Piotr, handing over his ID. 'Researching an article on the latest generation of baby pouchers. Dr Quentin was supposed to meet us.'

'He told you to come here?'

'No. We don't know where he is. He didn't turn up to our meeting, so we're looking for him.'

Eva noticed the cases stacked in the hall, along with black bags meant for charity or perhaps the dump – it looked a little like her own hall did, at the moment. But she knew from the woman's straight back and sharp, brittle eyes this wasn't packing done after someone had died. This was done after someone had left.

'Did he leave a message?' Piotr was saying. 'Or did he tell you—'

'He's giving me information on FullLife,' Eva said, ignoring Piotr and talking to the woman standing in the doorway. 'Something is going wrong, and he has the proof. I'm sorry if you didn't know.'

'Oh, he told me,' Julianne said.

Eva took a step forward. 'Is someone . . . are you going away?' she asked, trying to sound caring, though she didn't even know this woman's name. Using Mrs Quentin would seem to be a mistake. She reached out, but the sharp intake of breath told her that her comfort wasn't welcome. Eva stepped back – whatever had happened, this woman's anger was making her cold, and Eva didn't want to touch it. She'd spent a long time dealing with her own anger, she didn't want anyone else's. They should leave.

Piotr, though, was moving closer. She almost pulled him back, but didn't. Piotr, with his broad chest and big eyes and overgrown curly hair, was asking the woman if she was OK, was offering to make her a cup of tea. Did she just say her name was Julianne? And, good heavens, thought Eva, how on earth did that happen? Because suddenly she found she was following Piotr and Julianne into the house.

As she sat holding her mug of tea, trying to look sympathetic but staying out of the conversation, she wondered when Piotr had learned the skill of appearing genuine. She didn't think he'd had it when they were together. Sharp, yes. Cutting sometimes. He'd known how to steer a conversation and had a knack for understanding what people meant rather than what they said. But sympathetic? It was unlikely he was being genuine, so he must have worked out how to appear so. Perhaps it was all an act with her, too, the way he kept waiting for her to decide what they'd do next. Although he'd been the one to step up here, so maybe it was just a new variety of leadership. Waiting in the wings until he could shine. Was he trying to impress her? No, he seemed oblivious to her now.

Julianne was talking about thirty years of marriage. How he'd never seemed like the kind to do something so rash, but then perhaps you really never can tell? She was talking in a matter-of-fact voice. He hadn't been like himself for months, now that she thought about it, but you have ups and downs, don't you, in a marriage? She'd thought if she just gave him more space . . . And she herself needed space. They'd never lived in each other's pockets. But to start going on about having an affair . . .

Eva looked up from her tea, as it suddenly dawned on her that all of this had nothing to do with FullLife, but plenty to do with her.

'Who . . . ?'

Piotr shook his head, just subtly, and Julianne simply sighed.

'What does it matter?' she said. 'I won't be jealous. I won't behave like that. I've packed all his stuff and he's gone.'

'If we find him—'

'Don't tell me,' she said. 'I don't want to know.'

Eva was impressed with her composure. She wished she'd been as confident, as able to draw a line under their relationship, when she left Piotr. Not that he'd given her any choice. She felt a stab of anger, but swallowed it down.

'We do need to find him though,' she said, her tone a little too formal for the mood that Piotr had created. 'He has information, about FullLife . . .'

She trailed off, expecting to be met by the stare of Julianne Quentin. But Julianne was looking at Piotr.

'Perhaps he's left some clues in his study . . .' he said.

So that was his play.

'Or on his computer?'

'Empty,' said Julianne. 'And wiped.'

'You wiped his computer?' asked Eva, unable to help herself.

'Do you have some family you could call?' said Piotr simultaneously.

'The twins will be home this evening . . .'

'Someone who'll understand?'

'There's my brother. He's divorced.'

'Yes, call your brother. That's what I'd suggest . . .' he smiled apologetically. 'But what do I know?'

'Oh, that's a good idea,' she smiled back. 'After work. But I really do have to go . . .'

Perhaps they could rescue some information from the hard drive, thought Eva, if they could get hold of the computer after she'd gone. They might have to break in.

'We'll walk you to the station,' Piotr said. 'If you don't mind the company?'

And ten minutes later, Eva was standing on the platform watching Piotr and Julianne wave goodbye to one another, waiting for him to turn to her and suggest returning to the house, to see what they could salvage. But he didn't say anything.

'What now?' she asked. 'We could break a window?'

He laughed, a big belly laugh with no criticism in it, only warmth.

'Come on,' he said. 'We can go back to my flat.' He looked at her as if offering but not wanting to suggest she would join him. She'd always assumed he wouldn't be living in the *same* flat. Something in his expression told her he was. But it was just a building. She wouldn't let herself be upset by a building. If he could stand living in it after everything they'd been through, then she could stand visiting it.

'OK, but what then?' she said, businesslike and brusque.

'Then I need to feed my cat,' he replied.

Chapter 12

EVA WALKED CONFIDENTLY UP THE stairs to the flat she had once shared with Piotr. She didn't want to show any hesitation, didn't want him to think she could still be hurt by the memories. The building was dimmer than she remembered. In her mind it was always filled with daylight. Not today. Despite the glaring sun – there was not a cloud in the sky, she'd searched – inside it was dark and she had to focus on where to step. Her hand stayed on the banister.

Turning the last corner on the third flight of stairs, she stopped, static, bristling. Staring at her was an old woman that she recognised so hazily it felt as if she'd known her a very long time ago. Why did that unflinching face feel so familiar?

'Piotr!' she called, and cringed as it came out louder than she'd intended. Her voice seemed to echo, shrill, in the stairwell. He was two flights behind her – he'd stopped to pick up some post by the door.

She cleared her throat.

The old woman was standing up now, slowly, as though it cost her some effort to do it. She seemed to be rubbing her behind.

'Are you . . . OK?'

'You try sitting on those stairs for two hours.'

Eva looked over her shoulder.

'Piotr,' she called, softer.

He passed the final corner and stopped beside her, astonished.

'Well, it took you long enough,' the old woman said.

Eva watched her, still hoping for a sign of who she was.

Piotr hadn't replied.

'You know where Freida is,' the old woman said, facing Piotr now and ignoring Eva completely.

'No,' he said, shaking his head, 'I know . . . Nothing really. Hints, rumours, that's all. Is that why you're here?'

Oh my God.

'Well, I know things,' said Holly Bhattacharyya. 'Things that she's said to me, and comments she made when she thought I wasn't listening. There was a postcard, once. Also, I have an idea about why she left.'

Eva raised her eyebrows.

'So if we put it all together,' Holly said. 'We might have something.'

Holly didn't seem like a woman who had just lost her grandchild. Great-grandchild. But then what does that look like? Different for everyone, Eva knew. And personal. And not something you necessarily display on your face.

'Well, are you going to invite me in?' she said. 'I've brought a big map. I like maps.'

She produced a large map of the UK and waved it at them, impatiently.

'Yes,' Piotr replied, his voice like a sigh. 'It is good to see you, Holly.'

Her eyes narrowed.

'Please,' he said. 'Please, come in.'

*

Holly cleared her throat, loudly and unnecessarily. They were seated in a row on a cat-hair-covered sofa in a shabby living room with the blinds drawn. Piotr still hadn't introduced the woman who was with him, so Holly got tired of waiting and did it herself.

'I'm Holly,' she said. 'Who are you?'

'Eva.'

She looked this Eva in the eye, trying to see what she could make of her. Eva looked back. Eva wasn't scared of her, that was for sure. Still, people weren't usually scared of her, apart from Piotr Filipek in that interview. Ha!

'Why are you looking for Freida?' Eva asked.

'You know who she is then?'

'Of course.'

'And how much has he told you?' Holly said, nodding her head towards Piotr, who seemed to be making a pot of tea.

'Actually I found out more than him all on my own,' Eva said.

'Ha!'

Holly allowed herself to laugh out loud – a pleased, but restrained, single note accompanied by an exhale.

'So.' She straightened her back and clasped her hands together. 'You'd better start by telling me everything you know.'

There was something in Eva's accent, in the way she tilted her head, that seemed familiar. Holly had known a lot of people in her life, though. She had advised a lot of women – she offered her support freely, especially in the early days, wanting to pass on the revelation of the pouch experience. But Eva wasn't one of those women. Eva was hostile. And didn't like her, Holly realised with a smile, as Eva said the words:

'It has happened before.'

At first Holly didn't know what she meant. And then, like the sudden blare of a car horn, she did. She wasn't smiling any more.

'But I would have been told about it.'

'No one was told about it.'

'How is that possible?'

'FullLife keep their research as confidential as their mistakes.'

'But surely the parents would have . . . ?'

Piotr was back, carrying an old-fashioned teapot with a tea cosy tucked under his arm. It was yellow, Holly noticed, with a pattern of sheep on it. White sheep, and black sheep, together. God, she missed Will.

Piotr put the teapot on the low table, the tea cosy on top of the teapot, and said gently, raising his eyes to look at hers: 'Perhaps they found it too hard to talk about. Perhaps they were . . . ashamed.' He looked away.

'There have been five deaths, that we know of,' Eva said. 'The first one was three years ago. Most of them from used pouches.'

Piotr sat down opposite them. 'I think they've been encouraging the parents to blame themselves.'

'And not everyone is listened to,' Eva added, the edge to her voice audible.

Holly reached up and took her wide-brimmed hat off. It seemed wrong now, absolutely wrong, to be wearing it. She would leave it here, whatever happened next.

'Then we need to change that,' she said, a shake in her voice that she tried to dismiss. 'We need to find out what's wrong with the pouches.'

She opened up her map, one fold at a time, and spread it out on the table. On top of the teapot too – the Peak District had a large lump in it.

'I could just look it up on—' Piotr had his phone out already.

'No – we need to stay here,' interrupted Eva. 'We have to expose FullLife, tell people the truth.'

'What truth?' Holly said.

'That they're lying. That they're covering something up.'

Holly straightened her back. 'It would be best to know what, don't you think?'

'But how—'

'Freida will tell us,' Holly said firmly.

She looked from Eva to Piotr, who was sitting in the deep, well-worn armchair.

'You think it's been there from the start?' he said. 'A fault with the pouches, even back when Freida was involved?'

'I think it was why she left.'

'But . . .' Eva's voice trailed off.

'She's somewhere remote,' Piotr said, leaning forward now to look at the map on the table.

'And on the coast,' Holly said. 'She once mentioned a peninsula.'

'Scotland,' said Eva. 'I heard some people talking, when I was . . . some friends of my mum. One of them had met her, in Scotland.'

'OK.' Holly stretched out with a slight groan and pulled the map closer. 'See why a map's useful?' She spread her hands over the Highlands. 'Overview.' Then she reached into her bag and took out a faded postcard. It had been handmade – there was no location on the back, no county to help them. But there was the striking picture on the front. A tall, skinny, red-and-white-striped lighthouse. It was surrounded by nothing but thick grey cloud and wild sea, and that single beam of light, pulsing out to the right of the image.

Holly placed it on the map, somewhere between Glasgow and Edinburgh. Piotr ran his hands through his hair.

Eva was frowning. 'I don't understand,' she said.

'What do you mean?'

'I don't understand—'

'Eva?' Piotr leaned forward.

'I've been there before,' Eva said. 'I've been there with my mum.'

*

The jolt of the memory was so unexpected, so vivid, that it made her eyes sting. She was a child again, a girl of six or seven, running out to the black rocks that zigzagged through the sweet scent of heather and the prickly warning of yellow-flowering gorse, and her mum was young, beautiful, chasing her, shell-patterned flip-flops clutched in her hand so she could race barefoot through the bouncy moss of the peninsula.

Eva held on to a bucket and a net with a blue plastic rim. She was going to catch crabs in the rock pools, and the tiny black fish that darted faster than a blink below the surface. And a picnic, they sat on the rocks and ate cherry tomatoes and strips of carrot, watched the waves crashing into the jagged rocks below them – there was layer upon layer of those black and brown and rusty-coloured rocks, she'd never seen a landscape like it. And then, later, after all the fish had been returned to their rock pools and storm clouds were moving in from the east, her mother insisted they climb the tall, padlocked gate that led into the private garden of the lighthouse.

Eva felt like they were doing something wrong. There was a big sign saying keep out. The fence was high, and in places it had barbed wire. But her mum was not waiting for her – she went striding across the grass towards the heavy white door that led into the lighthouse. She raised her hand and knocked loudly with her knuckles, and then with the clenched fist of her hand. Eva was scared. She remembered now, she was scared then. She had been left behind. And so when she finally made it over the gate she started running – like she was running for her life – towards her mum, her mum's back, her long wild red hair that was whipping around in the wind and when she was about halfway across the grass and had nowhere to hide this terrible, loud, wailing noise came from the top of the lighthouse. She leapt with fright, didn't know where to run, and then the light was on too, insistent flashes that seemed so bright they could have blinded her. She started to cry. In fact that was the only time she could remember really crying in the all-encompassing way of a child. She collapsed into a pile on the grass. She howled. Eventually her mum came to comfort her, wrapped her up in her arms and sang to her the way she used to, when Eva had been much younger than she was.

No one had answered the lighthouse door.

'I know where she is,' Eva said.

Holly looked at her in astonishment.

'That's ... Damn, I can't remember the name. But that light-house,' she said. 'It is at the end of a peninsula. In the northern Highlands of Scotland. The something Ness Lighthouse.'

'Tarbat Ness?' Piotr said, showing them the screen of his phone. 'I think it's the Tarbat Ness Lighthouse.'

'Yes,' Eva said, staring at the postcard and frowning, a thought trying to surface.

'How do we get there?' Holly said impatiently.

'We can take a train.' Eva started laughing, but there was nothing carefree about it – there was pain behind it, and she needed to stop pretending it wasn't there.

'Freida will tell us everything,' Holly was saying.

'She might not remember,' Piotr replied.

'She'll know more than us.'

'How do you know?'

'She has to. Someone has to. We're going to fix this.'

'There is something else,' Eva said, quietly. It seemed like she had known James Quentin a long time ago now – it felt like a different version of herself who'd pressed him with questions and been dis-satisfied with the answers. 'I spoke to one of the scientists, just yesterday, and he was sure it only started happening in the last few years. He said he thought it was to do with the generations. The ... I'm sorry, Holly. The stillbirths seem to be connected with the third generation of people using the pouch. He said it wasn't the pouches themselves that were going wrong. He thought some-thing was being inherited. So maybe that could help?'

Eva looked up, surprising herself by hoping that Holly would be pleased with her - she didn't want assurance from this woman, surely. And she clearly wasn't going to get it. Holly's expression had changed completely. She didn't look determined any more, and the amusement that had seemed to dance in her eyes was completely gone.

'What's wrong?'

Holly didn't reply, and the longer they all seemed to sit there in silence the more concerned Eva became. Holly was quite old, really – was she ill? Was she having a heart attack? Suddenly she looked frail, transparent and, within that, angry. There was anger in her eyes; Eva recognised it.

'That can't be true,' Holly said finally. 'We have to talk to Freida.'

Eva didn't reply. After all, none of them actually knew what was going on.

'So you think Freida might know about that too?' asked Piotr. 'Even though she left before . . .'

'If she does, I'll kill her,' Holly said.

If the atmosphere hadn't been so chilling, Eva might have smiled. The idea of one old lady killing another – but there was nothing humorous about the expression on Holly's face. She looked like everything she loved had been destroyed.

'An assassination . . .' Piotr began, but Eva frowned at him and he stopped speaking, his voice trailing off like an apology.

'Don't you dare laugh at me,' Holly said. 'I might be an old woman, but you need to listen to me. She knows something, I know she does.'

'We'll try to find her,' Eva said, but what she'd intended to be soothing came out as patronising and her comment was brushed away with a swipe of Holly's hand.

'I think she knew the pouches were faulty years ago,' Holly said. 'And I think that's why she ran away.'

As Holly reached for her coat, Eva caught Piotr's eye – a question passed between them.

'Come on,' Holly said. 'I'm ready to go now. I don't want you slowing me down.'

Piotr stood, nodded. Checked for something in his jacket pocket.

Eva thought about saying she'd prefer to go home and pack a bag of overnight things, but she was too impatient to see where all this was going to lead.

'I'm ready,' she said, stepping back from the door, allowing Holly to head down the stairs first and taking the chance to whisper to Piotr: 'Why did she get so upset?' Piotr looked as confused as she was.

'We'll talk to her on the train,' he whispered back, his lips close to her ear.

They could hear Holly reaching the first-floor landing, her walking stick making a determined thump on every step.

*

Holly stood on the busy concourse of Euston Station and waited for the crowds of people to politely break around her – which is exactly what they did.

'Look,' she said. 'There's a direct train to Inverness. Leaving in twenty minutes.'

She sighed, impatiently, as Eva and Piotr looked up to study the board.

'I'm not senile,' she snapped. 'It's right there.'

'Oh, yes, I see,' said Eva.

Piotr's journalist's eyes were watching her. She still needed to keep a close eye on him, Holly thought. She hadn't been wrong before – he was a little wolfish. Dishevelled too. It would be easy to think he was bumbling, but she knew better than that. Perhaps it was some kind of disguise.

'Why don't you get us some tickets?' she said.

'But where do we go after Inverness?'

'The Far North Line,' both Holly and Eva replied, looking at each other in surprise as their words synchronised.

As he walked towards the ticket office, Holly turned to Eva and asked the question that had been in the back of her mind all afternoon.

'Do I know you from somewhere?' she asked.

Eva smiled in a way that Holly found secretive.

'I think you knew my mother, a little,' she said. 'You did an interview together, twenty years ago now. She was protesting against the pouch. She stayed in touch with you for a while after that I think – she liked to argue. She used to talk about you.'

Holly raised her eyebrows, went to adjust her hat before remembering that she had left it behind, and why.

'I remember, I think,' she said. 'Avigail, yes? Avigail Goldberg.'

'Goldsmith.'

'And you work there too, at her organisation?'

'I did,' Eva said. 'We've just closed down.'

Holly didn't smile or make any comment at first – she remembered liking Avigail, though she hadn't seen or heard of her for years. As the pouch had grown in popularity, the protesters had sort of disappeared, the way people do in London when other people stop listening to them. But Holly wanted to say something now that would be respectful, and besides, the truth usually fell out of her mouth whether she wanted it to or not.

'You might have to reopen,' she said. 'Once word of all this gets out.'

Eva looked surprised, like it hadn't crossed her mind.

'Isn't that the point of all this?' Holly said. 'You're here to expose FullLife, to make people scared of the—'

'Not scared,' Eva said. 'Just aware.'

Holly nodded. There was nothing wrong with that. People should be aware. She heard a scuffle and glanced over to the corner of the station, then found she couldn't look away. There was a young man over there. Cardboard on the floor. A sign. He had been begging. Holly hadn't seen a homeless person on the streets for years.

'What is it that *you* plan to do?' Eva asked her.

The ruckus she'd heard, it was the shelter team. Three of them. They were helping him up. At least that's what she thought they were doing. His eyes stayed focused on the ground as they collected the cardboard, removed the sign. Escorted him from the station. She wondered if he was ill. He'd be offered emergency care, she was sure, and taken to the shelter home complex.

'Holly? What do you intend to do?'

Holly didn't answer, and Piotr had returned with their tickets. She knew his presence made a difference to Eva, though she hadn't quite figured out why yet. He passed them their tickets one at a time, and as Eva reached out to take hers, Holly could tell she was trying not to touch his hand by mistake.

'Well, we've got five hours together on a train now,' Holly said under her breath. 'That should be enough time to work everything out.' Neither of them was paying attention to her any more though, which was absolutely fine. She was going to find Freida.

Audio log

19 Jan 2016 08:45

Well, today is his day. I have waited patiently for two weeks – there has been no word from him and no sign of you. But today he is *due*. That makes a difference, I think.

The difference between hoping for something with no promise, and hoping that a promise will be kept.

Do you realise that I'm about to tell you why I'm here? I always knew I would have to tell someone, sooner or later. So today is going to be my day, too. My memories are not particularly coherent any more, but they are still strong. Images. Feelings. A sort of dread . . .

I'll start with that.

I remember that their garden path was so neat I found myself wondering if my feet were unusually large. They're not – I'm an average size five. But you know the type of path I mean – so neat and trim that feet seem to crush it. Seem *unwelcome* on it. My presence was spoiling the illusion of their perfect home. Heaven forbid I forget to watch where I'm going and stand on that manicured grass.

You see, I made a point – in fact, I made it a point of pride – to visit every couple who applied for the pouch when we started working with the general public. It was so important to make sure that it wasn't misused. We had a duty to make sure. I had done all this for women, you understand; I wanted to help women. And so we didn't give it out to just anyone, far from it.

I expected their doorbell to play a tune, and so the way it rang like an old-fashioned alarm made me jump – loud, jangling, clashing notes. I pulled my finger away fast but the noise seemed to resonate. I could hear voices but not words, and then the door was answered.

I took them both in with a sweep of my eyes – she stood in front of him, holding the door, smiling nervously, and he stood behind, a possessive hand on her shoulder. Her hair was light brown with a slight auburn sheen. His was blond, very blond, with pale eyelashes and a scattering of pale freckles to match.

That is one of the images I have, of that visit – the visit that changed everything for me. The clasp of her hand on the door frame. The way I knew, at first sight of her, that she was afraid. That he was dangerous. Also, a pot decorated with Chinese dragons in the hall.

Their sofa was pale, plush cream leather – it looked untouched. I sat on it and sank.

He sat in the large chair opposite me, pulled it close.

She sat on the chair in the corner, with her hands neatly folded on her lap. Her face looked darkened now, particularly around one eye, one cheekbone, and I wondered whether it was coming from a shadow or a bruise beneath her perfect make-up.

I had never found it difficult to start the informal interview before but I did then. His face seemed big to me, it blocked out hers – the more I tried to focus on her expression the more I could only see his. I needed to ask them why they wanted to use the pouch. I needed to know *how* they would use the pouch. He answered my questions, and he answered them well. But she said not a word.

Tiny legs of insects were scampering over my forearms, my shoulders, my throat. I addressed my questions to her, and he answered them. Again. Different questions. Same result. The familiarity of it, the recognition of something I had always known – in the quieter places of my mind – I would one day have to confront. By the time I had asked all my questions I had no doubt that she was being coerced. He was forcing her into this, so that he would have control of their unborn child. I watched her while he talked, and I thought I saw her cringe. She was silently begging me to make this stop.

What had I done?

What could I do?

I searched her face, her bare arms – she was still sitting neatly in the corner – for undeniable signs of abuse, for something tangible that I could use.

She remained passive, and he continued to talk.

Eventually I got up to leave. I gave her my card, and I asked her to phone even though I knew she wouldn't. I felt helpless. And yet there was something he wanted from me that I could choose not to give. I controlled the pouch. I decided who was allowed to use it. That is what I told myself.

But I remember walking back down the path, away from their house. I was still afraid to step on that manicured grass.

I made sure they would not be given a pouch, but I soon realised that was not enough. Having provided the world with the means for such manipulation, I held myself responsible for it. I went to see Sylvia, to tell her what I had witnessed, to tell her I believed we had to stop. More people were applying for the pouch every day, and we couldn't possibly monitor them all. Looking back, I don't think FullLife had any intention of doing so.

Sylvia *smiled*. It wasn't my choice to bring her in as director, to let her make the decisions, but someone had to run FullLife and I didn't want to – I was a scientist. I was just a scientist. Even so, I expected her to listen to me.

I was not so naive as I sound, but my worries about FullLife had been pushed to that same, quiet place in my mind. I didn't want to think about worst-case scenarios. But that had to stop. They became the only thing I could think about.

I told her that a man, whom I had just met, was using the baby pouch to increase the power he had over his wife.

I told her that she didn't want to use the pouch at all, that it was his idea – that he was stealing from her and she would be left with nothing.

I told her that I could see she was afraid.

My words seemed to echo in the room. But when I spoke next my voice was quieter.

Think about what I'm saying, I said. Think deeply about the implications of what I'm saying.

I paused. I waited for her to think.

We have to slow down, I told her. We have invented a whole new form of abuse. We have given men the ultimate power over women. The risks are too great and we cannot monitor them and if we can't control it then we'll have to stop.

She was serene. She listened to me. But at the same time I knew she was preparing her reply. Her calmness angered me and I became less eloquent. How could anyone stay calm about this, I thought – how can you not be horrified? How can you not want to be sick? The pouch, my pouch, being used to control women, to abuse women.

Do you think, she said to me, that if we take away the baby pouch this man will stop abusing his wife?

I tried to breathe but I wanted to cry.

Do you imagine, she said to me, that society is going to improve on its own?

I've reported him to the police, I said.

And what about all the others?

My eyes were stinging, and now I didn't want to cry, I wanted to scream.

We are bringing about change, she said to me. This technology, your technology, will bring about change.

It will only be a good change if people don't abuse it.

That is true of everything, she said.

I began to realise that I had given up my own power. I realised, too late, that I did not control the technology I had invented. I knew that Sylvia would not always be director, but I knew that someone would be. They would always be women – I wrote that into the patent contract, at least I did that much – but they would be FullLife women. They would not share my doubts. I could see already that I had lost that battle. How stupid I was. How ignorant.

But perhaps we are all ignorant, us inventors. That is what we do – we make a physical reality by combining our dreams and our ignorance. Our ambition too.

Still, I didn't stop trying to get FullLife to slow down.

I didn't stop vetting every man who applied for the pouch – in fact, I was more determined than ever. I was no longer afraid of trampling on their manicured grass. I created long lists of those who should not be allowed. Some of them got lawyers. Some of them won the right to the pouch. But still I tried to stop them.

I didn't run away, that's what I want you to understand.

I didn't run away.

Not until there was no one left to listen.

Chapter 13

AS THE TRAIN LEFT THE city, light struck the edges of the tables in confident beams. The windows were clean. No faces drawn in smudged remnants of condensation, no patterns of rain left in streaks of dirt. The train carriage was disappointingly like those that never left London, except, Piotr thought, a little older – here and there he could see the signs. The armrest, when he pressed on it, rattled against the chair, and twice now the door between the carriages had opened when no one was standing there. Perhaps this train was a little rougher around the edges. He was glad, after all, that they had a table seat.

He'd originally got them economy tickets – pricey enough, at the last minute – but they couldn't find seats together. Holly had stomped her way through the carriages, her walking stick resounding against the floor, until Eva suggested they just pay the extra and sit in first class.

'I've got this,' she'd said as the ticket inspector came by, half an hour later.

'No, no,' Holly had piped up. 'I'll pay. I have plenty of money, you know.'

Piotr had rolled his eyes then let them work it out between themselves.

Now, opposite him in the comfort of first class, Eva and Holly sat side by side. Holly had the window seat. She was staring out but her eyes were still, looking into the distance. He was a little worried about her. Something had changed with Eva's mention of the third generation – her certainty was gone, replaced by a worried frown.

It struck him that he was the only member of their trio who didn't mind whether the pouch remained popular or not. If they found a way to fix it, then they would fix it. If they found there was no way to fix it then he'd make sure everyone knew, and people would stop using it. But it didn't actually affect him. Did it? He felt his inside jacket pocket. The three photos were still there, wrapped in that old letter and stowed next to his wallet. He looked up at Eva. Her face was softer than Holly's. Where Holly had a fixed stare out of the window, Eva seemed to be watching the people in the train, her eyes moving back and forth, never settling for too long in one place. Her expression was distant, though. She wasn't watching the people, he realised, she was thinking. She was running something over and over in her head, trying out different versions.

She'd always been able to do that. Piotr, well, he knew how to do that – you had to be able to approach different stories in different ways – but the ability to write a really good article lay in choosing an angle and sticking to it. You couldn't play devil's advocate with yourself or the result would be a mixed message. His writing had to be on point. But Eva didn't agree. He'd stopped giving her his work to read early on in their relationship – just quietly, he didn't want to have to explain why. The reason was that her response was usually the same, and he found it unhelpful. You're only giving one side of the story, she'd say. Where's the other point of view?

But the thing was, after everything had collapsed the way it did, he found himself unable to keep writing any single point of view. His editor said he was always second-guessing himself, and started sending him off on puff pieces where there was no point to make at all.

A trolley wheeled up – they were offered tea, coffee, snacks. He asked for a coffee. Holly shook her head. Eva looked up at him, then her eyes flicked over to the train attendant and she asked if she could have a cup of tea, please, with milk. And somewhere in between looking at him and looking at the train attendant she smiled in a beautifully warm way. Piotr was smiling too, now, as he accepted the coffee she bought him and nearly spilled it because the cup was so hot. He tipped in two sugars, stirred with the small plastic spoon, and resisted the urge to tell Eva that he still loved her. He did though, of course. He had never stopped.

When they'd come home from the hospital that last time, along with the deep emptiness, Piotr had felt so helpless he'd looked down at his feet, at the half-shell of a pistachio nut he'd dropped onto the carpet the week before, rather than look into Eva's eyes as she cried. She'd gone through labour knowing that her baby was already dead. He couldn't imagine that pain. He had no idea how to make it better.

Sitting on the sofa, side by side, not touching, staring out of the window at the buildings opposite for hours. The way the noise of the street seemed to scratch his skin, and hers, too – the sense of life elsewhere so invasive it could hurt. The way she slumped forwards, clutching her stomach, he could see she was in pain, severe physical pain, though she made no mention of it. She made no noise at all.

He had tried to move, first. He'd offered her things. Do you want some tea? Shall I put on some music? She'd scowled at him with a cross between disbelief and hatred. He'd left the room, sat at his computer and started asking it questions, though he'd already tried that with the doctors. They didn't know, they said. Perhaps there was a problem with the placenta. But they hadn't detected anything. So they couldn't be sure. They didn't know. It happens sometimes. They were sorry.

As he read page after page on the causes of stillbirth, he listened for any sound of Eva moving around. There was none. He researched for the first time in depth what the placenta actually did, how the umbilical cord worked, the risks of haemorrhage and pre-eclampsia, the many types of chromosome alterations. The statistics terrified him. Why had he not read this before? Studies suggest that 60% of stillbirths are unexplained, that 1 in 200 babies are stillborn when using natural birth – so many? So many? How could he have let this happen? He wasn't aware of crying, except that his vision was blurred as he sped through more websites. Those offering help or support were quickly ignored, it was the science he wanted. The numbers. The answers.

Darkness crept in around him, but he didn't turn on the lights. The computer screen lit the words he read, and that was enough. He was there long into the night and for the hours that he read he was able to keep his own pain away from the conscious part of his mind. He thought it was making him feel better.

But sometime after midnight, he became hungry. It was the sound that got him. He heard his stomach make a loud grumble, and from a distance he realised what the sound was. He didn't want to eat but his body was hungry. It made him feel unworthy, as he crept to the kitchen. It made him feel ashamed. He ate three slices of toast and the remaining Cheddar cheese in the fridge. Gulped down a pint of fruit juice. Walked quietly – he thought – towards the living room where he assumed Eva would be sleeping. But she wasn't sleeping. She was still sitting there, staring out of the window that was now a black, empty square, with nothing but the lopsided reflection of the side lamp interrupting its darkness.

He sat beside her. Took her hand.

'How, erm . . .' He cleared his throat. Closed his eyes for a moment, breathed out, then in. Tried again. 'How are you feeling?'

She was sitting up straight. He could feel her staring at him, not looking away from him the way he had been looking away from her. She was sallow, exhausted. He wondered if he should get her something to eat. She hadn't eaten. She hadn't moved. He tried to pull her into a hug but she gasped like it hurt. There were damp patches on her T-shirt.

'I want to try again,' she said.

'Try what again?'

She pulled her hand away from his and recoiled from him, just slightly.

'You mean . . . ?'

'We can't give up,' she said. 'I won't give up. We have to try again.'

He didn't respond, he didn't know how. There was too much they didn't know, how could she possibly . . . It was way too soon, too early to even think about it. What if it happened again? What if it was something . . . the risks were too great, surely she could see that. No, wait. She must mean . . . But then she hated it so much, would she really put that aside? But actually, she didn't hate the pouch. She just thought it was wrong. That was different. Perhaps he should ask her what she meant. Just to clarify. They had to be able to talk to each other – he'd always felt they could.

'You mean with the pouch?'

'No!'

She was on her feet, moving to the window. Piotr felt a wave of exhaustion hit him, like he couldn't face it, couldn't face talking about it, couldn't face getting anything else wrong. But then she was crying again and she came and sat next to him and put her hand, this time, on his leg as if she wanted to comfort him, or perhaps as if comforting him could comfort her as well.

'Remember that bird?' she said.

He did, though he wanted to pretend that he didn't.

'What bird?'

'That little bird, the long-tailed tit. One of the ones with the tiny round bodies, you know the ones I mean?'

He nodded, reluctantly.

'There was one,' she continued, 'the one I mean, that flew into the window and then lay there on the ground. For ages it lay there, unable to move. I thought it was going to die.'

'I'm not sure what this has to do with . . .'

'You told me it would be OK,' she said, looking up at him as if she was seeing him in a new way. 'You said it was stunned, but it would recover. I didn't believe you.'

'I didn't know what I was talking about.'

'But you were right,' she said. 'It was OK in the end, wasn't it? It got up again and flew off.'

'I can't . . . I can't allow another baby to die.'

She shook her head violently. 'Shut up and listen,' she said. 'There's no reason to think that would happen. Next time it will be OK. It has to be.'

'It will be if we use the pouch.'

He could see she was getting more upset.

'It's safer . . .' he persisted. 'I can show you the statistics. Natural birth is unsafe, we can't make that mistake again. I won't let it hap—'

He thought for a moment she was going to slap him, but she didn't.

'That bird died,' he said.

The pause was awful. Horrible. He wanted it unsaid. He knew he would want it unsaid even as he said it. He didn't know why he couldn't stop himself. But he didn't say it to be cruel, it was just that false hope seemed such a fake thing right now, such a useless thing. And now he'd started, he had to explain himself.

'The bird didn't fly off, during the night. I'm sorry . . .' He swallowed, staring at his hands again. Why had eye contact become so hard? 'When I got up in the morning I found it lying there. It was dead. I picked it up, held it in my palm – I wanted to be sure, you know? I'd hoped it would be OK . . .'

'But it was gone,' she said. 'It had flown away.'

'I took it to the back of the garden and buried it. So you wouldn't have to know . . . I wanted to protect you.'

'By lying to me?'

Her voice was still quiet, but there was an edge to it.

'It wasn't really a lie. I was—'

'You were lying!'

He'd wanted to protect her. That was all. He'd thought he was being kind.

'It's ridiculous,' she said, loud and angry now. 'You're ridiculous,' she shouted. 'And now we have the proof. You can't protect me, can you.'

She said it coldly - like she intended to hurt him. And he responded in kind.

'We should have used the pouch,' he said. 'A late-stage transfer, at the very least, and everything would have been OK. And we have to use it now. We cannot go through this with another child.'

Her eyes, staring at him, just staring.

'If you want to try again, we have to use the pouch. That's that.'

He recognised what it was, her expression, as he stopped talking long enough to notice the sound of his own breath, and hers, held tight into her chest. She was looking at him with disgust. They had fallen apart then, and neither of them had been able to find a way back together.

And now she was sitting across the table from him in the half-empty train carriage. But there was something - a thought, a fear - forming in his mind. Because in all his frantic research after their baby's death, through all his pain and anger, there was one thing he'd never thought to blame: the pouch itself. They'd been having a natural birth, so he tried to blame the natural birth, but . . .

The realisation came slowly. He had been born via a pouch. Eva had been born via a pouch. The parents affected by the stillbirths had all been pouch babies. Could it be . . . was it possible that it wasn't a problem with the pouches, at least not the ones they'd all been thinking about. Could it be that the problem was a change in biology, taking a generation or two to appear . . . that it was there already, in everyone born via the pouch, in Rosie, in Kaz, in . . . ?

'Are you all right?' she said, standing up, stepping around the table and sitting down next to him.

'No,' he replied. And that was all he could manage, right then – though he would tell her everything he'd been thinking, when he felt able to speak without breaking down – and it was enough for now, because it was the truth.

*

Daphne knocked on her mum's door. It had taken her a while to do it. She'd thought that perhaps her mum needed space, so she'd left her alone.

In a way she'd been glad to spend time with Rosie, without Holly constantly trying to show her how to mother better. It was unusual for her mum not to come down for breakfast – Sunday breakfast too, always a family gathering – but it was not unheard of. She'd been alone for hours now, though, and the past two days had been so hard and perhaps her mum's feelings had been lost among it all. Perhaps her mum was hurting too, and no one had noticed. Had she forgotten to show kindness to her mother?

She knocked on the door, a little louder this time.

'Mum?' she called. 'I'm making tea. Do you want a cup?'

There was no answer. So Daphne did what she'd done the day before for Rosie – she opened a closed door and stepped inside.

Except her mum was not there.

The room wasn't that big. And clearly it was empty.

Daphne looked at the bed, which was neatly made. The window, which was closed. She looked at the wardrobe with the long full-length mirror and opened the door to check. Her mum was – unsurprisingly – not hiding inside.

'Mum?' she called again as she took the stairs two at a time. She wasn't worried though – she knew her mum could take care of herself. She'd be out in the garden, or on her way to the shops. She would be absolutely fine. She wasn't that old, not yet.

Sitting at the kitchen table, the kettle on, Daphne checked her emails on her phone. She'd already told the embassy she needed a few days off. Hadn't told them why. She typed a few searches, to see if any of the websites had said anything yet. The press that had been waiting for them by the birthing centre would surely start asking questions soon.

The family asks for privacy, one said. *But why now?*

And there was something else, a column about how the top floors of the birthing centre were out of bounds, the director of FullLife refusing interview.

She sat up, but then checked the date – it was from six months ago. OK. But why was it being shared today? She followed the links. And there it was, the brand-new headline she had been hoping not to see:

POUCH DEATH

Her eyes scanned for Rosie's name, for any mention of her family, but there was none, this was about . . .

She sat back. It was a different family. She'd never heard of them, knew nothing about the case, but it was ongoing. They had lawyers. That was what the report said. They had just announced they were going to court. Not in London, they were from Newcastle. Maybe FullLife had been keeping it away from the press, while they tried to reach a settlement? It must have been an accident, she thought. Perhaps one of the doctors had made a terrible mistake . . . It made her nervous, seeing people suing health facilities like that. She'd sometimes wondered if it was the lawsuits that had finished off the National Health Service. Where was Holly?

She checked outside in the garden but there was no sign of her, searched from room to room in the house. Then slowing down, taking a deep breath. There was only one place left to check.

Daphne knocked gently on Rosie's door. Maybe Rosie had seen her nana; maybe Holly was in there.

'Come in,' Rosie called, her voice still quiet but steadier than it had been before.

Yes, Holly must be in there with her, she must have been able to help Rosie in a way that Daphne hadn't. Though she'd tried to offer support in the best way she knew how – she had listened to her daughter. She had held her as she cried.

But when Daphne pushed open the door she saw that Rosie was not with her nana, and she was not OK. Not in any way. Clothes were strewn all over the floor, posters ripped from the walls. Rosie was still wearing her pyjamas and holding torn pages of her book of designs; she loved that book of designs. They were her plans, her ideas, her creativity. She spent hours working on it. As Daphne watched, Rosie tore up another page. Let the ripped pieces of her future scatter onto the floor.

'I just . . . I'm just checking in, love,' Daphne said. 'How are you?'

'Everything is over.'

Rosie spoke sharply, her voice different, her expression closed. Daphne felt useless. This was worse than yesterday.

'Where's Kaz?'

Rosie shrugged.

Daphne tried to remember when she'd last seen him, but her mind went blank. He wasn't at breakfast either, and she hadn't seen him yesterday at all. Had he been out in the garden? Had he left the house?

'Maybe he went to his parents?'

Rosie ripped another page. She looked destroyed, desperate. Painfully young. Daphne had always told her it was her choice – that being a young parent was a valid option. And it was, she still believed that. Besides, was there any age at which this would be easier?

'If you like, we can go over there and check?' she tried.

'No,' Rosie said.

Daphne felt a worry tugging at her chest, something worse than she had felt yesterday. Something worse than she'd felt a few minutes ago.

'Where do you think he is?'

Rosie threw her book at the wall.

'Who the hell knows! I told him to leave me alone, and so he's gone.'

*

Eva often reminded herself of all the reasons why she no longer loved Piotr, but it had been a long time since she'd thought about the reasons that she loved him in the first place. Sitting next to him on the train, their legs beneath the table, their hands clasped around hot drinks, she wasn't trying to avoid her memories any more. She just accepted the silence between them and let the train journey transport her.

When she closed her eyes she felt like she could will herself back to the pivotal moments of her life. That moment when she decided – no, it wasn't a decision, there was nothing else she could have done – that she would leave the flat she shared with Piotr and move back in with her mum. The moment five years before when she had stormed into his office, her anger, her attraction; the feel of his hair under her chin as they lay in bed and she felt an overwhelming urge to protect him, to forgive him. Don't think of Piotr, she willed herself, and instead she heard her mum telling her she had cancer. Sitting beside her as she shivered and sweated and vomited. Seeing her pull on a wig of wild, orange hair and turning to her. Eva, do you think this needs some extra blue streaks?

Eva looked up as Holly leaned over the table to get her attention. She noticed, for the first time, that the old lady appeared to be dressed as a spy – a long trench coat was wrapped around her body, tied with a brutal double knot. She was reaching a hand towards her but Eva pulled away. It was too much intimacy.

'Tell me,' Holly said. 'Why don't you like the baby pouch?'

There was no venom in her voice. If anything her eyes looked sad. It was the first time in a long time that anyone had asked her such a straightforward question, and it was phrased in such simple language Eva wanted to give an equally simple response. Not simplistic – but honest. Why didn't she like the baby pouch?

At fourteen years old, sitting in a school classroom with the spring rain making a rhythmic backdrop to the emphatic words of her biology teacher: We have found a better way. They were taught about natural birth, they were even shown a video – screams of pain, the red-faced woman, hair plastered to her forehead with sweat, and that man telling her to push, push, *push*, as if she could move the horror show along by just trying harder. And then they were shown a pouch. Encouraged to try it on. So clean, so soft that it was hard not to want to cuddle with it. And the video for that, the parents smiling serenely at the camera, the neat birthing process as the pouch was delicately cut open, the fluids drained away, and a baby introduced to the world with calm orchestral music. In the Q&A afterwards they were told they could choose their own music, they could even write their own. It was impossible not to think that the whole process was far better – far healthier – for the baby as well. Because the struggle was gone.

'It's fake,' she said to Holly. 'I think it's . . . fake.'

'No, it's real. Just like the people who are born are real.'

'Something is not necessarily better just because it's easier.'

'Nor is it necessarily worse. What's the virtue of putting women through pain?'

Eva shook her head.

'Well? The pouch has eradicated the pain of childbirth.'

'Instead of fearing the pain of childbirth,' Eva said, 'perhaps we should be celebrating the strength of women.'

Arriving home from school, sweat pricking through her grey jumper and her woollen tights falling down, Eva dropped her bag inside the porch and pushed through the door to the living room. She saw her mum, deep red hair pulled up into a high ponytail and falling down around her shoulders, laughing with a group of friends who sat on the bright mismatched cushions strewn around the floor. But Eva didn't sit down. She walked into the middle of the room – always her mum's domain, Eva hated being in front of a crowd – and made her announcement.

'My teacher says you're wrong.'

Her mum had smiled as though she were delighted, and the soft laughter that rippled around the room made Eva want to hide, to disappear with the embarrassment, but she stood her ground. She expected a telling-off, but it didn't come. Instead, her mum put her arm around her and said Eva was ready to join the group. So Eva sat on one of the cushions and for the first time felt like she was a grown-up, with her questions and her ability to disagree. Not everyone should be the same, they said. Equality comes from respecting differences, not eliminating them. As Eva questioned, they listened, and they responded, and she began to love the process of arguing so much she didn't notice that her opinions were changing as they talked.

'Next time you have that teacher, are you going to ask about propaganda?' her mum said, and Eva blushed as she realised the look in her mum's eyes was pride.

'Can I dye my hair purple?' she said. 'We're not supposed to.'

'You can dye your hair any colour that you want.'

Although, today, Eva's hair was dyed red, a beautiful deep red, just like her mum's had been, and Holly's hair was silver grey and Eva was glad, for a second, that neither of them were being anything but themselves.

'We have bypassed nature,' she said.

'No,' said Holly. 'We cannot bypass nature. We are a part of nature.'

'The things we invent are not natural.'

'Yes they are. Everything we build, everything we create.'

They'd laughed at her at school. With her purple hair that had gone wrong – patches of bright purple between patches of brown, and a ruddy tint to her scalp, her hairline. They'd laughed when she told them what her mother believed, and her teacher had given her a detention and she'd known, even though she was too embarrassed to explain, she'd known that one day she would find a way to fight for natural birth. Because Eva felt, in that moment, that she had to protect something that was being lost. That was how it started – a feeling. The logic, the implications for fertility, the long-term effects, even the care homes, those arguments came later. At the beginning, she just wanted to protect.

She looked at Holly. Was it old age that made people so convinced the opinions they held were right? Was it the repetition of telling yourself what you believed, year after year, that brought conviction? When you think about something, it creates a pattern in your brain. When you rethink it, the pattern gets stronger; hazy memories start to feel like recent experiences. Opinions can start to seem like fact.

'There is too much you don't know,' she said to Holly. 'The technology arrived before society was ready for it. All the ways it can be misused—'

'No, the technology changed the society. Without it, society would never have been ready for change.'

'But things were changing.'

'Too slowly.'

'Slowly is the best way.'

Holly shook her head. 'People were in pain,' she said. 'Don't you realise how many people were in pain?'

'It's dangerous, what you've done. You and Freida. And FullLife.'

'We're not going to win with philosophy,' her mum had said. She was pacing the length of the room, bay windows to back doors, her socked feet stamping on the wooden floor creating a rhythmic thud thud thud in time with her words. We're *not* going to *win* with philosophy. She turned and looked at Eva, held her arms out. 'We're going to win with science,' she said. 'They've moved too fast, I know it – something is going to go wrong. I dreamed about it last night.'

Eva smiled – obviously her mum didn't really dream up the direction of their group, her mum was brilliant. Her mum knew more than anyone about FullLife. And she was right. Arguments didn't help, debating didn't help. They needed facts. They needed to find where FullLife had cut corners, faked research, skipped the required number of trials. Made promises they couldn't keep. Together they had searched, for years, for that something. Then her mum had fallen ill. Piotr had appeared. She had fallen in love. Her baby had died. The answer had arrived too late for them to find it together.

'Don't you know how many things can go wrong?' she was saying now, turning to the science just like her mum had taught her – and somewhere she had lost her temper with this stubborn, arrogant old woman – 'Can't you see how much you don't know? How *dangerous* it is?'

Had the whole carriage gone quiet?

'Have you any idea how many generations it might take to even reveal the dangers? The long-term effects?'

She was aware of a movement beside her, but she ignored it – she wouldn't listen to more of Piotr's statistics now. God, the man was a buffoon. There was something important in what she was saying. She was working something out . . .

'Will we lose the ability to reproduce altogether? Become completely dependent on technology outside of ourselves? Will we cease to be . . . Oh my God. It's genetic. That's why it's showing in the third generation, that's why James was so terrified. We're inheriting a new type of infertility, a predisposition to miscarry, developing it in the pouch and passing it on to our children – an inability to be born, like the babies' bodies are rejecting the process, preventing it – it's there already, in everyone born via the pouch, so we can't . . . the damage is done. We might never be able to fix it.'

She turned towards Piotr. He'd thought about it too, she realised, he had been thinking about it here, on this train, and so he must have the same question.

'Our baby . . . ?' she said, needing him to look at her now.

But Piotr was leaning over the table. Piotr was taking Holly's hand in his – no, Holly's hand was lying flat on the table, palm down, he was placing his hand over hers, he was offering comfort. Eva looked at him in disbelief, in anger – he was taking sides. He was taking *sides*? No, he wasn't taking sides. He was reaching for her hand too. He was holding both of their hands over the table. Hers and Holly's. And she felt, at last, all the ways that they were the same. Holly's eyes looked blurry. She looked old, not arrogant, she looked sad and lost, staring at her the way Eva had once stared out of a window with no words to describe how lost she felt. It is terrible, the way what you believe in can let you down with such devastation.

She felt suddenly ashamed. But as she looked at Piotr, as she noticed that her arm was leaning against his and that there was a familiarity about his skin, about his smell, she realised that somewhere between losing her and not quite losing himself, Piotr, whom she had once loved, whose hand was gently resting over hers, had become kind.

*

As Cris sat down beside him, Karl felt the warmth of his leg next to his own. He'd not spoken in days. It was a hard habit to break, though. He wasn't sure if it was because he didn't know what to say, or because he'd forgotten how to speak in the first place.

No, that was indulgent. He just found it hard, when he was trying not to break down, trying to hold it together. But for whom?

'Stop, now,' Cris said. And he held Karl's face and turned it towards him. 'You don't have to do this alone,' he said, although it hadn't occurred to Karl that he was doing anything alone. He'd thought he was being useless.

'I've done nothing,' he said. And it was a way to start, which helped.

'Then let's do nothing together, for a while,' Cris said. 'But do you mind if I talk? I find it helpful, to talk.'

Karl nodded. 'I'm sorry.'

'I know.'

'I'm really sorry,' and he leaned in closer, and held him.

'I went to see Kaz yesterday,' Cris said.

Karl looked up in surprise.

'While you were sleeping.'

'I'm sor—'

'You needed to sleep,' Cris said. 'And I needed to see Kaz. So stop apologising.'

Karl swallowed. 'OK.'

They were holding hands.

'How is he?'

Cris shook his head a little. 'He's chopped down a silver birch and cut it into little pieces with an axe.'

'Kaz?'

'I know,' he said. 'It doesn't seem like him, does it? Didn't think he even knew how to use an axe.'

'I don't know how to use an axe,' Karl said.

'It's easy actually,' Cris smiled. 'You just hold it high and let it fall.'

Karl pictured the movement, the transfer of energy, the arc of it. Perhaps it did make sense. He would like to use it in his choreography. The thought made him change slightly, as though his mind had shifted. Ideas had the power to do that.

'But . . .' Cris said, and Karl's mind switched back again. He felt his stomach sinking. 'I'm worried. He seems to think . . . He kept saying it was his fault.'

'It wasn't his fault – why would he think that?'

'Apparently some of the staff were asking questions when he took . . . when they brought the . . . at the autopsy.'

'The staff at the birthing centre?'

'At FullLife, yes. They might not have meant—'

'That's outrageous.' Karl wanted to stand up, to pace, or run, or do something. He wanted some action, after days of inaction. He had to do something. 'How could they blame him?'

'It used to be fairly common to blame women, I think.'

'I don't understand.'

'I mean in our parents' generation.'

Karl looked at him, not getting it. Truth was, he'd never really thought about it. There had never been a need.

'There were all these rules, you know – pregnant women had to eat certain things, sleep a certain way, avoid pain relief, and if something went wrong . . .'

'People used to blame the women?'

Cris nodded.

'And FullLife are blaming our son?' He was standing up now, and he had a new idea. 'I'll tell you whose fault it is. FullLife, that's who. I'm going to give them a piece of my mind.'

Cris smiled, warmly. 'I'm not sure that's a good idea, Karl.'

'I'm not letting them get away with this.'

'We don't know the full story—'

'We know enough.'

Karl had picked up his wallet, was searching the side table for his car keys and glasses, neither of which he could find. He wasn't entirely sure how to give a thirty-storey building full of people a piece of his mind – he'd never really given anyone a piece of his mind in his life – but it seemed, in that moment, to be the best, the only thing he could do. Cris was saying something about going to visit Kaz, but he wasn't ready for that yet – he had to prove that he was able to do something. That he had stood up for his son. He found his glasses, which were on his head, and his car keys, which were in Cris's hand.

'Well, I'd better come with you,' Cris said. 'And to be honest, I think I'd better be the one to drive.'

The ground outside was frozen but the car started easily. Karl could feel his pulse beating in his neck. As they drove towards central London, he squinted through sunlight that made the world both hazy and impossible to look at straight on. It didn't seem real. He was clutching his wallet, which had in it a photo of his family, of him and Cris and Kaz, and he kept picturing his father driving to help him, but the sun was in his eyes and he wasn't able to see him as the cars passed each other on the reflective road.

'It's icy,' Cris said at one point, and Karl supposed maybe that was why the road was shining. He wished the weather would turn already, with sleet and clouds and darkness. And then, suddenly, there they were, standing outside the FullLife birthing centre, people gathered over by the trees, the sun, the glass, and Cris was asking him what he wanted to do. Karl was reaching for Cris's hand and clasping it tight and finding the car keys there, transferring them to his own hand and pulling away. Cris was saying his name, like he didn't know what he was up to, and so Karl moved fast, darted back to the car, turned the ignition, blared the horn, and

drove their family hatchback up onto the pavement, over the concourse with the little blue lights set into the concrete, between the
neat flower beds, and straight into the pristine, shining, tall, splintering, shattering glass of the building that seemed to be reaching
beyond the sky.

As the car came to a stop halfway inside the reception area, Karl
came to his senses. He looked behind, anxious, and was relieved to
see that no one was hurt. The damage was minimal. Shards from the
front pane of glass twinkled on the floor like droplets. They weren't
sharp, he noticed, stepping out of the car. It was safety glass. As he
turned, a young woman who'd been passing raised her phone and
took a photo of the car, half lodged into the birthing centre, and the
broken glass twinkling in the sun. Then she posted it online.

Karl, meanwhile, was gently ushered to the seats by the receptionist, a young man who assured him that he just needed to sit still
for a second and help would be on its way. Cris joined them, and
they sat in a row on the comfy chairs, watching as the lift doors slid
open and a sympathetic-looking white woman walked towards
them. Security had appeared by the front of the building.

'Come in,' she said, holding out an arm to invite them towards
the lift. 'Please, come upstairs, both of you.' Her eyes seemed to glisten. 'I want to explain.'

Karl stood up and took a few steps. He felt a hand pressed, gently
but firmly, on the curve of his back, guiding him towards the lift
and whatever was going to happen next.

Chapter 14

JAMES QUENTIN WAS HOLDING THE yellow post that ran the length of the glass panel beside his seat. He was on the Circle Line. He always liked to be on the seat nearest the exit. He wondered what that said about him. He'd been holding the post, which was smooth plastic and clean, for quite a while now – it had become warm under his palm, absorbing the heat of his skin in a comforting way. He didn't want to let go. Having left both his job and his home there was no building he could think of spending time in, and no person alive he could think of spending time with. So he had opted for transport.

The Circle Line travelled through the stop he would have taken for the birthing centre, and passed the stop he would have used on his journey home. As each stop went by he found himself less and less able to leave the train. And that was OK by him. He didn't want to leave the Tube. He would sit here for a while longer.

He was thinking about the last time that he saw Avigail. There was snow, in London. One of the few times in his life he had seen heavy snow in London. It glistened on the rooftops and fell in mini snowstorms from tree branches. The twins had started at primary school and he'd dropped them off before walking to work, the crunch under his feet begging him to stay outside. The snow in the middle of the pavement was trampled to brownish sludge already but at the edges – if he kept close to the wall, under the shelter of the buildings' overhang – he could crunch through untrodden snow one foot-width at a time. He wanted to jump in it. If it had been deeper he would have. Being outside, the freshness of it all, was making him want to laugh – it was only the knowledge that people would turn and stare that stopped him. You didn't laugh for no reason on the street. But then, with a bright flash of colour against the white, there she was. It hit him so fast, so thoroughly, that he had not the slightest chance of walking away.

She hadn't seen him. She was in her long red coat with her multicoloured scarf billowing out behind her, and he knew from her body language that she was about to turn the corner, and then she would be gone. He ran towards her. Her name repeating in his mind. All he knew was this feeling – it could not be ignored. His foot landed in a puddle, splashing his trousers, soaking through his shoe, but none of it mattered. He reached out and touched her arm.

'Avigail,' he managed, though it came out as a whisper through his racing breaths.

She turned quickly, pulling away from the unexpected touch. The first glimpse he had of her expression showed annoyance. He let go of her coat. Started to stammer an apology. But then her expression changed, the anger vanished, and he saw her eyes lighten as she recognised him. Her hair was stripes of pink and purple blowing in the breeze.

'Oh, hello, James,' she said. 'It's been a while.'

She held out her hand, and he took it. Her soft leather-gloved hand in his bare palm, held beneath his fingers.

'Oh,' he said. It was all he could manage. He swallowed. Felt a warmth in his chest, spreading through his body. He was shaking now. His knees.

She pulled her hand away, gently, and looked at him. Her eyes, that deep brown sparkling with gold. In that moment, if she'd asked him to leave his wife and children and follow her across the world, he would have said yes.

But at the same time he hardly knew her at all. Not in the way that he knew Julianne. Avigail was brighter than everything else because she was out of reach. It wasn't logical. In fact it was absurd. The colours of her eclipsed the rest of the city. They eclipsed the sky. He didn't know how it was possible to feel such a deep longing for something he had never had.

She took a step back. Her eyes were different again, kinder, and he realised he had been staring, standing and staring and reaching out his hand towards hers even though she'd pulled away. A gust of wind blew her hair into her eyes and she pushed it out of her face and held it back against her head. The need he felt for her. For just a touch. Once she had ruffled his hair, as you might a child - he'd take that. Or, another time, she'd grabbed his arm when he was about to step out into traffic. He imagined her touching his face, where his chin curved to his neck. If this was to be the last time, could he kiss her cheek, the way friends did, these days, in London?

She was shaking her head a little, her eyes squinting in the brightness of the sun.

'Take care, James,' she said, turning, leaving him standing in a slush of what was once beautiful snow. He felt the colours drain out of the world, her bright red coat dimming as she walked away. So he closed his eyes, scrunched them tight and told himself the feeling filling his body was relief. Nothing would have to change. He could live his life the way he'd planned. He opened his eyes and walked, briskly, avoiding the puddles, to work.

As he thought about that, sitting on the Tube somewhere between Temple and Blackfriars, he was amazed at how he had been able to walk with such purpose. How he'd been able to convince himself so quickly that keeping going was the answer. It helped having something he believed in. He'd lost that, now. He didn't even have the energy to stand up.

He had wanted to explain things – to explain himself, properly – to Julianne. But he had failed. She didn't understand. Not about Avigail, and not about the pouch. She thought they were going to fix it. That it was something they could fix. But he knew better than that. In a way, he was glad he wouldn't be around to see the look on their faces when they finally understood. His family. He wouldn't have to see the blame in his children's eyes when they realised what all this meant. That was it, he knew now, that was the reason he'd been lying to everyone. He couldn't stand the blame.

Even yesterday morning he'd still thought there was an answer to find, a problem to fix. He'd believed – or, at least, had been able to convince himself enough to keep going – that he could find a solution. But he saw it clearly now; what they had been witnessing for the past few years was just the beginning. More babies were going to die. Of course they were. It would start in a few isolated cases in the third generation but soon enough the numbers would grow. Exponentially, he predicted. And what was the cause? He didn't know. But it was genetic. It had to be. The genetic material so carefully incubated in the pouches was becoming corrupt. Small unnoticeable problems were being passed down, and amplified with each subsequent generation of pouch use. Were the chromosomes developing incorrectly in the foetus? Something like Down's, but a different aberration, one that had never been seen before. Perhaps it was good that the babies died, he thought, then realised that he sickened himself.

He closed his eyes, as he had done once before, on a street in London, in the snow, scrunched them tight and tried to transport himself back through time. He could feel it rewinding around him. He was a young man again, with an idea to design a new audio system that would let people play music to their babies in the pouch.

He was presenting to the board, sweating with nerves, stammering his way through until he got to the videos, when he was able to step back and see the smiles as they turned to applause. He credited Julianne at the end. With a modest smile of his own, a nervous laugh. It was all my wife's idea, he said. She wanted to play the twins some salsa. And of course a photo of her, with the pouch. The twins, everyone knew, were a sign they had used IVF from the start. The photo was a nice touch of intimacy.

And there had been a wonderful closeness, while they were pregnant with the twins. So different from anything he had felt with Avigail. A sense of combined purpose, knowing that they were both together on this – that they were partners. That was the most contentment he'd felt in his life.

The most desire though, that was before he was married. That was sitting in Avigail's back garden, not far out of London but at the same time far beyond everything else, on a September evening that was warmed with soft light and skies of a deeper blue than he could remember seeing since. He'd taken her several research reports about the pouch, the monitoring of different nutrient mixes that would be put on the market – actually he'd cleared it with his supervisor before leaving, but he didn't tell Avigail that. She'd smiled when he handed them over, left them sitting on the kitchen table and led him outdoors. He started to speak but she put her finger to her lips.

'Eva's sleeping upstairs,' she whispered, and gestured to the outdoor chairs clustered around two low tables near the cherry tree, each with unlit candles on. 'We won't wake her, if we talk here,' she said. Although whatever words he'd been about to speak, he had forgotten the second he felt her whispered breath on his ear. She reached forward with some matches. She was in an unusual mood. Avigail was rarely this subdued – she liked to argue, to question him. She didn't usually want to sit outside watching the flickering light of candles.

'My daughter was adopted,' she said. 'Have I told you that before?'

'No,' he said, surprised. She'd rarely told him anything personal, and something like that you would remember.

'It's not a secret,' she said. 'Eva knows, and that's all that matters really.'

'I'd thought . . . because . . .' Well, because she was an activist for natural birth he had always assumed she had given birth to Eva. He'd wondered about the father – been jealous of the father. It was good to let go of that jealousy. Perhaps there was no man in Avigail's life. But he knew that didn't mean she wanted him.

'I was writing an article about how the pouch was changing our society, looking at the change in abortion rates. You'll know about that, of course. FullLife love to use that one, don't they?'

He waited for what was coming next.

'Who needs to have an abortion when they could just transplant to the pouch? But there's another side to that, isn't there?'

And he knew that there was. Of course, they all knew about the care homes, about how adoption rates were decreasing as well. The homes were overcrowded already. No one knew what was going to happen to all those children.

'They have no parents,' she said. 'No family. My God, the younger ones don't even have names.'

He looked down at his hands, thought how to phrase his belief that society was still in the process of change – and that society would work it out. He was a scientist, not a politician. But when he looked up, Avigail was crying.

The sky was darker now, a velvet texture to the evening, and her skin looked luminous. Her expression was sadder and more unveiled than he'd ever seen it. He knew, for the first time, he was looking at the real Avigail. He didn't think about what he wanted, he just reached out with his fingertips and didn't touch her cheekbone where it was glistening. She closed her eyes. His hand moved around to the side of her face and gently rested on her cheek, as he reached in and kissed her eyelashes.

It overtook him, all the things he didn't know, all the ways she was out of reach and all the ways she was here beside him. He let his hand run through her hair as he had imagined doing since he first saw her, since that moment in the lift to the museum. What he was doing and what he was imagining collided as he moved closer to her, unaware of the chair toppling over behind him, kissing her neck, her lips. Her hands were holding his head now and she said his name. It sounded both distant and close, formal but their own form of intimacy, his surname, 'Quentin', with a hint of kindness and a hint of laughter. His eyes opened, and he was kneeling in front of her on the grass. Had he kissed her? She smiled at him. 'Come on,' she said. 'Get up. This isn't real, you know.'

He got up. His lips felt dry, broken. His hands were shaking. The world was darker, but his longing intensified. He wanted to make it stop.

He stumbled to the door, still clasping onto the yellow handrail, and leaned his head against the glass pane as the train pulled into the station.

The door opened.

But he could not step out onto the platform.

Time had collapsed. He could see in the faces of two utterly different women, both of whom he loved, simultaneous disappointment in him. He could see their pity and feel their blame. And he could remember the extraordinary closeness of carrying the pouch, just as clearly as he could remember the horror of holding a baby's lifeless hand in the lab. In that instant the pouch was warm and soft and intimate and life-changing and made up of cold inhuman substrates neatly sliced apart in autopsy. It was possible, he thought, to love two people at once. It was possible to feel wonder and horror in equal measure.

Could he be wrong? About the third generation? There was that case, after a stillbirth, when the second baby was healthy . . .

Could it be something else?

No. He wouldn't cling on to false hope any more.

He didn't know what to do next.

Maybe he should get off the train. Then he could jump.

But as the doors closed he edged backwards, into the carriage, and as the train began to move he sat back down, in the same seat he had been in before. He closed his eyes, and the train continued to travel the Circle Line. It could, after all, keep going around like that forever.

*

Holly still couldn't, wouldn't, believe it. Freida would not have run away if the pouch was causing some kind of inherited infertility. If everyone born via the pouch would inevitably miscarry their children . . . No. Not the Freida she knew. They had to be leaping to the wrong conclusion. What did Eva know, after all? What did James Quentin know? Not as much as Freida. There had to be something else going on. There had to be a way to fix the problem. The pouch had changed everything; it had made society better. For the first time in history, women had true equality.

Beyond York the fields stretched flat and far to the horizon. To one side greens and browns, dull yellows edged with low hedges, to the other, lavender. Holly reached to the top pocket of her coat and pulled out her large, tortoiseshell-rimmed sunglasses. She placed them, carefully, on her face, making sure to free the strands of hair that were caught behind her ears and touching the bounce of her grey fringe. She wished Will was with her. Will would have understood. He would have worn a trench coat.

The day they met she was wearing a white pleated skirt and a yellow shirt, her favourite bright green belt pulled tight at the waist. Her long dark hair was plaited on either side of her face and she was smiling at the boy called William who'd offered to buy her a drink. It was nearly two years after she'd seen Freida give that lecture in London, a lecture that had changed her life, offered a glimpse of a new way for women to live. And just before she started at university – the beginnings of her own new life that Freida had made possible.

'I don't need you to buy me a drink,' she said to Will, full of confidence. It was the first conversation between them, and she knew as soon as the words were spoken that she was flirting. He looked pleased.

'What is it that you need, then?' he said.

Holly shrugged, crossed her legs, looked away. 'I don't need a single thing.'

She liked his eyes, though, his expression – suddenly she wanted to know exactly what he thought about everything. And to tell him exactly what she thought, too.

'But I'd like to buy *you* a drink, instead,' she said.

He grinned. His glasses were too big for his face. Big frames, like Buddy Holly. Dimples when he smiled. And he wasn't scared, or surprised, or taken aback by her.

Holly was leaning her head against the glass, pressing her face towards the sea she could glimpse now through the woods, and she was reaching out her hand to touch Will's knee, both of them talking excitedly, neither of them able to stop touching each other, to let go of that contact that fizzed and sparked like ideas. She had never met a man so open to ideas in her life – and he wanted to *try* things, wanted to *change* things. He welcomed new ideas as fervently as her parents clung to the old ones.

'They're paying for me to go to university,' she said. 'Full scholarship. Living costs. Everything.' She wouldn't even have been able to afford to rent a flat without the scholarship money – she'd still be living in her parents' estate, probably. Going nowhere. The money from FullLife had changed everything.

'And you'll be involved with what they're doing?'

She grinned. 'I'm going to be living a whole new kind of life.'

With a whole new kind of man, she thought, imagining already that Will could be the one to share it with her. She couldn't wait to tell Freida about him.

Holly lifted her sunglasses, pushing them up on her head because the clouds were denser now; they were approaching the border and she felt like things were about to change. Opposite her Eva had her eyes closed and her head was bobbing down and up as the train rocked. She looked peaceful. Piotr, though - as she watched Piotr she couldn't help smiling. She was convinced that he was only pretending to sleep. He was staying perfectly still, so Eva could sleep beside him. And sure enough, as the train rounded a bend, her head slipped down to his shoulder, and there it stayed. No smile flitted across Piotr's face, but Holly thought she saw his eyelids flutter, just for a second.

As she watched them, neither aware they were in Scotland now, Holly was fairly certain that Piotr was in love with Eva. What she didn't know yet was if Eva was in love with Piotr. Though she hoped - because she had come to rather like him after all - she hoped that Eva loved him back. Love could be such a kind thing, when reciprocated, and such a cruelty when not.

Freida was delighted for her and Will, at first. Holly had bounded into her office during her final year at university, so sure of what she wanted. She wasn't just going to donate some eggs for the research - she and Will had decided they wanted to be the parents. And they wanted to do it now. It was going to be beautiful!

'Oh, Holly,' Freida said, pulling her in for a hug then stepping back to look into her eyes. 'Are you quite sure? It's a big decision . . .' She spoke quietly, thoughtfully, under the murmur of excitement that was spreading through the room. Two of her colleagues were there, doctors that Holly recognised. They'd been working on the pouch with the primates, and were leading the team for human trials. She nodded at them both, smiled – and then turned her gaze to the final woman in the room.

'I'm Sylvia. I founded the company,' the woman told Holly as she introduced herself – Holly realised that her eyebrows had been raised, and she lowered them again. 'I mean, Freida and I founded the company,' she smiled at Freida reassuringly. 'FullLife. With the university, of course, and backing from the government. We'll be working alongside the NHS. Sort of in parallel,' she laughed. 'I won't bore you with the jargon.'

Holly shook her hand.

'You couldn't possibly bore me,' she said with her most charming smile.

She felt a part of the team – they all believed in what they were doing. Things started moving fast: a graduation, with her mum there, and Will's parents, all of them together that warm June day, all except her dad. The incredible moment of trying on the pouch for the first time, feeling it snug and soft against her body, the surge of love it inspired. Will's face whenever he held it, as he cupped his hand around the curve of their baby in the second, the third trimester.

'Thank you,' he said to her, a few weeks before their due date, as they held their hands together to feel another of Daphne's kicks.

Holly reached in for a kiss. 'What are you thanking me for?' she said. 'We've done this together.'

'We have, haven't we?' He grinned, and she reached a fingertip to each of his dimples. 'But I suppose I meant . . . I can feel her feet, her hands, against my body. Near my tummy, sometimes, or near my ribs. Do you think she's trying to tickle me?'

Holly laughed. 'I think she's exploring her world.'

'But then, I imagine *not* having felt that . . .' He shook his head. 'What I mean is, thank you for sharing.' He laughed almost nervously and her heart leapt to him.

They had a big celebration, after Daphne was born, at FullLife – a birth day party for Daphne, they called it, but of course they were celebrating more than that. It was a celebration of achievement, of hope, of the future, of Freida's dream. After the champagne and Sylvia's speech, Holly found Freida hiding out in the corridor.

'You should be taking the credit,' Holly whispered with a grin. 'You are the one who achieved all this.' She had been such an inspiration.

Freida just smiled.

'All I care about is that Daphne is OK.'

'Daphne is wonderful!' Holly exclaimed. 'And you knew she would be. You promised.'

'You mean Sylvia—' Freida began.

'And you were right,' Holly said. 'Everything you've said has been proved right. You're my hero!'

Freida laughed at that, shaking her head but delighted all the same, Holly could tell.

'Now let's go celebrate, OK? This is your party.'

'Anything for you, Holly.'

So Holly turned and walked purposefully back to the smiles and cake and balloons, to Will and their new baby. She climbed onto a table to get everyone's attention and then, in front of all the staff of FullLife, she made a speech of her own. Because she needed to say thank you to Freida, who had changed her world.

The train passed a winding river that glinted between hills of forest. The trees glowed red and orange in the strange light that filled the sky. Overhead there was a textured deep-water grey, not the sharp clear blue they'd had in London for most of the winter – this was different.

What had Eva said to her, that had made her mind sink into itself?

Can't you see how much you don't know?

And there was a lot Holly didn't know. Even now. She wasn't afraid to admit that – she was never a scientist. She believed in the ideas, though. She believed in her family.

Can't you see how dangerous it is, when there is so much we don't know?

Words playing over in her mind, as the younger version of herself suddenly seemed headstrong, foolish – so sure she was right. Her father had called her silly. Had she been silly? To trust Freida, Full-Life? To believe that her happiness was something more than luck, that it could be shared? She'd been trying to do something good. She knew that with every part of herself – not just her heart, but with her mind too. She still had all her faculties, whatever some people might think. Images flitted through her mind of Will holding the pouch, so in awe. She gave him that. Karl too, with his thank-you letter. He was grateful, he'd said.

And Rosie and Kaz . . . Her insides twisted as she forced herself to remember. Why had it happened? It was true that they didn't know the long-term effects – you could never really predict long-term effects. That was the risk they'd all taken. Would Rosie ever be able to have a child? Could the pouches be fixed? Had she rushed in? Oh, good heavens, had she done all this to prove a point? But no, she would not have her life dismissed like that.

The train was slowing. She felt herself judder against the glass of the window before sitting back firmly, keeping her eyes on the scene outside. Because she wasn't ready to face the two people sitting opposite her. And because they were pulling into Pitlochry station and the world, suddenly, was dusted with snow. Tree branches edged in white, streets soft with icing sugar. In the distance, snow-capped mountains reached up to the sky, their contours illuminated with shafts of sunlight and deep ravines of shadow, and Holly decided that she was not going to blame herself, as women had been doing for so many generations before her. No, she was not going to blame herself, and she was not going to give up on her better world. Not while there was still a chance to save it.

Audio log

19 Jan 2016 17:32

Sylvia is getting angry with me now. It's because I won't shut up. I think I spoiled her precious board meeting but they had to be told. I've built up a dossier of all the abuse cases I could find – the pouch being used to threaten, to manipulate. Women too terrified for the life of their unborn child to stand up and speak. Society was not ready for my invention. We have to take it away. We have to stop. There is even a group of them, in the States, men who believe women are redundant. The pouch gave them the last of our power. Men who want the world to themselves. Men who hate.

I go to their birthing centre and talk to the scientists, because I imagine them to be my friends. 'You're responsible,' I tell them. 'You're responsible for what you create.' I hear whispers when my back is turned. Someone has called Security and I am politely escorted from the building.

I take things further. I write to newspapers, to reporters, and I tell them – report this! A man refusing to let his girlfriend carry the pouch – report this! A woman afraid to leave the pouch with her husband – report this! But they fill their pages with statistics about equality at work, joint parental leave, about women in politics. Someone actually takes out a restraining order on me. Me! No one notices as the NHS slips away. Hooray for the UK! These women, these rising stars, see only how their own lives have improved. Sylvia takes me to one side, like she is trying to be my friend.

'You have to look at the whole picture,' she tells me. 'We are making things better, don't you see? You are upset about a few individual cases, but overall we are making things better.'

'Make the pouches stronger,' I tell her. 'Give them a protective coating. Something non-biological, plastic, rigid—'

'Like a cage?'

'If it keeps them safe.'

'You know it has to be soft.'

'But the way it can be misused—'

'You've lost your case,' she says. 'Men have the same rights to the pouch as women.'

'It's too dangerous.'

'Actually,' she says, and she's changed now, she's not pretending to be my friend, 'what's dangerous is the way you selectively presented your results on mouse reproduction.'

Fear crawls under my skin.

'I'm sure it was because you believed in what you were doing.'

How does she know?

'I'm sure you just wanted to be taken seriously. We have all done things, in order to be taken seriously. As women in a man's world. I understand.'

I thought my rodent trials were confidential. And there was no sign of any problem in the primate trials. It was a one-off. Before the technology was perfected. I just hadn't been able to find my mistake.

'But you see,' she says, 'if people learned that you'd fudged your data to get noticed . . . that your experimental procedures were so inaccurate . . .'

Oh my God.

'An unexplained risk of death, during the birth of mice after artificial gestation. That was something you should have shared.'

I know.

'And right at the start of your career,' she said. 'Imagine everything that you've done since. All your work . . .'

The thought is awful. 'You mean the pouch?' I say. 'Is there a risk . . . ?'

'Don't be absurd,' she says. '*We* have made the pouch perfectly safe. Our research practices are far more robust and accurate than yours were.'

'It was just—'

'If people found out, you would be discredited.'

I know.

'Nobody wants that, Freida. Nobody. But you've given over the rights to the pouch now, and so you have no power here, do you see?'

It is true. I wanted no part of the selling. No part of the PR. None of the money. I am a scientist, not a politician. The mice were an aberration, that's all.

'And you're embarrassing us now. You're embarrassing yourself. There is no evidence whatsoever to suggest that the pouch increases incidents of domestic abuse. Quite the opposite.'

I have lost my fight.

'We have a job to do, and you're getting in the way. So I suggest you just leave, OK? Go away, and take what's left of your reputation with you.'

Knock, knock, knock. I need to talk to you; I need to talk to my daughter. It has been too long. It has been years. Let me in! Please, sweetheart, please. But her eyes are cold as ice and red raw as she tells me what she's seen. 'Hundreds of children,' she says. 'Unwanted children, hundreds of them, living in homes outside the city. Hidden away. No one visits them. No one talks . . . Hundreds of them, already! Do you see what you've done? Women persuaded not to abort, to transfer to the pouch but then what? Then what? Have you any idea what you've done?'

And I haven't any more, I have no idea. I try to speak but the words won't come. I can't explain. Not to you, not when you're looking at me like you hate me.

'It's your fault! All those children . . .'

'But I want to help.'

'You want to help me, is that it?'

The bitterness in your voice breaks my heart.

'I know about pouch abuse,' I try. 'I've got a case file, a husband and wife that I visited last year . . .'

She looks at the paperwork.

'I know them already.'

'What?'

'He's in jail for domestic abuse, and she's working with me.'

'With you?'

'Of course with me!' You are so angry. 'Don't you even know what I do? You turn up here, five years we haven't spoken, and you say you can help me. You know nothing about my life.'

'But I'm your mother,' I say.

You're shaking your head and it's awful, the look in your eyes, I can't stand it.

'Those poor children,' you say, 'I am just one of those children you've created.'

'Please . . . Don't . . .'

'Like them, I have no mother.'

The door slams, and I disappear.

I disappear to the edge of the land. To a lighthouse built on a witches' coven – a strip of rock reaching out in blacks and browns to the crashing waves – and no one comes to find me.

Until now. I can hear it. I thought I was imagining it but I can hear it. Someone is knocking on my door. A steady and slow knock. Knock. Knock.

From where I am sitting I can see a shadow of a man at the door. The letter box flap just rose and fell again, making the clanking noise that it does – a noise that I had forgotten. I suspect he was just looking in.

Now I can see the Asda van outside and I can see the Asda man, who is not my Asda man, who is a stranger, stacking up crates outside my front door. I left a note with instructions, just in case. I said I did not want to be disturbed.

Perhaps I should go and talk to this stranger, to ask him where my Asda man is and if he will ever come back. But I won't. Because now you know that I chose silence when I should have screamed, that I gave up when I should have stayed to fight. Now you know that I am a coward.

I am a coward, and I made a mistake, and I do not feel well today.

Chapter 15

EVA WOKE UP WITH THE rhythmic sound of the waves hitting the rocks beyond the campsite and felt her head pressed snugly between the curve of her camping pillow and the warmth of Piotr's shoulder. Beside her Piotr was sleeping, she could tell from the rate of his breathing and the weight of his arm around her – when he woke, the first thing that happened was that his arm became lighter. She didn't know if it was subconscious or if he was being considerate, but she loved it either way. The sun hadn't risen yet and she held Piotr's arm tight around her, breathed in the smell of him.

She felt the carriage jolt and immediately her cheeks were burning. She couldn't pretend to be sleeping now – her head had lurched – but she could pretend to be unaware of where she was. As the train juddered she sat upright, hand to her head, pretending not to know she'd been sleeping on his shoulder, her face almost on his chest. She opened her eyes and stretched her legs into the aisle. Holly was facing out of the window with sunglasses on her head. Piotr wasn't moving beside her. She swallowed, then laughed.

'Sorry,' she smiled, turning to him.

He wasn't smiling, but he was looking at her. His eyes seemed soft, different. He shook his head gently. She could still feel the warmth of his chest on her cheek. She put her hand to her face, turned the gesture into one of pushing her hair back.

'Where are we?' she said.

'Scotland,' he replied. 'We're in Scotland.'

And suddenly she saw it, the hills and mountains of cloud, purple, grey, lines of gold layering the sky in a way that she'd never seen before. She leaned closer to the window – her arm pressing against Piotr's, but that didn't seem to matter any more – so that she could get a better view. There was a fence to the right, criss-crossed beams that had fallen into disrepair, and their weathered wood was topped with pristine snow. A sheep looked up at the train as they passed, its black face pretty and petite amid its tattered and muddy-white fleece.

'We're north of Edinburgh? We're nearly there?'

Piotr shrugged, and then Holly replied.

'We've passed Pitlochry,' she said. 'We're heading for the Cairngorms.'

Eva smiled. She'd been wrong to imagine they were on opposite sides. She liked Holly. Holly made her feel better. There was no need to argue with her. And the sky really was extraordinary. It was years since she'd really looked at the sky. That was another thing that her mum had made her do.

Sitting outside together, Eva and her mum, late into the night, both of them aware that there wasn't much time left, giving themselves this moment to lie back and look up at the full moon and see craters and ravines despite the hazy orange glow of London in the distance.

'Sometimes I wonder,' her mum said, sitting up. 'I wonder if we've been tricked.'

Avigail often had arguments running through her mind and would invite Eva in only halfway through, expecting her to pick up the thread. But Eva had been thinking about her old sofa, that she'd left in the flat with Piotr, and she didn't think now that she could face going to collect it – asking him to give back what was hers. She'd just leave it there. It didn't matter. But she knew that if their situations had been reversed, she would have arranged for it to be returned to him. That was the problem. She would have been thoughtful, and he was being thoughtless. That was why she was bothered by the lack of her sofa.

'It's as if the whole of society,' her mum continued, 'has fallen for a bad joke. Eaten it up, like a greedy python.'

'What are you talking about, Mum?' Eva said with a smile, lifting the blanket that had fallen from her mum's shoulders and wrapping it around her again. Her mum had become so thin recently.

'We wanted to be treated as equals, that's all.'

Eva sighed fondly. She should have known. 'Most people feel that we are,' she said. 'This world is not so bad, Mum. Things could have turned out worse.'

'We gave up everything we had, so that they had to give up their unfair advantage.'

'Yes, I know, Mum.'

'And then we said thank you.'

'I don't know what more I can do.'

'Tell that man to give you back your sofa.'

Eva laughed and her mum moved closer, rested her head on Eva's shoulder.

'The moon is beautiful tonight,' she said.

'It's not worth fighting for the sofa,' Eva replied.

But perhaps, she thought now, she had been wrong about that.

She looked sideways at Piotr, who was in silhouette with the evening light behind him. Steep hills were rising from the barren moorland either side of the tracks; hunched shoulders and crags, lined with steep black ravines between layers of snow. Above them the clouds hung so close she couldn't tell where the mountaintop became the sky.

'I want my sofa back.'

'Of course,' he said. 'I'm sorry I kept it.'

She nodded.

'I'll have it delivered.'

'Thank you.'

'Although . . .'

As he paused, Eva could feel her anger returning, her fight, and she knew that if he dared try to keep it, to say it was practically his after all this time, if he—

'. . . I think there might be some cat hairs on it,' he said. 'I'm sorry about that, too. If you like I can get it cleaned first?'

'That's OK,' she said, to her surprise feeling like she could cry if she were alone. 'That's OK,' she said again, and turned her eyes to look back out of the window.

As they approached Aviemore the light vanished, leaving them in stormy darkness. The windows were blasted with sleet that sounded from inside the carriage like gravel hitting the glass. Holly finally took the shades from her head, placed them on the table. The train stood at the station for a couple of minutes and Eva watched a group of people on the other side of the platform, hats pulled low, collars pulled high, laughing together. And then their train pulled away and the landscape changed again. As suddenly as it had arrived, they passed the worst of the storm and a new light emerged, a thunderous gold that split the sky above the Moray Firth.

It was the last of the light. It hadn't occurred to her they'd be travelling the last part of their journey in the dark. But they would. They needed to take the Far North Line from Inverness. They were not here to see the city of the Highlands; they were here to see the peninsula of jagged rock that Eva had visited as a child on what she'd once thought was a holiday with her mother. But it must have been something else.

And there, in her peripheral vision, was Holly Bhattacharyya. She was more than the first woman to use the baby pouch, of course, that was just fluke really, an accident of timing. What had made her famous – a hero, really – was the way she'd made everything seem so natural. She was calm. She was nurturing. Strong and determined too – she must have been, to go through with it – but she was petite and pretty and non-threatening and in all the photos she was surrounded by her beautiful family. Despite the pouch and the remaking of society that had followed, there was something very traditional about Holly and her life. Something content.

Even now, as Holly sat straight-backed with her hands clasped in her lap, there was something maternal about her that Eva knew was absent in herself. Eva was not offering comfort to anyone. That had never been her way. Here she was, next to Piotr, and she knew that they had loved each other once, that they were now as fractured as two people could be and she felt a wave of failure sweep over her. Was it possible that she was wrong? That she was angry, and frustrated, and tired, and lonely, because she'd been fighting for the wrong thing?

But no, this was bigger than her. She was just one person, after all. And if the pouch was malfunctioning, or worse, if babies in the pouch were developing a new type of infertility that meant their children could never be born, then it was not what she believed or what Holly believed that mattered. It was about a technology that had gone wrong, and it was about finding a solution – whatever that would be. So no matter what happened when they got to that lighthouse, this was not about Eva or Piotr, it was not about Holly or her children or her grandchildren, and it was not about the deep silent ache that Eva felt every time she thought about them.

*

Karl hesitated, standing at the back of the lift, Cris and the director in front of him. What had she said her name was? He couldn't remember. The inside of the lift was panelled with mirrors – wherever he looked there it was, his face staring back at him, in between the stranger and his Cris. Karl's black beard, which he always kept trimmed, kept rounded, was more grey now than anything. His usually wide-open brown eyes seemed watery in this light. He was starting to look old, he thought to himself. He was heading fast into the latter half of middle age. Not that he minded. Until this week he'd been rather enjoying the thought of growing old. He'd pictured himself sitting in his reclining chair with Will – a toddler now, perhaps, or a confident crawler, climbing up to sit on his lap, or sliding back down his legs again. Reading a picture book, perhaps, about the colours of the world or the times of the day, Will cuddled in under his arm the way young children did when they were almost, but not quite, ready to go to sleep.

Cris was trying to catch his eye in the mirror, to give him a smile of reassurance. They were still rising through the building – according to the button lights they were going to the top floor. He didn't know what they'd find there. He closed his eyes, blocking out his reflection, and saw instead the dead body of his grandson. He felt something pulsing uncomfortably through his arms – adrenaline, anger. Someone was to blame for what had happened, but not Kaz, not Rosie. He was sure of that. He stretched out his fingers, then curled them tight into his palms.

As the lift doors slid open, they revealed a well-lit and carpeted internal corridor. It was so calm, so quiet. Such a reassuring sort of space – was that the intention? All the corridors in the birthing centre were internal, so that all of the rooms could be flooded with natural light. Cris and the director had already stepped out of the lift and he followed them, turning right as they did. They were heading for the room with the closed door up ahead. There were no other doors in sight.

Along one side of the corridor they were passing framed, crayoned children's drawings, each one mounted as though it was a work of art. Or perhaps they were works of art. They were lovely, he thought, with a sharp twist of loss, but he didn't look at them for long. On the other side of the corridor a fish tank was set into the wall, emanating a fluorescent blue glow and housing intricate pieces of orange and red coral. Among them, striped purple-and-white tropical fish darted gracefully.

The director was holding a key card in her hand. She was of average height. Kind of nondescript hair. Clearly, she wasn't going to give anything away – she was too controlled for that. When he looked at her clothes, he found that he had instantly forgotten what she was wearing. Perhaps she didn't want to stand out. He was a little nondescript himself, he thought, except when he was dancing, when he was creating movement. He wondered what it was that would make the director stand out. She opened the door and held it wide, with a gentle smile, for Cris and Karl to step inside.

Oh, he gasped, the glass. On three walls of the room were floor-to-ceiling panels of glass looking out over central London. His first thought was of the smashed glass downstairs but the light here was softened, the glare was gone. He could open his eyes fully, he could see St Paul's, the Thames, curved and glittered, Tower Bridge. The Globe, over the river. He found himself approaching the window, staring out, following streets and paths between low red-brick houses, bare-branched trees decorated with light.

'Have a seat, when you're ready,' the director was saying. Cris was sitting down already – the view didn't seem to have affected him in the same way. But then he wasn't the one who'd just driven a car into a glass building. 'Have some herbal tea,' the director said, standing beside him now. 'Camomile, perhaps? Or green tea?'

'Whatever you're having,' he said coldly, and she turned to the corner of the room, disappearing from view. His eyes followed her, and he realised that the room ran the length of the building. On the fourth wall, behind the sofa, there were large digital screens, all of them switched off. He sat down next to Cris. Taking his hand, he saw a piece of the shattered glass lodged in his palm. Cris winced.

'Sorry . . .' he whispered, but Cris just shook his head.

Three china cups of green tea were placed on the low table between the sofas, and the director held hers in both hands, as though she needed to warm up – though it was quite warm in here. Karl was sweating. But then she put down her cup, and looked at each of them in turn.

'I am sorry for your loss,' she said. 'There are no words to make it better.'

Suddenly, Karl was completely focused on her.

'I should have invited you here before, to explain everything. I thought it would be better to give you all some time but . . . I know you're angry,' she said. 'And, unfortunately, you are not the first.'

'What?' Karl's voice came out sharp and loud. He felt Cris move beside him.

'You are the first to ram the building with a car, though,' the director smiled. 'That's all yours.' She didn't laugh, laughter would have been completely inappropriate, but there was warmth to her smile. Karl wasn't going to let that change anything.

She paused and sipped her tea.

They were going to blame Kaz, he thought. *She* was going to say Kaz did something wrong, he knew it.

'Don't. You. Dare . . .' he began, then stopped as Cris placed a hand on his knee.

He noticed the silence. The soundproofing. In this building full of newborn babies you never could hear anything beyond what was happening in your own room.

'The truth is,' she said, holding out her hands as though she wanted to hold theirs. They both ignored the gesture. 'The truth is, in recent years we've had a small number of tragic deaths. I don't know of a gentler way to put it. It is very unusual, but it happens. And we don't know why.'

Karl swallowed. Was she saying that others had died?

'What we do know is that, occasionally, a child has died in the pouch during the birthing process. We don't think it's because of the birth itself . . . They seem to be a little like cot deaths, in some respects, in that there's no sign that anything is wrong.'

She leaned forward, looking first into Karl's eyes, and then Cris's. There was a slight shake in her voice. Karl swallowed, but returned her gaze.

'I want you to know that we're trying to find the reason,' she said. 'But, mostly, I want you to know that this was no one's fault. No one knows why it happened. No one could have prevented it. I am so sorry.'

It was what he'd wanted to hear, but something was very wrong. 'Is that it?' he said, his voice reverberating around the room after the soothing tones of hers. So they weren't blaming Kaz. But . . . 'Are you telling me, us, that you knew about this risk?'

'There have been a small number of tragic—'

'You knew this could happen?' he interrupted, his voice getting louder as the full impact of what she had said sunk in. Something felt like it could burst from his chest. If they had known . . . 'You knew, and you didn't tell us?' He was standing, his legs knocking against the coffee table, his tea spilling into its saucer, and he had a sudden vision of hurling the cup against their perfectly muted windows, shattering every pane of glass in this false building, tearing it to the ground. 'You didn't tell us!' he was shouting now; he heard something smash but ignored it. 'You've been lying to everyone! If we'd known, if Kaz and . . . If we'd known that this might happen . . .'

'Then what?' she said, gently.

He stared at her, realised that his hands were clenched into fists. He unclenched them.

'You promised us it was safe,' Cris said quietly. 'Everyone. You promised—'

'Actually, I didn't,' she said. 'I've only been here for three years. People have believed, assumed, it was perfectly safe for forty, fifty—'

'So it's our fault?'

'No, no.' She shook her head, and for the first time Karl noticed her expression was deeply sad. 'I thought it was perfectly safe, too. I had my daughter . . . But there was no legal guarantee . . . I mean, they were just advertising campaigns.'

'What about the previous director?' asked Cris, keeping his voice soft. 'The people who founded the company?'

She shook her head again. 'For the pouch to be accepted, people needed to know it was safe . . . To believe in it completely.'

'So you – FullLife – let them believe a lie?' Karl said.

'I don't know.' She reached for her cup. It rattled just slightly in its saucer. 'Perhaps they had no idea . . . But since it started happening – and it was just recently, I promise you – we've been trying to understand . . . trying to work out why. At first it was just one isolated case. We had no reason to think it could happen to others. But then . . .'

'People need to be told.'

Karl wasn't shouting any more. He looked down at the floor, and saw the famous photo of Shulamith Firestone looking up at him from the cracked glass of a glossy black frame. He'd knocked it off the wall.

'But it might not affect everyone—' she began.

'*Everyone* needs to be told.' He looked at Cris for support. 'And Kaz and Rosie, they need to know the truth. People need to understand that the pouch isn't safe and then . . .'

'Then what?' she said.

The alterative, it struck him, would have been Kaz and Rosie choosing natural birth, and all the risks it comes with. The alternative for him, for Cris . . . ? The pouch had made their family possible.

'The pouch is worth protecting, I think,' she said, almost under her breath. 'Especially now we're offering natural birth as well. People will be able to choose.'

Karl was staring at the director now, and Cris was staring at her too. She looked calm again, but the quieter she spoke the more her words seemed to resonate. Karl sat back down, felt a sudden stinging behind his eyes.

'It is a good thing, that the pouch was accepted,' she said. 'I believe that. I believe the world is better, for many people, for all sorts of people, because we are here.'

'Our family . . .' Cris said.

'Yes, like your family.' She looked between them, one to the other and back. 'Many other families, too. Parenthood finally, truly, shared. Men at last able to experience carrying their child. Women who would have been unable to carry a child naturally, for any reason, illness, genetics . . . I became a mother at fifty-one. The pouch gave me that.'

Karl knew that what she was saying was true. And he didn't want to shout any more.

'I'm sorry I smashed your photo frame.'

'It's OK,' she said. 'A frame can be replaced.'

He held his head in his hands.

'You can sit here for a while,' she was saying. 'If it would help.'

But the stinging behind his eyes was worsening and he didn't want to be here, in this beautiful room, with this extraordinary view over London, discussing how the pouch had made his family possible, or how it had caused them so much pain. He wanted to go home, and *be* with his family.

'I am so sorry for your loss,' she said again. 'I wish there was something more I could do. I wish you both strength.'

He stood, though he was shaking, and he stumbled against the table again, this time mumbling an apology, and then he was in the lift with Cris, who was holding him tight. But Karl was slipping, now his anger had gone, he was slipping down onto the floor and making a noise that he didn't understand until they were out in reception and he was upright again, and at last he understood that he hadn't needed to blame. He had needed to cry.

Looking up, he saw his car had been neatly reversed out of the birthing centre and was waiting for them to drive it away. The number plate was cracked. One of the headlights had smashed. The bonnet didn't quite close properly. But the damage looked superficial. Beyond the space where there had once been a glass panel, there was a large group of people clustered, watching the building, but he didn't pay them any attention. He didn't notice the colour of the sky or the flash of the cameras, he only knew the warmth of Cris's hand held tight in his own.

'Karl!' one of the group shouted. 'I know who you are! Cris! Karl!' It was a young man running up to them, buttoned shirt, piercing blue eyes, expression determined, unabashed. 'What happened?' he demanded. 'Can you tell us anything?'

Karl looked at him, confused. Who were these people? What right did they have to be making demands of him? He noticed that young woman again, the one who'd been taking photos with her phone – she was with them.

'My grandson died,' he said simply. 'Now leave us alone.'

Cris put his arm around him, and he was grateful, and together they walked away.

Karl was silent in the car, but not withdrawn – as Cris drove, calmly, through London he watched his face, marvelling at how much he loved him, and how rarely he told him. 'I'll get the glass out of your hand,' he said. 'We've got antiseptic and . . . I'll make sure it's OK.' He reached up to stroke his arm, and Cris smiled without taking his eyes from the road. And then as they pulled into their driveway they noticed, at the same time, that the lights inside the house were on.

He ran up the path and fumbled for his keys.

'Kaz?' he was shouting, 'Kaz?' There was a shadow in the living room, blocking the light through the blinds. Too high to be someone sitting down. Was it too high to be someone standing? Karl felt his insides twist. 'Kaz?' he whispered, dropping the keys, picking them up again.

Finally he got the door open and ran inside, Cris close behind him, and they burst into the living room and there was Kaz, standing on a stepladder. He was positioning a photograph on the wall. It was a picture of them, of their family.

'You're here,' Karl said, out of breath, and Kaz turned. He had been crying.

'Do I have this up straight?'

'It's perfect,' Cris said, soft concern in his voice. 'It looks good, son.'

Slowly, Kaz climbed back down the stepladder, turned to face his dads and took a deep breath. Karl felt his heart fracture again.

'I don't know what to do,' Kaz said, words suddenly tumbling between sobs that turned into deep gasps for air. 'Everything is broken and Will's gone and now I can't see, I can't imagine and I don't know . . . I don't know what to do . . .'

But finally Karl knew what to do. He put his arms around Kaz, and Cris put his arms around them both.

*

Holly was sitting in her mum's kitchen, eighteen years old and oblivious to the freshly opened daffodils in the small square vase on the breakfast table. Her dad was pacing. It was the first announcement that the university had made – at least, the first that made it into national newspapers rather than specific peer-reviewed journals. It was the first announcement that the public were supposed to read. It was the flurry of excitement, the press conference, the moment of promise and change. They'd had successful births of mice, sheep, and now chimpanzees. They'd been given a licence to start preparing for human trials. They predicted the first human pouch birth would be within five years. Their company would be leading the way, their non-academic, research-led, public-facing company. Freida had told her about them already – none of this was news to Holly. They would be called FullLife.

'You have to admit it's a good name,' Holly said as her father slammed the paper onto the breakfast table and sat down. That was when she noticed the daffodils. The way their beaming yellow heads rocked on their stems.

Holly watched as her mum picked up the paper in turn – she always read it second – and as she, too, learned about the baby pouch, and the potential for the first human trials. She tried to deduce her mum's thoughts from her expressions as she read. It was hard to tell though, behind her calm face, behind the resignation, the willingness to wait in line. Holly hoped that her mum would express an opinion first.

'Nonsense!' cried her dad, as her mum put the paper down on the table. 'Can you believe it?'

'It's hard to believe . . .' her mum said.

'It's ridiculous.'

'It's not ridiculous,' said Holly.

'Why is this even necessary? Of all the things we could be doing!' He laughed, shaking his head now. 'What silly girl would sign up for something like this? It'll be over before it's started, Harshini.'

'*Holly*,' said Holly.

'It does seem like rather an odd thing to want to do . . .' said her mum.

Her mum was looking at her, and Holly wondered if somehow she knew already. But she'd been very careful, kept all the paperwork away from the family home. Avoided talking to Freida on the phone. Avoided talking too much to her parents, too, for the last six months. But she didn't want to carry on like that. She wanted them to know what she was going to do. She wanted them to be proud of her.

'I've applied,' she said.

'Applied for what?' her dad asked.

And Holly found herself rephrasing the truth in her mind, reworking the angle so it would sound different. Sound more palatable, to them.

'They want to talk to people. People of my age and . . . To see how we feel about the different designs for the pouches. To be involved.'

But she wanted so much more than that. She wanted to try one out. She wanted to make it possible. She was going to find a better way for women whether her parents could understand it or not.

'*Why?*'

'Because women don't have equality,' she said. 'Because I'm sick of how you sit there and laugh instead of trying out new ideas, or listening to mine.'

Her dad looked like he was about to speak, but she didn't stop.

'Because we have to evolve –' and she knew that her voice was raised now, but she couldn't stop – 'because it is *unfair* the way all this pressure is put on women – the childbirth, the pain, the whole nine months of it. Because it shouldn't be men doing one thing and women doing another, we should be equals. We should be partners!'

She felt herself looking away from her father, and she felt her own confrontation changing to judgement as she turned her eyes to her mother. Seeing the sadness in her face. Or maybe she was just tired. Or maybe all she wanted to do was avoid another argument. Then she heard the table judder as her dad stood up again – whether to walk away from the fight or project his voice louder she didn't know. It was only afterwards that she realised what she'd heard though, in the quiet voice to her left. Her mum's voice that so rarely said what she really thought.

'Actually, I rather loved giving birth to my children,' was what she said, though neither Holly nor her dad replied.

'I won't allow it,' was what her dad had said next.

And Holly had shouted, and they both had shouted, and they hadn't seen each other afterwards until everything was changed and he was lying in a hospital bed, and she was filled with thoughts of how she could have done things better. But now what Holly could remember most clearly were the words that her mother had spoken. Actually, I rather loved giving birth to my children, she had said. And although her mum had been dead for many years and she'd never asked her about it while she was alive, Holly wondered if when her mum spoke those words she was telling the truth, her own truth, and no one was listening.

*

Now this, thought Piotr, was a train. There were no tables on the Far North Line so Holly had commandeered a double seat for herself while Eva and Piotr sat behind, to give her some peace and quiet. The dark had fallen fast and deep, and to Piotr there was nothing but their own reflections visible in the windows. Inside it was all threadbare carpet and old-fashioned armrests on the seats, the kind that you had to press a little button on to make then move up and down.

'It's incredible,' Eva whispered, nudging him in the ribs.

'What?' he whispered back. 'The dirt on the windows?'

'No, you arse,' she said. 'The moonlight on the water.'

'There's water?'

He'd had no idea.

'Take the seat behind. Block out the lights, and shut up. And look.'

Piotr did exactly as he was told.

She was right. She was so very, very right. The water spread out into a shimmering expanse of black, and in the distance there was a bridge, lit, low, curving its way over the water. He looked up, and the stars began to appear between the clouds. The wind was strong, the sky changing rapidly, and he could hear the gusts howling against the windows of the carriage.

'Sounds a bit wild out there,' he whispered, and though she didn't turn round he was fairly sure that she was smiling. That she understood.

Locals got on and off as the train wound its way through the windswept villages on the Cromarty Firth, getting emptier the further they got from Inverness. Filling with the hushed quiet of a library. Soon the only people in their carriage were the three of them – the passengers from London. They'd bought some sandwiches for dinner at the station, and they ate them in silence. Outside there were no more homes to see, no more bridges or harbour lights, only the darkness of woodland and winter fields. Piotr pulled out his ticket and checked the name of their destination. The journey was almost over, at least the easy part of it. He put on his jacket and joined Eva by the doors. They were pulling in.

Holly, Eva and Piotr stood on the platform watching the empty train as it disappeared from view. There were no buildings. No information. The way out was through a small, empty car park, and beyond that: nothing. Piotr took a few steps into the night, hoping his eyes would adjust and give him some clue where to go next. Eva strode past him, locating a grassy track beside the road. The light of the station didn't reach far into the countryside, but the sky – it felt bigger than any he had seen before. Layer after layer of stars between the silver outlines of fleeting clouds, on a backdrop of deep, limitless black.

'I'm sorry,' he said, suddenly realising Holly was standing alone, looking uncertain. He took the phone from his pocket and turned it on as a torch. The thin white light lit the ground by her feet – an ineffectual guide, but it was all he had. 'We're going to have to walk.'

'How long will it take?' Holly asked. 'Not that I mind walking,' she added before either of them could reply. 'I just want to know, that's all.'

'Maybe about an hour, I guess,' Piotr said.

'A little more, I think,' said Eva. 'But it's possible.'

'Everything's possible,' Holly said, as she planted her walking stick firmly on the ground. 'Which way, then?'

Eva pointed. 'Look,' she said. 'Wait, for a few seconds, and look.'

And there, in the distance, after about ten seconds of darkness, came the guiding light that Piotr had forgotten about, and the warning – the warning of the dark treacherous rocks, the warning that beamed beyond the waves – that was the three distinctive flashes of light sent out, every thirty seconds, every night for the past two hundred years, from the Tarbat Ness Lighthouse.

Audio log

7 Feb 2016 18:32

—I hear the wind shaking the window glass and feel the air thickening around me. I know that it is no use. The dense purple clouds have reached the black rocks now and I made my choice a long time ago and I understand that the storm has finally arrived. It is here, after all my waiting. Here, in the middle of my last recording. Though it is not the storm I expected. It is internal, of course. Perhaps all the greatest storms are.

This is my final audio log, and I was talking about the indigo hamlets and I'm a bit worried now about them, about how they will survive if there is no one to check they have the right degree of turbulence. They are such extraordinary creatures, so much better than us, I think, in so many ways. I would love to be with them now, swimming through the warm salt waters of the Caribbean.

If you had answered my letter, I might have been able to help. Did you ever think of that? You wanted nothing to do with me because of what I had created but now – now – I want nothing more to do with what I have created. That's not true though, because deep down I still think . . . Well, I still hope. Do you see? It wasn't because of you that I invented the pouch, and it wasn't to get away from you that I worked so hard to complete it. I remember the way you looked at me, just after the first baby was born, and you said, 'You must be *proud* of yourself now.' As if you thought I was never proud of you; never proud of being a mother to you. It hurts to remember it.

But the numbness in my fingers is spreading. It is the cold, perhaps, but it's moved up over my wrist and my elbow and now my arm is almost frozen with it. The cold . . . So cold I can hardly move at all. I would put the fire on but with dizzing . . . No, I . . . With the dizzy feeling I mean. With the dizzy feeling I am not sure I want to get up. This is my final audio log and I want to finish saying what I am saying. I don't need my arm to be not numb.

And I don't believe any more that my Asda man will ever return, but if he did, I think I would tell him about my arm and how I can't feel this . . . about how the numb feeling is gone now but that . . . Maybe I won't tell him.

It would be nice to have the option to tell him.

Now I want him to come, and I know that he is not . . .

Have I done everything wrong?

I am so sorry, if I have done everything wrong.

Science is not perfect, you know. I never really tried to claim that it was. Sylvia was the one who wanted perfection – she stole my work. She set up her company and stole my ideas because of my doubts.

Sometimes I imagine what would have happened if . . . had I chosen differently. If I'd walked away, left his hand un-shook . . . never become a scientist . . . but sooner or later, the pouch would have been invented anyway. All the pieces were . . . Well, I tell you . . . If men had been having babies for as long, they would have invented it generations ago . . . it would have preceded the bomb!

Though I pushed things forward.

Oh. Just wait . . .

One person can make a difference.

One person.

I made a difference.

But it would have happened, eventually . . . without me. Walking away would have . . .

Slowed things down . . .

Would some extra time have helped?

. . . made any difference?

Perhaps I am still not ready to admit that I was wrong.

But there's more than right or wrong, don't you think? Life is not so . . . so neat as that.

He is not coming, of course. And you are not coming . . . Love.

No one is . . .

. . . But it is OK.

I'm just—

Chapter 16

THEY WALKED IN SILENCE, ALL of them – at times – looking up to the extraordinary expanse of sky and all of them – at times – stumbling over the rocky ground, in muddy ditches, against the sharp gorse that encroached on the path leading to the tip of the peninsula.

Eva walked on the other side of the path to Piotr and Holly. She wanted the space around her, and she wanted the time to listen. She listened to the sounds she could hear in between her own steps, as her confidence built with every new beam from the lighthouse. There was the regular thud of Holly's walking stick – usually a thump on rock but occasionally the gulp of it sinking into mud. She could hear the swish of Piotr's jacket sleeves as he walked ahead of her – that was less regular as he strode forwards alone then caught himself and waited for Holly to catch up. She could hear him breathe, too, when he paused and waited, when he looked up at the constellations. Like he was breathing in the sky. And behind all of that there was the constant, distant, crash of the waves.

She'd read somewhere that the sound of water is soothing, for humans – that it makes us feel like we're in a place where we could survive. She focused on the waves as she walked, the waves that were white and silver and loud, now, the loudest thing she could hear. Then the lighthouse appeared, its white stripes showing up in its beams of light, the contours of the land leading them out to where it stood, tall and thin, alone, the only thing stretching up from the flat featureless land.

They arrived at a gate.

Beyond the gate was an overgrown patch of grass and gorse that had once, as far as she could make out, been a garden. Through the garden was a low rectangular outbuilding, painted white and catching the starlight, the remnants of a small, broken window the brightest point on the structure. Beyond that, past a drystone wall, was the lighthouse.

Holly and Piotr were just standing, staring. Eva thought Holly was leaning on her walking stick, and wondered if she was out of breath. But Holly hadn't complained, or slowed down, so it seemed patronising to ask if she was OK. Instead, Eva pushed on the gate – waist-high, wooden slats – and it opened easily, inwards. Almost too quickly, they were in front of the lighthouse itself. It towered over them.

Eva knocked first.

There was no answer.

She checked her phone – the night was dark but it wasn't that late. If someone lived here, they wouldn't be asleep yet.

Then Holly knocked. Called out: 'Freida? It's me. It's Holly.'

Nothing.

Eva pushed on the door, gently. There was no handle – she couldn't see how to get in. She pushed again, harder. Then Piotr leaned against it, gingerly at first, then using all his weight. He stepped back, took a short run at it.

'Ouch,' he said.

The door, of course, hadn't budged.

'I'll need to take a longer run-up.'

'Piotr,' Eva said, touching him gently on the shoulder, 'look.'

She pointed, and they all looked beyond the lighthouse to the low building nestling behind it in the shadows. The cottage of the lighthouse keeper.

'That's where someone would live,' Eva said. She walked up to the door and pushed it. It opened.

She stepped into a tiled porch, through an inner door of dirty yellow glass and peeling woodwork, to find herself standing in a small, dark hallway. To her surprise, the light overhead came on as soon as she tried the switch. A door to the left was open, and inside it, on the wall facing them, was a large framed photograph that had been cut out from a newspaper article. It showed a young, happy Holly holding her newborn daughter. Eva knew what it said. The picture was familiar to everybody: *The first couple to give birth using the new and still controversial baby pouch.*

'Good heavens, not here too,' Holly pronounced, as she strode past Eva and knocked the frame off the wall with her walking stick. 'What on earth is going on?'

*

Daphne opened the door to a room that had been many different rooms over the years. It had been her bedroom, when she was a child, painted bright purple and filled with picture books. Then her dad's study, his white bookshelves double-stacked with biographies and novels. They were the readers of the family, Daphne and her dad. Everyone else liked to be out, doing, playing, but Daphne and her dad preferred to be inside reading. Then it became the empty room, for a while, after her dad died, after she and her mum had found the collective strength to go through everything on those bookshelves, save what they couldn't let go and donate the rest to charity. But for the past nine months it had been the baby's room, and she had decorated it herself, for the party, for the moment that never came.

The balloons had lost their lift, each of them by slightly different amounts, so now they were hanging around the floor or bobbing below the windowsill. One was lying on the small chest of drawers like a deflated skin. She would have to throw them away, but there was too much air in them to fit them in a black bag. They needed to be popped first. So, collecting a needle from her own room along the hall, that was what she did.

The Happy Birth Day sign was peeled down from the wall. The toys she placed in the cot – there had been colourful toys all around the room – because Rosie might want to keep some of them. But the decorations, the gold and silver and purple ribbons, she collected up so that the pain of removing them would be hers and no one else's.

She wished Rosie and Kaz would talk to each other. It was strange, particularly for her, that she took comfort in knowing that her child had a partner – the sense of peace she'd felt during their wedding had taken her completely by surprise. Daphne herself had never wanted a partner, and certainly never believed that anybody needed one. She'd always felt like she was most complete, living as the best possible version of herself, when she was single. She'd tried a few people out, of course, boys and girls while she was at school, men and women during her twenties, but she'd always felt relief when the relationships ended, as though she could return to being herself again. So when she decided she wanted to have a child, she did that on her own, as well. Though she had her family. Her mum drove her mad, but her gratitude ran deep.

It had always surprised her that FullLife focused so much on traditional families in their publicity. Given that they wanted the support of the majority of the population, though, it made a certain kind of sense to advertise the pouch as the way to create an ideal version of the existing family unit. It was how they got mainstream popular opinion behind them so fast: the pouch gave women equality and allowed men to experience complete parenthood. It fitted with society's image of happiness, of success. Even now, many parents were still heterosexual couples and lots of conceptions happened naturally – by choice – people opting for the embryo to be implanted in the pouch a few days later. But the real value was what the pouch offered to the non-traditional family. Single women and men empowered to become parents. Gay couples able to carry their own child. Trans people. Older couples. Women with health difficulties. People who wanted to live in groups. The possibilities for moving society away from its narrow view of family were beautiful. Though, apparently, it was going to take more than fifty years. Whether through biological or sociological change, human progress wasn't linear; there would inevitably be problems along the way.

As for worrying about the selection during IVF, you could drive yourself mad thinking about all the potential lives that never were, from the eggs never fertilised, the embryos that did not survive. You could drive yourself mad worrying about choosing one over the other, but they were just cells. She believed that. After all, for every child that was born there could be another, potential child that would never be conceived the night after. It was the child that was born that mattered. The life that was lived.

Picking up the basket she kept by the back door, she headed out into the garden despite the dark. Light from the house lit the grass, and the glow of London was reflected in the winter colours as she selected stems of rich green leaves and red berries. Indoors, she arranged two vases and took the first quietly to Rosie's room. She was lying on the bed now, the walls bare, the curtains drawn, but she sat up as Daphne placed the flowers by the window. They would catch the sun in the morning.

'Thanks, Mum,' Rosie said, her voice weak and quiet, but genuine.

'You're welcome, sweetheart.' Daphne kissed her on the forehead. 'Any word from Kaz?'

Rosie shook her head.

'He'll come home when he's ready. And so will Nana.' Daphne didn't know if that was true, but she'd always thought it best to deal with one problem at a time, and right now Rosie was exhausted. 'Try to get some sleep, love.' She went to pull the door over as she left the room, but Rosie called her back.

'Leave it open, Mum?'

Daphne smiled and nodded. 'I love you very much, sweetheart.'

Downstairs again, Daphne looked at the second vase she had arranged, added one more sprig from the spare cuttings in the sink and some extra plant food. Then she carried it up to the attic, to her mum's room, and arranged it on the dressing table between the family photos that Holly kept either side of the mirror she used when curling her hair. It felt wrong, this room being empty. Like a vital part of her was missing. But her mum would come home soon too, Daphne reasoned, and when she did, she'd quite like her to see that she'd brought her some red berries, some prickly holly, and some of the unexpected winter flowers from their new purple daphne.

*

Holly stood in the middle of Freida's room – part office, part lounge, part dining room – with the framed newspaper article celebrating her past at her feet. Eva and Piotr were looking decidedly scared of her now. Ha!

She wasn't amused, though. She was cold, deep in her bones cold, and the damp of the ground and the mud had seeped through her trainers hours ago – she could feel it, congealing around her toes. What in all of heaven's name was Freida doing, moving to a place like this? No, she wasn't amused, she was angry.

'Freida?' she called. 'Freida!'

'I think this house has been empty for a while,' Eva said gently.

The dust, it was true, was in such a thick layer that no one could have lived here without feeling the urge to wipe it up, surely. But then there were still books on the shelves, glasses and vases in that old-looking cabinet by the sofa – it reminded Holly of the furniture her parents used to have. It looked like an old woman had lived here. No, it looked like an old woman had died here.

'Do we think she's dead, then?' Holly said.

Piotr and Eva just looked at one another, and she had to fight the urge to bang their heads together.

She pushed past them and checked every room of the cottage – bungalow, in fact, with a kitchen at the front, and that hideous dark hall with its ugly yellow glass doors. She passed a bathroom on her way to the final room, presumably that would be the bedroom, but she wasn't expecting what she saw inside. There was no one there, of course – but the windows! The whole far end of the room was composed entirely of windows looking out, uninterrupted, over a black expanse that led to the violent sea that was thrashing against the coast. As she looked out into the darkness, the wilderness of it, Holly was hit by a sudden wave of homesickness.

She missed her beautiful, comfortable home, her Rosie, with her morning cookies and wide eyes, she missed the Thames, the reflections of the bridges' lights, the cathedrals on the skyline, the domes and glass arcs that nestled beside Elizabethan theatres. Was there any city in the world so old and new, so full of contradiction? But there was no contradiction here, in this lighthouse bungalow, in this uncompromising view that had been left unchallenged for millennia – it was single-minded. It was awful. The other two seemed to like it here. Acting like they were on an adventure, but that wasn't what this was for Holly, despite her trench coat and her trusty walking stick. This was no adventure for her. She wanted everything to be OK again, and she wanted to go home. Hearing Eva's footsteps behind her, she turned.

'We've found something,' Eva was saying. 'Piotr's trying to play it.'

'What?'

But the silence that followed was soon broken by a voice, too loud – far too loud – filling the low-ceilinged room.

'Sorry,' Piotr called, as the voice disappeared, then started up again, quieter but still audible. Eva held her arm out, offering Holly the chance to walk ahead of her, but Holly shook her head. She waited until Eva had reached the office door and then, slowly, started making her own way down the hall. About halfway along, opposite the vile avocado-green bathroom, she stopped and leaned against the wall, listening.

It was Freida's voice.

Freida's voice was talking about how she had written a letter but no one had answered. She sounded frail. She sounded disappointed . . . But there had been no letters to Holly for decades. Freida had said not to contact her at all. Holly didn't even have her address! If there was a problem, Freida should have stayed to face it – she should have told Holly what was going on. She'd written a letter? So what! It had never arrived! But where had she been all these years? They were supposed to be on the same side.

But her voice, even so much older, was familiar. Holly could remember the sparkle in her words as she described the pouch – so unlike anything the *men* would have come up with, she'd said, laughing. I'll make it soft and warm. No sterile containers and coloured fluids, no uniform pods – I'll make it personal, she'd said. And she had. Everyone experienced the pouch individually, everyone knew how personal it was – the love saw to that. The love you felt for your baby in the pouch was acutely intimate.

And here was Freida's voice, saying she thought the foundation of FullLife was a mistake – the whole company – implying she regretted giving away her patent, the patent that she had left to Holly, for the family. Freida had never wanted money, Holly knew that, and Holly had needed it then. She'd thought it was an act of generosity. But now Freida's voice was complaining that Holly cared more about her family than her.

And then there was Freida's voice, going on about those tropical fish again, and Freida's voice, describing a collection of burned gorse – is that what she did now, Holly thought, had she given up one of the most important careers in a century, walked away leaving a technology that she knew was flawed, that had hurt Rosie, so she could collect useless scraps of wood and obsess about sea bass and supermarket deliveries?

There is no greater patriarchy than London.

'It was Jean Rhys,' said Eva, replying to Freida's question as though she were right there.

'What?' said Holly, annoyed that her thoughts had been inter-rupted. But now, there was Freida's voice again, shaky, describing a room at King's. Describing a choice that she made, that she wished she could remake. There it was, recorded. Undeniable. She regretted what she'd created. They'd found her hiding place but she had dis-appeared, again, leaving no answer, only this record of the fact that she thought FullLife was wrong; she thought Holly was wrong. Her whole life. Holly's whole life.

Holly wanted to be sick. But Eva was there again.

'There's something else,' she said.

Piotr had followed her out to the hall now – was looking at Eva again with that admiration that was starting to make Holly want to scream.

'There's a note,' she was saying, and then she was handing it to Holly, who read:

I have left my lighthouse and gone to live with Declan Ross. If you want me, you can phone me, and I might even answer. 01862 4365117.

Holly looked at Piotr, who looked at Eva, who looked at Holly.

'Who in heaven's name is Declan Ross?'

Chapter 17

DECLAN ROSS WAS CONCERNED ABOUT his rhubarb. True, it was December, but it was a mild winter, it had barely dropped below freezing, and back in November he'd been walking along the beach in no more than his shirtsleeves. So he had expected, reasonably, he felt, to get another crop of rhubarb before Christmas.

He was down on his hands and knees, in his garden trousers, in his wellies, inspecting the rhubarb patch when Bea came out with the phone. Why he'd ever let her persuade him to go cordless was a mystery – a phone wasn't supposed to reach you in the garden. It was wrong, all wrong.

'Is it a bit dark for gardening, Dec?'

Bea, it seemed, was wielding his torch as well as the cordless landline.

'Not at all,' he said, peering at the ground and pretending not to have seen the phone.

'You can have the torch,' she said. 'If you take the call.'

She was swinging the torch back and forth by its strap, looped over her little finger.

'Or you can come in for tea,' she said.

'You drive a hard—'

'If you take the call.'

Something in her tone made him look up and forget about his rhubarb.

'I think you'll want to speak to them,' she said, offering him an arm so he could pull himself up. 'They're asking for Freida.'

'Good lord.'

Declan stood up, stretched his back. Thought about what she'd just said.

'Are you sure, love?'

She nodded.

'Good lord.'

He took the phone and held it to his ear. Bea waited, her arm looped through his.

'Good lord,' he said, into the phone. And then, as if realising he was now speaking on the phone for the first time, 'Hello?'

Five minutes later he was driving to collect the crazy Londoners from the lighthouse in his muddy 4x4. He hadn't yet made up his mind whether to be impressed or amused by their walk from the station to the edge of the peninsula, but it showed some determination, he would give them that. It was a short enough drive, he'd be there in fifteen minutes, but by the same token it was a miserable enough walk, at night, with the wind up as it was and the rain all of last week. Boggy, that was the word. He dipped his headlipghts and turned in towards the gate, where he saw the huddle of them emerging from Freida's old bungalow round the back. He wound down a window.

'Evening all,' he called.

'Good evening,' shouted the man, a little louder than he needed to, despite the wind. Big chap. He got in the front seat and held out his hand. 'Piotr Filipek,' he said. 'Thank you for this.'

'No bother,' Declan said with a nod and a shake of his hand.

'I'm Eva,' the younger woman said, climbing into the back seat. 'Yes, thanks.'

'Awful night,' said the older woman, slamming the door with some force.

Eva had short bright red hair, kind of spiky, and piercing eyes – Bea was going to like her. The older one was dressed like Humphrey Bogart. Declan reversed out the way he had come, and put the radio on for a bit of company as he turned back towards the main road.

'I live on the coast, near Edderton,' he said. 'Which you'll not have heard of, I imagine,' he chuckled.

None of them seemed to know what to say.

'But we've got a good view,' he said. 'Me and Bea. We can see right across to the lighthouse. Beautiful at night, you know?'

None of them seemed to know.

'And in the day,' he said.

Thank God the A9 was empty, he thought to himself, putting his foot down and accelerating past seventy. He could have told them about Freida in the car, or before they even set off from the lighthouse, but every time he caught the old woman's eyes in the mirror he knew this wasn't the time. And he was finding it difficult to broach the subject. He didn't like to upset folk, didn't want to be the one to deliver the news. He might never have heard of these people, Freida might never have spoken of them, but they knew her. He was sure of that. And judging by the tense silence in the back of the car, there seemed to be a lot riding on their finding her, even if it was seven years too late.

*

Julianne Quentin arrived home after dark to find a police car parked outside her front door. Her steps slowed. She hoped, as she approached, that they'd start the engine and drive away. But she saw them notice her, the way they sat up straighter as she walked towards them – they were here to see her. She'd knock on their window, ask if they needed her help with something. But before she could the door opened and two uniformed officers stepped out. It had been such a long time since she'd seen the police that they almost looked like they were in fancy dress. But at the same time she knew that they wouldn't be here unless there was a reason.

'Would you like to come in?' she said, keeping her voice calm and authoritative, as she did in every situation she found herself in.

They nodded and thanked her – although they didn't smile – and followed her into the house where she sat them down on the sofa, and took the single chair opposite.

'There's been an accident,' they began. 'I'm so sorry, Mrs Quentin. There's been an accident on the Tube . . .' And somehow it felt like she'd known what they were going to say, as though this had been coming, and she'd been waiting, rehearsing her side of the script. Except that she didn't have any words.

As a young woman, Julianne had spent a long time thinking about what she wanted her life to be. There were ideas there years before she understood the practical realities of them. She loved flying – ever since she was too young to remember, according to her parents – and so she studied the subjects that could bring her closer to flight. She always knew she would work with aeroplanes, and she did.

She always knew she would have a family, too. Though, just as running down a hillside didn't teach her much about the equations of motion, the idea of having a family and the way it was achieved seemed very far apart, when she was little. Perhaps it was the shock that made her determined to understand how everything worked as an adult. She got her PhD in eighteen months, a record for her department. She knew that knowledge meant power.

So although her instinct told her that she never wanted to be pregnant, she spent a long time considering the options. James working at FullLife didn't make it inevitable – she always made up her own mind. She wasn't afraid of childbirth the way some women were; in fact she would have relished the challenge. But the idea of carrying a growing life inside her for nine months just felt wrong. It felt unfair. She wanted to take the best possible care of her baby but she also wanted to work fifty per cent of the time, equally with James. She didn't want to be the only one worrying during pregnancy – she wanted the worry to be equally shared. So it seemed far more sensible for the baby to be safely cocooned outside their bodies, where they could take joint responsibility for its care.

And James was such a gentle kind of man. He loved carrying the pouches. He practically glowed with pleasure when he felt a kick, when the warmth of the pouch was pressed against him and he'd lean down to whisper about how miraculous our understanding of life was. And it had been wonderful, once the children were born, to see how close they were. She wasn't sure if they'd have been so close, had he not carried them in the pouch. FullLife understood, of course, they'd built their company on it.

So they'd both had the careers they'd wanted, and been the kind of parents they'd wanted. After the twins were born she'd been appointed to the board of directors at the airport. James had been offered more supervisory roles, but he turned them down. He just loved working in that lab. He was even more inspired once he was a dad – he used to talk about finding ways for the babies in the pouches to experience all the beauty of the world. Sensory inputs became his main focus. Well, until he was moved into a new lab to study what was going wrong. And he'd lied to her about it. Why did he do that?

Was it because he'd become ashamed?

There was always an uncertainty in him, she thought. He had never been one hundred per cent certain about anything. Well, except their family. But even there, it seemed, he'd had his doubts. She used to find it irritating, the way he would say one thing and then qualify it with the possibility of the opposite also being true. And all those nervous habits, really, for such an intelligent man, what did he have to be so nervous about? But then, she would overhear someone who wasn't nervous, someone who talked without acknowledging the possibility that they could be wrong, and she would feel this sort of . . . what was it, that she was proud of him? That she recognised it was better to doubt yourself than to never doubt at all?

The police officers had stopped talking now and it was strange that although they were in her house, and sitting on her sofa in her living room, she felt like she had to be the one to stand up and leave. She still hadn't spoken, and she didn't want to speak. But there had to be something in life that was certain, and for her it had been James and so she stood up and turned away from the police officers and took a single step away from the table they were seated around, and that was when it hit her. As her right foot landed on the carpeted floor and she felt a splintering inside her chest, even though she kept walking away, her head high and she didn't stop and didn't break down, that was the moment when Julianne Quentin realised that she had loved her husband.

*

A woman with long, curly grey hair and large tortoiseshell-framed glasses opened the door. She looked at Holly. Holly looked back.

'This is Bea,' said Declan, touching her hand. Eva and Piotr walked down the hallway first, and as Holly followed them Bea was by her side.

'You're Holly Bhattacharyya,' she said.

Declan paused, turned to look at Holly, the recognition warming his expression.

'She used to tell us stories about you,' Bea smiled.

Holly knew, from the way Bea spoke, that Freida was dead. She was gone. And it seemed that before she died she had found a place where she could belong, after all.

In the warm living room, with the wood-burning stove crackling in the corner, Holly sat quietly, her knee aching again, as Declan stumbled his way through the bad news. He was doing his best, and he must have been caught off guard by their arrival, after all this time. Seven years ago, did he say? Had she really died seven years ago?

And no one even knew, Holly thought.

But of course, that was wrong. These people knew. The people she had chosen to know. Had Holly done anything so bad, for her best friend to cut her out of her life, so completely? Bea said Freida had told her stories. Holly wasn't sure she wanted to know what they were.

'She did leave some things for you,' he said. 'Well, for anyone who came, I think.'

Holly breathed in, then out.

'So I guess they're for you.'

He was looking at her, not at those other two. Piotr and Eva had been minding their own business. They'd said early on that they had never even met Freida. Piotr had said that. It was good of him. Otherwise they could have been the ones holding this file, and sitting in front of this computer screen. Perhaps, in some way, she wished they were.

'I recorded the video for her,' Declan said. 'She asked me to. And she asked me to keep it here until someone came looking. She didn't say who that would be.'

Then he leaned over Holly's shoulder and selected the final recorded message that Freida had left behind.

Freida's face filled the screen, close up and distorted, a massive nose taking up the bulk of the picture. Her eyes – which appeared very small in comparison to the nose – seemed to be searching left and right, and then what was presumably a hand waved in front of the camera and blocked everything.

'Oh, good heavens!' said Holly as Eva stifled a laugh. She and Piotr had gathered round behind her, to watch.

'Where's the camera?' a voice, now familiar in the way it seemed to boom from electronic devices, asked the room. 'Hello? hello? Is this thing working?'

Declan's voice could be heard, off camera, saying it was right in front of her face.

'Not on top of it,' he said. 'There, there.'

'Oh, right,' said Freida. 'Why didn't you just say so?'

At last, she sat back and realised there was a small square showing her what was being recorded.

'That's me there, is it?' she said.

Off camera, Declan replied that it was.

'Right. Edit that first bit out for me, will you?'

'I can start the recording again?'

'No, no, don't do that. We're here now, let's get on with it. Just edit it out later.'

Holly glanced at Declan, who was standing beside her, watching the video like it was a home recording of a happy family holiday. Smiling, he caught her eye and shrugged to tell her he had no idea how to edit a video.

When Holly turned back to the screen, she finally saw her friend. She saw Freida, and recognised her as the woman she had once been. Older, yes. Much older. Her skin was red and patchy, from the wind out here. But those dark eyes, staring defiantly into the camera, were the same. Holly nodded, in greeting, and almost reached out a hand to touch her face.

Video log

24 August 2017 16:12

There was a reason, you know, why I went for an audio log before.
Who wants to see my face, really? No one. And besides, my face has
nothing at all to do with it. But I suppose it'll prove that I am, in
fact, alive. Well, that I was alive when I recorded this. The last time
I made an audio log I think . . . When was it?

. . . That's right, last year.

Last year I had my stroke.

Horrible feeling, it was. Creepy. Felt like I was turning
into a ghost, the way my arm seemed to disappear, and then
everything was spinning and I couldn't make sense of things,
couldn't order my thoughts. And then I really did think I was a
ghost for a while, slipped down off my chair and seeing the
room from the floor like that, and next thing I know I'm in a
hospital. Never wanted to end up in a hospital, but then nobody
does, I suppose. And sitting beside my bed – no, not at first, at first
there was no one and then the nurse who came when I started
pressing every buzzer I could find – but after that, sitting by my
bed and asking me how I felt, was the Asda man. It was such a
shock!

And now he's standing there listening to me. Can you see him
in the video? He wants to hear his name recorded for posterity, I
expect. Is that right?

I can leave, if you—

No, no, don't go. You know I'm only joking. You've a right to hear this as much as anyone. More so, actually. You saved my life.

After they let me out of the hospital – and gave me the bill, of course – I went back to my lighthouse. My Asda man dropped me home with some fresh milk and all those pills the doctors gave me. I managed on my own for a few weeks, though, before I realised I wasn't managing at all. Couldn't really walk, you know. Couldn't get out to the black rocks. Couldn't lift the kettle. Silly things like that. And he came round, after every shift, wanting to check – he said – just checking in. Sometimes offering me the spare room that they'd made in the garage for Bea's dad, before he'd passed away. I said no to that, at first, and no, and thank you but no, then one day I said yes. Finally I learned to appreciate the people who were actually there, in my life.

There were flowers in the room when I arrived, you know. Daffodils, just on the cusp of opening.

But there are other reasons why I'm making this recording. There's some information that I'd like to pass on, should anyone come looking for me. I've made a folder, and if I die then Declan will look after it until you arrive. Perhaps this is my last chance to explain.

I was fighting with FullLife because of the risk the pouch poses to women. All women. It's not really about the technology, or the pouch. It is about society. No one wanted to hear what I had to say before. I can't blame them – the benefits were so great they seemed to outweigh the risk. But sooner or later, people will want to hear. And maybe, once I'm dead, you'll be ready to forgive me. So, in the folder I've put the details of all the cases I know of. You'll be familiar with some of them already, I expect. They show the pouch being used by men to control women.

Imagine the kind of people who believe a woman's only role is to reproduce. What are women worth to them now? Imagine men

who used to run businesses, newspapers, even countries
unchallenged. Imagine them losing their jobs to women. Their
sense of importance. Their version of the world. They have been
staying quiet, but they are not gone. FullLife pushed them aside,
with influence, with popular opinion, with money, but that was
never going to last. We wanted to pretend we'd solved all our
problems, but all we did was make them harder to see. There is
resentment bubbling. I can feel it. And I still believe now what I
believed then: some people should not be allowed to carry a pouch.

But despite that, I still believe in science. I believe in its power to
change the world for the better, as long as our ethics can keep up
with our invention. We are responsible for what we create.

And that reminds me. There's something else. I'm ashamed of
what I did, but it was such a long time ago . . . When I was working
with mice at the university, I found a small risk of fatality towards
the end of term. It wasn't there at all to begin with, but it started
to appear after two or three generations. Then it stabilised. It was
unrelated to any previous illness – there were no signs anything
was wrong. And the same two mice could go on to have perfectly
healthy offspring. So I knew it wasn't infertility, or any kind of
inherited inability to reproduce or survive to term. But it was a
risk, a small statistical risk of unexplained fatality . . . and I wasn't
completely honest in the way I presented my data. I thought it was
just a mistake I was making, in my experimental procedures and
so . . . I only published my results from the healthy births, talked
of error bars arising from our equipment and our interpretation.
But I never admitted that I'd seen a mouse die during the birthing
process for no reason that I could explain. You see, the results were
so exciting. People were listening to me! I was going to change the
way we lived! We moved on to primates, built a huge research
group, everyone wanted to be involved; my invention was encased
in a private company as quickly as possible.

At first it was wonderful. I pushed aside any doubts I'd had. After all, we'd assembled the best team of scientists in the country, perhaps in the world! The technology worked without fail for the primates, and we moved on to human trials. The university was out – this was FullLife now. Sylvia was in charge.

Then things started to change.

I thought we were making the pouch available to the general public too soon. I thought we needed to slow down our expansion, have a more robust vetting process before deciding which parents could use a pouch. But FullLife had no intention of slowing down. I was pushed out. They threatened me, you see, with my early research. Said they would discredit me if I spoke out against them. That was one of the reasons I left. But it wasn't until years later that I started to think . . . to wonder how much Sylvia was hiding . . . to suspect that humans might develop a small risk of fatality towards the end of term as well. Maybe my mice weren't an aberration caused by my mistakes at all. I'd always told myself that my methods must have been flawed – but perhaps it was the opposite. Perhaps my results were showing a fundamental truth.

Anyway, FullLife didn't tell anyone about my earlier work, even though they had all the data. Their research teams published outstanding success rates and their advertising implied certain guarantees . . . They claimed perfection. Scientists should have known better. And so should I. So in the folder I've put my original data about the number of stillbirths in mice, and extrapolated that to primates and humans. Like everything in our world, technology is not perfect. Sometimes things go wrong during natural birth, and maybe one day something will go wrong during pouch birth as well. I think perhaps it is nature's way of evening the playing field. We don't get to create perfection. Sooner or later, we'll find the cure for everything – cancer and heart disease and meningitis and HIV – but in their place something new will arise, because we are living creatures and we cannot beat death.

I could be wrong. It might never happen. I hope it will never happen. But with all this information combined, you should be able to make FullLife look pretty bad, if you want, and me along with them. I guess I've not been very responsible, but I'm telling you everything now, and you can use it in any way that you choose. No one would have believed me anyway – one rogue inventor against their teams of scientists? But I am passing my suspicions on, and I'm an old woman, and I think it is the best I can do.

Besides, society does seem to have got better, over the past fifty years. My invention has brought about some change. Maybe I did well. Maybe I did something good. Or, something that was complicated, but that had the potential to be good. So that's what I wanted to tell you.

That, and the fact that I've decided that not everything has to be a fight any more. Not for me, anyway – I have finished with fighting. Despite what's in that folder, perhaps there is more hope for humanity than I used to think.

I had to say goodbye to my beautiful indigo hamlets. That's OK, though. I have something better now. It seems that I prefer not to live entirely without other people, after all.

But I wouldn't want you to make the mistake of thinking this is a happy ending. The nights are dark here, and the wind is vicious out to sea. Sometimes, when storms are wild enough, I find myself out beyond the lighthouse again . . . scrambling over the brittle rocks and knowing the feel of a twisted ankle, a knee cracking into stone. I find myself standing at the unapologetic end of this fractured piece of land, and at the same time I am standing in a room, in a basement, with dark wood all around. I can smell chemicals in the sea salt and hear men singing hymns beneath the resonating hum of the wind.

My hand is held out. I see it there. I feel it aching in the cold, but it lingers, neither reaching nor falling. I do not care that splashes of icy water are numbing my knuckles, or that the longer I hesitate the ruder I might appear. Because my hesitation is more important than my joints or my reputation. My hesitation is everything.

I still don't know if I did the right thing.

A different kind of life could have been equally worthwhile, I believe. And equally compromised.

But I want you to know that is where I'll be – that is where my mind will be – on the day that I die. I will be standing on the fractured black rocks beside the crashing waves of the Tarbat Ness Peninsula, and at the same time I will be standing in that office among the deep wooden shelves facing my undetermined future. My hand will be held out in front of me and I will still be standing there, with my indecision.

Chapter 18

HOLLY STARED AT THE SCREEN long after Freida had stopped talking. Stopped telling them about her doubts, about her uncertainty. Her concerns, which were justified. Her compassion, which was just barely implied.

And not about her pride, she didn't mention that – though Holly could hear it between the lines – how it can change you, to feel like you're not needed any more. How impossible Freida found it to admit her own mistakes. But she was also saying the risk was not about infertility, it was not something being inherited. Was that right? She seemed to be saying it was arbitrary, it was . . .

Had she got that right?

'Play it again,' Holly said, trying and failing to keep her voice calm. 'Can we play it over again?'

And yes, Freida was saying that there might be a risk, but it was *not* a genetic inability to have children. They'd been jumping to the wrong conclusion, they must have been. There was a better explanation. The answer was there, in her research on mice, and in that folder she was holding – the mice weren't becoming unable to reproduce, they could still have perfectly healthy offspring. And Freida said the same could apply to people. Her research from over fifty years ago explained what they'd been seeing, and explained it better than any of their fears had. There was no reason to think there was anything biologically the matter with Rosie, with Kaz . . . The pouch hadn't done any permanent damage. It wasn't a perfect technology that had harmed humanity. It was an imperfect technology that carried a natural risk.

'Oh, thank God,' she said, her hand flying to her mouth as Eva gently touched her shoulder.

'Has, erm . . .' Declan spoke quietly. 'Has something happened? To bring you here, I mean.'

Holly nodded.

'To do with pouch abuse?'

'No,' she said. 'No, not that.'

He looked confused, or perhaps concerned, but she didn't explain. He'd hear about what had happened soon enough, one way or another. She wasn't ready to talk about baby Will.

'Can I watch it one more time?' she asked, afraid that she might cry.

But she didn't cry. Instead she listened to Freida talking about her life, here. How she had grown old and left her lighthouse, found a new friend, and allowed herself to stop struggling. Gradually, it sank in that everything might be OK.

Looking through Freida's files later that evening, it dawned on Holly that she was grateful. Freida had left her exactly what she needed. She hadn't told the truth about her research, all those years ago – and she bloody well should have – but by leaving, she hadn't made things any different to what they would have been anyway. The risk was always going to be there. But, once it was acknowledged, it was a risk that people could choose to take, if they wanted to.

It was not a new form of infertility. Holly felt herself lighten, as her fear lifted further from her shoulders.

It was just a risk.

It meant, Holly thought, that Rosie and Kaz could try again.

It meant that her own life was not built around something that was broken. Just something that was imperfect.

She could live with that. She'd never wanted to be perfect, anyway. She'd just wanted to be brave.

'I've made up a bed in the spare room,' Declan said, looking from Holly to the others. 'It's just a single.'

'Oh no, it's . . .'

'We're, no, just . . .'

Eva and Piotr spoke over each other, then thankfully shut up.

'That would be ideal, thank you,' Holly said, calmly standing up. Eva looked lost, and Holly could think of only one thing to offer her. 'Here,' she said. 'You can have the file, if you want. You can tell everyone the truth. All of it.'

Eva took the file from her outstretched hand.

'But what then?' she said. 'People depend on the pouch. FullLife own the patent. How can we really hold them to account, when they have a monopoly?'

'Actually,' said Holly, pausing in the doorway, 'they don't own the patent. They were guaranteed exclusive rights for the first twenty years, and now they lease it from me.'

Eva stared at her.

'I didn't want it to get into the wrong set of hands,' she said. 'But maybe . . . perhaps just one set of hands is always going to be the wrong set.'

Declan was already pulling the coffee table out of the way. 'You two can get a sofa each,' he said. 'I'll grab some sleeping bags.' He looked over at Holly, then back at them. 'I'll give you a lift to the station tomorrow,' he said. 'I guess you'll be wanting to head home.'

But as he approached the door, Holly reached out and caught his arm. 'Where is Freida buried?' she said. 'I mean, is she . . . ?'

'Oh, aye,' he said. 'She's buried out in the Edderton church. I can take you there, if you like. Before the train?'

Holly nodded. 'I'd like that, yes,' she said. 'I'd like to say goodbye.'

'In the morning then,' he said quietly.

Holly smiled. 'In the morning. Thank you, Declan Ross.'

*

That night, the director of FullLife left her office late, and took the mirrored lift down to the front entrance that she always used. They'd done a good job of clearing up the glass. The new panel looked pristine, you'd think there was nothing there at all, except for the stillness of the air inside.

As she approached the turning doors, she thought she saw some movement outside, but it was so dark she couldn't really tell. It was probably just some of the other staff leaving work late. She was trying to look calm, even though there was no one in the lobby to see her, but it was an act. She hadn't been able to settle to anything all afternoon, her worry seeping into every task she attempted. Karl's anger, Cris's pain – they had every right to be upset. A baby had died, in her care; that was how she saw it. Every time she thought about it, she wanted to curl up into herself.

Why was it happening now? If she'd known before, she would never have accepted the job in the first place. She didn't want to have to cope with this. She didn't know how. She was going to have to write some kind of press statement, some kind of public apology. She'd hoped so desperately that they'd find the problem, fix the pouches, and be able to tell people everything was OK. But it wasn't OK, and they hadn't fixed anything. And now the care homes were running out of money. Someone had to take responsibility. The government was refusing to help – they'd made health care private for a reason. FullLife were about to lose public faith in the pouch when they most needed their support. She didn't know what to do.

She was walking through the lobby, looking out at the darkness towards the river, when the voices outside started getting louder. She stopped still. There was increased movement too, people pressing closer towards the doors, and there were flickering lights, low down on the concourse in front of the building. What was going on? She almost turned away, almost went for the back door that only the staff used. But no – she had walked through the rotating front doors every day that she'd worked here, and she wasn't going to stop now. The doors slowly began to turn as she stepped towards them, the voices got louder as the air got colder, and though she instinctively wanted to hold her arms up to protect herself from the crowd, she did exactly the oppo-site. She held her head high and stepped out of the building.

'What are you doing here?' She hoped there was authority in her tone.

'It's her,' a voice shouted from near the front of the group, and they began surging forwards, all of them, women and men, teenag-ers, City workers, people in jeans and suits and dresses, with banners and signs and—

'Why has the pouch gone wrong?'

'What happened to—'

'Have you been lying?'

Some of them looked like journalists, some students, phones thrust forward to record her reply over the shouts. There were cam-eras too, held up to video the scene.

'Step back,' she said, using her calmest voice, her most soothing voice. 'Please, you need to let me pass now.'

She'd been pushed beyond the doors; behind her was the fresh panel of glass – there was nowhere to go but forwards through the crowd. More people were arriving all the time, she could see a group crossing the bridge and heading her way.

'You have to answer our questions.'

It was a young woman, touching her arm, her phone held up.

'You can make an appoint—'

'I tried that already. This afternoon, after the crash. Your secur-ity wouldn't let me in.'

'But there's no secur . . .'

The car, the smashed glass – she had called in security today.

'They wouldn't let any of us in!'

'I'm . . . There's nothing I can say right now.'

The director tried to push her way through the crowd, but every time she moved more bodies pressed into her, their questions shouted above the ruckus, all of their eyes staring at her, demanding answers she didn't have.

'Let me through.'

Her arms were up now, trying to protect her face as she made her way forwards. And then someone grabbed her. They grabbed her hand away from her face, and held it, and tried to pull her closer, and she was going to have to defend herself, to push them away and run and—

'Please,' a voice said.

She looked up and saw a young man, mid-twenties maybe, carrying a pouch. He shouldn't be here, she thought. It's not safe, in this crowd, anything could . . .

'Please,' he said again. 'Is our baby at risk?'

Suddenly her eyes were stinging.

'I don't know,' she said. 'I don't know. I'm sorry . . .'

And then she was beyond the crowd, the winter chill fresh on her face. She could breathe again. If she was quick – though she didn't want to run, that might make them want to follow – and if she stayed calm then she could get over the road. What were those other voices? Not the shouts, not the questions. She stopped, suddenly recognising what she could hear. There was singing. She turned round. By the front of the building people had been placing flowers. Someone had hand-painted a sign that read 'Will Bhattacharyya'. There were teddy bears and roses and bouquets piled up outside the birthing centre and people were sitting in a circle on the ground, candles flickering beside them. Singing.

The crowd weren't following her. Some of them were watching, or talking among themselves, a few describing what had happened into the phone cameras held out in front of them. It was windy; she was suddenly aware of the cold, of her hair blowing into her eyes. A van with a TV crew pulled up alongside the building, but the director didn't want to speak to them. She had no idea what she could possibly say.

Instead, she walked towards the group of people sitting by the flowers. To her surprise, a couple of them moved over to give her space.

'Thank you,' she said.

The building was providing some shelter – the candles flickered but remained alight.

She sat down on the ground, and joined their circle.

*

Eva tiptoed to the back door in her socked feet, pulling her coat from the stand in the hallway and picking up her ankle boots from the busy row of mats on the floor. The rest of the house was still sleeping but she'd been up as soon as the sky lightened. Careful not to wake Piotr on the sofa by the fire, she'd peeked out of the curtains and seen the world in the crisp white of an undisturbed night of snowfall.

She opened the back door and welcomed the pure air into her lungs, inhaling deeply and enjoying the sting of it on her teeth, the newness of such a clean cold spreading through her body. It would have been easy, looking at the sky directly overhead, to think it was a grey day, to think rain would soon pour from the textured layers of cloud, but that was only if you didn't look down. Near the horizon – which from Declan's back garden was beyond an expanse of water that reflected the hazy snow-covered hills in the distance – the clouds thinned out, became wisps and ribbons that let the golden light through.

Reading the file last night, she had seen it immediately – and she'd known that Piotr had seen it too, from the way his breath fell from his lips. Freida predicted that, after the first few generations, approximately 1 in 200 pouch pregnancies could end in some form of late-term miscarriage. It was the same. The statistics were the same. For the pouch as for natural birth. Piotr had shouted those statistics at her once, and in the weeks, the months and years afterwards, she tortured herself with them. She had blamed herself, for a long time, for choosing the risk of nature over the safety of science.

But now she'd seen the proof. The risks were the same.

It was almost difficult, letting go of that blame. But this morning that was what she was going to do.

As she walked further into the garden her footsteps left the only marks that were on the snow-covered lawn, each one sinking several inches through to reveal the promise of fresh green grass. She held her arms wide, closed her eyes and tilted her head back so that the whole world became the expanse of air, the silence of dawn in the Highlands. She turned like that, eyes still closed, not spinning as she would have done as a child, but taking her time to turn in a deliberate circle, with the touch of ice on her face.

When she opened her eyes, she saw Holly at the window. She raised an arm in a stationary wave, and Holly did the same.

The clouds near the horizon were edged in silver and copper now, revealing the sun as a globe of light, magical in the haze of snow about to fall. As Eva walked back to the house, her return footsteps followed beside her outgoing ones, making it look as though two people had walked together, one striding straight ahead, and the other moving slowly backwards, eyes fixed on where she had been.

When she got to the door, Piotr opened it for her. He was dishevelled, like he'd just woken up and come to find her. He was watching her as though she was everything in the world.

There was snow on her shoes. In her hair.

She looked at him; she looked at him and she didn't look away.

Tentatively, he reached out and stroked her cheek.

His hand was warm. She felt her body exhale.

They stood there as the snow fell.

*

Holly had woken with the feeling that she would be the next person to die. It wasn't a gloomy thought – she'd never needed sympathy. But as she slept it had sunk in, deeply, that there was no one left in the generation above her. Freida was dead. Her mum was dead. And her dad – he'd been the first to go, from a stroke. The same thing that had killed Freida, in the end.

She could remember standing outside the hospital doors, letting the summer sun warm her shoulders, before she plucked up the courage to step inside. She was just twenty years old. She was not a mother yet, or a grandmother. But she was, and always would be, a daughter. She hadn't spoken to her father in over a year.

She had written the number of the ward, and directions to reach it, on the back of an envelope. It was the first thing she'd grabbed when her mum phoned. It was the practicalities she'd focused on: Is he stable? Where is he? Can I come today? Just like it was the practicalities she focused on as she navigated the twisting hospital corridors that smelled of antiseptic. Every T-junction had a sign. That was useful. The floor tiles squeaked underneath her shoes.

She knocked on the door of the ward, even though it was open.

Her mum had told her that the stroke had paralysed the left side of his body, that he could only open one eye, and that he dribbled. She'd said she wanted her to be prepared. Holly was grateful for that. But her mum had gone home to get some rest. Holly was here on her own, to see her father, to make things right, if she could.

She had finally told her parents about meeting Freida. About what she was working on.

They had been disgusted. They'd argued, again. She hadn't been surprised. No one had won. Holly hadn't been home since. It had been terrifyingly easy, to choose Freida over her parents.

She pulled a chair close to the bed, took her father's hand. It was clammy, frail.

'Dad,' she said. 'It's me. Holly.'

He turned towards her, and she saw what must have been a smile twist his lips. Her mum had been right about the drooling. She couldn't lean forwards and mop it up though – she couldn't be the one to make her dad feel as though he needed help. So instead, she started talking to him as if there was nothing wrong – as if they were sitting on the old concrete patio and the aeroplanes overhead were drowning out the birdsong.

She didn't think about what she was going to say. She just wanted to be the same way she'd always been with him, because that would have meant he was all right. That he was still strong, argumentative, stubborn. Old-fashioned. A little domineering, even. She could handle that. She could handle arguing with her dad. So she started talking and didn't think about what would happen next.

'I'm going to university, Dad,' she said. 'Paying my own way.'

He was watching her, so she continued.

'I've got a scholarship, through Freida. Remember, I told you about Freida?'

Her dad reached down and pressed the button on the side of his bed that slowly raised his head. Holly watched as his face became level with hers, and held his hand gently over the bedclothes. His skin looked older, weathered, wrinkled around the neck and joints. She could see a blue pulse in the back of his hand.

'And what . . .' he said.

'I'll be studying psychology,' she smiled.

He let out a fast breath that could have been disapproval, but she decided to assume it meant the opposite.

'So you'll have to get better. You need to come to my graduation in three years' time.' She didn't mention what she'd be doing after that.

'And what will this scholarship cost you?' he said.

She knew it was his way. Suspect, question – but just for once it would have been nice if he could have been pleased for her, first.

She had no intention of hiding, though.

'I've agreed to take part in the first trial,' she said, sitting up straighter. 'The last few years have been revolutionary, Dad. I'm donating my eggs for use in the first baby pouch.' She knew she should stop talking but she didn't. 'We're going to change the world, me and Freida,' she said, her voice getting louder now. 'This inequality can't last. I can't live with it. So we've found a way to change things.'

'She's changing things,' he said. 'You'll be a medical trial.'

'I think that's a rather negative—'

'Don't, Holly,' he said. 'Please . . .' He sounded weak, but she didn't want to compromise, not now. Wasn't that what women had been doing for centuries? Putting up with it, out of obligation, or kindness. 'Don't,' he said. 'You're being . . . this is . . . *silly*.'

She pushed her chair back.

'It's not, Dad. Not in the slightest. And I'm going to university. That's right – just like my brother. Except I've found a way myself, since you didn't think I was worth it.'

Did he cringe, when she said that?

'And I'm going to have a child. But I'm doing it as an equal. And you – you were wrong. When you said boys and girls were different, when you tried to prove it was right to treat us differently. You didn't even know how to interpret the behaviour of children, let alone adults. But I do. I'm fixing the problem.'

'I . . . try to . . .'

She couldn't hear his words, and suddenly her outburst seemed childish, arrogant. She leaned forwards, the word sorry resting behind her lips. The side of his chin was slimy, glistening in the bright light streaming in between the slats of the blind.

'You don't have to talk, Dad,' she said. 'I know you don't agree with what I'm doing, but it's my choice, isn't it?'

She thought his body was convulsing, or was he turning away from her?

'. . . No, I . . .'

'Yes it is, Dad. It's my choice.'

If he was in pain she wanted to help him. She looked around for a nurse but saw only an emergency cord and it seemed melodramatic to pull on that. There was no emergency here. Just a heartbreaking decline.

He was shaking his head again, moving in one direction and letting it flop back against the pillow. She gently touched his forehead. She didn't want him to strain his neck.

'We . . . try . . .' he said.

'It's OK.' Holly shook her head now. 'I always knew I was lov—'

He pulled her hand, hard, and she stopped talking. Her words were making him uncomfortable. They never were a family for spoken affection.

'We tried,' he said, his voice stronger.

Holly frowned.

'We tried to be fair,' he said. 'To let you choose.'

He let out a sigh that made the effort of speaking suddenly unbearably clear to her, and at the same time she saw it – the hurt, in his eyes.

'You were,' she found herself saying. 'You were always . . . I always felt I could speak up,' she said, 'and I always . . .'

His smile was tired now, resigned, and his right eye, which had been open, connecting with hers, closed over.

'It's OK, really, you were . . . wanting me to get married and . . .

and not sending me to university . . . that stuff doesn't matter now.' Though it did, it mattered to her. She reached for his hand. 'You were a wonderful father.' And a man of his time, she thought, but didn't say. It is true of us all, sooner or later, whether we like it or not.

'It's OK,' she said. 'I love you, Dad.' And she kept clutching his hand as the room dissolved.

*

Freida had a whole row to herself in the small graveyard that was boarded by a drystone wall and dusted with snow. Beyond the wall a field of sheep led gently down to the water's edge, the oranges and browns of the rocks appearing and disappearing like miniature islands in the lapping waves. Pointing her gravestone out to them, Declan said that the new graves would join her one day – they were filling the rows in order.

'But I asked them to put her out there to stand on her own for a bit,' he said. 'I thought she'd like that.'

'Yes, I think she probably does,' Eva said.

He left them alone then, walking to another grave closer to the church, where he laid a waterproof sheet on the ground and sat down. She could see his big green wellies sticking out to the side of what she assumed was his parents' grave. We have all lost someone, she thought.

The church was a small white chapel with a grey-tiled roof and in front of it were graves that looked centuries old, with large cross-shaped stones and engravings so faded she couldn't make out the names. She realised she was alone, that Holly and Piotr were walk-ing towards Freida, and for some reason she thought she ought to be walking in between them. So she followed their path, feeling a new flurry of snow falling on her hair, on her neck. It was cold, but not unwelcome.

Standing at the graveside, Holly was looking at the neat stone decorated with white and purple flowers and three golden baubles. She seemed tiny, standing there, and her head was low. Eva suddenly felt like a giant, conscious of her own strength. Poor Holly. She was just one person, who was trying her best – as they all had been. Gently, Eva reached out and rested her arm around Holly's shoulders. Holly didn't respond, but she didn't pull away either, and Eva took that to mean she had done the right thing.

Piotr nodded at her, just slightly. She had been wrong before, when she'd thought he was diminished. He had simply learned to hesitate. To Eva, at that moment, he seemed far stronger for it. He reached into his jacket pocket, and pulled out the photos she had given him. On the top, their ultrasound. Perhaps it was a good moment to stand together in a graveyard and remember.

But it wasn't the photos he was looking at. He'd had them wrapped in something – a letter. It was one of her mum's old letters of support. He read it. Looked up at her. Quietly, he handed it to her.

Avigail, I am asking you to visit me.

Eva looked up at Piotr, but she already knew what he had just worked out.

It has been a long time and I know you are angry. But I'm asking you to put that aside, if you can, and visit me. There is so much I'd like to tell you. But I will not come knocking on your door. You made your feelings very clear the last time I did that.

It is very beautiful here. I'd like to show you.

The letter had not been signed, but Eva understood. It was from Freida, to her daughter. She knew what that meant. Perhaps she'd known all along. She heard herself breathing as she held the letter. She wanted to be angry with her mum for keeping her family hidden, but she couldn't do that, it was far too late. It wasn't a rival they'd come to confront, on that visit to the lighthouse when she was a child. It was her grandmother.

But why hadn't she opened the door?

Perhaps she was down at the black rocks. The coast that she loved so much.

Eva realised she was holding all the answers she had been searching for. She had found her family, in this graveyard in Edderton, and she had found a way to fight FullLife as well. In the folder she was carrying, she had proof enough for a major court case and a public scandal. But she still wasn't quite sure what she was trying to achieve.

She'd been telling the truth yesterday, when she'd told Holly that people were dependent on the pouch. People had been helped by it, too. And standing here at her grandmother's grave, finally knowing the woman who had invented the pouch, she recognised what she owed it. Eva was alive because of the pouch. Her grandmother, though she had never met her, had invented the technology that had saved her life.

Eva wasn't aware that she was crying, not until she tried to read the words on Freida's gravestone and found that she could not. Everything was blurred; the snow and the sky, the mountains and the clearest water she had ever seen. Piotr stepped forward and reached out his arm, gently placing it around her shoulders, just like her own arm was still resting around Holly's. That was how they stood, the three of them, in front of Freida's grave.

Chapter 19

ALL THE WEBSITES CARRIED NEWS of the protest, and of the tragedy of Will Bhattacharyya. Holly went home to her family, Eva got straight back to work, and Piotr published an article about FullLife's misguided privacy policy – and Freida's prediction of the risk of fatality. Suddenly journalists from all over the country were digging deeper. It was like they'd been waiting for permission to speak and now they were speaking, on every topic, from every point of view:

Vigil Continues; Fears Over Pouch Safety; Bhattacharyya Family Thank Public For Support; Care Home Closure; Fatal Used Pouches; Biological Class Divide.

They had interviews with families who couldn't afford the Full-Life plans, and interviews with the other parents who had lost their babies over the past three years.

Piotr published photos from the care homes outside London; dozens of children, toddlers to teenagers, crammed into huge dormitories. One reporter had figures – though it wasn't clear where she'd got them – of higher instances of Down's syndrome, cystic fibrosis and haemochromatosis in the homes than in the general population. The care pouches were used of course, the oldest on the market. Were they getting the same screening and health care? Were they becoming faulty with overuse?

One by one the FullLife board members resigned as memos were leaked and more documents appeared proving the cover-up. The way they had panicked after the first pouch death, the scale of research funding hidden in the accounts, even minutes of the meeting where they decided to offer natural birth as an alternative, just in case. For three years they'd tried to keep the growing risk of pouch death away from the public, and the addition of the NaturalBirth plan to their portfolio showed just how calculating they had been – they were trying to retain customers by putting an alternative in place before announcing the truth about the pouches. Four legal cases were pending, though it was widely assumed they would settle out of court. Piotr suspected more cases would quickly follow.

So far as he had been able to find out, none of the current board members had known there were similar problems with the earliest pre-clinical mouse trials. The founder of the company, Sylvia Ash, was the only one who had known – and it seemed she'd even destroyed Freida's research in her determination to make the pouch seem perfect. She was the one who should have been prosecuted. But she had been dead for twenty years. He and Eva focused on making sure everyone knew the truth, understood the risks; and that they understood the risks were the same as with natural birth, too. There was no safer alternative here. The pouch was not to blame.

The director herself was the last to resign, though given her lack of public comment and continued support of the protesters it had seemed inevitable. Her statement said she valued every second she had spent at FullLife, but that she was not the right woman to lead the company forwards. Details of the break-ins came out too, including the one from a few weeks ago. All that had been stolen from FullLife was a box of red fleece pouch covers. Piotr thought it was probably poor parents who'd just wanted their pouch to look festive for Christmas. But he also wondered what else the police might be keeping hidden.

Eva had given interview after interview – denying Piotr's request for a never-ending exclusive – talking about everything from the risks of abuse to the long-term effects on human fertility. She questioned the accessories, the optional extras, the paid-for extras. But she made it clear that she thought that the pouch should remain available to the people who needed it. And to the people who chose it.

Together, Holly and Piotr had written the announcement about cancelling FullLife's exclusive lease of the baby pouch patent. From now on, the design would be available for free to any and all registered hospitals. It wasn't clear yet how any other hospitals would be able to afford to make it, but at least now they had a chance – and FullLife knew their monopoly was not going to last.

Then, on the day the director issued her resignation, Eva got a phone call. She told Piotr it was one of the strangest phone calls of her life. She was being invited to FullLife. They'd all expected that FullLife might want to talk to them; they were talking to everyone who had ever disagreed with them at the moment, trying to rebuild their image. But FullLife must have been more frightened than Piotr, or Holly, or Eva had realised. Or perhaps they genuinely wanted to make things better. Either way, they were inviting Eva in for more than advice.

*

Rosie wasn't sure if she liked the idea. But she had to think about it – really think about it – after everything that had happened. It was just so *different* from how she'd imagined things would be. But then she didn't think she'd want to go through it the same way again. She closed her eyes and tried to picture it, to feel it, the movement and the weight and the closeness. A baby inside her body. Sometimes you could feel their little hand, their curled fist, between your ribs. She'd read that yesterday. Was that beautiful or was it gross? She didn't know. And there'd be no such thing as a break from it, if she didn't like the feeling. But then, there was no such thing as a break from being a parent, was there? And perhaps she would love the feeling of being pregnant. Perhaps it would be beautiful.

She'd sent Kaz a text message the day after she'd told him to leave her alone, after he'd inexplicably chopped up their tree and she'd angrily ripped up her book of designs. *I didn't mean it*, she'd written. *I love you. Come home?*

He'd arrived back from his dads' house with red eyes and a potted plant, of all things.

'It's a hazel tree,' he'd said, holding it out to her on the doorstep as though he doubted being invited in. 'I thought that, maybe . . . Well, maybe once it's a bit bigger we could plant it in the garden, for Will.'

She'd pulled him into her arms, mumbled yes through her tears. He'd come back, and that was what she'd needed. They'd been inseparable since.

She knew Kaz would be a wonderful father, however they decided to try next time. She had no doubt of the equality between them. But that was what the pouch had achieved, wasn't it? Without that, she wouldn't be considering what she was considering. Could she do it, though – did she really have the strength to do it? She'd have to go through labour. She didn't know how much pain she could take.

She'd been reading a lot, these past few weeks. They both had. Watching videos together, too. Absorbing different points of view. She'd heard her mum and nana talk so often about the pouch, but she hadn't heard anyone really talking about the alternative. And now she wanted to. There was a woman in the States, a midwife for natural birth, who said that the key to a happy delivery was laughter. That we shouldn't fear it, we should laugh through it. Her smile was so warm it was hard not to wish to share her views – Ina May, with her long grey hair and her kind voice. Rosie had memorised what she said, she thought it was so good. 'It's very easy to scare women about childbirth,' she said. 'But it's not very nice. It's bad manners. So let's not do it.' Was that what FullLife had been doing, quietly, subconsciously, for three generations?

Rosie didn't want to be afraid. She didn't want any woman to feel afraid.

She looked up at Kaz. His face was soft, hopeful – like when they had first talked about having baby Will. She placed her hands on her belly and imagined the shape there, and suddenly Kaz was kneeling down by the side of the bed and doing the same. With their hands, they made the shape of Rosie's pregnant belly. Kaz blew it an air kiss. He looked quite ridiculous, she thought, and then she smiled. But it didn't feel right – not yet. She needed more time. She pulled Kaz up to sit next to her on the bed and she hadn't really meant to do it, but she found that her hands now made the shape of the pouch around his belly. He was doing the same. He was holding his belly, where he had carried Will, his arms wrapped around himself, and he was rocking, silently, on the bed.

'I know,' she said. 'I know.' And then they were both crying, crying for their lost baby. They curled around each other on the bed and they cried.

*

When Holly thought about Will, it was mostly his laughter that she remembered. She had laughed with Will. They had laughed so often and so much. You had to, with three kids under the age of ten. She could still see him now, Aarav held under his arm as he scrambled to climb up on his back, the girls playing their version of crawl-football between his legs, and he would be cheering them on with Leigh grabbing onto his knees and Daphne – always Daphne – being the one to say, stop now, everyone, I think Daddy needs a sit-down. Hands on hips. She was in charge, even then, her confident eldest child. The baby who changed it all.

They'd laughed the next time Will had asked her to marry him too, so many years after his first proposal that had been met with absolutely not and a kiss and a lifetime spent as partners. They were both in their fifties then, Leigh already in Delhi and Aarav had just moved down to Brighton, and they were alone in their house for the first time, acknowledging that no one else was coming home any time soon.

'What are we going to do now?' she said. Although by that point she was two years into her five-year research grant and Will was writing a book, which he never did finish. He loved writing it, though. It was the kind of memoir no one would ever want to read but them. In reply to her question he got down on one knee and asked her: 'Will you, Holly Bhattacharyya, be the next Mrs William Bold?'

And she'd said, 'Yes, yes, I believe I will, but I have just one question. No, two questions. Who is William Bold, and where do I find him?'

'It's my name, woman,' he said. 'My name is William Bold.'

'But they always call you Will Bhattacharyya,' she said. 'What a funny thing. How confused the world must be.'

'Never mind the world,' he said. 'Will you marry me?'

'I can't see the point in marrying you,' she said. 'And now I think about it, I don't really want to be a wife.'

'That's a good point,' he replied. 'Now I think about it, I don't really want to be a husband.'

'Let's stay who we are then,' she said.

'Yes, let's. But we should have a ceremony.'

'There's no one here to attend.'

'There's you, and there's me,' he said. 'I'm happy with that.'

And so was she, Holly had said, and she'd thought it very often since, too. There was nothing more that she could have had. Nothing more that she wanted. She was so content that she'd never really questioned the decisions she'd made, until now. How could they have been wrong, when they had brought her so much happiness?

'Are you OK, Mum?' Daphne asked, sitting down beside her. It was unusual for neither of them to select the armchair closest to the fire, with its cushions and its solitary comfort – unusual but nice, to be sitting next to each other like this.

'I was just thinking that my part in this story is all a little false.'

'What do you mean?'

'I mean that perhaps I made no difference at all,' Holly said. 'Perhaps I am just an irrelevant old woman who was once in the right place at the right time. Or the wrong place at the wrong time.'

'To me it looks like you made a huge difference, Mum.'

Holly smiled but she didn't agree – there were plenty more women ready to do what she had done. They would all have done it in their own way, and their own stories would have played out, and sooner or later someone would have snapped after losing a child and someone would have found Freida's files and the risks would have come out and the world would be exactly where it was. Though she wouldn't have had Daphne, if she'd made different choices – she would have had a different family. So perhaps her choices were pretty good. She certainly wouldn't change a single one of them now.

FullLife would be paying compensation, but Rosie and Kaz had already decided they wanted to donate all of that to charity. Maybe to the care homes, Rosie had said. She'd had a big talk with Eva. And FullLife were changing their advertising policy too; from now on every advert would carry details of the risks. It was something.

'Freida's lighthouse was brutal,' Holly said.

'However did she run a lighthouse all on her own?'

'She didn't. It was fully automated and managed from Edinburgh, apparently.'

Daphne smiled. 'So she liked the idea of running a lighthouse rather than the reality?'

'Maybe so,' Holly said. 'Mostly I think she wanted to be near the waves.'

They lapsed into silence for a moment, both of them enjoying it. Aarav was coming up at the weekend, with Drew and the kids, so the peace and quiet would be replaced by the noise of family soon enough.

'Would you have done the same, in my place?' Holly asked her daughter. 'Would you have volunteered to be the first woman to use the pouch?'

'I hope so,' Daphne said. 'I think you were brave.'

Holly shook her head. 'No. It was fairly easy, my part in the whole thing. I wanted to make society better as quickly as possible, and other people had invented a way to kick-start the change. But is it any better?'

'In some ways it is, yes. In a lot of ways, in fact. And you made things infinitely better for me.'

'Really?'

'Oh, Mum. I thought you knew that. You gave me choices. Thanks to you I always knew I had options. That made all the difference in the world.'

'Well, then I'm proud,' Holly said.

'Me too, Mum.'

Holly smiled and Daphne took her hand, and mother and daughter sat together for a while, watching the clouds blowing past the sun as it sank behind the tall glass buildings in the distance.

'After all,' Holly said, turning on the lamp in their living room and leaving the outside to its increasing darkness, 'I've had a beautiful life. I have lived such a very fortunate life.'

*

Standing outside the FullLife birthing centre, Eva could tell that the front panel of glass had recently been replaced. There was a piece of cream-coloured tape still visible along one edge, the kind that window fitters use to seal the glass against the frame during installation. She hoped that no one else had noticed it – she didn't want it to be removed. It gave the building a certain fragility. For once, you could see how easily it could shatter. How carefully it might need to be repaired.

Behind her, the Thames glittered in the morning light and she could hear the waves lapping against the boats moored along the water's edge.

In front of her were the rotating doors that led into the FullLife reception hall. There was no turning back now.

Eva strode confidently across the lobby and took the lift up to the top floor. It had never been open to the public, or to the press. There were fish tanks all along the walls – indigo hamlets, her grandmother's favourite. She wondered if the director had had any idea why they were here, or what they'd once meant to someone. In her bag she had Freida's folder, several of her own, some of her mum's old letters – including the one from her grandmother – and the photo of her mum and Piotr, with paper hats on their heads, taken years ago. Everything else she'd arranged to be sent over yesterday, though she still didn't quite trust these people, and as she pushed open the door to the director's office she felt a little queasy.

The room had been divided into an open-plan office, as they'd promised, with several desks, tables and sofas, just like she'd requested. She'd told them that she wasn't doing this alone, and she had absolutely meant it. And there, beside the desk nearest the window, was her old chair. She sat down in it, leaned back, and felt it adjust in exactly the way that she needed.

She wished James Quentin were here. He'd have been a good partner, with his uncertainty and his conscience; he was such a natural scientist. She hadn't known him for very long, but she missed him. Eva didn't understand why the wrong people so often had to pay the price.

She'd spent yesterday afternoon with the director – or former director, as she was now – who had apparently decided that changes should be made.

'You'll need to talk about the care homes,' she'd said, taking Eva's arm as though she were an old friend. 'I think they're the biggest challenge we face, and no one knows what to do. We thought we could cope with the numbers, but we can't. It's increasing every year.'

Of course it was, Eva thought.

'At first, it seemed such a good thing to offer the pouch as an alternative to abortion. A number of . . . well, interested parties, offered financial support.'

Eva raised her eyebrows, but made no comment.

'But now . . . Basically, they've changed their mind. The money is gone and the homes need help, in the short term. In the longer term, we need a solution, and that means debate, legislation . . .'

'You know it will open other debates,' Eva said, with sharpness in her tone. 'Sterilisation. Cryogenics . . .'

'Yes.' The former director was nodding.

'Genetic modification.'

'We have strong ethics laws in place—'

'Genetic selection.'

'Yes, absolutely,' she'd said, smiling and leaning back in her chair. She was wearing casual clothes, a knitted jumper; she looked different to before. 'I'm so glad it's you taking over. Debate everything.'

And that was exactly what Eva intended to do. She was going to start with the care homes. And natural birth. The risks and the choice. The money. The inequality.

She opened her email and saw 1,439 messages already waiting for her. Glancing through the first few pages, she saw they were emails from staff and from scientists, from new parents and would-be parents, old people, schoolchildren; on the second page of her inbox there was an email from Holly. Probably just one of many – Holly was having a lot of ideas. They all had ideas. They had questions, they wanted to understand what had happened, and to ask her about what they could do next. She gently swivelled her chair away from the computer and stood up. On the wall were several large blank screens. The former director had used them for photos of her baby, but now Eva set up each one to display the notes she'd prepared yesterday. It was her statement of intent. Her list of what needed to be done. The NaturalBirth plans, the care homes, education, research into long-term effects, the many and varied risks – there was still so much they didn't know. The government had to start contributing again. Some kind of universal health insurance. The new hospitals needed help, equipment and supplies. And the options had to be available to everyone, not just those who could afford them.

It was going to be hard. The extensive range of private health plans, the accessories, the covers, the add-ons, were how FullLife stayed afloat. She knew it. Not to mention the court cases pending. People had been lied to. People were angry. She had inherited a fractured company, to say the least.

She knew there was a black market internationally, that pouches were being misused and civil unrest was rising. She knew that natural birth was still preferred in some countries, and that while the UK had embraced the pouch others had voted to make it illegal. The world was divided. She knew the pouch was involved in some domestic abuse cases, even today, and FullLife had to take a stronger role in prevention and survivor support. Perhaps she'd push for new legislation. Taking Freida's folder out of her bag, she placed it on the desk and let her fingers rest briefly on the pages.

Her phone was ringing, and when she picked it up the receptionist started talking before she'd even had the chance to say hello.

'Oh good, you're there, all set up? I'm holding a queue of fourteen people on the phone lines, and we've got a dozen or so already down in the lobby, asking to talk in person. Bethan, new director of research, is going to start some one-to-ones, if that's OK with you – I figured you might not have time for that today – and the press have arrived. Will I send them up?'

'Send them up,' she said, still standing, and aware that this was the last moment of peace she was going to have for quite some time. She wanted to take a moment to look out at the sky. The clouds were low, a deep vibrant grey, strikingly beautiful.

Then they were at the door. Thirty, forty people, she wasn't even sure how many, came crowding into the room, all speaking. It was the first time the press had ever been allowed in here. And among them, she saw Piotr. She felt the blush spreading to her cheeks, even though she'd been having breakfast with him just two hours ago.

'I'm never going to change my mind,' she'd said.

'I know.'

'I have given it a lot of thought,' she'd said.

'Eva, I know.'

They'd discussed it the night before, so when he said that he knew, it was true. She just wanted to be sure. People had a habit of expecting others to change and she didn't want him imagining he could change her. Though she was fairly certain that he didn't want to. But with or without him there was a lot of work to do and Eva, it turned out, was not someone who could walk away leaving it undone.

'I'm not having a child,' she'd said, speaking forcefully because of how important it was to be believed. 'If you want a child—'

Piotr shook his head.

'I know,' he said.

And she had considered it. Of course she had, they both had – there were options. It might have been too late for her to have a child the way she wanted, but it wasn't too late. She'd tried to imagine it, closed her eyes and tried to picture herself with a pouch, but it still felt wrong to her. Deeply so. She didn't know what it was, or where it came from, this desire to have children, but she knew it was to do with creating, or recreating, family. And she had a family. Her mother had saved her once, and her grandmother had saved her too. The care home where she'd spent the first three years of her life was somewhere she'd be spending a lot more time from now on. Looking at the photo she'd placed on her desk, she knew she was ready.

Eva sat down on her chair, and took a deep breath. And then it began.

'Are used pouches less safe?'

'How many babies—'

'—risks of natural birth—'

'Where is the financing—'

'—support new hosp—'

'—lawsuits—'

'But the dangers are—'

'—appoint to the board?'

'One thing at a time,' she said, raising her voice to make herself heard above the commotion. 'I will listen to everyone, one at a time.'

Piotr wasn't shouting with the rest though. He was standing still in the middle of the huddle, and he smiled at her as she began to explain, to answer their questions as best she could, to tell them everything she knew. On the wall, her plan was written clearly for everyone to see, along with her naivety, or perhaps her optimism, or perhaps her life's work. Glancing at it, she felt suddenly afraid. She didn't know if she was doing the right thing. She didn't know if she could make any difference. Except that something was different already, because she was here. And now she was surrounded by all these people; by this humanity, and its questions.

Acknowledgements

This story would not exist the way it is without the advice, feedback and inspiration of Jane Alexander, Viccy Adams, Margaret Callaghan, Michael Gallacher, Alison Hennessey, Kirsty Logan, Katy McAulay, Ally Sedgwick, Chris Sedgwick, Brigit Sedgwick, Andrew Thompson, Kate Tough, Mark Buckland, Simon Cree, Harry Josephine Giles, Gill Tasker, and everyone at Scottish Book Trust. This book would not exist the way it does without the skill, talent and belief of my agent Cathryn Summerhayes and my publishers Liz Foley, Anna Redman, Mikaela Pedlow, Julia Connolly, Candice Carty-Williams, Katherine Fry, Nicky Jeanes, and Shabana Shakir. And I would not exist the way I am without the love and support of my family and my partner Michael. To all of you, thank you.